RESOUNDING PRAISE
FOR *NEW YORK TIMES* BESTSELLER
SUSAN ELIZABETH PHILLIPS
AND HER NOVELS

The Great Escape

"Flawlessly written romance . . . another jewel from one of the genre's most incandescent stars."
Booklist (★Starred Review★)

"Full of wit, humor, and her trademark emotionally compelling characters . . . not to be missed."
Kitsap Sun

Call Me Irresistible

"A delightful romantic-comedy romp."
Washington Post

"A laugh-out-loud and romantic story."
Publishers Weekly

"Reading this novel was like opening a box of expensive chocolates—once I'd started, I couldn't stop. . . . If you're down or busy or distracted, I have the cure: *Call Me Irresistible* is guaranteed to put a smile on your face. I loved this book."

Kristin Hannah

By Susan Elizabeth Phillips

THE GREAT ESCAPE
CALL ME IRRESISTIBLE
WHAT I DID FOR LOVE
GLITTER BABY
NATURAL BORN CHARMER
MATCH ME IF YOU CAN
AIN'T SHE SWEET?
BREATHING ROOM
THIS HEART OF MINE
JUST IMAGINE
FIRST LADY
LADY BE GOOD
DREAM A LITTLE DREAM
NOBODY'S BABY BUT MINE
KISS AN ANGEL
HEAVEN, TEXAS
IT HAD TO BE YOU

SUSAN ELIZABETH PHILLIPS

The Great Escape

AVON

An Imprint of HarperCollinsPublishers

AVON BOOKS
An Imprint of HarperCollins*Publishers*
10 East 53rd Street
New York, New York 10022-5299

Copyright © 2012 by Susan Elizabeth Phillips
ISBN 978-0-06-228016-9
www.avonromance.com

First Avon Books mass market international printing: July 2013
First William Morrow paperback printing: April 2013
First William Morrow paperback international printing: July 2012
First William Morrow hardcover printing: July 2012

FOR DAWN

Even though you're prettier and dress better,
I still love you, dear friend.

Still, for the millionth time Lucy wished she could have a real family. All her life, she'd dreamed of having a dad who mowed the lawn and called her some kind of lame pet name, and a mom who didn't get drunk and keep losing jobs and having sex with everybody.

From First Lady

Chapter One

Lucy couldn't breathe. The bodice of her wedding gown, which had fit so perfectly, now squeezed her ribs like a boa constrictor. What if she died of suffocation right here in the vestibule of the Wynette Presbyterian Church?

Outside, an international army of reporters stood at the barricades, and the sanctuary inside bulged with the rich and famous. Only a few steps away, the former president of the United States and her husband waited to escort Lucy down the aisle so she could marry the most perfect man in the world. The man of everyone's dreams. The kindest, the most considerate, the smartest . . . What woman in her right mind wouldn't want to marry Ted Beaudine? He'd dazzled Lucy from the moment they'd met.

The trumpets rang out, announcing the beginning of the bridal procession, and Lucy struggled to pull a few molecules of air into her lungs. She couldn't have picked a more beautiful day for her wedding. It was the last week of May. The Texas Hill Country's spring wildflowers might have faded, but the crepe myrtle was in bloom, and roses grew outside the church doors. A perfect day.

Her thirteen-year-old sister, the youngest of the four bridesmaids in her unfashionably small wedding party, stepped off. After her would come fifteen-year-old Charlotte, and then Meg Koranda, Lucy's best friend since college. Her maid of honor was her sister Tracy, a beautiful eighteen-year-old so smitten with Lucy's bridegroom that she still blushed when he talked to her.

Lucy's veil fluttered in front of her face, suffocating layers of white tulle. She thought about what an incredible lover Ted was, how brilliant, how kind, how amazing. How perfect for her. Everybody said that.

Everybody except her best friend, Meg.

Last night after the rehearsal dinner, Meg had pulled Lucy into a hug and whispered, "He's wonderful, Luce. Everything you said. And you absolutely can't marry him."

"I know," Lucy had heard herself whisper in return. "But I'm going to anyway. It's too late now to back out."

Meg had given her a fierce shake. "It's not too late. I'll help you. I'll do whatever I can."

Easy for Meg to say. Meg lived a completely undisciplined life, but Lucy wasn't like that. Lucy had responsibilities that Meg couldn't begin to comprehend. Even before Lucy's mother had taken the oath of office, the country had been fascinated by the Jorik menagerie—three adopted kids, two biological ones. Her parents had shielded the younger children from the press, but Lucy had been twenty-two at the time of Nealy's first inauguration, which made her fair game. The public had followed Lucy's dedication to her family—the way she served as a surrogate parent to her siblings during Nealy and Mat's frequent absences—her work in child advocacy, her sparse dating life, even her less-than-exciting fashion choices. And they were definitely following this wedding.

Lucy planned to meet her parents halfway down the aisle as a symbol of the way they'd come into her life when she was a rebellious fourteen-year-old hellion. Nealy and Mat would walk that final stretch with her, one on each side.

Charlotte stepped out onto the white runner. She was the shyest of Lucy's sibs, the one most worried about not having her older sister around. "We can talk on the phone every day," Lucy had told her. But Charlotte was used to Lucy living in the same house, and she said it wouldn't be the same.

It was time for Meg to step off. She glanced over her shoulder at Lucy, and even through yards of tulle, Lucy saw the concern that dragged at Meg's smile. Lucy longed to trade places with her. To live Meg's carefree life, running from country to country with no siblings to help raise, no family reputation to uphold, no cameras shadowing her every move.

Meg turned away, lifted her bouquet to her waist, plastered a smile on her face. And got ready to take her first step.

Without thinking, without asking herself how she could consider doing something like this—something so awful, so selfish, so unimaginable—even as she willed herself not to move, Lucy dropped her bouquet, stumbled around her sister, and grabbed Meg by the arm before she could go any farther. She heard her voice coming from a place far away, the words thready. "I have to talk to Ted right now."

Behind her, Tracy gasped. "Luce, what are you doing?"

Lucy couldn't look at Tracy. Her skin was hot, her mind reeling. She dug her fingers into Meg's arm. "Get him for me, Meg. *Please.*" The word was a plea, a prayer.

Through the suffocating tulle shroud, she saw Meg's lips part in shock. "*Now*? You don't think you could have done this a couple of hours ago?"

"You were right," Lucy cried. "Everything you said. You were completely right. Help me. Please." The words felt alien on her tongue. She was the one who took care of people. Even when she was a child, she'd never asked for help.

Her sister Tracy spun on Meg, her blue eyes flashing with indignation. "I don't understand. What did you say to her?" She grabbed Lucy's hand. "Luce, you're having a panic attack. It's going to be okay."

But it wouldn't be okay. Not now. Not ever. "No. I—I have to talk to Ted."

"Now?" Tracy echoed Meg. "You can't talk to him now."

But she had to. Meg understood that, even if Tracy didn't. With a worried nod, Meg lifted her bouquet back into position and started down the aisle to get him.

Lucy didn't know this hysterical person who'd taken over her body. She couldn't look into her sister's stricken eyes. Calla lilies from her bouquet flattened beneath her stilettos as she moved blindly across the vestibule. A pair of Secret Service agents stood by the heavy front doors, their eyes watchful. Just beyond, a crowd of onlookers waited, a sea of television cameras, a horde of reporters. . . .

> Today, President Cornelia Case Jorik's oldest daughter, thirty-one-year-old Lucy Jorik, is marrying Ted Beaudine, the only son of golf legend Dallas Beaudine and television newswoman Francesca Beaudine. No one expected the bride to choose the groom's small hometown of Wynette, Texas, as the site for her wedding, but . . .

She heard the purposeful strike of male footsteps on the marble floor and turned to see Ted striding toward her. Through her veil, she watched a beam of sunlight play on his dark brown hair, another ray splash across his handsome face. It was always that way. Wherever he went, sunbeams seemed to follow. He was beautiful, kind, everything a man should be. The most perfect man she'd ever known. The most perfect son-in-law for her parents and the best imaginable father of her future children. He rushed toward her, his eyes filled—not with anger—he wasn't that sort of man—but with concern.

Her parents were right behind him, their faces masks of alarm. His parents would appear next, and then they'd all come pouring out—her sisters and brother, Ted's friends, their guests . . . So many people she cared about. Loved.

She searched frantically for the only person who could help her.

Meg stood off to the side, her hands in a death grip on her bridesmaid's bouquet. Lucy pleaded with her eyes, prayed Meg would grasp what she needed. Meg started to rush toward her, then stopped. With the mental telepathy shared by best friends, Meg understood.

Ted caught Lucy's arm and swept her into a small antechamber off to the side. Just before he shut the door, Lucy saw Meg take a deep breath and stride purposefully toward Lucy's parents. Meg was used to dealing with messes. She'd fend them all off long enough for Lucy to— To do what?

The long, narrow antechamber was lined with hooks holding blue choir robes and high shelves bearing hymnals, music folders, and musty, ancient cardboard boxes. A trickle of sulfurous sunlight oozed through the dusty windowpanes in a door at the end and somehow found his cheek. Her lungs collapsed. She was dizzy from lack of air.

Ted gazed down at her, those cool amber eyes shadowed with concern, as calm as she was frantic. Please let him fix this like he fixes everything else. Let him fix her.

Tulle stuck to her cheek, held there by perspiration, by tears—she didn't know which—as words she could never have imagined speaking tumbled out. "Ted, I can't. I—I can't."

He lifted her veil just as she'd pictured, except she'd pictured him doing it at the end of the ceremony, right before he kissed her. His expression was perplexed. "I don't understand."

And neither did she. This raw panic was unlike anything she'd ever experienced.

He cocked his head, gazed into her eyes. "Lucy, we're perfect together."

"Yes. Perfect . . . I know."

He waited. She couldn't think of what to say next. If only she could breathe. She forced her lips to move. "I know we are. Perfect. But . . . I can't."

She waited for him to argue with her. To fight for her. To convince her she was wrong. She waited for him to take her in his arms and tell her this was merely a panic attack. But his expression didn't change except for an almost imperceptible tightening at the corner of his mouth. "Your friend Meg," he said. "This is because of her, isn't it?"

Was it? Would she be doing something so unimaginable if Meg hadn't appeared with her love, her chaos, and her swift, brutal judgment? "I can't." Her fingers were icy, and her hands shook as she tugged at her diamond. It finally came off. She nearly dropped it as she pushed it into his pocket.

He let her veil fall. He didn't beg. He wouldn't know how. Nor did he make even the slightest attempt to change her mind. "All right, then . . ." With a brusque nod, he turned and walked away. Calm. Controlled. Perfect.

As the door shut behind him, she pressed her hands to her stomach. She had to get him back. Run after him and tell him she'd changed her mind. But her feet wouldn't move; her brain wouldn't work.

The knob turned, the door opened, and her father stood there, with her mother just behind, both of them pale, tense with concern. They'd done everything for her, and marrying Ted had been the best thank-you gift she could have given them in return. She couldn't humiliate them like this. She needed to get Ted and bring him back. "Not yet," she whispered, wondering what she meant, knowing only that she needed a moment to pull herself together and remember who she was.

Mat hesitated and then shut the door.

Lucy's universe collapsed. Before the afternoon was over, the world would know that she'd dumped Ted Beaudine. It was unthinkable.

The sea of cameras . . . The herds of reporters . . . She'd never leave this small, musty room. She'd live the rest of her life right here, surrounded by hymnals and choir robes, doing penance for hurting the best man she'd ever known, for humiliating her family.

Her veil stuck to her lips. She tore at her headpiece, welcomed the pain as the combs and crystals pulled her hair. She was crazy. Ungrateful. She deserved pain, and she ripped it all off. The veil, the gown—snaking her arms behind her to work at the zipper until the white satin lay in a puddle around her ankles and she stood gasping for breath in her exquisite French bra, her lacy bridal panties, blue garter, and white satin stilettos.

Run! The word shrieked through her brain. *Run!*

From outside the chamber she heard the crowd noise grow momentarily louder and then muted again, as if someone had opened the front doors of the church, then quickly closed them.

Run!

Her hand grasped one of the dark blue choir robes. She jerked it from its hook and pulled it on over her disheveled hair. The cool, musty robe slipped along her body, covering her French bra, covering her tiny panties. She stumbled toward the small door at the end of the antechamber. Through the dusty windowpanes, she saw a narrow, over-grown walkway enclosed by a cinder-block wall. Her hands weren't working properly, and the lock didn't give at first, but she finally managed to open it.

The walkway led toward the rear of the church. The cracked pavement grabbed at her stilettos as she made her way past an air-conditioning unit. Spring thunderstorms had blown trash into the gravel at the side of the path: smashed juice boxes, bits of newspaper, a mangled yellow shovel from a kid's sandbox. She stopped when she reached the end. Security was everywhere, and she tried to think of what to do next.

She'd lost her Secret Service detail a few months earlier, at the end of her mother's first year out of office, but the agency still guarded Nealy, and since she and her mother were so frequently together, she'd barely noticed the absence of her own detail. Ted had hired private security to supplement the town's small police force. There were guards at the doors. The L-shaped parking lot overflowed with cars. People were everywhere.

Washington was her home, not this Central Texas town she'd failed so miserably to appreciate, but she remembered that the church sat on the edge of an old residential neighborhood. If her legs could carry her across the alley and behind the houses on the other side, she might be able to get to one of those side streets without anyone seeing her.

And then what? This wasn't a well-planned escape like the one Nealy had pulled off from the White House all those years ago. It wasn't an escape at all. It was an interruption. A suspension. She needed to find a place where she could get her breath back, pull herself together. A child's empty playhouse. A hidden nook in someone's backyard. Someplace away from the chaos of the press, from her betrayed bridegroom and bewildered family. A temporary hideout where she could remember who she was and what she owed the people who'd taken her in.

Oh God, what had she done?

A commotion on the other side of the church caught the guards' attention. She didn't wait to see what it was. Instead she stumbled around the end of the cinder-block wall, rushed across the alley, and crouched behind a Dumpster. Her knees were shaking so badly she had to brace herself against the side of the rusty metal bin. It exuded the fetid stench of garbage. There were no cries of alarm, only the distant noise of the crowd packing the bleachers that had been set up in front of the church.

She heard a thin cry, like a kitten's mew, and realized it was coming from her. She made herself creep along the row of shrubs that separated the old Victorians. The shrubs ended at a brick-paved street. She rushed across it and into someone's backyard.

Old trees shaded the small lots, and detached garages opened into narrow alleys. She pulled the choir robe tighter as she moved blindly across the yards, from one to another. Her heels sank into the soil behind freshly planted vegetable gardens where marble-size green tomatoes grew on the new vines. The smell of pot roast wafted through an open kitchen window; the sound of a television game show came from another. Soon that same television would broadcast the story of former president Cornelia Case Jorik's irresponsible daughter. In the space of one afternoon, thirty-one-year-old Lucy had blown seventeen years of good behavior. Seventeen years of proving to Mat and Nealy they hadn't made a mistake by adopting her. As for what she'd done to Ted . . . She couldn't have hurt him more.

A dog barked and a baby cried. She stumbled over a garden hose. Cut behind a swing set. The dog's barking grew louder, and a rusty-haired mutt charged the wire fence that marked the next yard. She backed around a statue of the Virgin Mary toward the alley. The toes of her stilettos filled with pebbles.

She heard the roar of an engine. Her back straightened. A beat-up black and silver motorcycle spun into the alley. She ducked between two garages and flattened her spine against peeling white paint. The bike slowed. She held her breath, waiting for it to pass. It didn't. Instead, it crept forward, then stopped in front of her.

The rider gazed into the space between the garages to the place where she stood.

The motor idled as he took his time studying her. One black boot hit the gravel. "'S'up?" he said over the engine noise.

'S'up! She'd crushed her future husband, mortified her family, and if she didn't do something quickly, she would become the country's most infamous runaway bride, yet this guy wanted to know what was *up*?

He had too-long black hair that curled past his collar, cold blue eyes set above high cheekbones, and sadistic lips. After so many years of Secret Service protection, she'd grown used to taking her safety for granted, but she didn't feel safe now, and the fact that she dimly recognized the biker as a guest at last night's rehearsal dinner—one of Ted's odd assortment of friends—didn't exactly reassure her. Even semi-cleaned-up in a dark suit that didn't fit well, a rumpled white shirt open at the collar, and motorcycle boots that appeared to have received nothing more than a dusting, he didn't look like anybody she wanted to meet in an alley. Exactly where she happened to be.

His nose was blunt, square at the tip. A wrinkled necktie poked out of the pocket of his ill-fitting suit coat. And that long, wild hair, all curls and tangles, looked like a finger painting of a van Gogh night sky made from a sloppy pot of black ink.

For more than ten years, ever since Nealy's first presidential campaign, she'd tried to say the right thing, do the right thing, always smiling, forever polite. Now she, who'd long ago mastered the art of small talk, couldn't think of a thing to say. Instead she felt a nearly irresistible desire to sneer, *'S'up with you?* But of course she didn't.

He jerked his head toward the rear of his bike. "Wanna go for a ride?"

Shock radiated through her body, shooting from vein to capillary, piercing skin and muscle into bone. She shivered, not from cold, but from the knowledge that she yearned to get on that bike more than she'd wanted anything for a very long time. Get on that bike and flee from the consequences of what she'd done.

He shoved his necktie deeper into the pocket of his suit coat, and her feet began to move. It was as if they'd detached from the rest of her body. She tried to make them stop, but they refused to obey. She came closer to the bike and saw a battered Texas license plate along with a dog-eared bumper sticker that covered part of the worn leather seat. The print had faded, but she could still make out the words.

GAS, GRASS, OR ASS. NOBODY RIDES FOR FREE.

The message hit her like a shock wave. A warning she couldn't ignore. But her body—her treacherous body—had taken control. Her hand tugged on the choir robe. One foot came off the ground. Her leg straddled the seat.

He handed her the only helmet. She pulled it on over her wretched bridal up-do and wrapped her arms around his waist.

They shot off down the alley, the choir robe billowing, her bare legs catching the edge of the wind, his hair flying, whipping her visor.

She tucked the robe under her legs as he cut from one alley to the next, took a sharp right turn and then another, the muscles in his back flexing under the cheap material of his suit coat.

They rode out of Wynette and down a two-lane highway that stretched along a craggy limestone bluff. The helmet was her cocoon, the bike her planet. They passed lavender fields in bloom, an olive oil factory, and some of the vineyards that were springing up across the Hill Country. The wind pulled at her robe, exposing her knees, her thighs.

The sun dipped lower in the sky, and the growing chill cut through the robe's thin fabric. She welcomed the cold. She didn't deserve to be warm and comfortable.

They barreled over a wooden bridge and past a decrepit barn with a Lone Star flag painted on its side. Signs for cave tours and dude ranches flashed by. The miles slipped away. Twenty? More? She didn't know.

As they reached the outskirts of a one-stoplight town, he turned toward a shabby convenience store and parked in the shadows at the side of the building. He jerked his head at her, indicating she was to get off. She tangled her legs in her robe and nearly fell.

"You hungry?"

Even the thought of food made her nauseated. She eased her stiff legs and shook her head. He shrugged and headed for the door.

Through the helmet's dusty visor, she saw that he was taller than she'd thought, about six feet, longer in the leg than the trunk. With his wild blue-black hair, olive complexion, and rolling gait, he couldn't have been more unlike the congressmen, senators, and captains of industry who populated her life. She could see part of the store's interior through the window. He walked toward the cooler at the back. The female clerk stopped what she was doing to watch him. He disappeared for a few minutes, then reappeared to set a six-pack of beer on the counter. The clerk tossed her hair, openly flirting with him. He placed a few more items by the register.

Lucy's shoes were rubbing a blister on her feet. As she shifted her weight, she caught a glimpse of her reflection in the window. The big blue helmet swallowed her head, hiding the small features that always made her appear younger than her age. The robe hid the fact that prewedding stress had left her normally slender figure a little too thin. She was thirty-one years old, five feet four inches, but she felt tiny; stupid; a selfish, irresponsible waif.

Even though no one was around to see, she didn't take off the helmet but lifted it slightly, trying to ease the pressure on the hairpins digging into her scalp. Normally she wore her hair almost to her shoulders, straight and tidy, generally held back with one of those narrow headbands Meg detested.

"They make you look like a fifty-year-old Greenwich socialite," Meg had declared. *"And unless you're wearing jeans, ditch those stupid pearls. Ditto your whole stupid-ass preppy wardrobe."* Then she'd softened. *"You're not Nealy, Luce. She doesn't expect you to be."*

Meg didn't understand. She'd grown up in L.A. with the same parents who'd given birth to her. She could wear all the outrageous clothes she wanted, dangle exotic jewelry around her neck, even have a dragon tattooed on her hip, but not Lucy.

The store door opened, and the biker emerged carrying a grocery sack in one hand, beer in the other. She watched with alarm as he silently stowed his purchases in the bike's scuffed saddlebags. As she imagined him drinking the whole six-pack, she knew she couldn't let this go on. She had to call someone. She'd call Meg.

But she couldn't summon the courage to face anyone, not even her best friend, who understood so much more than the rest. She'd let her family know she was safe. Soon. Just . . . not quite yet. Not until she'd figured out what to say.

She stood in front of the biker like a big, blue-headed alien. He was staring at her, and she realized she still hadn't spoken a single word to him. How awkward. She needed to say something. "How do you know Ted?"

He turned back to fasten the clasps on the saddlebags. The bike was an old Yamaha with the word WARRIOR written in silver across the black fuel tank. "We did time together in Huntsville," he said. "Armed robbery and manslaughter."

He was baiting her. Some kind of biker test to see how tough she wasn't. She'd have to be crazy to let this go on any longer. But then she was crazy. A bad kind of crazy. The crazy of someone who'd fallen out of her skin and didn't know how to crawl back in.

His shadowed eyes, heavy with another kind of threat, slid over her. "You ready for me to take you back?"

All she had to do was say yes. One simple word. She pushed her tongue into the proper position. Arranged her lips. Failed to force it out. "Not yet."

He frowned. "Are you sure you know what you're doing?"

The answer to that question was so obvious even he could figure it out. When she failed to respond, he shrugged and climbed back on the bike.

As they pulled out of the parking lot, she wondered how riding off with this menacing biker seemed less chilling than facing the family she loved so much. But then she didn't owe this man anything. The worst he could do was— She didn't want to think about the worst he could do.

Once again the wind tore at her robe. Only her hands stayed warm from the body heat radiating through his thin suit coat. Eventually he turned off the highway onto a rutted trail. The bike's headlight cut an eerie pattern across the scrub, and she held tighter to his waist even as her brain screamed at her to jump off and run. Finally they reached a small clearing at the edge of a river. From a sign she'd seen earlier, she guessed it was the Pedernales. A perfect place to dispose of a dead body.

Without the roar of the engine, the silence was suffocating. She got off the bike and backed away. He pulled something that looked like an old stadium blanket from one of the saddlebags. As he dropped it on the ground, she caught the faint scent of motor oil. He grabbed the beer and grocery bag. "You gonna wear that thing all night?"

She wanted to keep the helmet on forever, but she took it off. Pins tumbled, and a wedge of oversprayed hair poked her in the cheek. The quiet was dense and noisy with the rush of river over rock. He lifted the beer in her direction. "Too bad this is only a six-pack."

She gave a stiff smile. He popped the top, sprawled on the blanket, and tipped the longneck to his mouth. He was a friend of Ted's, wasn't he? So he had to be safe—despite his threatening appearance and boorish manner, despite the beer and the frayed bumper sticker.

GAS, GRASS, OR ASS. NOBODY RIDES FOR FREE.

"Have one," he said. "Maybe it'll loosen you up."

She didn't want to loosen up, and she had to pee, but she hobbled over anyway and took a bottle to keep him from drinking it. She found a spot on the far corner of the blanket where she wouldn't brush against his long legs or breathe in his general air of menace. She should be drinking Champagne now in the bridal suite of the Austin Four Seasons as Mrs. Theodore Beaudine.

The biker pulled a couple of cellophane-wrapped sandwiches from the grocery bag. He tossed one in her general direction and opened the other. "Too bad you didn't wait until after the big wedding dinner to dump him. The food would have been a lot better than this."

Lump crab parfait, lavender grilled beef tenderloin, lobster medallions, white truffle risotto, a seven-tier wedding cake . . .

"Really. How do you know Ted?" she asked.

He ripped off a big corner of his sandwich with his teeth and spoke around the wad in his mouth. "We met a couple of years back when I was working a construction job in Wynette, and we hit it off. We see each other when I'm in the area."

"Ted hits it off with most people."

"Not all of them good guys like him." He wiped his mouth with the back of his hand and took another noisy swig of beer.

She set aside the beer she wasn't drinking. "So you're not from around here?"

"Nope." He balled up the cellophane sandwich wrapper and flipped it into the weeds.

She hated people who littered, but she wasn't going to mention that. Devouring his sandwich seemed to require all his attention, and he didn't volunteer any more information.

She couldn't postpone a trip into the woods any longer. She took a napkin from the grocery bag and, wincing with every step, limped into the trees. When she was done, she returned to the blanket. He chugged some more beer. She couldn't stomach her own sandwich, and she pushed it aside. "Why did you pick me up?"

"I wanted to get laid."

Her skin crawled. She looked for some indication that this was his crude attempt at a joke, but he didn't crack a smile. On the other hand, he was Ted's friend, and as odd as some of them were, she'd never met any that were criminals. "You're not serious," she said.

He skimmed his eyes over her. "It could happen."

"No, it couldn't!"

He burped, not loud, but still disgusting. "I've been too busy for women lately. It's time to catch up."

She stared at him. "By picking up your friend's bride while she's running away from her wedding?"

He scratched his chest. "You never know. Crazy women'll do anything." He drained his beer, burped again, and tossed the empty into the bushes. "So what do you say? Are you ready for me to take you back to Mommy and Daddy?"

"I say no." Despite her growing apprehension, she wasn't ready to go back. "You haven't told me your name."

"Panda."

"No, really."

"You don't like it?"

"It's hard to believe that's your real name."

"No skin off my nose whether you believe it or not. I go by Panda."

"I see." She thought about it while he ripped open a bag of chips. "It must be nice."

"How do you mean?"

"Riding from town to town with a made-up name." And a big blue bike helmet to hide beneath.

"I guess."

She had to stop this, and she gathered her courage. "Do you happen to have a cell I can borrow? I . . . need to call someone."

He dug into his suit coat pocket and tossed her his phone. She failed to catch it and had to fumble in the folds of her robe.

"Good luck getting a signal out here."

She hadn't thought about that, but then her ability to think logically had deserted her hours earlier. She hobbled around the clearing on her now-torturous heels until she found a spot near the riverbank where she picked up a weak signal. "It's me," she said when Meg answered.

"Luce? Are you all right?"

"Matter of opinion." She gave a choked laugh. "You know that wild side of me you're always talking about? I guess I found it." Nothing could be further from the truth. She was the least wild person imaginable. Once maybe, but not for a long time.

"Oh, honey . . ." The signal was weak, but not weak enough to mute her friend's concern.

She had to go back to Wynette. But . . . "I'm—I'm a coward, Meg. I can't face my family yet."

"Luce, they love you. They'll understand."

"Tell them I'm sorry." She fought back tears. "Tell them I love them, and I know I've made a horrible mess of everything, and that I'll come back and clean it up, but . . . Not tonight. I can't do it tonight."

"All right. I'll tell them. But—"

She disconnected before Meg could ask her any more questions she had no way of answering.

A crushing fatigue swept over her. She'd slept badly for weeks, and today's awful events had used up whatever energy she had left. Panda had disappeared in the woods, and as he came out, she decided to let him get drunk in peace. She gazed at the blanket spread on the hard ground and thought of the narrow, comfortable beds in the private presidential quarters of *Air Force One* and the blackout shades that covered the windows with the push of a button. She gingerly lay back on the farthest edge of the blanket and gazed at the stars.

She wished she had a biker name to hide behind. Something tough. Something strong and menacing. Everything she wasn't.

She fell asleep thinking up biker names. Snake . . . Fang . . . Venom . . .

Viper.

Chapter Two

⁂

THE DAMP MORNING CHILL AWAKENED her. She eased her eyes open to see straws of peach pushing through the low clouds. Her body ached everywhere; she was cold, dirty, and as nauseated now as she'd been when she'd fallen asleep. This was the first day of what should have been her honeymoon. She imagined Ted waking up, thinking the same thing, hating her . . .

Panda slept next to her in his wrinkled white dress shirt. He lay on his back, his wild, irresponsible hair in chaotic twists and snarls around his head. Blue-black stubble covered his jaw, and a dirty smudge marred his blunt-tipped nose. She hated being so close to him, so she came awkwardly to her feet. His suit coat slipped off her and dropped to the blanket. She winced as she wedged her feet into her stilettos and limped into the trees. On the way, she spotted six empty beer bottles tossed in the weeds, sordid symbols of what she'd gotten herself into.

Ted had rented a honeymoon villa on the beach at St. Barts. Maybe he'd go by himself, although what could be worse than a honeymoon for one? Not even waking up at the side of a river in the middle of nowhere next to a surly, hungover, potentially dangerous biker.

When she came out, he was standing by the river, his back to her. Last night's fantasy of Viper, the tough-talking biker girl, faded away, and it seemed rude to ignore him. "Good morning," she said quietly.

He grunted.

She quickly looked away, afraid he'd decide to pee in the river while she watched. She yearned for a hot shower, clean clothes, and a toothbrush, the exact comforts she would have been enjoying if she'd walked down that aisle. A pot of coffee. A decent breakfast. Ted's hands on her body, coaxing those delicious orgasms from her. Instead she was surrounded by empty beer bottles and a man who openly admitted he "wanted to get laid." She hated the mess, the uncertainty. She hated her panic. He still hadn't turned, but she didn't see him fumbling with his fly, so she risked a question. "Are you . . . going back to Wynette this morning?"

Another grunt.

She'd never been comfortable in Wynette, although she'd pretended to love it as much as Ted did. But whenever she was there, she could feel everybody judging her. Even though she was the adopted daughter of the former president of the United States, they made her feel as if she weren't good enough for him. Of course she'd proved them right, but they hadn't known that when they met her.

Panda continued to stare at the river, his long body silhouetted against the limestone cliffs, his shirt a mass of wrinkles, the tail hanging out on one side, everything about him disreputable. Her shoes were torturous, but she wanted the punishment of pain, so she didn't pull them off.

He abruptly abandoned his lookout duty to stalk toward her, the heels of his boots grinding into the dirt. "Are you ready to get back to your screwed-up life?"

More than ready. She was done with postponing her responsibilities. Even as a fourteen-year-old, she'd been responsible. How many times over the past seventeen years had Nealy and Mat told her they couldn't do their jobs if she weren't such a good caregiver to her siblings?

She'd worked hard at her own job, too. At first she'd used her bachelor's degree in social work to counsel troubled teens while she got her master's in public policy. But after a few years, she'd left the casework she loved and begun using her famous name for the less satisfying—but more impactful—task of lobbying. Thanks in part to her, important pieces of legislation had been passed that helped disadvantaged kids. She didn't plan to give up her lobbying work after she was married either, no matter how tempting. She'd fly to Washington for a few days every month and do the rest of her job from her Texas base. It was long past time to face the consequences of what she'd done.

But her stomach didn't agree. As the churning got worse, she hurried into the woods and made it into the trees just in time to throw up. She hadn't eaten in so long that it was painful.

The spasms eventually stopped. He barely looked at her as she came out of the trees. She stumbled toward the river, her heels catching on rocks, then sinking into the sand. She knelt beside the water and splashed her face.

"Let's go," he said.

She rested back on her calves, river water dripping down her cheeks. Her voice came from a place far away, a place she hadn't inhabited since she was very young. "Did you leave many of your things in Wynette?"

"What do you mean?"

"Clothes? Suitcase?" *Your Mensa card?*

"I travel light. A pair of jeans, a couple of T-shirts, and a box of condoms."

People were always on their best behavior with the president's family. Hardly anyone other than Meg or one of her father's seven sisters ever told her a dirty joke or made even a vaguely crude reference. People's stiff courtesy had always annoyed her, but now she would have welcomed even a little of it, and she pretended she hadn't heard. "So there's nothing I couldn't compensate you for leaving behind?"

"What are you getting at?"

Her family knew she was safe. Meg would have told them. "I really can't go back to Wynette while the press is still there." The press wasn't her main concern, but she wasn't telling him that. "I'm wondering what your immediate plans are."

"Getting rid of you." He rubbed his stubbly jaw. "And getting laid."

She swallowed. "What if I make it worth your while?"

He dipped his eyes to her breasts, which her extravagantly expensive French bridal bra had improved. "You aren't my type."

Ignore him. "I meant, what if I make it worth your while not to do either?"

"Not interested." He whipped the blanket off the ground. "I'm on vacation, and I'm not spoiling another day. You're going back to Wynette."

"I'd pay you," she heard herself say. "Not today. I don't have any money with me, but I'll take care of that soon." How? She'd have to figure that out. "I'll cover gas, food, all your expenses. Plus . . . a hundred dollars a day. Agreed?"

He balled up the blanket. "Too much hassle."

"I can't go back now." She unearthed a shred of the bravado she'd possessed in such abundance as a teen, before the weight of her responsibilities had straightened her out. "If you won't take me with you, I'll find someone who will."

Maybe he knew she was bluffing because he practically sneered at her. "Trust me. A chick like you isn't cut out to spend eight hours a day on a bike."

"Maybe not. But I can manage it for a day."

"Forget it."

"A thousand dollars, plus expenses."

He carried the blanket over to the saddlebags and stuffed it in. "You think I'd trust you to pay up?"

She twisted her hands in front of her. "I'll pay. You have my word."

"Yeah, well, Ted had that, too, and it didn't turn out to be worth much."

She cringed. "I'll put it in writing."

"Too bad your fiancé didn't think of that." With a scowl, he snapped the saddlebags closed.

ALTHOUGH PANDA DIDN'T TAKE HER up on the offer, he also didn't ride off without her, which she took as a positive sign. She needed food, but more than that, she wanted comfortable shoes and a change of clothes. "Would you go back?" she shouted in Panda's ear as he buzzed past a Walmart. "I'd like to get some things."

Either she hadn't spoken loud enough or he didn't hear her because he didn't stop.

As they rode, she let her mind drift and found herself remembering the day Mat Jorik had shown up at that ratty rental house in Harrisburg where she'd been hiding out with her baby sister during those terrible weeks after their mother's death. He'd loomed at the front door, angry and impatient. She had a dead mother and a year-old baby sister to protect, so even though she'd been fourteen and scared to death, she didn't let him see it.

"We got nothing to talk about," she'd said after he'd bullied his way inside.

"Cut the crap . . . Unless you shoot straight with me, Child and Family Services will be here to pick you up in an hour."

For six weeks, she'd used all the resources a fourteen-year-old could muster to keep the authorities from finding out she was the only one caring for the baby she'd called Button, the baby who'd grown up to be Tracy. *"We don't need anybody taking care of us!"* she'd shouted. *"We're doing great by ourselves. Why don't you mind your own damn business?"*

But he hadn't minded his business, and before long, he, Lucy, and Button were on the road, where they'd met up with Nealy and gone on a cross-country trip in Mabel, the beat-up Winnebago that still sat on her parents' property in Virginia because none of them could bear getting rid of her. Mat was the only father she had ever known, and she couldn't have found a better one. Or a better husband for Nealy, a love match Lucy'd had more than a small hand in bringing about. She'd been so courageous in those days. So fearless. She'd lost that part of herself so gradually she'd barely been aware of the change.

Panda wheeled into a dirt lot in front of a white frame building with a sign over the door that read STOKEY'S COUNTRY STORE. The windows displayed everything from shotguns to mixing bowls to kids' Crocs. A Coke machine sat near the door, along with a garden gnome and a postcard rack.

"What size shoes d'you wear?" He sounded angry.

"Seven and a half. And I'd like—"

He was already taking the steps two at a time.

She got off the bike and tucked herself behind a delivery truck, helmet firmly in place, while she waited. She wished she could pick out her own shoes, but going into the store looking like this was unthinkable. She prayed he wasn't picking up more beer. Or condoms.

He emerged with a plastic sack and thrust it at her. "You owe me."

GAS, GRASS, OR ASS. NOBODY RIDES FOR FREE.

"I said I'd pay you."

He uttered another of his caveman grunts.

She glanced inside the sack. Jeans, gray cotton T-shirt, cheap navy sneakers, and a ball cap. She carried it all behind the building, took off her helmet, and changed where she couldn't be seen. The jeans were stiff and ugly, baggy in the hip and leg. The T-shirt had a University of Texas logo. He'd forgotten socks, but at least she could get rid of her heels. Unlike him, she didn't litter, so she stuffed the choir robe and shoes back into the plastic sack and came out of the trees.

He scratched his chest, his expression vacant. "The television was on in the store. You're big news right now. They're saying you're staying with friends, but I wouldn't count on not being recognized."

She clutched the plastic bag with the choir robe inside and pulled the helmet back on.

Half an hour later, he was parking behind a Denny's. She wanted a real bathroom with hot and cold running water, which outweighed her dread of anyone recognizing her. While he pocketed the ignition key and looked around, she took off the helmet and gathered her stiff, sprayed hair into a facsimile of a ponytail, which she pulled through the hole in the back of her ball cap.

"If that's your disguise," he said, "you're not gonna get far."

He was right. She yearned for the helmet. With a quick glance around to make sure no one was watching, she took her ruined shoes out of the plastic bag, leaving the wadded choir robe in it. She bunched up the bag and stuffed it under her roomy T-shirt, securing part of it in the waistband of her jeans so it wouldn't fall out.

This was the same disguise Nealy had used all those years ago when she'd fled the White House. Maybe it would work for Lucy. If she was lucky, no one would connect the former first daughter with a cheaply dressed pregnant girl walking into a Denny's. She'd look like one more stupid female who'd fallen for the wrong guy.

Panda gazed at her plastic-bag pregnancy. "Here I am, about to be a father, and the sex wasn't even that good."

She fought the urge to apologize.

He only seemed to have two expressions, vacant or scowling. Now it was a scowl. "You don't even look legal."

She'd always appeared younger than her age, and her current outfit had to make her look even younger. *I'm sure I'm not your first teen-ager.* That's what Meg would have said to him, but Lucy turned away, dumped her ruined stilettos in a trash bin, and headed cautiously into the restaurant.

To her relief, no one paid any attention to her, not because of her bad clothes or pregnancy bump, but because everyone looked at Panda. He was like Ted in that way. They both had a big presence—Ted's good, Panda's not.

She made her way to the restroom, cleaned up as best as she could, and rearranged her pregnancy bump. When she came out, she felt almost human.

Panda stood by the door. He wore the same wrinkled shirt, but he smelled like soap. He studied her bump. "It's not too realistic."

"As long as you're around, I don't think anybody will pay much attention to me."

"We'll see."

She followed him back to the table. More than a few people in the room were watching as they slid into the booth across from each other. They ordered, and as they waited for their food to arrive, he studied the ball scores scrolling on a TV hanging in the corner.

"While you were in the john, the news said your family's back in Virginia."

She wasn't surprised. Staying in Wynette would have been unbearably awkward for them. "They're going to Barcelona tomorrow for a conference with the World Health Organization."

He didn't look as though he knew what a conference was, let alone the World Health Organization. "When are you calling Ted to tell him you screwed up?"

"I don't know."

"Running away's not going to solve whatever problems a rich girl like you thinks you have." His slight sneer said he didn't believe anybody like her could have real problems.

"I'm not running," she retorted. "I'm . . . on vacation."

"Wrong. I'm on vacation."

"And I've offered to pay you a thousand dollars plus expenses to take me with you."

Right then, their food appeared. The waitress set a bacon cheeseburger, onion rings, and a garden salad in front of her. He shoved a fry into his mouth as she left. "What're you going to do if I turn you down?"

"I'll find someone else," she said, which was nonsense. There was no one else. "That guy over there." She nodded toward a rough-looking man sitting in front of a platter of pancakes. "I'll ask him. He looks like he could use the money."

"His mullet tell you that?"

Panda was hardly the person to criticize another man's hairstyle, although the other women in the restaurant didn't appear as critical as she was.

He didn't seem to be able to do two things at once, and for a while, he chose thinking over eating. Finally he took a too-large bite and, mouth full of burger, said, "You'll guarantee me a grand even if you don't last through today?"

She nodded, then picked up one of the crayons left on the table for kids. She wrote on a napkin and pushed it across the table to him. "There. We have a contract."

He studied it. Shoved it aside. "You screwed over a decent guy."

She blinked against the sting in her eyes. "Better now than later, right? Before he found out he might be a victim of false advertising." She wished she'd kept silent, but he merely upended the ketchup bottle and slapped the bottom.

The waitress returned with coffee and eyes for Panda. Lucy shifted position, and the plastic bag rustled under her T-shirt. The coffeepot stalled in midair as the waitress turned to look at her. Lucy ducked her head.

He wadded up the napkin contract and swiped his mouth with it. "Kid doesn't like it when she eats too fast."

"You girls get pregnant younger all the time," the waitress said. "How old are you, honey?"

"Legal," he said before Lucy could answer.

"Barely," the waitress muttered. "When are you due?"

"Uhm . . . August?" Lucy had made it sound like a question, not a declaration, and the waitress looked confused.

"Or September." Panda leaned back in the booth, eyelids at half-mast. "Depends on who's the daddy."

The woman advised Panda to get himself a good lawyer and walked off.

He pushed away his empty plate. "We can be at the Austin airport in a couple hours."

No plane. No airport. "I can't fly," she said. "I don't have an ID."

"Call your old lady and let her take care of it. This jaunt has cost me enough."

"I told you. Keep track of your expenses. I'd pay you back. Plus a thousand dollars."

"Where are you getting the cash?"

She had no idea. "I'll figure it out."

LUCY HAD GONE TO THE party knowing there'd be drinking. She was almost seventeen, none of the kids was going to narc, and Mat and Nealy would never find out. What was the big deal?

Then Courtney Barnes passed out behind the couch, and they couldn't wake her up. Somebody called 911. The cops showed up and took IDs. When they found out who Lucy was, one of them drove her home while the rest of the kids got hauled into the police station.

She'd never forgotten what the officer had said to her. "Everybody knows what Senator Jorik and Mr. Jorik did for you. Is this how you pay them back?"

Mat and Nealy refused preferential treatment for her and hauled her back to the police station to sit with the others. The press covered the whole thing, complete with op-ed pieces about the wild children of Washingon's pols, but her parents never threw that in her face. Instead they talked to her about alcohol poisoning and drunk driving, about how much they loved her and wanted her to make smart choices. Their love shamed her and changed her in a way their anger never could have. She'd promised herself never again to let them down, and until yesterday, she hadn't.

Now she stood in a small-town discount store that smelled of rubber and popcorn. She'd adjusted the plastic bag under her shirt so it didn't rustle, but she looked so mangy after hours on the road that no one was giving her a second glance, although Panda was attracting the same wary attention he'd garnered in the restaurant. A young mother even pulled her toddler into the next aisle to avoid him.

Lucy glanced at him from under the brim of her ball cap. "I'll meet you at the register."

He held up a cheap pink training bra. "This looks about your size."

She gave him a tight smile. "Really. I don't need any help. You can do your own shopping now. It's on me."

He tossed down the bra. "Damn right it's on you. I'm keeping the receipts."

But he still didn't move. She added some ugly white granny panties to her shopping basket because she wasn't going to let him watch her choose anything else.

He pulled out the granny panties and tossed in some neon-colored nothings. "I like these better."

Of course you do. But since you'll never see them, you don't get a vote.

He slipped his hand under his T-shirt and scratched his stomach. "Hurry up. I'm hungry."

She needed him, so she left the trashy nothings in the shopping basket and let him steer her to the single aisle that served as the store's men's department.

"I like to get input from the ladies when I shop." He grabbed a navy T-shirt and studied the illustration, a cartoon drawing of a woman with enormous breasts and a rocket launcher between her legs.

"That would be a definite no," she said.

"I like it." He tossed it over his shoulder and began thumbing through a stack of jeans.

"I thought you wanted my input."

He stared at her blankly. "Why'd you think that?"

She gave up.

A few minutes later as she set her meager purchases by the register, she experienced a stab of yearning for her pearls and headbands, her slim summer dresses and neat little sandals. They were the objects that anchored her. In her ballet flats and cashmere sweaters, a cell phone tucked to her ear, she knew who she was, not only the adopted daughter of the former president of the United States but a crackerjack lobbyist and first-rate fund-raiser for important causes that help children. Her stomach started to hurt again.

Panda shot her a sullen look as he paid for their purchases. Once they were outside, he shoved everything into the cheap gray nylon duffel he'd bought, wadding up her neon panties with his charcoal gray boxer briefs, and secured the duffel to the Yamaha with a bungee.

Panda didn't like interstate highways, she'd discovered, and they rode east on dusty secondary roads that ran through dying towns and past run-down ranches. She didn't know where they were going. Didn't care. As evening began to fall, he stopped at a twelve-unit motel next to an abandoned driving range. The first thing she spotted when he came out of the motel's tiny office was the single key dangling from his big hand. "I'd like my own room," she said.

"Then you pay for it." He tossed his leg over the bike and, without waiting for her, rode toward the last motel unit. She walked, her legs wobbly. At least straddling that big leather vibrating seat had made her feel nominally alive—right up to the moment she remembered those broad shoulders she was forced to stare at all day belonged to a man who communicated with grunts, ate with his mouth open, and was only putting up with her for the money. A man she was about to share a seedy motel room with.

All she had to do was make a phone call. One phone call and this insanity would be over.

She kept walking.

He was unfastening the bungee cord from the back of the bike when she reached their motel unit. He freed the duffel that held their recent purchases, then flipped open one of the saddlebags. As he pulled out that night's six-pack, she spotted another bumper sticker, this one plastered to the inside of the flap.

The message was so over-the-top vile, it took her a moment to absorb what it said.

NEVER TRUST ANYTHING THAT BLEEDS 5 DAYS A MONTH
AND DOESN'T DIE.

He slapped the flap shut and raked her with those half-lidded eyes. "Are you ready to call Mommy and Daddy yet?"

Chapter Three

THE SPACE BETWEEN THE TWO double beds was no wider than the battered nightstand that separated them. Lucy chose the bed closest to the door in case she needed to run screaming into the night.

The room smelled of cigarette smoke and cheap pine air freshener. Panda plunked the six-pack on what passed for a desk. He had a bad habit of looking at her as if he could see through her clothes, and he did it now. No one ever looked at her like that. They had too much respect. But he was a primitive life-form. He scratched, belched, grunted. Focused on food when he was hungry, on beer when he wanted to drink. And when he wanted sex, he focused on her.

She tried to watch him without his noticing. He grabbed a beer. She waited for him to snap off the bottle cap with his teeth, but he found an opener somewhere. His jeans fit a lot better than hers. If he weren't gross, stupid, and scary, he'd be hot. What would it be like to have sex with someone like him? There'd be no finesse. No courtesy or consideration. No insecurities over whether she was as good in bed as her Texas beauty queen predecessors.

She'd nearly forgotten what sex felt like. Three months ago, she'd told Ted she didn't want them to sleep together again until their wedding night so it would be more special. Ted said he'd go along with them not sleeping together—as long as it didn't interfere with their sex life. But in the end, he'd done as she'd asked with only a minimum of complaining. Now she wondered whether she'd put him off out of sentimentality or because her subconscious was sending her a message.

She took her things from the duffel. Panda kicked off his boots, carried the beer to his bed, and picked up the remote. "I hope they've got some porn."

Her head shot up. "Tell me more about your life in prison."

"Why?"

"Because . . . I'm interested," she said in a rush. "I used to be a social worker."

"I did my time," he said. "I don't believe in looking back."

Surely he was lying. "Has . . . your prison record impeded your career goals?"

"Not so as you'd notice." He flicked through the channels. Fortunately, the motel didn't seem to offer porn—the cross on the wall might explain why—and he settled for NASCAR.

All day she'd been looking forward to a shower, but the idea of stripping naked behind that flimsy bathroom door with him on the other side wasn't appealing. She grabbed her things anyway, carried them into the bathroom, and shot the flimsy lock.

She'd never appreciated a shower so much, despite her uneasiness over sharing a room with him. She shampooed her hair and brushed her teeth, reveling in the sensation of being clean again. Since she hadn't thought to buy pajamas, she dressed in her new T-shirt and shorts, both of which fit her better than the clothes he'd bought for her. As she came out Panda shoved something in his pocket. "TV here sucks." He flipped to a show about monster trucks.

I'm sure life without porn is challenging for a man with your vast intellect. "Sorry about that," she said.

He scratched his chest and nodded.

He was exactly the kind of guy her biological mother would have gone for. Sandy had drunk too much, slept with too many men, and ended up dead when she was only a few years older than Lucy. They had the same green-flecked brown eyes, the same delicate features, and now the same irresponsibility.

She needed to prove to herself that wasn't entirely true. "Could I use your phone?"

His eyes stayed glued to the monster truck rally as he leaned on one hip and pulled his phone out of the same pocket she'd seem him slip it into moments before. She took it from him. "Were you talking to someone?"

His eyes didn't leave the screen. "What do you care?"

"Just wondering."

"Ted."

"You talked to Ted?"

He glanced up at her. "Figured the poor son of a bitch deserved to know you're still alive." His attention returned to the trucks. "Sorry to break the bad news, but he didn't say anything about wanting you back."

Her treacherous stomach did its customary death spiral at the thought of Ted, but if she started picturing what he was going through, she wouldn't be able to function, not that she was functioning all that well now. And then another thought struck her. What if Panda was lying? What if he'd been calling the tabloids instead of Ted? Her story would bring him more money than he could make in a year. Years.

She itched to check the call record on his phone, but she couldn't do it with him watching. The moment he went into the bathroom, she'd check. In the meantime, she had to let Meg know she was still alive, but when she started to carry the phone outside, Panda growled at her. "Stay here. Unless you don't care about making friends with some of those characters I saw hanging around in the parking lot."

"A problem decent hotels never seem to have," she couldn't help but point out.

"Wouldn't know about that."

She punched in Meg's number and kept the call brief. "I'm fine." "Not sure what I'm going to do." "Rather not say." "Tell my folks." And finally, "I've got to go."

Over the years, she and Meg had talked about so many things, but she couldn't do that now. Fortunately, Meg seemed preoccupied and didn't press.

It wasn't even nine o'clock when she hung up. She had nothing to read. Nothing to do. When she'd returned from her honeymoon, she'd planned to start work on the writing project about Nealy that her father was spearheading, but she couldn't concentrate on anything like that now, and she definitely couldn't think about the lobbying work she intended to resume in the fall.

She moved to the far side of the unoccupied bed and pushed the pillows against the wobbly headboard. The truck show finally ended. She jumped as the springs squeaked next to her. Panda grabbed some of his things and disappeared into the bathroom. She got up to look for his phone but couldn't find it. It must still be in his pocket.

The shower went on. She hadn't noticed him buying pajamas either. Viper, the biker girl she wished she could be, would take something like that in stride, but the idea of a naked Panda made Lucy nervous.

Sleep offered an escape from her enforced confinement. She rearranged the covers and sandwiched her head between the pillows. As she told herself to go to sleep, she heard the bathroom door open. Once again, she thought about how much Sandy would have loved Panda. He was swarthy, surly, and dense. Guys like Panda explained how her mother had ended up with two daughters by different fathers.

Sandy's vague memories of Lucy's sperm donor had included the words "stoned frat boy." Tracy's jerk of a father had died in the same car accident that had killed Sandy.

A hand curled around her shoulder. She shot up, the pillow falling off her head. *"What?"*

He stood over her, wearing nothing but a splash of shower water and a clean pair of jeans. Her heart pounded. His bare chest was rock hard—too hard. He hadn't bothered to fasten the snap on his jeans, and they barely clung to his hip bones. She saw a flat abdomen, a narrow arrow of dark hair, and a sizable bulge.

He rubbed his thumb on her shoulder. "So . . . You want to get it on or what?"

She jerked back. *"No."*

"You've been acting like you do."

"I have not!"

He ran the flat of his hand over one pectoral and glanced toward the TV. "Just as well, I guess."

The crazy part of her wanted to know why it was "just as well." She clenched her teeth.

He returned his attention to her. "I like it rough, and you don't seem the type." He snapped her thigh with his thumb and second finger. "You sure you don't want to change your mind?"

She wrenched her leg away and rubbed the sting he'd inflicted. "Positive."

"How do you know you won't like it?"

He was still looming over her, and her heart was thudding. Nine years of Secret Service protection had allowed her to take her safety for granted, but there was no friendly agent stationed outside the motel room door now. She was on her own. "I just know, that's all."

His thin lips twisted. "You're fucking up my vacation. You understand that, right?"

"I'm paying you."

"Yeah, well, I've decided you're not paying me enough. I was straight with you from the start. I told you I wanted to get laid." He reached for the sheet she'd twisted around her body.

She grabbed at it. "Stop right there! Back off."

Something disturbing flickered in his eyes. "You'll like it. I'll make you like it."

It sounded like a line from a bad movie, but he looked as though he'd thought it up all by himself. She couldn't believe this was happening. She hauled herself up against the headboard, frightened and furious. "You're not going to touch me, and you know why? Because if you do, the full power of the United States justice system is going to come crashing down on you."

"Your word against mine." He curled his lip.

"Exactly. An ex-con and the president's daughter. You figure it out."

She'd finally penetrated that thick skull. With a dark mutter, he shot her a sneer and retreated to his cave.

She stayed upright, her spine pressed to the headboard, her blood still racing. She clutched the sheet to her chest, as if that would protect her if he changed his mind.

It was over. He'd made the choice for her. She couldn't spend another day with him, not after this. First thing tomorrow, she'd call her family, find an airport, and fly home. Her adventures as Viper, the biker girl, were over.

Fly back home to what? Her family's disappointment? The job she'd started to hate?

She tucked the sheet around her body, feeble armor. Why couldn't he be a harmless drifter who'd let her hitch a ride without giving her any trouble? She pressed her head between the pillows again, trepidation and resentment churning inside her. Through the slit of light, she watched him across the narrow space that separated their beds. The walls were thin. She was afraid to shut her eyes. If he made another move, she'd scream. Surely even in this seedy motel, someone would hear her.

He lay on his back with his ankles crossed, the remote propped on his chest, his hair inky against the pillow propped behind his head. He'd switched from monster trucks to bass fishing, and he looked perfectly relaxed, not at all like a man with rape on his mind.

Perfectly, totally relaxed . . .

Maybe it was a trick of the flickering light from the television, but she swore she saw the faintest smile of satisfaction lurking at the corners of those thin lips.

She squinted. Shifted the pillows ever so slightly. It wasn't her imagination. He looked smug, not sinister.

He looked like a man who'd figured out the perfect way to get rid of an unwanted nuisance and come out a thousand dollars richer.

SHE GOT DRESSED IN THE bathroom the next morning and didn't speak to him until they'd been served at a pancake place wedged between a service station and a thrift shop. Some of the diners were women, but most were men wearing caps that ranged from the trucker variety to sports teams. They eyed Panda suspiciously, but no one paid any attention to either her or her pregnancy bump.

He took a noisy slurp from his coffee mug, then dug into his pancakes, chewing without bothering to close his mouth. He noticed her staring at him and frowned. Her conviction that he'd been manipulat-

ing her last night wavered. She was almost certain he'd been deliberately trying to scare her off, but her instincts weren't exactly foolproof
these days.

She studied him closely, paying particular attention to his eyes as
she spoke. "So, have you raped a lot of women?"

She saw it. A flicker of outrage camouflaged almost immediately by
half-closed eyelids and a noisy slurp from his coffee mug. "Depends on
what you mean by rape."

"You'd know it when you did it." She took the plunge. "I have to
admit last night was interesting."

His brows slammed together. "Interesting! You think that was interesting?"

Not at the time she hadn't. But now? Definitely. "Maybe if you were
a better actor, you could have pulled it off."

He grew wary. "I don't know what you're talking about."

She ignored his scowl. "It's obvious you want to get rid of me, but
was that the best you could do?" Those sinister lips pulled tight, and
his expression became so ominous she had to muster all the bravado she
could find to set her elbows on the table and meet his gaze. "I'm not
going anywhere, Panda. You're stuck with me." A small devil prodded
her, and she pointed to the corner of her own mouth. "You have a little
food right there."

"I don't care."

"Are you sure? A fastidious eater like yourself?"

"If you don't like it, you know what you can do."

"Yes. Fly home and send you a check for a thousand dollars, plus
expenses."

"You're damned right, plus expenses." He swiped at his mouth with
his napkin, more a reflexive motion than capitulation.

She curled her fingers around her own coffee mug. He could have dropped her off on the side of the road anytime and disappeared, but he wanted the money, so he hadn't done it. Now he intended to scare her off and still collect the cash. Too bad for him.

She set down her mug. All this time she'd assumed he had the upper hand, but it was just the opposite. "You're big and bad, Panda. I get that. And now that I get it, would you mind knocking it off?"

"I don't know what you're talking about."

"The leers. All those references to 'getting laid.'"

He pushed away his plate, leaving his pancakes half eaten, eyeing her with distaste. "Here's the way I see it. Rich girl thinks she can add a little excitement to her life by slumming it with a guy like me. Am I wrong?"

She reminded herself who had the upper hand. "Well, the experience is definitely making me rethink the importance of decent table manners." She gave him the same dead-eye look she gave her sibs when they misbehaved. "Tell me where we're going."

"*I'm* going to Caddo Lake. If you know what's good for you, you'll be going to the airport."

"Excuse me." A sixtyish woman in a peach pantsuit approached their booth. The woman gestured toward a nearby table where a jowly man with a walrus mustache pretended to look in the opposite direction. "My husband, Conrad, said I should mind my own business, but I couldn't help noticing . . ." She stared at Lucy. "Has anybody ever told you that you look like the president's daughter? That Lucy character."

"She hears it all the time," Panda said. He looked across the table at Lucy and said in fluent Spanish, *"Ella es otra persona que piensa que te pareces a Lucy Jorik."* And then, to the woman, "Her English ain't too good."

"It's amazing," the woman said. "'Course, now that I'm closer, I can see she's a lot younger. Hope she doesn't grow up to be like her."

Panda nodded. "Another spoiled brat who thinks the world owes her."

Lucy didn't like that at all, but peach pantsuit lady was on a roll. "I used to admire the way President Jorik raised her kids, but obviously she missed something with that Lucy. Running out on the Beaudine boy. I see his mama's television show all the time. And Conrad's a big golfer. He never misses watching any tournament where Dallas Beaudine's playing."

"I guess some women don't know what's good for them," Panda agreed.

"Confidentially, neither does Conrad." She smiled at Lucy. "Well, y'all have a nice day. Sorry to have bothered you."

"No bother," he said, as courteous as a small-town preacher. But the moment she disappeared, he crumpled his napkin. "Let's get the hell out of here before more of your fan club shows up. I don't need this crap."

"Snarl all you want," she told him. "You're the one who invited me on this joy ride, and I'm not calling it off."

He tossed some bills on the table a lot harder than he needed to. "Your funeral."

Chapter Four

❧

THE SMALL RENTAL HOUSE SAT on one of Caddo Lake's hidden bayous. A pair of aging window air conditioners protruded from the faded mustard-colored siding, and a square of artificial turf covered the front stoop. They'd spent the previous night at a motel near Nacogdoches, where Panda had made a point of ignoring her. Early this morning, they'd headed northeast toward the lake, which sat on the Texas-Louisiana border and, according to the pamphlet she'd picked up when they stopped for gas, was the largest freshwater lake in the South—and surely the spookiest, with its primordial swamps rising out of brown water.

The house was shabby but clean, with a small living room, two even smaller bedrooms, and an old-fashioned kitchen. Lucy chose the room with twin beds. The orange plaid wallpaper curled at the seams and clashed with the cheap purple and green floral quilted bedspread, but she was too grateful to have a wall between her bed and Panda's to care.

She changed into her shorts and made her way to the kitchen. It was outfitted with metal cabinets, worn countertops, and a gray vinyl floor. The window above the sink looked out over the bayou, and a nearby door led to a small wooden deck that held a molded plastic table, webbed lawn chairs, a propane grill, and some fishing gear.

She found Panda gazing out at the palmetto banking the bayou, his feet propped on the deck railing, a Coke can curled in his palm. At least he hadn't hunkered down with another six-pack. He didn't acknowledge her as she checked out the grill, then examined a fishing pole. His silences were unnerving. "It's hot out here," she finally said.

He took a swig of Coke without bothering to reply. She averted her eyes from the disagreeable T-shirt she'd been pretending all day not to notice. Panda's concept of sartorial elegance didn't extend further than a shower and a clean pair of jeans. She felt an unwelcome pang for Ted, the sweet, sensitive, even-tempered bridegroom she'd thrown under the bus.

"A shade umbrella would be nice," she said.

Nothing but silence.

She spotted an excursion boat in the distance, cutting through bald cypress webbed with Spanish moss. "If I were a biker, I'd have a better name than Panda."

Viper.

He crumpled his Coke can in his fist and stalked off the deck into the backyard, pitching the can into a black plastic trash bin on his way. As he walked toward the lake, she slumped into the chair he'd abandoned. Ted was a great conversationalist and the best listener she'd ever known. He'd acted as though he was fascinated with whatever she said. Of course, he acted that way with everybody, even crazy people, but still...She'd never known him to be impatient or short-tempered—never heard him utter a harsh word. He was kind, patient, thoughtful, understanding, and yet she'd dumped him. What did that say about her?

She pulled one of the matching chairs closer with her heels, feeling bluer by the minute. Panda reached the dock. An overturned canoe lay on the bank, and an osprey skimmed the water. He hadn't told her how long he planned to rent the house, only that she was free to leave anytime, the sooner the better. But did he really want that? She was growing increasingly convinced that he was smarter than he let on, and she couldn't let go of her nagging fear that he was talking to the tabloids. What if he'd figured out he could make a lot more than a thousand dollars selling them her story?

She headed down the steps and toward the water, where he'd stopped by the canoe. She scuffed the heel of her sneaker in the dirt. He didn't look up. She wished she'd chosen a traveling companion who didn't indulge in oppressive silences and favor loathsome bumper stickers. But then, she wished for a lot of things. That she'd picked a different fiancé to abandon, one who'd done something—anything—to justify being ditched at the altar. But Ted hadn't, and some ugly part of her hated him for being so much better than she was.

She couldn't stand her thoughts a moment longer. "I like to fish," she said. "I throw everything back. Except when I went to Outward Bound. I kept the fish then because—"

"Not interested." He straightened and gave her a long look—not undressing her with his eyes; he'd stopped doing that—but looking at her in a way that made her feel as if he were seeing every part of her, even the parts she didn't know were there. "Call Ted and tell him you're sorry. Call your folks. It's been three days. You've had your adventure. It's time for the rich girl to go home."

"I've heard enough rich-girl cracks."

"I call it like I see it."

"Like you want to see it."

He studied her for an uncomfortably long moment, then tilted his head toward the canoe. "Help me get this thing in the water."

They flipped the canoe and slid it into the lake. She grabbed one of the paddles without waiting for an invitation and stepped in. She hoped he'd stalk off, but he picked up the other paddle and climbed in, the motion so graceful the canoe barely moved.

For the next hour, they glided through the water, steering clear of the water hyacinths that choked the swampier areas. As they paddled from one hidden bayou to the next, through eerie cypress forests draped with Spanish moss, he barely spoke. She glanced back at him. The play of his muscles stretched his white T-shirt over his chest as he paddled, highlighting the message written in black letters. The shirt wasn't one of his recent purchases but something that must have been stashed in the bike's saddlebags when he'd left Wynette. If only it had stayed there. "Those awful bumper stickers are bad enough," she said, "but at least a person has to be close to your bike to see them."

He watched an alligator lolling in a patch of sunlight on the far bank. "I told you about the bumper stickers."

She turned around in her seat, resting the paddle on her knees and letting him steer. "You said the bike's previous owner put them on. So why didn't you let me peel them off?"

He shifted his paddle to the other side. "Because I like them."

She frowned at the message on his T-shirt: IT ONLY SEEMS KINKY THE FIRST TIME.

"It was a gift," he said.

"From Satan?"

Something that looked almost like a smile flickered across his face and then disappeared. "You don't like it, you know what you can do about it." He cleared another snarl of water hyacinths.

"What if a child saw that shirt?"

"Seen any kids today?" He shifted his weight slightly on the seat. "You're making me sorry I lost my favorite one."

She turned back to the bow. "I don't want to hear."

"It says, 'I'm all for gay marriage as long as both bitches are hot.'"

Her temper sparked, and the canoe wobbled as she twisted back around. "Political correctness is obviously a big joke to you, but it isn't to me. Call me old-fashioned, but I think there's value in honoring the dignity of everyone."

He pulled his paddle out of the murky water. "Damn, I wish I'd brought the one I got a coupla weeks ago."

"A terrible loss, I'm sure."

"Want to know what it said?"

"No."

"It said . . ."—he leaned toward her and spoke in a slow whisper that carried over the water—"'If I'd shot you when I wanted to, I'd be out by now.'"

So much for conversation.

When they returned to the house, she made herself a sandwich from the groceries they'd picked up, claimed an old paperback someone had left behind, and closed herself in the bedroom. Loneliness wrapped around her like a too-heavy overcoat. Had Ted done anything to find her? Apparently not, considering that he hadn't tried to stop her from leaving the church. And what about her parents? She'd called Meg twice from Panda's phone, so it couldn't be that hard for the Secret Service to locate her.

What if Mat and Nealy had written her off? She told herself they wouldn't do that.

Unless they were so disgusted with her that they didn't want to see her for a while.

She couldn't blame them.

SOMETHING ODD HAPPENED OVER THE next few days. Panda's manners underwent a marked improvement. At first she didn't notice the absence of all those belches, slurps, and scratching. It was only when she saw him cut a piece of chicken neatly from the bone and carefully swallow his first bite before he asked her to pass the pepper that she became thoroughly confused. What had happened to that open-mouth chewing and using the back of his hand as a napkin? As for any suggestions of sexual violence . . . He barely seemed to notice she was female.

They went into the town of Marshall for groceries and supplies. She bought sunglasses, kept her hat pulled low, the baby bump she'd grown to detest in place, and with Panda close by, no one noticed her.

He worked on his bike, taking things apart, reassembling. Bare chested, and with a blue bandanna wrapped around his forehead, he lubed and polished, checked fluid levels and changed brake pads. He set a radio in an open window and listened to hip-hop, except once she'd gone outside and heard an aria from *The Magic Flute*. When she'd commented on it, he accused her of messing around with his radio and ordered her to change the damn station. Occasionally she'd catch him talking to someone on his cell, but he never left his phone around, so she had no opportunity to check his call records.

At night, she sealed herself in her bedroom while he sat up, sometimes watching a baseball game on television, but more frequently sitting on the deck, staring out at the water. The numbness from the first few days began to fade, and she found herself watching him.

PANDA DRAGGED THE MUSKY SCENT of the bayou into his lungs. He had too much time to think—too many memories crowding in—and each day his resentment burrowed deeper.

He hadn't expected her to last more than a few hours, yet here she still was, seven days after he'd picked her up. Why couldn't she do what she was supposed to? Go back to Wynette or run home to Virginia. He didn't give a damn where she went, as long as she was gone.

He couldn't understand her. She'd seen right through that stomach-churning bogus rape he'd staged their second night out, and she acted as if she didn't hear half the insults he hurled at her. She was so controlled, so disciplined. What she'd done on her wedding day was clearly out of character. And yet . . . Beneath those good manners, he kept catching glimpses of something—someone—more complicated. She was smart, maddeningly perceptive, and stubborn as hell. Shadows didn't cling to her like they did to him. He'd bet anything she'd never woken up screaming. Or drunk until she blacked out. And when she'd been a kid . . .

When she'd been a kid, she'd been able to do what he couldn't.

Five hundred dollars. That's all his kid brother had been worth.

Through the cry of a swamp creature, he heard his eight-year-old brother's voice as they'd walked up the broken sidewalk to still another foster home, their current social worker climbing the creaking porch steps in front of them. *"What if I pee the bed again?"* Curtis whispered. *"That's what got us kicked out of the last house."*

Panda hid his own fear beneath a fifteen-year-old's swagger. "Don't worry about it, jerkface." He delivered a sucker punch to Curtis's scrawny arm. "I'll wake up in the middle of the night and take you to the bathroom."

But what if he didn't wake up like he hadn't last week? He'd promised himself he wouldn't fall asleep until he got Curtis up to pee, but he'd dozed off anyway, and the next day old lady Gilbert had told Social Services they had to find someplace else for Curtis.

Panda wouldn't let anything separate him from his kid brother, and he told their social worker he'd run away if the two of them got split up. She must have believed him because she found a new house for them. But she warned him there weren't any more families willing to take them both.

"I'm scared," Curtis whispered as they reached the porch. "Are you scared?"

"I'm never scared," he lied. "Nothing to be scared of."

He'd been so wrong.

Panda gazed out at the dark water. Lucy had been fourteen when her mother had died. If he and Curtis had fallen in with Mat and Nealy Jorik, his brother would still be alive. Lucy had accomplished what he couldn't pull off—she'd kept her sister safe—and now Curtis lay in a grave while the sister Lucy had protected prepared for her first year of college.

Curtis had hooked up with a gang when he was only ten, something Panda could have prevented if he hadn't been in juvie. They'd let him out long enough to go to his little brother's funeral.

He blinked his eyes hard. Memories of Curtis only led to other memories. It would be easier not to think if he had music to distract him, but he couldn't listen to the heavy drama of *Otello, Boris Godunov,* or a dozen other operas with Lucy around. With anybody around.

He wished she'd come out and talk to him. He wanted her close; he wanted her farther away. He wanted her to leave, to stay, to take off her clothes—he couldn't help that. Being with her all day would test any man, especially a horny bastard like himself.

He rubbed the bridge of his nose, pulled his cell from his pocket, and carried it around to the side of the house where he couldn't be overheard.

PANDA KEPT GOADING HER INTO going for morning runs, and even though she held him back, he refused to run ahead. "The second I'm out of sight, you'll start walking," he said.

True. She walked for exercise and had a gym membership she used semi-semi-regularly, but she wasn't a running enthusiast. "When did you make yourself my personal trainer?"

He punished her by kicking up the pace. Eventually, however, he took pity and slowed.

Her conviction that he wasn't entirely the Neanderthal he wanted her to believe had grown along with her curiosity about him, and she embarked on a fishing expedition. "Have you talked to your girlfriend since you've been gone from wherever you're gone from?"

A grunt.

"Where is that, by the way?"

"Up north."

"Colorado? Nome?"

"Do you have to talk?"

"Married? Divorced?"

"Watch that pothole. If you break your leg, you're on your own."

She pulled some extra air into her burning lungs. "You know the details of my life. It's only fair that I know some of yours."

He moved ahead again. Unlike her, he wasn't out of breath. "Never been married, and that's all you're getting."

"Are you involved with anybody?"

He looked at her over his shoulder—faintly pitying. "What do you think?"

"That the pool of lady alligator wrestlers isn't big enough to give you a lot of dating opportunities?"

She heard a sound—either amusement or a warning that he'd heard enough stupid questions—but all she'd learned was that he was single, and he could be lying about that. "It's so strange," she said. "As soon as we got here, your manners improved. It must be the swamp air."

He cut to the other side of the road. "The question is," she said, "why bother with all that spitting and scratching since—and I have to admit I was surprised about this—it doesn't seem to come naturally?"

She expected him to dodge the question, but he didn't. "So what? I got bored when I realized you were too much of a nut job to be scared into doing what you should have done right away?"

No one had ever called her a nut job, but since the insult came from him, she didn't take it to heart. "You were hoping when I saw the contrast between you and Ted, I'd realize what I'd given up and go back to Wynette."

"Something like that. Ted's a good guy, and he was obviously in love with you. I was trying to do him a favor. I stopped when I realized the biggest favor I could do him was to keep you from going back."

That was true enough to hurt, and they finished the run in silence.

When they returned to the house, he pulled his sweat-soaked T-shirt over his head, grabbed the hose, and doused himself. His hair clung to his neck in wet black ribbons; the sun poured over his face as he tilted his head to the sky.

He finally set the hose aside and used his palm to sluice the water from his chest. His swarthy skin, blunt-tipped nose, and wet, big-fisted hands made an unsettling contrast to Ted's perfect male beauty. Panda might not be as crude as he wanted her to believe, but he still existed completely outside her realm of experience.

She realized she was staring and turned away. Her female body was clearly drawn to what she saw. Fortunately, her female brain wasn't nearly as foolish.

One day drifted into another until they'd been at the lake for a week. She swam, read, or baked bread, one of the few foods that tasted good to her. What she didn't do was call Ted or her family.

Each morning after their run, Panda appeared in the kitchen, his hair still wet from his shower, his curls temporarily tamed, although she knew they'd quickly reassert themselves. He picked up what she suspected would be the first of several warm slices of the oatmeal bread she'd just taken from the oven, tore the bread neatly in half, and spread each piece with a spoonful of orange marmalade. "Did Ted know about your baking skills when he let you dump him?" he said after he'd swallowed his second bite.

She set aside her own piece of bread, no longer hungry. "Ted doesn't eat a lot of carbs." That wasn't true, but she wouldn't admit that she'd never gotten around to baking for her fiancé.

She'd picked up her adult cooking skills under the funnel-shaped stainless steel lights that hung in the White House kitchen, the place where she'd escaped when her siblings' squabbles had gotten on her nerves. There, she'd learned from some of the country's best chefs, and now Panda, instead of Ted, was the beneficiary.

He twisted the lid back on the marmalade jar. "Ted's the kind of guy who was born under a lucky star. Brains, money, polish." He slapped the jar in the refrigerator and shoved the door closed. "While the rest of the world screws up, Ted Beaudine sails free."

"Yes, well, he was trapped in a pretty big screwup last weekend," she said.

"He's already over it."

She prayed that was true.

NEAR THE HOUSE, CADDO LAKE was shallow with a muddy bottom, so she couldn't swim there, but when they were on the lake, she swam off the small outboard that came with the rental house. He never went in the water with her, and eight days after their arrival—eleven days since she'd fled—she asked him about it as she swam alongside the drifting boat. "Odd that a tough guy like you seems afraid to go in the water."

"Can't swim," he said as he propped his bare feet on the boat's splintering rail. "I never learned."

Having observed his love of being on the water, she found that strange. And what about those jeans he always wore? She flipped to her back and took another approach. "You don't want me to see your skinny legs. You're afraid I'll mock." As if any part of his body could be less than muscular . . .

"I like jeans," he said.

She dropped her feet and treaded water. "I don't get it. It's a sauna around here, and you'll take off your shirt at the drop of a hat, so why not wear shorts?"

"I've got some scars. Now shut up about it."

He might be telling the truth, but she doubted it. As he leaned back against the stern, sunlight gilded his swarthy pirate's skin, and his half-closed eyes seemed more languid than menacing. She felt another of those unwelcoming stirs of . . . something. She wanted to think it was merely awareness, but it was more than that. An involuntary arousal.

So what? It had been almost four months since she and Ted had made love, and she was only human. Since she had no intention of giving in to her wayward thoughts, what was the harm? Still, she wanted to punish him for making her mind wander where it shouldn't. "It's strange that you don't have any tattoos." She dog-paddled next to the stern. "No naked women dancing on your biceps, no obscenities etched on your knuckles. Not even a tasteful iron cross. Aren't you worried you'll get kicked out of the biker club?"

The flickering light coming off the water softened the hard edges of his cheekbones. "I hate needles."

"You don't swim. You hate needles. You're afraid to show your legs. You really are sort of a mess, aren't you?"

"You're not exactly the person to call anybody else a mess."

"True. Deepest apologies." She managed something almost approaching one of his sneers.

"When are you going to call your folks?" he said out of nowhere.

She went under and didn't come up until she had to. "Meg lets them know I'm safe," she said, even though she knew that wasn't the same as talking to them herself.

She missed Charlotte and Holly's spats, Tracy's dramas, Andre's rambling accounts of the latest fantasy novel he'd read. She missed Nealy and Mat, but the idea of picking up the phone and calling them paralyzed her. What could she possibly say?

Panda gave her a none-too-gentle assist back into the boat. Her cheap one-piece black swimsuit rode up, but he didn't seem to notice. He fired up the outboard, and they chugged back to the dock. As he killed the engine, she gathered up her flip-flops, but before she could climb out of the boat, he said, "I have to get back to work. We're leaving tomorrow."

She'd known this limbo couldn't last forever, but she still hadn't made plans to move ahead. Couldn't make them. She was paralyzed, caught between the focused, organized person she'd been and the aimless, confused woman she'd become. The panic that was never far away kicked up inside her. "I'm not ready."

"That's your problem." He tethered the boat. "I'm dropping you off at the Shreveport airport on my way."

She swallowed. "No need. I'm staying here."

"What are you going to do for money?"

She should have solved that problem by now, but she hadn't. Although she wouldn't admit it, she didn't like the idea of staying at the house without him. For a brooding and increasingly mysterious stranger, he was surprisingly relaxing to be around. So much more relaxing than being with Ted. With Panda, she didn't have to pretend to be a better person than she was.

He stepped out of the boat. "Tell you what. If you call your family tonight, you can ride with me for a while longer."

She scrambled onto the dock. "For how long?"

"Until you piss me off," he said as he tied up the boat.

"That might not get me to the next town."

"My best offer. Work with it."

She was almost glad he was forcing her to do what she should have done from the beginning, and she nodded.

That night she did her best to put off the phone call with various unnecessary chores until he lost patience. "Call them."

"Later," she said. "I have to pack first."

He sneered. "Chickenshit."

"What do you care? This doesn't have anything to do with you."

"Sure it does. Your mother was the president. It's my patriotic duty."

She snatched the phone. As she punched in the number, she wished she'd been able to get her hands on his phone just once when he wasn't watching. Even as she retreated to the deck, he could see her through the window.

Her heart hammered when she heard Mat's familiar gruff voice. She fought back tears. "Dad . . ."

"Lucy! Are you all right?"

"Kind of." Her voice broke. "I'm sorry. You know I wouldn't hurt you and Mom for anything."

"We know that. Lucy, we love you. Nothing could change that."

His words twisted the knife of guilt even deeper. They'd given her everything without expecting anything back, and this was how she repaid them. She struggled against tears. "I love you, too."

"We need to sit down together and discuss what happened. Figure out why you didn't feel like you could talk to us about it. I want you to come home."

"I know. How—how are the kids?"

"Holly's having a sleepover, and Charlotte's learning to play the guitar. Andre has a girlfriend, and Tracy's really pissed with you. As for your grandfather . . . You can imagine how he's taken this. I suggest a stiff drink before you call him. But first you have to talk to your mother. You might be thirty-one, but you're still part of this family."

He couldn't have said anything that made her feel worse about herself.

"Lucy?" It was Nealy. He'd passed over the phone.

"I'm sorry," she said quickly. "Really."

"Never mind about that," her mother said briskly. "I don't care if you're a grown woman. We want you home."

"I—I can't." She bit her lip. "I'm not done running away yet."

Nealy, of all people, couldn't argue with that, and she didn't try. "When do you think you'll be done?"

"I'm . . . not sure."

"Let me talk to her!" Tracy shrieked in the background.

Nealy said, "We had no idea you were so unhappy."

"I wasn't. You can't think that. It's just—I can't explain."

"I wish you'd try."

"Let me have the phone!" Tracy cried.

"Promise you'll stay in touch," her mother said. "And promise you'll call your grandfather."

Before Lucy could promise anything, Tracy grabbed the phone. "Why haven't you called me? This is all Meg's fault. I hate her. You should never have listened to what she said. She's jealous because you were getting married and she wasn't."

"Trace, I know I disappointed you, but this isn't Meg's fault."

Her baby sister Button had turned into a volcano of eighteen-year-old outrage. "How can you love somebody one minute and then not love them the next?"

"It wasn't exactly like that."

"You're being selfish. And stupid."

"I'm sorry I hurt you." Before she lost her courage, she needed to get the rest of this over with. "Put the others on, will you?"

In the next ten minutes, she learned that Andre still talked on the phone to Ted, that Holly was auditioning for a part in a play, and that Charlotte had mastered "Drunken Sailor" on the guitar. Each conversation was more painful than the last. Only after she'd hung up did it register that all three of them had posed the question her parents had never raised.

"Lucy, where are you?"

Panda came up behind her on the deck and took the phone before she could check his call log. Was he in touch with the tabloids or not? He disappeared back inside, and when she finally went in herself, he was watching a baseball game. "I need to make another call," she said.

He studied her. "Phone's been acting up lately. Give me the number and I'll put it in for you."

"I can handle it."

"It's temperamental."

She had to stop playing games. "I want to see your phone."

"I know."

"If you don't have anything to hide, you'll let me look at it."

"Who says I don't have anything to hide?"

He was enjoying himself, and she didn't like it. "You know everything about me, but I don't know any more about you than I did eleven days ago. I don't even know your real name."

"Simpson. Bart."

"Afraid I'll see the *National Enquirer* on your speed dial?"

"You won't."

"One of the other tabloids, then? Or did you contact the legitimate press?"

"Do you really think somebody like me is going to cozy up to the press?"

"Maybe. I'm a lucrative meal ticket."

He shrugged, extended his leg, and pulled his phone from his pocket. "Knock yourself out."

The fact that he was giving up the phone told her she wouldn't discover any secrets, and she was right. The only call on his log was the one she'd just made. She flipped the phone back to him.

As she walked away, his voice drifted toward her, quiet and a little gruff. "I see you as a lot of things, but a meal ticket isn't one of them."

She didn't know what he meant by that, so she pretended not to hear.

PANDA ABANDONED THE BASEBALL GAME he hadn't been watching and moved back out to the deck. It was time to have a serious talk with himself. As if he hadn't been doing that for almost two weeks.

Be the best at what you're good at. That had always been his motto. *Be the best at what you're good at and stay away from what you're not.* At the top of that list? Emotional crap.

But being closed up with her like this would drive any man nuts. Those shorts and T-shirts made her look like a damned fifteen-year-old, which should have turned his stomach but didn't because she wasn't fifteen.

He was trapped with his arousal, his resentment, his fear. He gazed out into the night, trying not to give into them. Failing.

LUCY STUDIED THE CURLING WALLPAPER in her bedroom. They were leaving here tomorrow morning, and Panda was as much a mystery to her as he'd been when she'd climbed on his bike. She didn't even know his real name. Most important, she didn't know whether or not he was selling her out.

She'd eaten barely any dinner, and she went into the kitchen to fix herself a bowl of cereal. Through the window, she saw Panda on the deck, where he was staring at the lake again. She wondered what he was thinking about.

She sprinkled some Special K in a bowl and carried it into the living room. *The American President* was playing silently on the television. As she started to sit, she spotted what appeared to be a business card wedged at the back of the seat cushion. She slid it out.

CHARITY ISLAND FERRY

RESIDENT PASS

3583

Your Pure Michigan Adventure Begins Here

Had this fallen out of Panda's wallet or had a previous tenant lost it? Only one way to find out. She returned the card to the seat cushion, leaving it just as she'd found it.

The next morning it was gone.

Chapter Five

❧

LUCY FINALLY KNEW SOMETHING ABOUT Panda that he didn't want her to know. That should have made her feel better, but she didn't want to leave Caddo Lake, and her mood was dismal as they rode away. She persuaded him to stop in Texarkana where, fake pregnancy in place, she pointedly purchased a prepaid phone of her own. She told him to put it on her expense account.

Right after they crossed into Arkansas, they had to pull beneath an underpass to wait out a rain shower. She asked him where they were going, not expecting him to answer. But he did, at least partially. "We should be close to Memphis by nightfall."

His bike had Texas license plates, he vacationed on the Louisiana border, they were headed for Tennessee, and he had a resident ferry pass to an island somewhere in Michigan. Were these the practices of an itinerate construction worker or simply the lifestyle of a wanderer? She wished she could be as mysterious, but it was hard to have secrets when your life had been laid out for public examination while you were still a teenager.

Their nighttime lodging was a backwater Arkansas motel near the Tennessee border. She took in the room's painted cinder-block walls and ugly puce bedspreads. "I'm sure there's a Hyatt someplace nearby."

He dropped his pack on the bed closest to the door. "I like it. It has character."

"Characters. We'll be lucky if those drug dealers lurking outside don't break in and murder us in our sleep."

"Exactly why you can't have your own room."

"Why I can't have my own room is because you like being difficult."

"True." He cocked his head and gave her his calculated biker's sneer. "Plus, this way, I might see you naked."

"Good luck with that." She grabbed the pajama shorts and T-shirt she'd bought when they were at Caddo and headed for the bathroom. Once she'd sealed herself in, she took a deep breath. She was flustered enough from spending the day plastered against his back with the vibrations from that big bike stirring her up. She didn't need him baiting her.

The flimsy shower stall was barely larger than a phone booth, and every time she moved, she banged her elbow into the plastic panels. She tried to imagine Panda attempting to wedge his body into such an uncomfortably small space.

His naked body.

She dropped her hands from the breasts she'd been soaping for too long. She was female. She couldn't help the way Panda stirred her baser instincts. There was something primal about him. He was earthy and carnal, all brawn and muscle. Made for sex. It would be rough and raunchy, so different from sex with Ted, who'd been the gold standard of male erotic perfection—polished, inexhaustible, selfless.

Only now could she begin to admit how taxing that selflessness had been. She'd wanted to give back as good as she got, but what she got was so perfectly executed that she had no idea how to return it in equal measure, and that kept it from being as good as it should have been. She'd worried that her moans were too loud, her movements too awkward, her caresses too tentative, too rough, not in the right place. What if she was taking too long or her breath was bad or her thighs were jiggling? What if she farted?

All that stress.

It would be so different with Panda, so easy. He'd only be out for himself. And who cared what she did or what he thought about it? She could respond or not respond, however she felt. She wouldn't need to worry about how her words, her actions, her moans—or lack of them—affected him.

The idea of simply taking what she wanted from a man who expected nothing except access to a female body tantalized her. All through high school and college, she'd fantasized about the wild men she sometimes encountered: the son of a wealthy socialite who'd supplemented his income dealing drugs, the college basketball player with the mile-wide grin who'd cheated on his exams, the guys with the cocky struts and cigarettes dangling from the corners of their mouths, the ones who drove too fast, drank too much, worked their bodies instead of their brains. And now Panda.

How would he react if she walked out naked? She couldn't imagine that he'd turn away.

This trip was nearly over. She understood that, even if he hadn't spelled out the exact timetable. Any day now, he'd be dumping her. Would she ever have a better chance for free, dirty, uncommitted sex? This was a once-in-a-lifetime opportunity. Was she going to let it pass her by?

Two weeks ago, she was engaged to another man—a man she still loved in so many ways. Jumping into bed with Panda would be unforgivable.

Still, the idea wasn't altogether repellent.

She felt an irrational urge to talk this over with Ted. He was always clearheaded, and she wasn't clear about anything right now.

Even as she dried off, she was still thinking about it. She knew what she wanted. Didn't know what she wanted. Finally she decided on a coward's compromise. She wrapped herself in the threadbare towel, opened the bathroom door, and said, "Don't look."

He looked. Not even being subtle about it but studying her in a way that made her skin hot. Long seconds passed before he spoke. "Are you sure about this?" No games. Straight to the point. Pure Panda.

"No."

"You must be fairly sure."

"I'm not."

He took more time thinking it over than she'd expected. Finally he rose from the bed and jerked his T-shirt over his head. "I need a shower. If you're still wearing that towel when I come out, lose it."

She didn't like this. Not the fact that he intended to shower—she knew exactly how grimy they were from their long bike ride—but she didn't like having more time to think than she wanted. Was this the best way to move on from Ted or the worst?

The bathroom door banged shut. He'd left his phone behind, proof that he'd wiped it out again. She made a call. "Meg . . ."

"Luce? Honey, are you all right?"

"I'm . . . fine."

"Why are you whispering?"

"Because . . ." Lucy paused. "Would I be . . . like . . . a total skank if I slept with another guy now? Like in about ten minutes?"

"I don't know. Maybe."

"That's what I thought."

"Do you like him?"

"Kind of. He's no Ted Beaudine, but . . ."

"Then you should *definitely* sleep with him."

"I want to, but . . ."

"Be a skank, Luce. It'll be good for you."

"I guess if I'd seriously wanted to be talked out of this, I'd have called somebody else."

"That tells you a lot, then."

"You're right." The water shut off in the bathroom. Panda had taken the fastest shower on record. "I have to go," she said in a rush. "I'll call when I can. Love you." She hung up.

The bathroom door opened. Now there were two of them wrapped in threadbare towels, Panda's draped so low she could see the entire plane of his stomach . . . and the bulge beneath.

He held his discarded clothes in one hand, his hair a long wet tangle, his lips thinned in something approaching a scowl. Water beaded on his chest and on his bare legs, which were—no surprise—free of any disfiguring scars. What was surprising, considering the lack of sunlight they received, was how tan they were. Even more surprising was how foul his mood seemed to be for a man about to get lucky.

He cocked his head in the general direction of her towel.

"I'm still thinking," she said.

"No, you're not. You made up your mind." He yanked his wallet from his jeans pocket, flipped it open, and pulled out a condom. "I only have one of these, so you'd better be good."

"Might be. Might not be," she said. "It depends on my mood." Her words exhilarated her.

He dropped his clothes, walked over to her, and dipped his index finger into the fabric between her breasts. With a single tug, the towel fell to the carpet. "Time to taste the forbidden fruit," he said in a barely audible rasp.

Who was the forbidden fruit? Herself or him? She didn't want to think, only to feel. He dipped his head to her shoulder, but she wasn't going to be the only naked person in the room, and she tugged off his towel. It fell across their feet as their bodies met. His lips touched her collarbone. He nipped. Moved onto her neck. He hadn't shaved, and his beard scraped lightly over her skin, leaving a trail of goose bumps.

She'd spent hours today pressed against his body, and now that she'd made up her mind to do this, she wanted to feel more of it. She splayed her hands against his chest. He lingered just below her earlobe. She didn't want him to kiss her, and she turned her head before he could reach her lips. The movement exposed more of her neck, and he accepted the invitation.

Before long, his hand went to her breast, his thumb to the crest. Hot blood rushed through her. He flicked it, and she did the same to him. His breathing came faster, and so did hers. He hooked his arms under her bottom, lifted her, and carried her to the bed she'd staked out for herself. No kisses. No endearments. Nothing that would remind her of Ted.

He flipped the covers back with one hand. As they fell into the sheets she accidentally scratched him. She didn't care. She dug her hands into his wild curls and tugged simply because she wanted to.

"Ouch."

"No talking," she said.

"Like it rough, do you?"

Yes. That was exactly how she wanted it. No solicitude or consideration. No tender caresses.

She slipped her hands between his legs and squeezed. Not hard enough to cause him pain. Just enough to make him feel the tiniest bit vulnerable.

"Watch it," he said.

"You watch it," she said.

He reared above her, one corner of those sadistic lips kicking up. "Aren't you full of surprises . . ." And just like that, he'd pinioned her wrists to the bed and pressed her into the mattress with his body.

A dangerous thrill shot through her.

He dragged his unshaven jaw across her nipple. The deliciously painful abrasion made her gasp. He did it again. She twisted beneath him, a movement that left her open and vulnerable.

"I was hoping for a little more foreplay"—he ripped the foil around the condom with his teeth—"but if that's the way you want it . . ."

She'd never imagined anyone could pull on a condom so fast. He recaptured her wrists. With one powerful thrust he drove inside her.

She gasped. Her legs fell open. He gave her no time to adjust to his size before he began to pump. He displayed no finesse. Only deep, powerful strokes that touched her very core. Strokes that required nothing of her but a submission she didn't feel like offering. She wrapped her heels around his calves. Bucked beneath him. His teeth gleamed as he smiled.

Before long, sweat beaded on his forehead, but still he thrust. Refusing to give in until she did.

But she wouldn't go first. She'd hold out forever. Die before she let him win this battle, which, like most wars, had lost its point. His dark eyes grew glassy. His weight heavy. A whimper slipped through her lips. Another. His grip slackened on her wrists. She curled both hands around his sides. Dug in her nails. She owed him nothing.

And with that knowledge, she gave him everything.

At the exact moment he lost his own battle.

His back arched, shoulders lifted, hips drove. Flurry. Quake. Flood.

❧

"WANNA BEER?" HE SAID AFTERWARD, not looking at her, every bit the great Neanderthal.

"No. I want to sleep. Alone." She pointed toward the other bed, as rude as she could be.

He didn't seem to care.

THE SOUND OF THE MOTEL room door awakened her the next morning. She forced her eyes open. Panda stood there, holding two cups of coffee he must have picked up in the motel office. Being a skank was a new experience—not nearly as much fun the morning after. She wanted to pull the sheet over her head and beg him to go away. She left the sheet where it was and reached for a little attitude. "I want Starbucks."

"Hurry up and get dressed." He set the coffee on the dresser.

Pretending last night hadn't happened would only make her feel worse. "Sex is supposed to be a mood enhancer. What happened to you?"

"Real life," he retorted, as prickly as his day-old stubble. "I'll wait for you outside."

So much for cozy chitchat, but what did she care? She'd broken one more link—the final link?—in the chain that bound her to Ted. He was no longer the last man she'd slept with.

Panda was standing impatiently by the bike, her helmet dangling from one hand, his coffee cup in the other, when she emerged from the motel room. A storm during the night had left the air heavy with humidity, but she doubted that was the reason he looked like a time bomb about to detonate. Trying to conjure up all the impertinence and bravado of her fourteen-year-old self—her fourteen-year-old *virginal* self—was useless in this case, but what about Viper, her biker chick alter ego? Her eyes narrowed. "Chill, dude."

Ohmygod! Had she really said that?

He scowled and pitched his cup into an overflowing trash can. "It's two weeks, Lucy. Time's up."

"Not for me, babe. I'm just getting started."

She'd thrown him off balance almost as much as she'd thrown herself off. "Whatever you think you're doing," he said with a glare, "stop it."

She grabbed her helmet from him. "Maybe you want to stand here all day and talk, but I want to ride."

As she strapped on the helmet, he muttered something she couldn't hear, and then they were off. It didn't take them long to cross the Arkansas border and reach the Memphis outer belt. Until yesterday, Panda had stayed off freeways, but not today. He blew past a sign for Graceland, switched lanes, and merged onto another freeway. Before long, he pulled off at an exit. The triumph she'd felt over her display of bravado vanished when she saw the sign.

MEMPHIS INTERNATIONAL AIRPORT

She squeezed his ribs and shouted, "Where are you going?"

He didn't answer.

But she knew, and the scope of his betrayal was so huge she couldn't take it in.

He pulled up in front of the airport departure area and stopped between two SUVs. "End of the road."

He said it as if it didn't matter, as if she should hop off, shake his hand, and breeze away. When she didn't move, he took over. He grasped her arm, and the next thing she knew, they were both standing next to the bike. "It's time for you to go home." He tugged her chinstrap free, pulled off her helmet, and secured it to the bike.

Her lungs had collapsed. This was the way Ted had felt. Blindsided and deceived. "That's my decision to make," she said.

Instead of responding, he unfastened her pack and set it on the sidewalk. He reached into the saddlebags, withdrew an envelope, and pressed it into her hands. "Everything you need is in here."

She stared at him.

"It's two weeks, Lucy. Two weeks. Do you know what I'm saying? I have another job waiting."

She couldn't—wouldn't—grasp his meaning.

He stood before her. Withdrawn. Indifferent. Maybe a little bored. She was one more woman. One more female body. One more job . . .

GAS, GRASS, OR ASS. NOBODY RIDES FOR FREE.

And then something shifted. The smallest furrow gathered between those dark eyebrows. His lids dropped, and when he lifted them again, she saw everything the man she knew as Panda had worked so hard to suppress. She saw the intelligence he'd kept so tightly veiled. She saw pain and doubt, remorse maybe. And she saw a soul-deep hunger that had nothing to do with smutty T-shirts and obscene bumper stickers.

He shook his head slightly, as if he wanted to clear away those vulnerable emotions. But he couldn't seem to do it because he lifted his arms and cupped her cheeks, his big hands as gentle as a butterfly's wings, those cold blue eyes tender and troubled. He slanted his head and did what she hadn't let him do last night. He kissed her. At first the softest touch, then something deeper, a hungry joining with her face protectively nested in his palms.

His mouth moved over hers as if he could never get enough. And then he let her go without warning, turned away before she could stop him. He straddled the bike and kicked the engine into life. A moment later, he was gone, roaring out of her world on a beat-up Yamaha Warrior plastered with bumper stickers that no longer fit the man she'd thought she'd known.

She stood on the sidewalk, her heart in her throat, her backpack at her feet, long after he'd disappeared. Car rental shuttle buses passed. Taxis pulled up. Eventually she gazed down at the envelope he'd handed her. She slipped her finger under the flap, opened it, and took out its contents.

Her driver's license. Her credit cards. And directions to the security office inside, where someone would be waiting to handle her trip back to D.C.

The evidence of her parents' wonderful, suffocating love stared back at her. She'd known they could find her if they wanted to. Now she understood why they hadn't. Because they'd known from the beginning exactly where she was. Because they'd hired a bodyguard.

Two weeks, Lucy.

She should have realized they'd do this. Over the years there'd been a few incidents where people had gotten too aggressive around her . . . A couple of wacko letters . . . Once she'd been knocked over—nothing serious, but enough to put them on edge. After she'd lost her Secret Service detail, they'd ignored her objections and hired private security for big events where they felt she'd be too exposed. Did she really think they'd allow her to go unprotected through a highly publicized wedding? Panda had been on her parents' payroll from the beginning. A short-term contract they'd extended to two weeks after she'd run off. Two weeks. Enough time for the worst of the publicity to fade and for their anxiety about her physical well-being to ease. Two weeks. And the time was up.

She gathered her pack, pulled on her ball cap and sunglasses, and made her way into the terminal. *Let her have the freedom she needs,* she imagined them telling him. *But keep her safe.*

Now she saw what she should have comprehended from the moment he'd so conveniently shown up in that alley. He'd never left her alone. Not once had he taken the boat out by himself. He'd dogged her whenever they'd gone into a store, and in restaurants he'd been lounging by the door when she'd emerged from the ladies' room. As for those motels . . . He'd insisted on one room because he was keeping guard. And when he'd tried to scare her into going home, he'd only been doing his job. Considering how much private security cost, he must have gotten a real kick out of the deal she'd struck to pay him a thousand dollars.

She stopped at a bench inside the terminal doors, her thoughts bitter. With no effort at all, Panda had picked up a great job perk last night. Maybe sex was a service he always provided his female clients, a little something extra to remember him by.

If she didn't get to the security office soon, someone would be out looking for her. They probably already were. But still, she didn't move. The memory of that kiss kept intruding, those troubling emotions she'd seen in his eyes. She only wanted to feel anger now, not this uncertainty. Why had he looked so troubled? So vulnerable? Why had she seen a need more complicated than desire?

Nothing more than a trick of the light.

She thought about the way he'd cradled her face, kissed her. His tenderness . . .

A self-created illusion. She didn't know anything about him.

So why did she feel as though she knew everything?

He should have told her the truth. Regardless of what his agreement was with her family, he should have leveled with her. But that would have involved being straightforward, something of which he was incapable.

Except just now, as they'd stood at the curb, he'd told her the truth with his eyes. That final kiss had told her these past two weeks meant more to him than a paycheck.

She grabbed her backpack and walked out through the terminal door just as she'd walked away from her wedding.

Half an hour later, she left Memphis in a rented Nissan Sentra. The clerk at the rental car desk hadn't recognized her name when she'd passed over her driver's license, but then he'd barely been able to operate the computer, and she knew she couldn't count on that kind of luck again.

She glanced over at the map spread out on the seat. On top of it lay the phone she'd just used to text her family.

Not ready 2 come home yet.

Chapter Six

L UCY STOPPED FOR THE NIGHT at a Hampton Inn in central Illinois. She registered under a phony name and paid with cash she'd withdrawn using the ATM card that had been tucked in the envelope and that she had no doubts her parents could trace. Once she reached her room, she pulled the detestable pregnancy padding out from under her shirt, tossed it in the trash, and withdrew the purchases she'd made a few hours earlier.

The idea had come to her at a rest stop near the Kentucky border where she'd watched two goth girls climb out of a beat-up Chevy Cavalier. Their dark makeup and crazy hair gave her an unexpected, but vaguely familiar, stab of envy, a feeling she remembered from high school when the alternative girls had passed her in the hallways. *What if . . .*

Mat and Nealy had never made her feel as though she needed to conform to a higher standard than other girls her age, but even before the drinking incident at the party, she'd known, so she'd sublimated her desire to pierce her nose, wear funky clothes, and hang around with the more disreputable kids. It had been the right thing to do then.

But not now.

She consulted the directions on the packages and started to work.

DESPITE HER LATE NIGHT, SHE awakened early the next morning, her stomach sour with anxiety. She had to turn the car around and go home. Or maybe travel west. Maybe search for enlightenment on one of those mythic road trips along what was left of Route 66. Her psyche was too fragile to probe the mystery of a surly, enigmatic bodyguard. And did she really believe that understanding more about him would help her understand herself?

She couldn't answer that question, so she climbed out of bed, took a quick shower, and pulled on the clothes she'd bought. The bleeding red rose that adorned her tight-fitting sleeveless black T-shirt clashed perfectly with her short, lime green tutu skirt, which was strapped at the waist with bands of black leather and a pair of buckles. She'd traded in her sneakers for black combat boots and applied a couple of coats of sloppy black polish to her fingernails.

But the biggest change was her hair. She'd dyed it a harsh coal black. Then, using the directions on the special jar of wax, she'd formed half-a-dozen random dreadlocks that she'd sprayed orange. Now she lined her eyes top and bottom in smudgy black, then clipped in a nose ring. A rebellious eighteen-year-old stared back at her. A girl who looked nothing like a thirty-one-year-old professional lobbyist and runaway bride.

Later, as she passed through the lobby on the way to her car, she pretended not to notice the covert glances of the other lodgers. By the time she'd backed out of her parking place, the tutu skirt was already making the back of her thighs itch. Her boots were uncomfortable, her makeup over the top, but she began to relax.

Viper, the biker girl.

PANDA TOOK A MORNING RUN along the lakefront path. Normally, the beauty of the Chicago skyline cleared his head, but that wasn't happening today.

Two miles turned into three. Three to four. He swiped at his forehead with the sleeve of his sweat-soaked T-shirt. He was back where he belonged, but after the quiet of Caddo, the city was too loud, too fast.

A pair of weekend idiots on Rollerblades blocked the path ahead of him. He swerved into the grass to pass them, then cut back onto the pavement.

Lucy was a smart woman. She should have seen it coming. But she hadn't, and that wasn't his fault. He'd done what he needed to.

Still, he'd hurt enough people in his life, and knowing he'd hurt one more—knowing exactly how far he'd stepped over the line—was something he couldn't forgive.

A biker sped past. Panda ran faster, wishing he could outrun himself.

Out of nowhere, an explosion ripped through the air. He threw himself off the path and hit the ground. Gravel scraped his chin and dug into his hands. His heart slammed against his ribs, and his ears roared.

Slowly he lifted his head. Looked around.

Not an explosion at all. An old junker of a landscaping truck had backfired.

A dog walker stopped on the path to stare at him. A runner slowed. The truck disappeared, leaving a trail of exhaust hanging over Lake Shore Drive.

Shit. This hadn't happened to him in years, but two weeks with Lucy Jorik and here he was. Flat on the ground. Dirt in his mouth. Something to remember the next time he tried to forget who he was and where he'd been.

As the miles rolled by, Lucy kept glancing at herself in the mirror, taking in the harsh makeup, dead black hair, and orange dreadlocks. Her mood began to lift. But was she really going to keep going? Even Ted, who was smart about everything, wouldn't be able to figure this one out. Neither could she, but she loved this feeling of slipping into a new skin.

Before long she left Illinois behind and headed into Michigan. Would Ted ever forgive her? Would her family? Weren't some things beyond forgiveness?

Near Cadillac, she abandoned the freeway for the secondary roads that led to northwestern Michigan. By evening, she was waiting in line with half a dozen other cars to drive onto the day's last ferry to Charity Island, a place she'd had difficulty locating on a map. Her muscles were stiff, her eyes scratchy, and her good mood fading. What she was doing was crazy, but if she didn't follow through, she'd wonder for the rest of her life about Panda and that kiss and why she'd fallen into bed with a virtual stranger two weeks after she'd run out on a man who'd been too good for her. Not an entirely logical reason to make this trip, but she wasn't exactly in the best shape these days, and it was the best she could do.

The old ferryboat, painted black with highway yellow striping, smelled of mildew, rope, and spent fuel. A dozen passengers boarded with her. One of them, a college kid hauling a backpack, tried to strike up a conversation by asking where she went to school. She told him she'd dropped out of Memphis State and walked away, her heavy combat boots thumping on the deck.

She stayed in the bow for the rest of the trip, watching the island gradually materialize in the fading light. It was shaped like a reclining dog—head at one end, harbor where its belly would be, lighthouse raised like a stubby tail at the other end. The island lay fifteen miles out in Lake Michigan, according to a tourist brochure. It was ten miles long by two miles wide with a year-round population of three hundred, a number that jumped into the thousands during the summer. According to its chamber of commerce, Charity Island offered visitors secluded beaches, pristine woods, fishing and hunting, as well as cross-country skiing and snowmobiling in the winter, but she only cared about finding answers to her questions.

The ferry bumped against the dock. She headed below to get her rental car. She had friends all over the country—all over the world—who would have given her a place to stay. Yet here she was, getting ready to disembark on an island in the Great Lakes on the strength of nothing more than a farewell kiss and a resident ferry pass. She pulled the ignition key from her backpack and told herself she had nothing better to do with her time, which wasn't quite true. She had amends to make, a life to rebuild, but since she didn't know how to do either, here she was.

The harbor was filled with charter fishing boats, modest pleasure craft, and an ancient tug anchored near a small barge. She drove down the ramp into a gravel parking lot bordered by a sign reading MUNICIPAL DOCKS. The two-lane main street—optimistically named Beachcomber Boulevard—held an assortment of stores, some weather-beaten, others spruced up with bright colors and kitschy window displays to attract the tourists—Jerry's Trading Post, McKinley's Market, some restaurants, a couple of fudge shops, a bank, and a fire station. Sandwich boards propped along the road advertised the services of fishing guides, and Jake's Dive Shop invited visitors to "Explore Nearby Shipwrecks."

Now that she was here, she had no idea where to go. She pulled into a parking lot next to a bar named The Sandpiper. Once she got inside, it wasn't hard to pick out the locals from the sunburned tourists, who had the glazed look of people who'd squeezed too much into one day. While they clustered around the small wooden tables, the locals sat at the bar.

She approached the bartender, who eyed her suspiciously. "We card here."

If she hadn't lost her sense of humor, she'd have laughed. "Then how about a Sprite?"

When he brought her drink, she said, "I'm supposed to be staying at this guy's place, but I lost his address. You know a dude named Panda?"

The locals looked up from their drinks.

"I might," the bartender said. "How do you know him?"

"He . . . did some work for this friend of mine."

"What kind of work?"

That was when she discovered Viper had no manners. "You know him or not?"

The bartender shrugged. "Seen him around sometimes." He went off to help another customer.

Fortunately a couple of seniors seated at the other end of the bar were more garrulous. "He showed up here a couple of years ago and bought the old Remington place out on Goose Cove," one said. "He's not on the island. I know for a fact he didn't come by plane, and if he'd been on the ferry or a charter, one of us would of heard about it."

Finally a piece of luck. Maybe she could get her questions answered without having to see him again.

The old man rested his forearm on the bar. "He don't talk much. Kind of standoffish. Never heard what he does for a living."

"Yeah, that's the way he is," Viper said. "Is Goose Cove far from here?"

"Island's only ten miles long," his pal replied. "Nothing's too far from here, although some places are harder to get to than others."

Their directions involved a confusing number of turns, as well as locating a boat shed, a dead tree, and a boulder somebody named Spike had spray-painted with a peace sign. Fifteen minutes after she left the bar, she was hopelessly lost. She drove aimlessly for a while and eventually managed to get back to the main road, where she stopped at a bait shop that was closing up for the night and got another set of directions, almost equally confusing.

It was getting dark by the time she spotted the battered mailbox with the name REMINGTON faintly visible on the driftwood sign above it. She turned off the road into the potholed drive and parked in front of a double set of garage doors.

The big, rambling beach house had started life as a Dutch Colonial, but over the years, it had been haphazardly expanded with a porch here, a bay there, another porch, a short wing. Its weathered shingles were the color of old driftwood, and twin chimneys poked from its jumbled roofs. She couldn't believe it belonged to Panda. This was a house de-signed for families—a place for sunburned kids to chase their cousins up from the beach, for moms to trade family gossip while their husbands fired up the charcoal grill, where grandparents stole naps on a shady porch and dogs lazed in the sun. Panda belonged in a run-down fishing cabin, not at a place like this. But the address checked out, and the men had been clear about the name Remington.

An unimpressive front door stood to the right of a two-car garage. On the landing, a chipped clay flowerpot held some dead soil and a faded American flag from a long-forgotten Fourth of July. The door was locked. She followed an overgrown path around the side toward the water, where she discovered the heart of the house—a sprawling screen porch, an open deck, and rows of windows facing a sheltered cove with Lake Michigan just beyond.

She made her way back around the house looking for a way to get in, but everything was locked. She'd seen a couple of inns while she was driving around, some guesthouses and bed-and-breakfasts, so there were plenty of places to stay. But first she wanted to see inside.

She reached through a piece of torn porch screening and unfastened the hook latch on the door. The boards creaked as she wove between some chaise longues with mildewed canvas cushions that had once been a bright marine blue. A broken wind chime made of spoons hung crookedly in one corner, an abandoned cooler sat in another. The door to the house was locked, but that didn't stop Viper. She broke one of the small glass panes with a rusted garden trowel, reached inside, and opened the lock.

The musty scent of a closed-up house met her as she stepped into an old-fashioned kitchen. At some point, the tall wooden cabinets had been unwisely painted institutional green. They still bore what were surely the original cup handles and matching drawer pulls. An exceptionally ugly fake Victorian table sat in a breakfast nook too small for its size. The scarred white laminate counter held an old microwave, a new coffeemaker, a knife block, and a salt crock stuffed with bent spatulas and scorched plastic spoons. A ceramic pig dressed like a French waiter sat by the sink.

She turned on some lights and explored the downstairs, walking through a living room and a sunroom and sticking her head into a musty den before ending up in a large first-floor bedroom. The queen-size bed had a navy-and-white-patterned spread, end tables shaped like cable spools, a triple dresser, and two unmatched upholstered chairs. A pair of cheaply framed Andrew Wyeth prints hung on the wall. The closet held a windbreaker, jeans, sneakers, and a Detroit Lions ball cap. The sizes seemed about right to belong to Panda, but that was hardly conclusive proof that she'd broken into the right house.

The attached bathroom with its outdated robin's-egg-blue ceramic tile and fresh white shower curtain was no more revealing. She hesitated, then opened the medicine cabinet. Toothpaste, dental floss, Advil, an Atra razor.

She went back to the kitchen and inspected the one object that was out of place, a state-of-the-art German coffeemaker, exactly the sort of thing a highly paid professional bodyguard who loved good coffee might own. It was what she discovered in the refrigerator, however, that convinced her she'd found the right place. On a nearly empty shelf, she spotted a jar of orange marmalade, exactly the same brand she'd seen Panda slather on her homemade bread.

"Real men eat grape jelly," she'd said when she'd seen him pick up an identical jar at the grocery near Caddo Lake. "I'm serious, Panda. If you buy orange marmalade, you have to turn in your man card."

"It's what I like. Deal with it."

The refrigerator also held two six-packs of Coke. No beer. She'd spent countless highway miles thinking about that first morning when she'd awakened by the lake and seen the pile of empties from the six-pack Panda had bought the previous night. What kind of bodyguard drank when he was on duty? But try as she might, the only real drinking she'd witnessed involved his taking a few slugs before she'd gone into the trees and the sight of him draining the bottle when she came out. Then there was the six-pack he'd set on the dresser their first night in that motel. How much of it had she really seen him drink? Not more than a couple of sips. As for their time at Caddo Lake . . . He'd only drunk Coke.

She glanced toward the stairs that led to the second floor but couldn't work up any enthusiasm for investigating. It was fully dark now, and she still needed to find a place to stay. But she didn't want to go anywhere. She wanted to sleep right here in this big spooky house with its memories of summers past.

She returned to the main-floor bedroom. Ugly vertical blinds covered sliding doors that led to an open deck, and a sawed-off broomstick resting in the door track provided the only security. After more snooping, she found a stack of the same low-cut boxer briefs he'd bought during their shopping trip, along with a pair of black and white board shorts for swimming. She retrieved her things from the car, locked the bedroom's outer door to keep the wild things away, and settled in.

Unexplained creaks disturbed her sleep, and toward morning, a troubling dream had her running through a house with too many rooms but no way out. The dream awakened her.

The room was cool, but her T-shirt stuck to her skin. Early morning light trickled through the vertical blinds. She stretched, then shot up in bed as she heard the click of a latch.

A boy came through the door she'd locked before she'd fallen asleep. "Get out," she gasped.

He seemed as shocked to see her as she was to see him, but he recovered faster. His wide eyes narrowed into a belligerent glare, as if she were the interloper.

She swallowed hard. Sat up. What if she was in the wrong house after all?

He wore a baggy pair of none-too-clean gray athletic shorts, a bright yellow T-shirt printed with an electric guitar, and scuffed sneakers without socks. He was African-American, his skin a couple of shades lighter than her brother Andre's. Small and scrawny—maybe ten or eleven—he had short, nappy hair, knobby knees, gangly arms, and a hostile expression designed to proclaim his toughness to the world. It might have worked if his antagonism hadn't been sabotaged by an extraordinary set of thickly lashed, golden-brown eyes.

"You're not supposed to be here," he said, thrusting out his chin.

She thought fast. "Panda said I could stay."

"He didn't say anything to Gram about it."

So this was the right house after all. Although her brain had recovered from the shock of his appearance, the rest of her hadn't stopped shaking. "He didn't mention you, either," she said. "Who are you?"

But even as she asked the question, she suspected she knew the answer. This was Panda's kid. And Panda's beautiful, pregnant, African-American wife was in the kitchen right now, getting the place opened up for the family's annual summer vacation, while his mother-in-law loaded the refrigerator with the groceries they'd bought on the way. All of which meant that Lucy, who'd won two good citizenship awards in high school and been president of the student body her senior year in college, was an adulterer.

"I'm Toby." He practically spit out his name. "Who are you?"

She had to ask. "You're Panda's son?"

"Yeah, right. You don't know him at all, do you? You're some druggie from the mainland, and you broke in here because you was scared to sleep on the beach."

His scorn was a relief. "I'm not a druggie," she said. "My name is . . . It's Viper." The word rolled off her lips, sang in her head. She wanted to say it again. Instead, she slid her legs over the side of the bed and glanced toward the door. "Why did you break in my bedroom?"

"It wasn't supposed to be locked." He scratched the back of his calf with the toe of his opposite sneaker. "My gram takes care of this place. She saw your car and sent me over to see who was here."

She refrained from pointing out that "Gram" was the world's lousiest housekeeper. From what she'd seen, the floors had been swept only in the middle, and Gram's dusting hadn't included more than a few tabletops. "Meet me in the kitchen, Toby. We'll talk there." She straightened her twisted pajama shorts and got out of bed.

"I'm calling the police."

"Go ahead," she countered. "I'll call Panda and tell him a ten-year-old kid broke into his bedroom."

His golden brown eyes grew indignant. "I'm not ten! I'm twelve."

"My mistake."

He shot her a hostile glare and sauntered out of the room before she could figure out how to ask him if he happened to know Panda's real name. By the time she got to the kitchen, he'd disappeared.

THE UPSTAIRS BEDROOMS HAD SLOPING ceilings, mismatched furniture, and a hodgepodge of old draperies. A large dormitory extended the width of the house, the light seeping through its dusty windows revealing four sets of scarred bunk beds with thin, striped mattresses rolled up at the footboards. Sand from long-ago summers still lodged in some of the floorboard cracks, and she imagined wet bathing suits abandoned wherever they'd been dropped. The house seemed to be waiting for the Remingtons to return from their life in Grand Rapids or Chicago or wherever they came from. What had possessed Panda to buy a place like this? And what possessed her to want to stay?

She carried the coffee she'd made in his fancy machine out the back door into the yard. The morning was sunny and the sky clear. The clean air brought back memories of precious mornings at Camp David, the sight of her sisters chasing one another around the stone pool deck at the Aspen Lodge, her parents setting off on a hike, just the two of them. Here an old oak sheltered a splintered picnic table, and a metal stake waited for a game of horseshoes. She curled her fingers around the coffee mug and breathed in the crisp lake air.

The house sat on a bluff with a long flight of rickety wooden steps leading down to an old boathouse and dock, both of them weathered a soft, sea gray. She couldn't see any other docks jutting from the rocky, tree-lined shore or any neighboring rooftops peeking through the canopy. The Remington house seemed to be the only one on Goose Cove.

The water in the cove was a painter's palette of colors, dark blue at the center, a grayer blue toward the edges, with streaks of tan marking the shoreline and the top of a sandbar. As the cove emptied into Lake Michigan, the morning sun flung silver spangles over the rippling surface.

A pair of sailboats reminded her uncomfortably of her grandfather, who loved to sail. She knew she couldn't postpone it any longer. She set aside her coffee mug, reached for her cell, and finally called him.

Even before she heard the patrician voice of James Litchfield, she knew exactly what the former vice president of the United States would say. "Lucille, I do not approve of what you're doing. I don't approve at all."

"That's a surprise."

"You know I detest sarcasm."

She tugged on the orange dread dangling near her ear. "Has it been awful?"

"It hasn't been pleasant, but Mat seems to have the press under control." His tone grew even colder. "And I suppose you're calling me because you want me to somehow aid and abet."

"I'll bet you would if I asked you to." Her eyes stung.

"You are so much like your mother."

He didn't say it as if it were a compliment, but she thanked him anyway. And then, before he could light into her, she pointed out what they both knew. "Running away made Nealy a better person. I'm sure it'll do the same for me."

"You're sure of no such thing," he snapped. "You simply don't know what to do next, and you don't want to face the consequences of your actions."

"That, too." She said to him what she hadn't been able to say to her parents. "I dumped the perfect man, and I'm not even sure why."

"I'm certain you had your reasons, but I wish you'd done it before I was forced to fly to Texas. You know how I detest that state."

"Only because you couldn't carry it. The election was almost thirty years ago. Maybe you should get over it?"

He harrumphed around, then said, "How long do you intend for this vacation of yours to last?"

"I don't know. A week? Maybe more."

"And I'm sure you won't tell me where you are."

"If I told you, you might be forced to lie about it. Not that you aren't really good at it, but why put an old man in that position?"

"You are the most *disrespectful* child. "

She smiled. "I know. I love you, too, Gramps." He hated it when she called him Gramps, but it was payback for that "Lucille." "I'm staying at a friend's house on an island in the Great Lakes," she said. "But then you probably already know that." If he didn't, he would soon, since she'd paid for that rental car with her credit card, and her loving parents were almost certainly keeping track.

"Exactly what is the purpose of this call?"

"To tell you I'm . . . I'm sorry I disappointed you. And to ask you to be nice to Mom. This is hard on her."

"I do not need reminders from my granddaughter about how to behave with my daughter."

"Not exactly true."

That precipitated a bristling lecture about respect, integrity, and the responsibility of those to whom much is given. Instead of listening, she found herself replaying a conversation she'd had with her mother a few months ago.

"You know I'm jealous of your relationship with him," Nealy had said.

Lucy had looked up from the wedge of coconut custard pie they'd been sharing at their favorite Georgetown restaurant. "He was an awful father to you."

"And he's hardly the world's best grandfather. Except to you."

It was true. Lucy's sibs avoided him at all costs, but he and Lucy had hit it off from the beginning, even though she'd been mouthy and rude when they'd first met. Maybe because of it. "He loves me," she'd said. "And he loves you, too."

"I know he does," Nealy replied. "But I will never, ever have as comfortable a relationship with him as you do."

"Do you really mind so much?"

She remembered Nealy's smile. "No. I don't mind at all. The old curmudgeon needs you as much as you need him."

Lucy still wasn't quite sure what she'd meant by that.

When her grandfather finally concluded his lecture, she told him she loved him, reminded him to eat right, and asked him not to growl so much at Tracy.

He told her to tend to her own business.

After she disconnected, she tossed her coffee dregs into the weeds and got up. But just as she started to turn back to the house, she heard an odd sound. A human sound. The sound someone makes when they trip and try to catch themselves. It came from the grove of trees that marked the north edge of the lawn where the woods began. As she turned to look, she caught the flash of an electric-yellow T-shirt disappearing into the pines.

Toby had been spying on her.

Chapter Seven

Toby raced through the trees, cutting to the left around the big stump, darting past the giant boulder, hurling himself over the trunk of the red oak that had come down in a storm last summer. Finally he reached the path that led to the cottage. Even though he was smaller than a lot of the other guys in his grade, he could run faster than any of them. Gram said his dad had been a fast runner, too.

He slowed as he reached the cottage. *She* was sitting on the back step smoking another cigarette and staring out into the yard the same way she'd been doing since she got here two weeks ago. It wasn't as if *she* had anything to look at. The yard sloped down to a gully, and except for the tomato and pepper plants Mr. Wentzel had put in, Gram's garden was nothing but a bunch of weeds. There were a couple of apple and pear trees behind the honey house, but they weren't near as good as the trees in Mr. Wentzel's cherry orchard.

The woman blew a long stream of smoke but didn't even notice he'd come back. Maybe she thought if she didn't look, he'd disappear, but she was the one who needed to disappear. He wished Eli and Ethan Bayner were still here so he could go to their house. They were his best friends—kind of his only friends—but they'd gone to Ohio for the summer because their parents might be getting a divorce.

She flicked her ashes in Gram's rosebushes. "It's going to rain," she said. "The bees are all heading inside."

He glanced uneasily toward the hives. Fifteen of them sat on the edge of their yard not too far from the border of Mr. Wentzel's orchard. Gram had loved the bees, but Toby hated getting stung, so he stayed far away from them. At first when Gram had gotten sick, Mr. Wentzel had taken care of the hives, but then he'd gotten sick, too, and he'd had to go live at this nursing home on the mainland. His son was in charge of the orchard now, and he didn't even live on the island—he just hired people to take care of the fruit. Nobody had checked the hives since Mr. Wentzel left, and if they got too crowded, the bees would start to swarm, something Toby didn't even want to think about.

He didn't want to think about a lot of things.

The lady crossed her legs and took a deep drag on her cigarette, holding the smoke in her lungs like she didn't know how bad it was for her. She had long red hair, and she was tall and real skinny with sharp bones that looked like they could cut you. She didn't ask him where he'd been. Probably hadn't even noticed he was gone. He was like Gram. He hated having strangers around. And now there was also the new lady at the Remington house. She told him her name was Viper. He didn't really think that could be her name, but he didn't know.

All morning he'd been spying on the Remington house in case Panda, the guy who owned it, showed up, too. Toby'd never met Panda, but he was pretty sure he'd stop sending the money if he knew it was Toby instead of Gram who'd been taking care of the house ever since

Gram got sick in January. Toby needed that money or his plan to live here by himself wouldn't work. The last time Panda had been here was two months ago, and he hadn't called Gram to complain about anything, so Toby figured he'd been doing an okay cleaning job.

She stubbed out the cigarette in a saucer she left on the steps. "Do you want me to fix you something to eat?"

"I ain't hungry." Gram didn't let him say *ain't*, but Gram wasn't alive now, and he had to make sure this lady knew he could take care of himself so she'd go away and leave him alone.

She stretched out her legs and rubbed her knee. Even for a white lady, her skin was really white, and she had little freckles on her arms. He didn't believe she really knew how to cook because all she'd done since she got here was heat up stuff Gram had left in the big freezer. Like he couldn't do that himself.

She finally looked at him, but it was like she didn't really want to see him. "I don't want to be here any more than you want me here." She sounded like she was really tired, but he didn't see how she could be, since she didn't do any work.

"Then why don't you leave?" he said.

"Because your grandmother left me this place and made me your guardian and I haven't figured out what to do about that."

"You don't have to do nothing about it. You can go. I can take care of myself."

She picked up her cigarette pack and stared at the honey house. It was like she'd lost interest.

He stomped past her and followed the flagstone path around the side of the house. Why wouldn't she go away? He could get himself to school and cook his own meals and wash his clothes and all that other kind of crap. Hadn't he been doing it ever since Gram got sick? Even those couple of weeks he'd stayed with Mr. Wentzel after the funeral, he'd done stuff. Gram believed in keeping to herself, so she didn't have a lot of friends except Mr. Wentzel and Big Mike, who used to drive her to the doctor's. Toby was the one who took care of about everything else.

He reached the front of the cottage. Him and Gram had painted it three summers ago—robin's-egg blue with light gray trim. Gram had wanted to paint it this purple color, but he'd talked her out of it. Now he wished he'd let her paint it any color she wanted. Just like he wished that he'd never talked back to her or tried to make her feel bad about not buying him a new game system or any of the other stuff he'd done.

He grabbed the bottom branch of the biggest tree in the front yard, a maple that Gram had said was older than she was. As he climbed he scraped his knee on the bark, but he kept going because the higher he climbed the farther he was from *her* and from the bees and from thinking about the lady in the Remington house. And the closer he was to Gram and to his dad in heaven. His mom, too, but she'd left him when he was a baby, and he didn't think much about her. Gram said she'd loved her daughter, but that she'd been sort of worthless.

Gram and his mom were white, but he was black like his dad, and as much as he missed Gram, right now he missed his dad more. He'd been four when his dad died. His dad was a tower dog, the most dangerous job in the world, ask anybody, and he'd died saving this other guy who'd gotten stuck on this big cell phone tower up by Traverse Bay. It had been in the winter, a couple of degrees below zero, and there'd been a snowstorm. Toby would give everything he had—he would even cut off his arm or his leg—if that meant his dad could still be alive.

LUCY FOUND THE EXPENSIVE MOUNTAIN bike in the garage and a fancy sea kayak in the boathouse, both too new to be castoffs from the Remingtons. After discovering the journey into town wasn't nearly as complicated as her first night's wanderings had led her to believe, she used the bike for transportation, carrying the groceries she bought in her backpack. Charity Island was used to all types, and her orange dreads, nose ring, and combat boots didn't attract much attention.

After a few days, she took the ferry to the mainland to get rid of her rental car. While she was there, she shopped for a couple of additions to her new wardrobe, as well as some incredible temporary tattoos.

By the end of her first week at the house, she'd cleaned the kitchen from top to bottom. Each time she entered, she hated the big table more. It was not only hideous and much too large for the alcove, but also painted an ugly shade of mint green that was supposed to match the walls but didn't. She'd even baked a few loaves of bread.

Other than occasional glimpses of the twelve-year-old spying on her from the woods, she had no distractions, which made it the perfect time to start the writing project for her father's book. Since she hadn't planned to resume her lobbying work until September, she'd originally intended to begin working on it as soon as she got back from her honeymoon. Mat said he was fed up with other people defining Nealy's legacy, and he believed future generations deserved a more personal history of the nation's first female president.

Her father was an experienced journalist, and he'd originally intended to write the book himself, but after a few months' work, he'd decided one viewpoint was too limiting. He wanted several perspectives, each highlighting a different aspect of Nealy's life, so he'd asked Nealy's father to write one section and Terry Ackerman, Nealy's longtime aide, to write another. Most of all, he wanted Lucy's viewpoint. She had been an inside witness from the time Nealy had first run for the Senate through her presidency, and she was to write about Nealy as a mother. Lucy had jumped at the opportunity, but so far she hadn't written a word. Even though her deadline wasn't until September, now would be a perfect time to get started.

She'd found a laptop computer in the den—a computer wiped

clean of any personal information—and after she'd finished breakfast, she carried it out to the porch. As she arranged herself on one of the chaises she had covered with a beach towel, she inspected the tattoo of thorns and blood drops that encircled her bicep. It was gloriously tacky, and she loved it, or maybe she simply loved the idea of displaying something like it, if only temporarily. The packaging said it could last up to two weeks, but she'd bought replacements as well as a few other tattoo patterns she might or might not use.

She pulled her eyes away from the bloody thorns and thought about what she wanted to write. Finally she set her fingers on the keys.

When my mother was president . . .

A squirrel chattering just outside the screen distracted her. She pulled her attention back to the keyboard.

When my mother was president, her working day started every morning before six with a stint on the treadmill . . .

Lucy hated treadmills. She'd rather walk outside in the rain and snow than on a machine.

My mother believed in the benefits of exercise.

So did Lucy, which didn't mean she liked it. The trick was to find something you didn't hate doing.

A trainer had designed her program, but she and my father were usually alone in the gym.

Lucy didn't like gyms, either.

They started their routine with easy stretches, then—

She frowned. Anyone could have written those boring sentences. Mat wanted something personal, and this wasn't it.

She deleted the file and shut down the computer. The morning was too beautiful to write anyway. She grabbed her baseball hat and climbed down the rickety wooden steps to the boat dock. The life vest in the kayak was too big for her, but she cinched it up anyway and took the boat out.

Even as she paddled around the rocky beach that marked the perimeter of Goose Cove, she had a hard time believing she was holed up on an island in the Great Lakes. She'd come here to unearth the secrets of the man her parents had hired to keep her safe, but the house hadn't yielded any clues, so why was she still here?

Because she didn't want to leave.

The wind picked up as she hit the open waters of the lake, and she turned the bow into the waves. She rested her arms for a moment, rubbed the bloody thorn tattoo. She didn't know who she was anymore. The product of a chaotic childhood? An orphan who'd taken responsibility for her infant sister? A celebrity child who'd become part of the symbolic American family? She had been an exemplary student, a dedicated social worker, and she was an accomplished lobbyist. She'd raised a lot of money for some very worthwhile causes and promoted legislation that had made a difference in a lot of lives. Never mind how much she'd grown to dislike that work. Most recently, she was a neurotic bride who'd turned her back on the man destined to be the love of her life.

Between her job, her family, and planning her wedding, she'd been too busy for introspection. Now that she had time for it, she didn't like the way it made her feel, so she headed back toward the house. She was paddling against the current, and she had to work harder, but it felt good. She reached the shelter of the cove and paused to rest. That's when she saw the lone figure standing on the end of the dock.

His features were indistinguishable, but she would have known that silhouette anywhere. Wide shoulders and narrow hips. Long legs braced for action, hair blowing around his head.

Her heart started to pound. She bought herself time by making an unnecessary detour to inspect a beaver lodge, then another detour to check out a tree that had fallen into the water. Taking it slow. Pulling herself together.

He should never have kissed her at the Memphis airport. Should never have looked at her like that. If he hadn't kissed her—hadn't looked at her with all those turbulent emotions churning in his eyes—she'd have gone back to Washington—gone back to her job—and he'd have been nothing more than her only one-night hookup.

The closer she got, the angrier she became, not just with him but with herself. What if he thought she was chasing him? That hadn't been it at all, but that's how it would look.

She slid the kayak up to the dock. The rocky shoreline made it hard for her to beach the boat, so as long as the weather was good, she generally tied it to the ladder. But she didn't do that now. Instead she secured the kayak loosely—too loosely—to the post at the end of the dock. Finally she looked up at him.

He loomed above her in his standard uniform of jeans and T-shirt, this one bearing the faded insignia of the Detroit Police Department. She took in those high cheekbones; that strong nose; those thin, sadistic lips and laser-sharp blue eyes. He glowered down at her.

"What the *hell* happened to your hair? And what are you doing out on the lake by yourself? Exactly who did you think was going to rescue you if you went in?"

"Your two weeks are up," she shot back, "so none of that is your concern. Now I'd appreciate it if you'd help me up on the dock. I've got a cramp."

He should have seen it coming. But he knew only Lucy, not Viper. He moved to the edge of the dock, a lamb to the slaughter, and reached down for her. She grabbed his wrist—braced herself—and, using all her strength, gave a sudden, sharp yank.

Dumb ass. He went right in. She went in, too, but she didn't care. She cared only about getting the best of him in whatever way she could.

He came up cussing and sputtering from the freezing water, hair wild and wet. All he needed was a cutlass in his teeth. She flipped her own dripping hair out of her eyes and yelled, "I thought you couldn't swim."

"I *learned*," he yelled back.

She swam away from the kayak, the life vest inching up under her armpits. "You're a jerk, you know that? A lying, money-grubbing *jerk*."

"Get it all out." He swam toward the ladder, his strokes long and powerful.

She swam after him, her own strokes choppy with anger. "And you're a first-class—" Viper found the right word. *"Asshole!"*

He glanced back at her, then mounted the ladder. "Anything else?"

She grabbed the bottom rung. The water hadn't lost its spring chill, and her teeth chattered so hard they hurt. "A liar, a fraud, a—" She broke off as she spotted the lump. Exactly where she expected to see it. She scrambled up the ladder after him. "I hope that gun is waterproof. No? Too bad."

He sat on the dock and peeled up the right leg of his jeans, revealing the black leather ankle holster that explained why he'd refused to wear shorts at Caddo Lake, why he wouldn't go in the water. He pulled the gun out and flipped open the bullet chamber.

"Are you back on duty?" She shoved her wet, dyed hair out of her eyes, her finger snagging on a dread. "Did my parents extend your contract?"

"If you have a problem with what happened, take it up with your family, not with me. I was just doing my job." He knocked the bullets into his hand.

"They hired you again. That's why you're here."

"No. I'm here because I heard that somebody was squatting in my house. Anybody mention that breaking and entering is a crime?" He blew into the empty chambers.

She was dizzy with fury. "Anybody mention that bodyguards are supposed to identify themselves?"

"Like I said. Take it up with your family."

She stared down at the top of his head. His hair was already starting to curl. Those wild curls. Thick and rancorous. What kind of man had hair like that? She fumbled with the buckles on her life vest, so angry with him—with herself—she could barely unfasten them. She'd come all this way because of a kiss that she'd convinced herself meant something. And she'd been partially right. It meant that she'd lost her mind. She tore off the vest. "That's going to be your defense, isn't it? You were just doing your job."

"Believe me. It wasn't easy." He stopped blowing into the bullet chambers long enough to take in her hair and the thorn and blood tattoo around her arm. "I hope none of that's permanent. You look weird."

"Screw you." Viper would have said, "Fuck you," but Lucy's lips couldn't quite shape the words. "I'm sure you liked that little job perk you picked up at the end? Nailing the president's daughter has to give you bragging rights in the bodyguard locker room."

Now he looked almost as angry as she felt. "Is that what you think?"

What I think is that I lost every shred of my dignity when I came here. "What I think is that you're a professional, so you should have acted like one. That meant telling me who you were. More important, it meant keeping your hands to yourself."

He sprang up from the dock. "I damn well did! All those days we were trapped in that shitty little hole on Caddo Lake. The two of us rubbing against each other. You running around in a piece of black cellophane you called a bathing suit and that pink top even somebody half blind could see through. I damn well kept my hands to myself then."

She'd pierced his armor, a small bandage to her pride. "You knew all about me, Panda—or whatever your name really is. You had a dossier full of information on me, but you didn't reveal one honest thing about yourself. You played me for an idiot."

"I didn't play you at all. What happened that night had nothing to do with the job. We were two people who wanted each other. It's that simple."

But it hadn't been simple to her. If it had been simple, she would never have come here.

"I did my job," he said. "I don't owe you any more explanations."

She had to know—had to ask—and Viper formed a sneer to hide the importance of her question. "Did your job include that pathetic, guilt-filled kiss at the airport?"

"What are you talking about?"

His confusion cracked another layer of her self-esteem. "That kiss had your guilty conscience smeared all over it," she said. "You wanted some kind of absolution because you knew exactly how sleazy you were."

He stood there stony-faced. "If that's the way you see it, I'm not going to try to change your mind."

She wanted him to change her mind. To say something that would make her feel better about everything that had happened since she'd jumped on the back of his motorcycle. But he didn't, and she'd only inspire pity if she said more herself.

He didn't try to hold her back as she left the dock. She stopped at the outdoor shower. With her clothes on, she shampooed the lake water out of her hair, then wrapped a beach towel around herself and went inside. A trail of wet footprints followed her across the kitchen floor. She shot the lock on her bedroom door, peeled off her wet clothes, and slipped into a black tank, her leather-belted green tutu skirt, and her combat boots. She took another few minutes to smudge her eyes in black and her lips in brown, and put in her nose ring. Then she stuffed everything she could fit into her backpack. The ferry left in half an hour. It was finally time to go home.

A late-model dark gray SUV with Illinois plates sat in the drive. Odd to think of him behind the wheel of a car. She climbed on the mountain bike and headed for town.

It was a hot, sunny afternoon. The summer season didn't launch into high gear until the Fourth of July, but tourists in shorts and flip-flops were already mingling with the locals on Beachcomber Boulevard. The smell of French fries wafted from Dogs 'N' Malts, a beach shack with a squeaky screen door and splintery picnic tables. She passed the Painted Frog Café, where just yesterday she'd picked up a cappuccino. Next door, a dog lounged in the shade by the entrance to Jerry's Trading Post. As she took it all in, she realized how much she liked this place, how much she didn't want to leave it.

Jake's Dive Shop doubled as the ferry's ticket office. It smelled of musty rubber and oily coffee. She bought a one-way ticket and stashed the bike in a rack at the municipal dock. Maybe Panda would find it there. Maybe not. She didn't care.

She joined the line of tourists just beginning to board. A mother jumped out of line to chase a restless toddler. How many times had Lucy imagined herself with Ted's baby? Now she wondered if she'd ever have a child.

She wished she'd asked Panda more questions, like what kind of reputable bodyguard thought it was a good idea to toss his client on the back of a motorcycle and take off on a road trip? The person in line behind her moved too close and bumped her backpack. She edged forward, but it happened again. She turned and gazed up into a pair of cold blue eyes.

"What I told you was true." His voice was gruff, his mouth unsmiling. "The bumper stickers were already on the bike. I didn't put them there."

He wore the same wet clothes she'd dunked him in, and his hair wasn't quite dry. She was determined to keep her dignity. "I so don't care."

"And I only wore those T-shirts to rile you." His gaze made its way to her tutu skirt and combat boots. "You look like a teenager turned hooker for drug money."

"Lend me one of your T-shirts," she retorted. "I'm sure that'll polish up my appearance."

He was receiving his customary amount of attention, and he lowered his voice. "Look, Lucy, this situation was a lot more complicated than you want to acknowledge." He moved with her as the line edged forward. "The whole world was covering your wedding. You needed your own security."

She wouldn't lose her temper. "Three words. 'I'm your bodyguard.' Not complicated."

They reached the bottom of the ramp. The chest-scratching doofus who'd picked her up had turned into Mr. No Nonsense. "Your parents hired me. They gave the orders. They knew you'd object to having private security, especially for your honeymoon, so they wanted you kept in the dark."

"My honeymoon?" she nearly shouted. "I was going to have security on my *honeymoon*?"

"How could you not have figured that out?"

She handed over her ticket. He flashed his ferry pass. She stalked up the ramp, her boots clattering on the boards. He followed right after her. "Ted knew it was necessary even if you didn't."

"Ted knew about this?" She wanted to stomp her foot, throw a tantrum, throw a punch.

"He's a realist, Lucy. And so are your parents. I called your father from the convenience store that first night. He told me not to identify myself. He said if I did, you'd figure out a way to ditch me. I didn't buy it, but he was the one who hired me, so no, I'm not going to apologize for following a client's wishes." Lucy tried to walk away from him, but he grabbed her arm and steered her toward the ship's stern. "As soon as your honeymoon was over and you got back to Wynette, we were dropping security. Except that's not the way it played out. You took off and media was everywhere. It was too big a story. Too much attention focused on you."

"Nobody recognized me."

"They almost did, and if you'd been by yourself, they would have."

"Maybe. Maybe not." The ferry blasted a warning as they reached the stern. One of the male passengers regarded her with concern. She remembered how young she looked, how threatening Panda looked, and figured he was trying to decide whether or not to intercede. He chose not to risk it. She pulled away. "You said you and Ted were friends."

"I met him three days before the wedding."

"Another lie."

"I do my job the best way I know how."

"You're a real pro," she shot back. "Is it standard bodyguard practice to stick a client on the back of a motorcycle?"

His jaw set in a stubborn line. "I'm not explaining anything else until you get off this boat."

"Go away."

"Look, I know you're pissed. I understand that. Let's get off, grab a couple of burgers, and talk this through."

"Now you want to talk? All right, let's start with your name."

"Patrick Shade."

"Patrick? I don't believe it."

"You think I'd make up my name?"

"In a heartbeat." She shoved her thumbs into the straps of her backpack. "Where do you live? Because you definitely don't live in that house we just left."

"I have a place in Chicago. And if you want to know more, you have to get off the ferry."

She did want to know more, but not as much as she wanted payback. "I'll admit I'm curious. But I'm not getting off." The whistle blew its final warning. "If you want to talk to me, we can talk right here. But first I need to find the ladies' room so I can throw up."

He decided not to push her. "All right. We'll talk here."

"See if you're competent enough to find us a place to sit where everybody won't stare at you." She headed into the ship's cabin, knocking her backpack against a fire extinguisher as she ducked around a corner. She wedged through the door on the other side and raced down the ramp just as they were getting ready to pull it up. Moments later, she was standing in the shadows by the municipal dock sign, watching the ferry chug away with Panda on board.

Knowing she'd gotten the best of him felt good, but it would have felt even better if she weren't stuck here until that same ferry returned, undoubtedly bringing Panda along with it. This was the kind of situation Meg got caught up in, not Lucy, but she couldn't regret it. At least she'd recovered a small measure of pride.

The dark gray SUV with Illinois plates she'd last seen at the lake house was parked in the municipal lot. She had an afternoon to kill until she could leave again, and she wasn't doing it in town.

As she biked back to the house, she passed a playground. She'd carried her infant sister ten blocks to a playground like this the day after their mother had died just so she could push Tracy in a baby swing—a fourteen-year-old's idea of what a good mother should do. Tracy had screamed the whole time.

Patrick Shade . . . What kind of name was that?

If she chartered a boat to take her to the mainland, she wouldn't have to see him again. Expensive, but worth it. She turned the bike around and went back to the dive shop.

"We're booked for the rest of the day," the guy behind the counter told her. "The *Mary J* and *Dinna Ken* are out, too. But if you want to go tomorrow . . ."

"That's okay," she said, even though it wasn't okay at all.

Maybe she wouldn't have to deal with Panda again. She'd made her point, and he wasn't the kind of man who explained himself more than once.

The house smelled faintly of cooking gas and the hamburger she'd made for dinner last night. How could he own a place like this and not put a single personal mark on it? She traded in the combat boots for flip-flops, grabbed a book she'd picked up in town yesterday, and carried it down the rickety steps.

He'd pulled the kayak up on shore. She sat on the edge of the dock, but she couldn't read, couldn't do anything except try to quell her panic. What would she do once she was back on the mainland? Where would she go?

A noise distracted her. She looked up and saw a man who definitely wasn't Panda coming down the steps from the house. He was tall, with a large frame. The steps were wobbly and he took his time, his carefully styled light brown hair glistening with an undoubtedly expensive hair product. "Hey there!" he called out cheerfully.

Although he was good-looking, everything about him was a little too loud—his voice, the crest on the pocket of his designer sports coat, the heavy gold bracelet and big college ring any intelligent man would have gotten rid of after his frat boy days ended. "I heard Panda's back on the island," he said, taking in her tattoo and hair as he came toward her on the dock. "But nobody answered the door."

"He's not here."

"Too bad." With a broad smile, he thrust out his hand. "I'm Mike Moody. Big Mike. I'll bet you've seen my signs."

She shook his hand, then regretted it as the pungent scent of his cologne clung to her skin.

"Big Mike's Island Brokerage," he said. "Anybody who buys or sells property on this island—house or boat, big or small. Hell, I've even sold a couple of horses. I take care of it all." His straight teeth had an iridescence achievable only in a dental chair. "I sold Panda this house."

"Did you?"

"I didn't catch your name."

"I . . . go by Viper."

"No kidding. That's some name. You're one of the hippie girls." Like a good salesman, he sounded more admiring than critical.

"Goth," she replied, which was beyond ridiculous.

"Yeah, that's right." He nodded. "I stopped because I've got a boat I thought Panda might be interested in."

Lucy was a big believer in being cooperative, but Viper didn't share her principles. "Come back after the six o'clock ferry gets in. I know he'll want to talk to you about it. Maybe bring a pizza along. That way the two of you can have a long chat."

"Thanks for the tip," Big Mike said. "Panda's a great guy. I don't know him well, but he seems like an interesting character."

He waited, hoping she'd provide a few details, and Viper decided to cooperate. "He's a lot different from the way he was before he went to prison."

Her troublemaking didn't go over nearly as well as she'd hoped. "Everybody deserves a second chance," Big Mike said solemnly. And then, "Holy cripes, but you look familiar."

While she speculated on what kind of man would say "holy cripes," Big Mike gazed at her more closely. "You been on the island before?"

"No. My first trip."

His gold bracelet gleamed as he stuck his hand in his pocket. "It'll come to me. I never forget a face."

She hoped that wasn't true. He looked like he wanted to linger for a chat, so she nodded toward the steps. "I have some things to do in the house. I'll walk with you."

He followed her, and when they reached the top, he pumped her hand again. "Anything you need, you let me know. Big Mike's services don't stop with the sale. Ask anybody on the island, and they'll tell you that."

"I'll remember."

He finally left. She began to walk toward the house only to stop as she heard a rustle in the trees that didn't sound as though it came from a squirrel. A branch snapped, and she glimpsed a bright red T-shirt.

"I see you, Toby!" she called out. "Stop spying on me!"

She didn't expect an answer, and she didn't receive one.

She made a sandwich, but tossed it out after only a few bites. She sent Meg a text that revealed nothing important, then did the same with her parents. She wanted to send Ted a text but couldn't imagine what she'd say. With hours still to kill, she wandered into the sunroom.

Three walls of dirty, square-paned windows extended in a large square bay from the wainscoting to the ceiling. Lumpy couches, wing chairs upholstered in fabrics popular in the early nineties, and scarred tables sat haphazardly around the big room. This must have been the family's primary indoor gathering place. Built-in bookshelves displayed the detritus that ended up in summer homes: yellowed paperbacks, videotapes of old movies, board games in broken boxes held together by dehydrated rubber bands. There was something about this house she'd loved from the beginning, and her inner Martha Stewart wanted to toss out all the junk and clean those windows until they sparkled.

She picked up a ratty dish towel she'd used to wipe up a Coke spill and rubbed one corner of the glass. Most of the dirt was on the outside, but not nearly all of it. She blew on the pane and rubbed again. Better.

Cooking wasn't the only homemaking task she'd observed during her White House years, and fifteen minutes later she was equipped with a squeegee she'd seen in the upstairs bathroom, a bucket of clean water with a few drops of dishwashing soap, and a stepladder from the pantry. Before long, she'd finished one section of the sunroom windows. She reached for a spot she'd missed, and when she was satisfied, climbed down only to trip on the bottom rung.

Panda stood just inside the door, a can of Coke in his hand, combat in his eyes. "I'll bet you were real popular with the Secret Service."

Chapter Eight

❦

SHE SHOULD NEVER HAVE COME back to the house, and she certainly shouldn't have let him catch her washing his filthy windows. She grabbed the ladder for support and tested Viper's sneer again. "Did I hurt your pride?"

"Destroyed it," he said dryly.

"Excellent. It's not every day I get to outwit a trained professional."

"I wouldn't say 'outwit.'"

"I would." His clothes had dried, but he kicked his shoes off, and she could have sworn his dark stubble had grown since she'd given him the slip. "The ferry's not due in until six." She patted her tutu skirt back in place. "Obviously you had better luck chartering a boat than I did."

"The gun helped."

She had no idea whether he was serious or not. She knew nothing about him. He ran his thumb around the curve of the Coke can and propped a shoulder against the doorjamb. "Now I see why your father was so insistent about me not identifying myself. You've had practice pulling your disappearing act."

"I've only slipped away a few times."

He jabbed his Coke in the general direction of her face. "If I'd really been on duty, you wouldn't have slipped away at all."

True. He wouldn't have let her out of his sight. Which meant her family really hadn't rehired him. "Who tipped you off that I've been staying here?"

"Let's just say I've kept tabs on you."

Her parents. "I'm touched."

He gestured toward the section of windows she'd been working on. "You want to tell me why you're doing that?"

"Because they're filthy." She laid one more grievance at his feet. "The whole place is a mess. If you're lucky enough to own a house like this, you should take care of it."

"I do. A woman comes in every two weeks."

"And you can see for yourself what a top-notch job she's been doing."

He glanced around as if he was looking at the place for the first time. "I guess it's getting a little mangy."

"You think?"

"I'll hire somebody else."

She wondered if his gun was back in its ankle holster. Firearms didn't bother her. She'd spent years being guarded by armed agents, although they tended to wear business suits instead of jeans and obscene T-shirts. So it wasn't the gun. It was the fact that she hadn't known about the gun or the two-week contract or any of the measly details she should have known about before she decided to drop that towel and jump into bed with him.

She tossed down the squeegee. "Why did my parents hire you? As opposed to someone reputable?"

That annoyed him. "I am reputable."

"I'm sure they thought so at the time." Viper smirked. "How did they find you anyway? Never mind. You're on one of those work-release programs the prisons offer."

He cocked his head, his expression puzzled. "What's happened to you?"

Her rudeness was giving her a rush. "Or maybe an aide spotted your name on a sex offenders registry and decided to play a little prank?" She wanted to go on like this forever, let her tongue run free, fling out one nasty after another, say whatever insult popped into her head without a care about how it reflected on the office of the president of the United States.

"You wanted to know about me. I'll tell you." The Coke can landed with a thud on the wobbly wooden table by the door.

"No need." She practiced her new Viper's smirk. "I don't care."

"I'm thirty-six. I was born and raised in Detroit. In and out of trouble until the army straightened me out. Pulled sweet duty in Germany, went to Wayne State for a degree in criminal justice—"

"You have a *college degree*? You can barely talk."

That made him angrier. "Just because I don't brag about my exclusive upbringing doesn't mean I can't talk."

"I never bragged—"

"I joined the Detroit police force. Resigned a couple of years ago to take over a private firm in Chicago that specializes in security for corporate executives, celebrities, athletes, and Wall Street crooks getting death threats they damn well deserve. Your parents hired me to guard you because I'm good at what I do. I've never been married and don't intend to be. I like dogs, but I'm gone too much to have one. I also like hip-hop and opera. Make of that whatever you want. When I'm not on duty I sleep in the raw. Anything else you'd like to know that's none of your business?"

"Patrick Shade? Is that name another of your many lies?"

"No. And there weren't that many lies."

"How about Huntsville prison?"

"Give me a break. You knew that was bogus."

She hadn't exactly. "Construction worker?"

"I worked construction for a while."

"A man of honor. My mistake."

He wouldn't back down. "Your parents hired me. I took my orders from them, and judging from what happened today, they made a good call when they told me not to identify myself."

"They're overprotective."

"You've gotten threatening letters. You've been knocked over a couple of times. And you were part of a high-profile wedding. There is such a thing as exercising reasonable caution."

"The only person who caused me any harm was you!"

He flinched, which should have made her feel better than it did. "You're right," he said. "I should have kept my hands to myself no matter how crazy you made me."

Knowing she'd made him crazy encouraged her to continue her attack. "Whose idea was Caddo Lake?"

"It was a good place to keep you out of sight. The rental house was isolated, and your parents wanted to give you time to sort things out and realize you'd made a mistake."

"All of you thought that sticking me on the back of a death machine was the best way to get me to Caddo?"

"I didn't plan on that."

"And here I thought you planned everything."

"Yeah, well, next time I guard a bride, you can be damned sure I'll anticipate that she might take off."

She couldn't listen to any more of this, and she headed for the door.

Before she reached it, he spoke again. "I got the bike from a guy in Austin. It was good cover. I rode into Wynette a few days before you arrived so I could hang out in the local bars without anybody getting suspicious. It gave me a chance to see if I overheard anything that made me uneasy."

"And did you?"

"Mainly I heard a lot of people saying that no woman was good enough for Ted. He's some kind of local god."

She frowned. "I knew they didn't like me."

"I don't think it was personal. At least I didn't think so at the time. I might have changed my mind about that."

She'd heard enough, but as she headed for the back door, Mr. Talky was right behind her. "When your great escape started," he said, "I figured it'd only last a couple of hours. How was I supposed to know you were having some kind of existential breakdown?"

His use of the word unnerved her. She wanted burps, not verbal erudition. "It wasn't a breakdown." She stalked across the kitchen floor and out onto the porch. But now that she didn't want to talk, he stayed with her, and he wouldn't shut up.

"I could have traded in the bike for an SUV the next day, but I'd have blown my cover, and you'd have tried to pull another disappearing act. Frankly, I didn't want to work that hard. And don't try to pretend you didn't love being on that bike."

She had loved it, but she wasn't admitting anything. She pushed open the screen door and stepped into the yard. "Unfortunately, the ferry doesn't leave for a few hours, so I'd appreciate it if you'd leave me alone. I'm sure you have things to do."

He moved in front of her, blocking her way. "Lucy, that night . . ."

She stared at his collarbone. He jammed his hands in his pockets, studied her nose ring. "I've never let anything like that happen with a client."

She didn't want to hear about his remorse, and she shot around him.

"You have a right to be pissed," he said from behind her. "I screwed up."

She spun back. "You didn't screw up. You screwed *me*. And don't think it's the sex that bothered me. I'm a grown woman. I can have all the sex I want." *Big talker.* "What bothers me is that I didn't know who I was having sex with."

"Loud and clear."

"Great. Now leave me alone."

"Fine."

But he stayed where he was. She couldn't bear hearing more apologies, and she thrust her finger in the general direction of the sunroom. "Try taking care of your house for a change instead of bothering me."

"You want me to wash windows?"

She hadn't meant that at all. She didn't care about the windows. "I suppose you could shoot them out," she sneered, "but that seems a little excessive. Still, it's your house. Whatever works for you." With that, she reached the staircase. But with every step she took, her resentment burrowed in deeper. She didn't want to leave this house. She wanted to stay, to eat breakfast on the screen porch, and take the kayak out, and hide from the world. He didn't deserve this house. If it were hers, she'd give it the love it deserved. But it wasn't hers.

She stomped back to the top of the stairs. "You don't deserve this house!"

"What do you care?"

"I don't. I—" It came to her in a flash. An impossible idea . . . She closed her mouth. Opened it. "When are you leaving?"

He regarded her suspiciously. "Tomorrow morning."

"And . . . Are you coming back soon?"

"Not sure. I'm starting a new job. Maybe September. What difference does it make to you?"

Her mind raced. She loved this house . . . this island . . . She swallowed. "If . . . you're not going to be using the house for a while . . ." She did her best to keep her voice even, not let him see how important this had become to her. "I might want to rent it. I have some things to do, and this is as good a spot as any."

"What kind of things?"

She wasn't telling him about the panic she experienced whenever she thought of going back to Washington. Instead, she shrugged. "Take a real vacation. Cook. I have some writing to do for my father. You can apply my cleaning fees to the first month's rent."

He regarded her stonily. "I don't think it's a good idea."

She wasn't giving up so easily. "So all that talk about how you screwed up was just talk, right? You don't have to back it up? Make some kind of atonement?"

"Atonement? That's what this would be?"

Atonement, but not forgiveness. "Why not?"

He stared at her for a long time, and she stared right back. "All right," he finally said. "You can have the place for a month. Rent free. And my sins are all forgiven."

Not by a long shot. "Deal."

A rabbit darted across the yard. She escaped to the dock, where she pulled off her boots and dangled her feet toward the water. The only deep emotion lurking behind that airport kiss had been guilt. Still, with the prospect of being able to spend more time on the island, she wasn't going to regret the impulse that had brought her to this place where she was free from everyone's expectations. She could be herself, even if she was no longer certain exactly who that person was.

With the sun beating down on the dock and her tutu skirt itching like crazy, she got too hot and climbed back up to the house. Panda was fixing the backdoor windowpane she'd broken. She decided to skirt the house and go in the front so she wouldn't have to talk to him, but on the way, she glimpsed a bright red T-shirt moving through the woods. Her nerves were already stretched too tight from the day's tension, she was sick of being spied on, and something inside her snapped. "Toby!" She ran into the trees. "Toby! You come back here!" He kept running, and she barely avoided a tangle of wild blueberries as she charged after him.

He knew the terrain better than she did, but she didn't care. She wasn't letting him get away. Just as she jumped over a thick patch of bracken, she heard something coming toward her from behind. Panda barreled past her. Moments later, he held the terrified twelve-year-old by the back of his T-shirt. "Who do we have here?" he said.

She'd forgotten about Panda and his bodyguard instincts.

Toby was too terrified to struggle. Panda's grip on the red T-shirt made it bunch under the boy's armpits, revealing his bony rib cage and a sizable gap at the waistband of his oversize camouflage shorts. They hung to his knees, his skinny legs jutting out beneath. As annoyed as she was about being spied on, she couldn't stand the fear in his eyes, and she touched Panda's arm. "I'll take care of this."

"Are you sure you're up to it?" he drawled. "The kid looks dangerous."

Toby's literal mind didn't recognize sarcasm. "I-I-I'm not dangerous."

"This is Toby," she said. "His grandmother is your housekeeper."

"Is that so?"

"Lemme go!" Toby cried. "I didn't do anything."

"That's not true," she said as Panda relaxed his hold on the T-shirt. "You've been spying on me for days, and I want it to stop."

Free of Panda's grip, Toby got his swagger back along with his belligerence. "I never spied on nobody. My grandma sent me over to make sure you didn't trash the place."

"I'm being policed by a ten-year-old?"

"Twelve!"

As she very well knew, but Viper wasn't as sentimental about kids as Lucy. "You need to find something better to do with your time," she said.

The boy jutted his jaw and stared her square in the eye. "I haven't been spying. You're lying."

Viper looked up at Panda. "Go ahead. Take him out."

Chapter Nine

P ANDA LIFTED AN EYEBROW AT her. "Take him *out*?"

Toby was a disagreeable little cuss, and she hated being spied on. Still, she couldn't help but like his spirit. "He's too much for me," she said. "It's the least you can do."

Toby stumbled backward in his effort to get away, only to slip on a patch of pine straw and go down hard. He scrambled to his feet and started to take off again, but Panda captured him by the seat of his baggy shorts. "Hold on, kid. This conversation isn't over."

"Let me go, you jerkoff!"

"Hey! What's going on here?"

Lucy turned to see Big Mike Moody approaching on the path, a large pizza box in his hands. She'd forgotten all about her invitation for him to return and annoy Panda. He must have spotted them through the trees.

"Big Mike!" Toby was back on his feet, still struggling to get away.

"Trouble here, folks?" The real estate broker flashed his shiny white teeth at Panda. "Nice to see you on the island again. Hope you're enjoying that house."

Panda gave him a brusque nod.

Big Mike gestured toward the boy with his free hand. "What's up, Toby? You in trouble? Toby's a friend of mine. Maybe I can help out here."

Toby shot Lucy an enraged glare. "She says I was spying on her. She's a big liar."

Big Mike frowned. "Best you settle down, boy. That's no way to talk."

Lucy stiffened. As annoyed as she was with Toby, she didn't appreciate hearing him addressed as "boy." Either Big Mike didn't know or didn't care how offensive that appellation was to African American males, regardless of their age. If her brother, Andre, had been around, Big Mike would have gotten a big lesson in racial sensitivity.

But the offense didn't appear to have registered with Toby. As Panda freed him, he rushed to Big Mike's side. "I didn't do anything. Honest."

Big Mike had already transferred the pizza box to his left hand, and he draped his right arm around the kid's shoulders, undoubtedly transferring his cologne in the process. "Are you sure about that?" Big Mike said. "Miss Viper here seems pretty upset."

Panda snorted.

The way Big Mike was taking her in said he was still trying to place her face. She looked down.

"I didn't do anything," Toby said again.

Lucy decided wearing a cologne-saturated T-shirt was sufficient punishment for Toby. "I don't want you spying on me anymore. If it happens again, I'll talk to your grandmother."

Toby screwed up his face. "My grandmother's not home right now, so you can't talk to her."

Not even a smart-aleck kid could ruffle Big Mike's amiability. "You know what I think, Toby? I think you owe Miss Viper an apology."

She wasn't a big believer in forced apologies, but Big Mike patted Toby's shoulder. "Don't you have something to say to her? Or would you rather wait till she comes to your house?"

The boy looked at his feet. "Sorry," he muttered.

Big Mike nodded, as if Toby had spoken from the depths of his heart. "That's better. I'll take Toby home now. He won't be giving you any more trouble, will you, Toby?"

Toby scuffed his feet and shook his head.

"I didn't think so." Big Mike still held the pizza, and he extended the box toward Panda. "The two of you go ahead and enjoy this. I can come over and talk to you later about the boat."

"The boat?" Panda said.

"A twenty-foot Polar Kraft. The owner only took it out one summer, and he's practically giving it away. Miss Viper told me you were in the market."

Panda glanced down at her. "Miss Viper misunderstood."

Big Mike knew how to roll with the punches, and his smile grew broader. "She seemed pretty sure, but hey— You have my card. When you're ready, you give me a ring. That boat's a real bargain. Now you two enjoy that pizza. Come on, Toby." He steered the boy along the path in the opposite direction from the house.

As they disappeared, Panda looked down at her. "You told him I wanted to buy a boat?"

"You might want to buy a boat. How was I supposed to know?"

He shook his head and turned toward the house only to stop and lift the box closer to his nose. "Why does this pizza smell like perfume?"

"Big Mike believes in marking his territory." She quickened her steps and left Panda to walk back to the house alone.

❧

BREE HEARD TOBY COMING THROUGH the woods before she saw him. It was almost seven, and once again she'd forgotten to fix him dinner. Usually when that happened, she'd go inside and find him sitting at the kitchen table eating a bowl of cereal from one of the many boxes Myra had picked up on her last trip to Sam's Club before she'd gotten too ill to travel to the mainland.

Bree told herself to get up off the step and do something—anything—other than smoke, stare at Myra's beehives, and think about those long-ago summers when she and Star ran back and forth like wild things from this cottage to the house. But she didn't have a lot of bright thoughts to choose from. Her shattered marriage? Nope. Her empty bank account? Definitely not. As for her self-esteem . . . How could she think about something that didn't exist?

This cottage, along with Myra's honey house, had once been her second home, but in the last three weeks, the place had become her prison. If only she could run to the summer house, curl up on the screen porch with her Walkman again, and listen to the Backstreet Boys while she watched her brothers and their friends race up and down the steps to the dock. David had been one of those beautiful boys that last summer, although during the day he'd worked a fishing charter while the rest of them played.

Bree stared at the bees and lit another cigarette just as Toby came out of the woods. Someone was with him. She shielded her eyes and saw a good-looking man walking at his side. He was big all over, tall, with wide shoulders and a broad chest. One of those attractive men who stood out in a crowd. The kind of man—

She sprang off the step.

"Hey there, Bree," he said. "It's been a long time."

Thirteen years fell away. His physical transformation meant nothing. She hated him now as fiercely as she had the last time she'd seen him. "Toby, get in the house," she said stiffly. "I'll be there in a minute."

"Hold on." He ruffled Toby's hair as if he had that right. "You remember what I said, Toby. Summer people are naturally paranoid. You can't keep going over there."

"I wasn't doin' nothing bad."

The hair tousle turned into a knuckle rub. "Sooner or later, he'll find out about your grandmother. And just so you know . . . You can't cash a check he's made out to her. Now you go inside while I talk to Bree."

Bree clenched her hand into a fist. Mike Moody ranked along with her ex-husband, Scott, as someone she'd never wanted to see again. She'd known Mike still lived here, since his face stared out from half a dozen billboards along the island's main road, but she'd intended to make sure she never ran into him. Yet here he was.

Toby stomped into the cottage. Mike came forward with his big suck-up smile and his hand extended to shake. "You're looking great, Bree. Beautiful as always."

She pressed her arms to her sides. "What do you want?"

He let his arm fall but didn't lose his phony smile. "Not even a 'hello'?"

"Not even."

He'd been a smelly, weaselly-eyed fat kid with bad skin and crooked teeth who'd tried unsuccessfully to worm his way into their group of summer kids each year. But the only islander they'd let in was Star. Mike was too loud, too uncool. Everything about him was wrong—his clothes, his snorty laugh, his unfunny jokes. The only one who'd tolerated him had been David.

"I feel sorry for the kid," David had said after one of her brothers had insulted Mike. "His parents are both drunks. He's got a lot of problems."

"We all have problems," Star had said. "You're only sticking up for him because you're kind of an outcast, too."

Had he been? Bree didn't remember it that way. From the beginning, David had fascinated them. He was charming, charismatic, good-looking. Raised in poverty in Gary, Indiana, he was attending the University of Michigan on a full scholarship. At twenty, he was the same age as her oldest brother, but David was more worldly. Although she couldn't remember any of them saying it out loud, they all thought it was cool to hang out with a black kid. Beyond that, there wasn't one of them who didn't believe David was destined for great things.

Mike gestured toward her cigarette. "Those coffin nails'll kill you. You should give that up."

He was still uncool, but in a different way. The crooked teeth, acne, and extra pounds might be long gone, but he still tried too hard. The scraggly, dirty blond hair of his teenage years had been tamed by an expensive cut, then overtreated with grooming products. His cheap summer wardrobe of ill-fitting shorts and T-shirts had given way to white slacks, a high-end polo shirt, and a belt with a Prada logo, all of it too ostentatious for casual island living, although not as objectionable as his heavy gold-link bracelet and college class ring.

Her cigarette burned close to her fingers. "What's this about?"

"Toby's run into some trouble with the new folks next door."

She tapped the bottom of the filter with her thumb and said nothing.

He jingled the coins in his pocket. "No one seems to have told the new owner that Myra passed, so he thinks she's still taking care of the place. But turns out Toby's been doing the job ever since Myra got sick. I didn't know about it till just now, or I'd have put a stop to it."

The cigarette burned her fingers. She dropped it and stubbed out the butt with the toe of her sandal. A twelve-year-old trying to do an adult's job. She should have paid more attention to his disappearances. Something else to make her feel incompetent. "I'll talk to him."

She turned away to go into the house.

"Bree, we were kids," he said from behind her. "Don't tell me you're still holding a grudge."

She kept moving.

"I tried to apologize," he said. "Did you get my letter?"

She was good at walking away from her own anger. She'd spent ten years doing exactly that. Ten years pretending she didn't know Scott was a serial cheater. Ten years avoiding a confrontation that would end her marriage. And look where it had gotten her. Exactly nowhere.

She whipped around. "Do you still spy on people, Mike? Are you still the same sneaky rat now that you were then?"

"I had a crush on you," he said, as if that justified everything. "The older woman."

A year older. She dug her fingernails into her palms. "So you went to my mother and told her you'd seen David and me together. Great way to get the girl."

"I thought if the two of you broke up, I'd have a chance."

"Never in a million years."

Once again, he dug his hands in his pockets. "I was seventeen, Bree. I can't change the past. What I did was wrong, and all I can do now is say I'm sorry."

She and David hadn't suspected Mike was spying on them that night when they hid in the dunes and made love. Mike had gone to her mother the next day, and Bree had been sent off the island that same afternoon into exile at her horrible Aunt Rebecca's in Battle Creek. Bree had never come back to the island, not until three weeks ago when she'd gotten word that Myra had died and left Bree responsible for her grandson.

Mike pulled his hands from his pockets. "Let me help you with Toby."

"I don't need your help. Leave us alone."

He rubbed his gold bracelet with his thumb. "I care about the kid."

"I'm sure it's good for your image in the community to pretend to watch out for poor orphans."

He didn't display even a flicker of shame. "I knew you wouldn't roll out the welcome mat for me, but I thought maybe we could work together on this."

"You thought wrong."

He gazed around at the weedy yard and small honey house with its peeling white paint and sagging tin roof. A gust of wind stirred the leaves but didn't disturb his expensive haircut. "You won't get much for this place if you try to sell it. There's no water view, no beach access, and the cottage needs work."

He wasn't telling her anything she hadn't already figured out. Unlucky in love and in real estate—that was her. The bank had foreclosed on the five-million-dollar house she and Scott had bought in Bloomfield Hills. The last she'd heard, they'd listed it for one-point-three million and still couldn't move it.

Mike wandered toward Myra's abandoned garden where young tomato plants were struggling to survive the weeds. "If you take Toby off the island, you'll destroy the only security he has."

"You don't really think I'm staying here?" She said it as if she had a dozen other options when, in reality, she had none.

He still managed to look innocent as he drove in the knife. "I heard you didn't get much in your divorce settlement."

She hadn't gotten anything. No help from her family, either. Her brothers had their own financial problems, and even if they hadn't, she couldn't have asked them for money, not when she'd turned a deaf ear to their warnings about Scott. As for her inheritance . . . That had been gone within a year of her mother's death.

"Here, you have a house," he said. "Myra kept Toby too close, so he didn't have many friends, but his roots are here, and there've been enough changes in his life. I think David would want you to stay."

She couldn't stand hearing him speak David's name, not even after all these years. "Don't ever come here again." She turned on her heel and left him standing alone in the yard.

Toby was sitting at the small drop-leaf table in the kitchen, eating another bowl of cereal. The kitchen, along with the rest of the cottage, had been redone in the days of pickled oak cabinetry and butcher-block countertops. A pair of open shelves held Myra's collection of honey pots and ceramic bees. Through the window over the sink, she watched Mike survey the yard as if he were appraising the property. Finally he walked away.

David had written her one letter.

I'll always love you, Bree. But this is the end. I won't be
the cause of trouble between you and your family . . .

She'd been devastated. Her sole comfort had come from her phone conversations with Star. Myra's daughter was her best friend, the only person who understood how much she loved David, how much more he was to her than a summer romance.

Six weeks after Bree left, Star got pregnant with David's baby, and David dropped out of school to marry her. Bree had never spoken to either of them again.

Toby picked up his cereal bowl and slurped the remaining milk. He set the bowl on the table. "Gram told me you were rich. I bet you lied to her."

"I was rich." Bree gazed out the window. "Now I'm not."

"Why?"

"Because I relied on a man to support me instead of figuring out how to rely on myself."

"I knew you didn't have any money." It was an accusation, another reminder of how much he hated her. Not that she was too crazy about him, either. "When are you gonna leave?" he said.

It wasn't the first time he'd asked the question, and she wished she had an answer. "I don't know."

He shoved back his chair. "You can't keep sitting around here not doing nothing."

He was right, and she needed to show him she had a plan. Something. Anything.

"I don't intend to." She turned away from the window. "I'm going to sell Myra's honey."

LUCY HAD NO INTENTION OF joining Panda for a chummy pizza dinner. Instead she put on her sneakers and headed outside. She hated to run, but she hated feeling like a slug even more, and she needed to work off her emotions from this miserable day.

From Goose Cove Lane, she turned out onto the highway. Eventually she passed an abandoned farm stand. Behind it, she glimpsed a small blue cottage. She heard another runner coming up behind her and didn't have to look back to know who it was. "You're not on the family payroll anymore," she said as he reached her side.

"Force of habit."

"I don't like running, and I especially don't like running with you."

"Tough. This road's too damn narrow. Get on the shoulder."

"You can hear a car coming a mile away, and I'm doing this because I want to be alone."

"Pretend I'm not here." He slowed to keep from passing her. "You're really not going back to Wynette, are you?"

"You're just figuring that out?"

"I'd have bet anything you'd change your mind."

"You'd have been wrong."

"There's always a first time."

"You're such a loser." She cut across the road, turned around, and started back to the house.

He didn't follow her.

When she got back, she biked to the beach at the south tip of the island and sat on top of a sand dune to watch the sun set over the lake. When she finally went back to the house, she found Panda sitting in one of the six mismatched chairs that surrounded the fake Victorian kitchen table she'd grown to hate, not just for its chipped green paint and ugly, too-bulky legs—one of which was propped up with a piece of folded cardboard—but because it symbolized everything that needed tending in this once-lively house.

Although the pizza box lay open in front of him, only a few slices were missing. He looked up as she came in, and the yellow light from the Tiffany-like shade hanging above the table shadowed his already swarthy skin. She addressed him impersonally, as if they were only the most distant of acquaintances. "I've been staying in your bedroom, and since you're leaving tomorrow, I'd rather not move out for just one night."

He propped his elbow on the back of his chair. "It's my room."

It was also the only bedroom on the first floor, which made it feel like a safe refuge from him. "I'll be happy to make up one of the other beds for you," she said.

"And if I object?"

"Then I'll move, and you can sleep on my dirty sheets."

He gave her his badass sneer. "Let me think about it."

She countered with cool formality. "I'd appreciate it if you'd think quickly. I've had a long day, and I want to turn in."

His sneer turned to a shrug. "Sleep wherever you like. I don't care. And I'll make up my own bed." He turned to the door, then stopped himself. "One more thing. Leave the house alone. Everything stays the way it is."

She'd see about that.

But he wasn't done giving her a hard time. Not long after she'd turned out the bedroom light, she heard a knock. "I forgot my toothbrush," he said through the door.

She got out of bed, retrieved his toothbrush from the medicine cabinet, unlocked the bedroom door, and pushed it through the crack.

From the angry way his jaw locked, she might as well have been holding a switchblade. "You locked the door?" he said in a voice that smoked like dry ice.

"Habit," she replied uneasily.

"You *locked* the door?"

She'd come off like a kid if she mentioned how spooky the house was at night, so she shrugged.

His brows slammed together, and the corner of his mouth cocked with contempt. "Babe, if I wanted to get in that room, no lock would keep me out. But why would I bother? You weren't that good anyway."

She sucked in her breath and slammed the door in his face.

PANDA WANTED TO PUNCH SOMETHING. Himself. How many times was he going to blow it with her? But she got him so pissed off.

Bitch deserved it. If she hadn't made me so mad, I wouldn't have hit her.

He'd heard exactly those words during hundreds of domestic violence calls where some asshole tried to justify beating the shit out of a woman with the same excuse. The fact that he'd used words instead of his fists didn't make him any better than they were.

He shoved his fingers into his hair. *Be the best at what you're good at.* But everything connected with Lucy Jorik had been one big screwup after another, right from the beginning. As soon as he picked her up in that alley, he should have taken her back to her family. All those games he'd played trying to scare her off had done nothing more than make him feel like a colossal jerk. One mistake after another, each leading to the biggest mistake of all. That last night.

It had been hard enough keeping his hands off her when they were at Caddo, but that last night in the motel had snapped his self-control. He'd spent too many hours with her pressed against his back, too many days watching those green-flecked brown eyes flash tornado signals at him whenever she felt vulnerable.

He raised his fist to knock on the door again, then let his arm fall. What was the point of apologizing? The last thing she wanted right now was to see any more of him.

He headed down the musty old hallway and up the stairs of this haunted house he hadn't been able to stop himself from buying. The life he'd lived had given him more than enough emotional shit to deal with. He didn't need more, especially not with the daughter of the fucking president of the United States.

He couldn't get off this island fast enough.

Lucy avoided Panda the next morning by slipping out through the sliding doors in her bedroom onto the deck that led to the backyard. She rode her bike into town and had coffee and a muffin at one of the Painted Frog's outside café tables. Other than some assessing glances at her hair and tattoo from a couple of teenage girls, no one paid any attention to her. The feeling of leaving Lucy Jorik behind was heady.

After she finished, she rode toward the north tip of the island. She loved the island's shabby edges. This was no playground for the rich and famous. Plumbers and shoe salesmen came here. Kids who attended state colleges and families pushing babies in Walmart strollers. If Mat and Nealy hadn't come into her life, a place like this would have been her fantasy vacation spot.

The Fourth of July was almost two weeks away, but boaters were already out on the water. She passed a farm, then a wooden shack with a hand-lettered sign advertising the BEST SMOKED WHITEFISH ON THE ISLAND. A small inland lake spiked with cattails lay on her left, a marsh spread to her right, with the bigger body of Lake Michigan beyond that. Gradually the hardwoods shading the road gave way to pine, and then the trees disappeared altogether as the road narrowed into the exposed point of the island.

A lighthouse rose from a bedrock landscape that had long ago been swept clean by glaciers. She abandoned her bike and picked her way along a path. She nodded at the lighthouse keeper tending some orange impatiens in wooden planters near the door. Beyond the building, a jetty jutted into the water. The lake was calm today, but she imagined this place during a storm, with waves crashing over the rocks.

She found a spot to sit among boulders already warming from the morning sun. The ferry was a moving speck on the water as it coasted toward the mainland. She fervently hoped Panda was on that boat because if he was still at the house, she'd have to move out, and more than ever, she didn't want to leave. The ugly words he'd flung at her last night still burned. People were never cruel to her, but Panda had been deliberately vicious.

She didn't care why he'd lashed out at her or even if he believed what he'd said. His words had destroyed any lingering nostalgia over their great adventure. And that, ultimately, was a good thing.

By the time she was back on her bike, she'd resolved to put herself on a regular schedule. She'd take advantage of the cooler mornings to go out on the lake or to explore the island. In the afternoons, she'd start writing the chapters she'd promised her father.

As she neared the turnoff to Goose Cove Lane, she glimpsed the same robin's-egg blue house she'd spotted yesterday. The island's undulating shoreline made distances deceptive, but this must be where Toby and his grandmother lived—not all that far from the Remington home as the crow flew.

A mailbox leaned at a precarious angle on one side of the driveway with an abandoned farm stand on the other. Although the house was several miles from town, it had a decent location for selling summer produce, since the highway led to the south beach, the largest on the island and the place where she'd gone last night near sunset. A faded sign dangling crookedly from a broken chain read CAROUSEL HONEY FOR SALE.

Impulsively, she turned into the driveway.

Chapter Ten

❦

B REE SCREAMED AND SPRANG AWAY from the hive.

"Oh, god . . . Oh, god . . . oh, god . . ." She moaned, hunched her shoulders, shivered. The mass she'd seen in the bottom of the brood box wasn't an arbitrary collection of debris. Oh, no. It was a mouse. A dead mouse, petrified inside the sticky mass of protective propolis the bees had deposited around it.

She shuddered, jerked off her stiff leather beekeeper's gloves, and retreated across the yard. According to Toby, Mr. Wentzel had given the bees a strong sugar solution last month, but now the hives needed to get new brood boxes. This was only the third hive she'd opened. What was she going to find inside the rest?

Maybe Star had it right after all. She'd hated working with her mother's bees. But Bree wasn't Star, and right from the beginning, the bees had fascinated her. Each summer she'd helped Myra with the hives. She'd loved the vague air of danger, the superiority of having a skill none of her brothers possessed. She liked the order of the colony, the strict rules that governed their society, the idea of a queen. Mainly, though, she'd liked being with Myra, who was quiet and private, so different from Bree's own frantic, self-absorbed mother.

Bree had been awake most of the night studying Myra's small collection of beekeeping books, but neither the books nor all her summers helping Myra had prepared her for this much responsibility. She'd even taken a beekeeping class a few years ago, but Scott had refused to let her put a hive in the yard, so she'd never done anything with it. And now here she was, with not a single hive to guard against rodents, parasites, and overcrowding but with fifteen of them.

She scratched her ankle with the toe of her opposite sneaker. Although Myra's jacket with its attached hat and veil fit, the matching overalls weren't designed for someone as tall and thin as she was, so she'd pulled on her own khaki slacks. Light clothing kept the bees calmer, since dark colors reminded them of predator animals like raccoons and skunks. Unfortunately, she'd forgotten to tuck her slacks into her socks, which accounted for the sting throbbing near her ankle.

She considered the possibility of persuading Toby to dispose of the dead mouse, but he shared his mother's dislike of bees, and it wasn't likely. After yesterday's spying incident, she'd intended to keep a better eye on him, but he was nowhere to be seen. What she did see was a teenage girl with dyed black hair and some messy dreadlocks coming around the side of the house. She wore a black tank top, shorts, and ugly boots. She was shorter than Bree, maybe five four, with small, even features and a generous mouth. If it weren't for the awful hair and hard makeup, she might be pretty. She also looked vaguely familiar, although Bree was sure they'd never met.

She pushed her veil on top of her hat. The girl's appearance made her uneasy, not just because of the tattoo and nose ring, but because nobody had bothered her until yesterday. She liked feeling invisible, and she wanted to keep it that way.

"I'm guessing you're not Toby's grandmother," the girl said.

Despite her tough appearance, she didn't seem threatening. Bree tossed her gloves down next to the smoker she'd been using to calm the bees. Myra used to work the hives with her bare hands, but Bree wasn't even close to being ready for that. "Toby's grandmother passed away at the beginning of May."

"Really? That's interesting." She extended her hand, an odd thing for a young girl to do. "I'm Viper."

Viper? Bree returned the handshake, but it felt odd. In her old social circle, hugs were de rigueur, even with women she barely knew. "Bree West."

"It's nice to meet you, Bree. Does Toby happen to be around?"

How did this girl know Toby? Once again Bree felt the scope of her incompetence. She didn't know where Toby was or what he did when he was out of her sight. "Toby!"

No answer.

"He's probably in the woods," the woman said with a kindness that made Bree realize she wasn't a teenager after all. "Are you Toby's mother?"

Bree's pale redhead's complexion had earned her the nickname Corpse from her brothers, and considering Toby's racial heritage, she thought the woman was being ironic. But she seemed sincere. "No. I'm . . . his guardian."

"I see." Something about her steadfast gaze made Bree feel as if she really did see—maybe more than Bree wanted her to.

"Can I help you?" Bree knew she sounded brusque, but she wanted her to leave so she could get back to the bees. More urgently, she needed a cigarette.

"We're neighbors," the woman said. "I'm renting the Remington house."

The Remington house? *Her* house. Could this be the woman Toby had been spying on? She pretended ignorance. "Remington house? I . . . only got here a couple of weeks ago."

"It's on the other side of the woods. There's a path."

The path she and Star had raced along a thousand times.

The woman glanced toward the hives. "You're a beekeeper."

"Toby's grandmother was the beekeeper. I'm just trying to keep the hives alive."

"Do you have a lot of experience?"

Bree laughed, a rusty sound that she barely recognized as her own. "Hardly. I worked with bees when I was growing up, but it's been a long time. Fortunately, these are healthy, established colonies, and the cold spring seems to have kept them from swarming. If I don't screw up, they should be okay."

"That's great." She seemed honestly impressed. "Would you mind if I borrowed Toby for a while tomorrow? I need help moving furniture. He's visited me a few times, and I thought he might like some work."

He hadn't been visiting. He'd been spying. "I . . . hope he didn't cause any trouble."

"An angel like Toby?"

Her ironically lifted eyebrow took Bree by surprise. Once again, she heard herself laugh. "He's all yours."

The woman who called herself Viper turned in the general direction of the woods and cupped her hands around her mouth. "Toby! I need help over at the house tomorrow afternoon. If you want to make some money, come see me."

There was no answer, but that didn't seem to bother her. She returned her attention to the hives. "I've always been interested in bees, but I don't know anything about them. Would it be presumptuous to ask if you'd let me watch you work sometime?"

Her vocabulary and manner were so at odds with her appearance that Bree was taken aback. Maybe that was why she found herself giving a brusque nod. "If you'd like."

"Great. I'll see you soon." With a smile, she headed back the way she'd come.

Bree turned toward the hives, then stopped as she was struck with a sudden thought. "How do you feel about mice?" she called out.

"Mice?" The woman stopped. "Not my favorites. Why?"

Bree hesitated, then gestured toward the last hive in the row. "If you're interested in beekeeping, there's something unusual you might be interested in seeing. Have you ever heard of propolis?"

"No. What is it?"

"This heavy, sticky substance bees collect to seal crevices in the hive. It has antibacterial qualities—some commercial beekeepers even harvest it." She tried to sound professional. "The bees also use it as a kind of hygienic seal around any hive invaders to protect the colony from infection. Go take a look."

The woman walked toward the hive, a lamb to the mouse slaughter. She stopped in front of the noisome lump and gazed down at it. "Gross."

But she didn't move away. She kept staring. Bree snatched up the shovel she'd propped by the step. "If you want to pick it up and throw it into the gully . . ."

The woman glanced over her shoulder.

Bree did her best to continue her bright, informative chatter. "The propolis has actually mummified the mouse. Isn't that fascinating?"

"You're conning me."

In the path of that steady gaze, Bree's posturing collapsed. "I—can do it myself. I'll have to. But . . . I hate mice, and you seem like the kind of person who's up for anything."

The woman's eyes brightened. "I do?"

Bree nodded.

"Excellent." She took the shovel, scooped up the mouse detritus, and tossed it into the gully.

It had been forever since another person had done something nice for her—even if she'd been manipulated into doing it—and Bree couldn't remember the last time she'd been so touched.

CURIOSITY ABOUT TOBY AND HIS grandmother had made Lucy stop at the cottage. Or maybe she'd simply been procrastinating because, if Panda's SUV was still in the drive, she had to pack up and leave. Still, as tense as she was, she couldn't be any more uptight than Toby's guardian.

Bree was a beautiful woman, despite being almost brittlely thin. There was an old-fashioned fragility about her sharply cut features and translucent complexion. Lucy could see her in Victorian dress, that long neck rising out of a high lace collar, auburn hair caught up on her head. Something told her the woman was carrying a boatload of trouble on her thin shoulders. But how did Toby fit into the picture?

It was none of her business, and she shouldn't have given in to the impulse to invite Toby to the house, but as soon as she'd heard that his grandmother was dead, she couldn't help herself. Gutsy kids were her weakness. Right along with throwing herself at the first man she'd met after she pulled her runaway act.

She rounded the last curve, held her breath, and turned into the drive.

His car was gone. She'd never have to see him again.

As she leaned the bike against the back of the house, she wondered if jumping into bed with Panda had been her twisted way of justifying running from her wedding. She couldn't have found a better way to prove to herself how unworthy she was to marry a man like Ted. Both a comforting and a disturbing thought. It would explain why she'd acted so out of character, but it was hardly a positive reflection on her character.

Determined to file away that short, painful chapter of her life forever, she let herself into the house with the key she'd unearthed from a broken wicker basket buried underneath expired pizza coupons, outdated ferry schedules, dead flashlight batteries, and a ten-year-old island phone book. She headed for the kitchen and found Toby sitting at the table, eating a bowl of cereal.

"Do make yourself at home," she drawled. The German coffeemaker had been freshly rinsed out, and she doubted Toby had done it. Other than that, she saw no signs that Panda had been here.

Toby gave her his customary hostile glare. "How much are you going to pay me?"

"How much are you worth?"

He munched another spoonful of Cheerios. "A lot."

"I'll pay you by the job. Now hand over that house key you've been hanging on to."

He was all bravado. "I don't need a key to get in here."

"Right. You used your Spidey powers." She marched over to him and held out her hand.

He scratched a mosquito bite on his arm, and she could see him trying to decide whether to brazen it out, but he finally dug into his shorts' pocket. After he'd given her the key, he poked his spoon around in the cereal. "How come you're not mad about my grandmother?"

"Who says I'm not mad?"

"You don't look mad."

"I'm good at hiding my feelings. Serial killers learn to do that."

"You're a serial killer?"

"Not yet. But I'm thinking about starting. Like maybe today."

The beginnings of a smile tugged at one corner of his mouth. He quickly reined it in. "You think you're funny, but you're not."

"Matter of opinion." She'd told herself she wouldn't get involved, yet here she was. Typical of those who didn't know how to deal with their own problems. They poked around in other people's troubles so they could feel better about themselves. She pocketed the key. "Bree seems nice."

He made a dismissive sound. "She's only staying with me till my dad gets home. He's a tower dog. They're the guys that put up stuff like cell phone towers. It's the most dangerous job in the world."

He was lying—she knew an orphan when she saw one. She poured some water from the tap and drank half of it. As she dumped the rest down the sink, she thought of how much she used to love working with kids like Toby. She'd been good at it, too, and giving up that job had been heart-wrenching. But as a caseworker, she could help only a few kids, and as a lobbyist, she helped thousands, something she always had to keep in mind whenever she was tempted to quit.

"Here's the thing, Toby. I have a brother and three sisters, so I know when a kid isn't telling the truth. If that's the way you want it to be between us, it's your choice. But it means I can't really help you if you ever need help." He opened his mouth to tell her he didn't need help from anybody. She cut him off. "And . . . it means I can never ask you for help if I need it. Because there's no trust. See how that works?"

"Who cares?"

"Apparently not you." There were no dirty dishes in the sink. Either Panda hadn't eaten or he'd washed up after himself. She took a banana from a bowl on the counter.

"My dad really was a tower dog," Toby said in a small voice from behind her. "He died when I was four. He was saving another guy who got stuck, and that's the truth."

She peeled the banana, deliberately keeping her back to him. "I'm sorry about that. I don't even know who my father was."

"What about your mom?"

"She died when I was fourteen. She wasn't a great mom." She concentrated on the banana, still not looking at him. "I got adopted, though, so I was lucky."

"My mom ran away not too long after I was born."

"It doesn't sound like she was a great mom, either."

"My grandma was great."

"And you miss her." She set aside the banana and finally turned to face him, only to watch tears gathering in his big brown eyes. Tears he wouldn't appreciate her witnessing. "We have a lot of work to do." She moved briskly toward the sunroom. "Let's get to it."

For the next several hours, Toby helped her carry broken furniture, moth-eaten cushions, and desiccated draperies to a spot at the end of the drive where she'd get someone to haul it away. Panda might not have any respect for this house, but she did, and if he didn't like it, he could sue her.

Toby tried to make up for his lack of muscle with a seriousness of purpose that touched her to the core. She never got to work one on one with kids anymore, not unless they were related to her.

Together she and Toby struggled to carry out an ancient television that no longer worked. He filled trash bags with the decades-old magazines and tattered paperbacks she handed him from the sunroom bookcases, then wiped the shelves as she rearranged what was left. Although they tried, the awful green kitchen table proved too heavy for them to move, and they both ended up with nasty splinters for their efforts.

When she'd had enough for the day, she carried some money out to the screen porch Toby had just finished helping her scrub down. His eyes widened when he saw what she was paying him. He quickly shoved the bills in his pocket. "I can come back anytime," he said eagerly. "And I'll clean the house, too. I know it didn't look too good before, but I'm a lot better now."

She regarded him sympathetically. "Panda's going to need a caretaker who's a grown-up." As his face fell, she went on, "But I have some other jobs in mind for you."

"I'm just as good as a grown-up."

"He won't see it that way."

He stomped across the porch and banged the screen door behind him, but she knew he'd be back, and he was.

Over the next few days, they swept up cobwebs and scrubbed floors. She covered the worst of the outdoor cushions with more beach towels and discovered the metal baker's rack that looked clunky in the front hallway fit perfectly on the porch. Gradually the ceramic pig, chipped canisters, and other detritus that had cluttered up the counters disappeared. She filled a blue pottery bowl with ripe strawberries and a jelly jar with roses she found growing on an old rambler behind the garage. The arrangement was a far cry from the incredible creations that came out of the White House flower shop, but she liked it just as much.

By the fourth day after Panda had left, they were ripping up the ugly carpet in the gloomy den. "You got any more bread?" Toby asked as they finished the job.

"You polished off the last slice."

"Are you gonna make more?"

"Not today."

"You should make more." He studied her newest accessory, a gorgeous dragon tattoo that curled from her collarbone around her neck with its fiery mouth pointing toward her earlobe. "How old are you anyway?"

She started to tell him she was eighteen, then stopped herself. If she wanted him to be truthful, she had to be straightforward. "Thirty-one."

"That's old."

They moved outside, and Toby held the stepladder while she pulled away the vines that had grown over the den's only window. Once this room wasn't so gloomy, it would be a good place for her to start writing.

Through the window, she could see the warm, honeyed tones of the hardwood floor. From the moment she'd stepped through the doorway, the house had called out to her. Panda didn't deserve this place.

BREE UNDRESSED IN THE TINY laundry room at the back of the cottage and dropped her dirty clothes directly into the washing machine, right down to bra and underpants. The smoker she used to calm the bees had left her smelling like she'd spent the day around a campfire. She wrapped a towel around herself and made her way to the bathroom shower. She'd never worked so hard in her life, and every muscle in her body ached.

For the last few days, she'd been outside from dawn until nightfall getting the hives ready for summer. Following the directions in the manuals she'd read, she moved frames, checked for queens, replaced the old brood comb with fresh comb, and added more brood boxes. She'd also cleaned the honey house from top to bottom, wiping the dust from hundreds of jars filled with last summer's harvest. When that was done, she'd attached Myra's labels.

Carousel Honey
Charity Island, Michigan

Bree had once dreamed of being an artist, and the illustration of the gaily beribboned carousel on the labels came from a watercolor she'd painted when she was sixteen as a birthday gift to Myra. Myra had liked the watercolor so much she'd asked to use it for her labels.

Bree dried herself off, working gently around the numerous bee stings she'd accumulated, the oldest of which were itching like crazy. But she hadn't gotten stung once today. It was nice to feel proud of something.

She found Toby sprawled on the living room couch playing with the Nintendo portable game player she'd brought as a gift when she'd arrived. The room had changed little over the years. Peach walls, a blue and navy floral carpet, overstuffed furniture, and a pair of ceramic Siamese cats on each side of the fireplace mantel. She and Star had named them Beavis and Butt-Head.

It was almost eleven. Toby should be in bed, but if she mentioned it, he'd pretend not to hear. She picked up a dirty cereal bowl. "I'm going to open the farm stand tomorrow." It sounded more like a question than a statement.

"Nobody'll stop," he said, without looking up from his game.

"It's on the main road to the south beach, so there's plenty of traffic. If we fix it up a little, I think people will notice." She had no idea whether they would or not. "I'll need some help, so you'd better get to bed."

He didn't move.

She had to be firmer, but she didn't know how, so she escaped to the kitchen. She hadn't eaten since breakfast, but even though she wasn't hungry, she made herself open the refrigerator. The shelves held only milk and lunch meat. She shut the door, glanced toward the pantry with its supply of canned goods, cereal, pasta, and beans. Nothing tempted her. Nothing except . . .

The single jar of honey she'd brought inside sat on the counter. Golden amber in the sunlight, it looked dark as maple syrup in the kitchen's artificial light. She picked up the bottle and studied the fanciful carousel label. Finally she twisted the lid. It opened with the lightest pop.

She touched the honey with the tip of her index finger. Shut her eyes. Brought her finger to her lips.

All the summers of her childhood came flooding back. She tasted the faintest hint of cherry blossom; a dash of dandelion, clover, and strawberry; a whisper of honeysuckle and touch of sourwood, all the flavors clean and fresh as a June morning. She dipped her finger again and tasted the days of summer growing longer as the bees gravitated toward lavender patches and blackberry brambles, bringing a complexity to the flavor notes. Then August arrived with summer nearing its end. The honey became rich and buttery from thistle, sage, and alfalfa.

Her weariness faded, and for a moment she felt as if all life's secrets clung to the tip of her finger.

THE NEXT MORNING, SHE COULDN'T get Toby out of bed, so she set to work alone. Her arms ached as she piled the old wheelbarrow with the brushes, rollers, rags, and paint cans she'd found in the storage shed. She maneuvered it awkwardly down the drive. The farm stand sat gray and weathered in the shade of a hundred-year-old oak. A sloping roof and rudimentary floor supported its three walls, and a pair of splintered shelves ran beneath a long wooden counter. With the exception of a small storage shed attached to the back, the whole thing could have fit inside her old kitchen pantry.

A blue Honda minivan whizzed by, followed by another just like it, both bearing families heading for the still-chilly waters of the south beach, the island's best swimming locale. She made two more trips back to the house for tools, the temporary poster-board sign she'd painted, and a dozen jars of last summer's honey. This year's crop wouldn't be ready for harvest until August. She hoped she'd be long gone by then, although she couldn't imagine where. She stomped to wake Toby up and discovered a deserted bedroom.

Her spirits lifted when the first car stopped just as she was sticking her poster board sign in the ground. "It's about time you opened up," the woman said. "We finished our last jar of Myra's honey a couple of weeks ago, and my arthritis is starting to flare up again."

They bought two jars. Bree was giddy from her success, but her euphoria gradually faded when no one else stopped.

She filled the time sweeping away cobwebs and old bird nests and nailing loose boards back into place. Finally she was ready to open the first of two cans of exterior paint she'd found in the shed, a buttery yellow shade she suspected Myra had chosen for just this purpose. She'd never actually painted anything herself, but she'd watched painters work, and how hard could it be?

Harder than it looked, she discovered after several hours. She had a crick in her neck, a splinter in her hand, and a nasty gash in her leg. As she swiped her forehead with her arm, smearing herself with even more paint, she heard a car slow. She turned to see a late-model red Cadillac come to a stop. Her excitement at finally having a customer faded when she saw who it was.

"You putting any paint on the wood or is it all ending up on you?"

Mike's obnoxious hardy-har-har laugh felt like fingernails on a chalkboard, and she snapped at him as he came toward her. "I'm doing fine."

Instead of leaving, he inspected what she'd done. "Looks like you're going to need more paint. The wood's really soaking it up."

Something she'd already noticed, but she didn't have money to waste on more paint, and she hadn't figured out what to do about it. He nudged one of the almost empty paint cans with the toe of an expensive cordovan loafer, then stepped away to examine the sagging shelf. "Why isn't Toby helping you?"

"You'd have to ask him." She dropped the paint roller into the tray, splattering even more yellow paint on her only decent pair of sandals.

"I just might. Where is he?"

If her resentment hadn't gotten the best of her, she wouldn't have answered. "Next door with his new best friend."

"He should be helping you." He chose a bottle of honey from the carton on the ground, tossed in a bill, and returned to his car with it.

As he drove off, she realized she was shaking. Just the sight of him flooded her with painful memories. Nothing in her life had ever really gone completely right since the night he'd spied on her with David.

Even though she left the rear of the farm stand untouched, she still ran out of paint. As she worked her brush around the bottom of the can, the Cadillac reappeared with a sullen Toby sitting next to Mike in the front seat. Mike rolled down the car's window as Toby got out. "He forgot he was supposed to help you today."

Toby's angry door slam indicated he hadn't forgotten anything.

Mike got out and walked around to the trunk. "Come on, boy. Grab these for me."

Even though Toby was only twelve, she didn't like hearing him addressed that way. David had gotten fired from one of the charter boats when he'd confronted a customer who'd called him "boy." But Toby obeyed Mike without protest. Was Toby afraid of him? She eyed the two cans of fresh paint Toby pulled from the car trunk. "What's this?"

"You were running out." Mike pulled a paint bucket, some brushes, and another paint roller from the trunk. "I got you some more. No big deal."

Her muscles clenched. "I don't want you buying me paint. I don't want you buying me anything."

He shrugged and turned to Toby. "Let's get that opened up."

"No," she said. "The paint's going back, along with everything else."

Toby shot her a disgusted glare, grabbed the screwdriver she'd left in the dirt, and shoved it under the lip of the can.

"Toby, I mean it. Don't open that—"

The lid popped.

She'd never been able to make anybody do what she wanted. She couldn't make Toby obey her or force Mike to leave her alone, and she hadn't been able to turn Scott into a faithful husband.

Mike poured some paint into the roller pan. "Toby, grab that brush and start putting a second coat on the trim."

Toby didn't offer a single protest. He wouldn't do the simplest thing for her, but when it came to taking orders from a racist ass, he turned into a model of cooperation.

"I'd help you myself," Mike said, "but . . ." He made an expansive gesture toward his immaculate gray summer slacks. "Oh, heck." He grabbed the roller, loaded it up with the buttery paint, and started to work.

She hated what was happening, but she didn't know how to stop it. Mike Moody, nosing in where he wasn't wanted, just like always.

"It's a nice color," he said.

She liked it, too, but she wasn't exchanging polite chitchat with him. "Don't work next to me," she said. "Your cologne reeks."

She'd finally managed to ruffle his phony geniality. "What are you talking about? Do you know how much this stuff costs?"

"You can't buy good taste, Mike. Just like you can't buy manners."

Toby threw down his paintbrush, his face contorting with anger. "Why can't you be nice to him?"

Mike didn't miss a beat. "I sure would like something to drink. How about it, Bree? You got some lemonade or something in the house? A cool drink would simmer everybody down."

Only Toby and Bree were simmering. Mike's phony affability remained unruffled. And then he stopped painting. Not because she wanted him to stop but because he'd spotted an approaching pickup truck. A truck he apparently recognized, since he hurried to the road to flag it down.

A big salesman's grin stretched his face as the truck stopped. "Jason, my man," he said to the long-haired kid behind the wheel. "Have you met Bree Remington?"

She was Bree West. She hadn't been Bree Remington in ten years.

The kid gave her a nod. Mike rested his hand on the roof of the truck. "Bree's selling Myra's honey now. I bet your mom would appreciate it if you brought her a couple of jars. Everybody knows Myra's honey's good for migraines."

"Sure thing, Mike."

And that was the way the rest of her afternoon went, with Mike alternating between rolling paint and flagging down customers. She stayed as far away from him as she could. Experience had taught her that whatever good deeds Mike Moody performed came with all kinds of strings attached.

By the time the day was over, the farm stand glowed under two coats of buttery yellow paint, and she'd sold eighteen jars of honey, but as Mike headed back to his car, she couldn't find a "thank you" anywhere inside her.

LUCY FOUND HERSELF WATCHING FOR Toby as she pulled up some weeds along the porch. She hadn't seen him in three days, not since Big Mike had taken him away. She decided to drop in at the cottage and check on him. Although she'd been out on her bike every day, she hadn't ridden into town in nearly a week, and she needed some groceries. When she returned, she'd get to work. Really, this time. Instead of just thinking about writing, she'd sit down and actually do it.

Instead of following the back road, she took the highway, and as she rounded the bend, she saw the farm stand, no longer a dingy gray but a soft yellow. Jars of golden honey sat on the counter, and Bree was painting a fanciful carousel horse on one side of a teepee-shaped wooden sign hinged at the top. As Lucy got closer, she read the royal blue script:

Carousel Honey
Best on the island
Our honey makes your world go round

Toby sat on the counter, watching Bree, his legs dangling, a sour expression on his face. As Lucy got off her bike, Bree put down her brush. She had a splash of bright pink paint on one cheek, a dab of lime green on the other. Her sleeveless top revealed an angry red bump on her pale, freckled arm.

Toby hopped off the counter and raced over to her. "Hey, Viper. You got work for me to do?"

"Not today." She studied the sign. "You're a real artist, Bree. It looks great."

"Thanks, but I'm just a dabbler." She began maneuvering the heavy sign toward the road, being careful not to smudge the fresh paint.

Lucy hurried to help her. "You must have been working hard. Everything looks great."

"I can be there early tomorrow," Toby said.

Bree adjusted the sign. "You have to watch the stand in the morning while I check the hives."

"I don't want to watch the stand!" Toby cried.

Lucy took the pressure off Bree. "I have some other things to do tomorrow anyway."

Bree stepped back from the sign. It was painted the same on the other side but had a slightly different message:

Carousel Honey
Memories of summer all year long

"We've only had ten customers all day," Toby protested.

"It's not even noon." Bree gazed down the highway. "Ten customers is more than we had this time yesterday. The sign is going to help."

She didn't sound convinced, and Toby wasn't buying it. "You need to get a real job," he said.

Lucy waited for Bree to tell Toby to knock it off, but Bree acted as if she hadn't heard, and Lucy had to bite her tongue to keep from telling him herself. Instead, she said, "I'm definitely buying some on my way back from town."

That embarrassed Bree. "You don't have to."

"Are you kidding? I love honey."

"It'd be really good on your bread," Toby said. And then, accusingly to Bree, "Viper makes bread all by herself. It's really good, too. The best you ever tasted."

"You bake your own bread?" Bree said.

"Sometimes. I'll bring you a loaf."

"That'd be— Thanks." She reached in her pocket, pulled out a pack of cigarettes, and lit up. Toby regarded her with disgust. She gave Lucy an apologetic grimace. "I didn't mean to start again. It just happened."

Lucy wasn't entitled to pass judgment on what people did when they were stressed. A dark green sedan whizzed by. "See," Toby said. "Your sign is stupid. Nobody's going to buy anything."

Lucy couldn't stand it. "Stop giving Bree such a hard time."

Lucy had sided with the enemy. With a scowl, Toby stalked up the drive toward the house.

Bree took a deep drag on her cigarette. It looked odd seeing someone who resembled a Victorian painting puffing away. Bree gazed at Toby's retreating figure. "I don't know anything about kids. As I'm sure you can see, we're sort of a mess right now."

"He's scared," Lucy said.

"I can't imagine what was in Myra's head making me his guardian."

"I'm sure she thought a lot of you."

"We were close when I was a kid, but after Star ran off—she was Toby's mother—we only talked on the phone every few months. Star and I . . . We were best friends." She flushed, as if she were embarrassed to have revealed this small bit about herself.

An ancient Crown Victoria slowed and pulled over next to Bree's new sign. Lucy left her to tend to her customer and biked on into town.

By the time she'd bought her groceries and two small pots of herbs for the baker's rack on the porch, her pack was too heavy to add more, so she stopped on her way back and told Bree she'd come over the next day to pick up her honey.

"Really. You don't have to." Bree smiled, the first Lucy had seen. "The sign's working. Three more cars have stopped. I've sold six jars. And your honey is on the house."

Lucy wanted to argue, but she understood this was Bree's way of thanking her for helping with Toby. Another customer slowed. Lucy waved at Bree and took off.

By the time she'd reached Goose Cove Lane, she'd made a mental note to bake bread first thing tomorrow so she could take some with her. She turned into the drive and laid on the brakes. A car was parked by the house.

A dark gray SUV with Illinois plates.

Chapter Eleven

Lucy was furious. She slammed the door behind her, dropped her backpack, and stomped down the front hallway, passing the empty wall space where the baker's rack should never have been in the first place.

Panda was in the sunroom, his back to the windows, his eyes on her. She hardly recognized him. His wild mane had been cut and tamed into something respectable, although she suspected that wouldn't last for long. He was clean-shaven, or as clean-shaven as he'd ever get, and he wore a neatly pressed gray dress shirt with equally neat dark gray pants, both a far cry from the cheap suit he'd worn to her wedding. It was disconcerting seeing him dressed like a reputable businessman, but she wasn't fooled. Beneath all that good grooming was a renegade biker who'd taken advantage of her, then called her a bad lover.

His gaze went to the fire-breathing dragon crawling up her neck, then to her fake pierced eyebrow, and two things were immediately clear. He was no happier to see her than she was to see him. And he wasn't alone.

A woman stood next to him, her back to Lucy, her attention fixed on the view of the cove through the sparkling windows. Lucy gave Panda her iciest glare. "Patrick."

He knew exactly how much she loathed seeing him, and his aloofness equaled her own, which made her even angrier. He had no right to act as though he'd been the injured party.

You weren't that good anyway.

"I told you not to make any changes." His displeasure couldn't have been more obvious, but she didn't care.

"Sorry, but I had orders from the health department." She pulled off her ball cap, revealing her freshly colored purple dreads. The clutter in the bookcases was gone, the shelves neatly arranged, and the grimy sisal rug that should have been thrown out years ago was nowhere to be seen. She'd edited the mishmash of shabby furniture down to a chest, a few tables, and the sofa and chairs she and Toby had dragged in from the living room. Even without new paint, the space was homey and inviting.

The woman, her spine ramrod stiff, still hadn't turned from the window. She wore an oversize black tunic top, black slacks, and stilettos. Her straight dark hair hung to her shoulders, and her ring-less hands looked too large for her wrists.

"Panda has assured me that I can count on you for discretion." She spoke in a low-pitched, slightly husky voice, but something about her authoritarian tone suggested she preferred full volume.

"No problem," Lucy said. "I'm leaving."

"You can't leave." The woman's large hands fisted at her sides, but she still didn't turn.

Lucy gave Panda a poisonous look. "If Panda tries something, you can always call the police."

"There has to be another female here," the woman said in her eerily quiet drill sergeant's voice. "I understand you've been through a lot lately, but I promise I'll make it worth your while."

So Panda had told her who Lucy was. Another indication that he had no moral compass.

"Normally, I'd offer to pay you," she said, "but . . . that seems a little insulting."

A little? The woman didn't appear overawed at being with a member of the former first family, which suggested she was accustomed to celebrities. Lucy's curiosity got the best of her. "Why is it so important?"

The woman's head came up another inch. "Before I explain, I don't suppose you'd consider signing a confidentiality agreement?"

She had to be kidding.

"Lucy has a lot of *faults*"—Panda leaned on that last word—"but she has too much at stake herself to go around blowing anyone else's cover."

"So you said." The woman straightened her shoulders. "I suppose I'll have to trust you, not something I'm good at." A gull swooped by the window. And then she turned. Slowly . . . Dramatically . . . A tragic queen facing the guillotine.

Enormous black sunglasses concealed much of her face. She was tall and statuesque, a little overweight underneath that voluminous tunic top. She wore no jewelry, nothing to call attention to herself except the inappropriateness of all that black on a warm June day. Her hand shook ever so slightly as she took off her sunglasses. She folded in the stems, then raised her chin and gazed at Lucy.

She was attractive—dark, almond-shaped eyes; good cheekbones; a strong nose—but her full mouth could have used a slick of lip gloss, and a little makeup would have done wonders for her sallow complexion. Not that Lucy was one to criticize anyone else's makeup application, since she was wearing brown lipstick and had thick kohl smudges both above and below her lashes.

The dramatic way the woman stood before her indicated she expected Lucy to say something, but since Lucy had no idea—

And then she understood. *Whoa.*

"Lucy, I'm sure you've heard of Temple Renshaw," Panda said, all business.

Temple Renshaw, the Evil Queen of the celebrity fitness gurus and star of *Fat Island,* a horrible reality show that shamed its participants by exiling them to a place "where no one has to look at you." She'd built her career on humiliation and degradation, and photographs of her panther-sleek body were everywhere—on the labels of her fitness drinks, her power bars, her extensive line of exercise wear. But those photographs only remotely resembled this woman draped in black—a woman with full cheeks and a plump little cushion of fat under her chin.

"As you can see," Temple said, "I'm obese."

Lucy swallowed. "I'd hardly say you were obese." Temple still looked better than most of the tourists who got off the ferry. But that didn't mean she was the lithe willow the public knew so well.

"No need to be polite," Temple said.

Panda spoke up. "Temple had some personal difficulties over the spring that caused her to gain a little—"

"Don't make excuses." Her drill sergeant's voice became a full-volume snarl. "I'm a fat slob."

Lucy looked at him. "Where do you fit into this?" She paused. "And are you armed?"

"Temple hired me to help her get back in shape," he said. "And none of your business."

"You're her trainer?"

"Not exactly."

"I don't need a trainer," Temple snapped. "I need a disciplinarian."

"Disciplinarian?" A series of images involving whips and paddles flashed through her head. Panda's lip curled in an unpleasant smile, as if he were reading her mind. Lucy gave him her back. "Exactly what does this . . . discipline involve?"

"Panda and I have that worked out," Temple said. "*Fat Island* starts taping in September, exactly three months from now. Since I'm clearly out of control, I've hired Panda to give me the structure I need to get back in shape."

Out of the corner of her eye, Lucy saw Temple's "disciplinarian" inspecting the neatly organized bookshelves. With his index finger, he flipped a copy of *Lighthouses of Lake Michigan* onto its side, disturbing the arrangement.

"And you're doing it here?" Lucy said.

"I can hardly check into a spa looking like this. I need complete privacy." And then, bitterly, "My own *Fat Island,* if you will."

With a flick of his thumb and a flash of an expensive stainless steel watch, Panda knocked over *Field Guide to North American Birds.* Lucy still couldn't get used to his *GQ* appearance. It felt so wrong.

"Panda has worked security for me in the past," Temple said. "When I remembered he had this house, I insisted we come here. It was all very *Mission: Impossible.* I flew in on a private plane. He met me at the airfield and smuggled me here in the back of his car."

"I understand why the two of you are here," Lucy said, although she didn't entirely, "but what makes you think I'd stay?"

"Because I need you for cover."

"Cover?"

"I'll require special food," she said. "Panda doesn't exactly look like a man who'd go into town to buy digestive teas and wheatgrass."

Lucy didn't see herself as a woman who'd buy those things either, but she was beginning to get the point, however ludicrous it might be.

Panda nudged a floor lamp out of place with his shoe, a stylish pair of immaculately polished tasseled loafers she'd like to stomp on with her boots.

"I'm going to be here for weeks," Temple said. "What if I want a copy of *Women's Health* or *Vogue*? How about moisturizer or hair products? Tampax, for god's sake."

Panda's foot stalled on the ladder-back chair he'd been about to push away from the corner.

"You can order those things online," Lucy pointed out.

"And I will, but some things I'll need immediately. And how do we account for the difference between the amount of garbage one person generates and two people? I like to air dry my workout clothes. Women's clothes. I want to be able to swim. If someone brings their boat into the cove and sees a woman in the water, I can't let them suspect it's anyone other than you. There are a hundred ways I can be exposed if there isn't another female in the house, and if that happens, my career is over forever. Now do you understand?"

Lucy wondered why Temple hadn't enlisted one of her friends. Then again, Temple didn't exactly look like the kind of woman who'd have a bevy of BFFs.

She tucked the stem of her sunglasses into the neck of her tunic. "Lucy, I realize you're an important person in your own right, and I understand this is a hard time for you. I also know you expected to stay here alone. My showing up is an intrusion, and I want to make that right, so. . . ." Her critical gaze swept from Lucy's dreads to her combat boots. "I'm going to train you for free."

Lucy was too appalled to respond.

"I charge my private clients six hundred dollars an hour. I know that's outrageous, but it does make people take their training seriously."

Temple's brows came together as she gazed at Lucy's upper arms—and not, Lucy suspected, to study her bloody thorn tattoo. From there, she assessed Lucy's thighs as they emerged from her shorts—thighs that were only beginning to return to their normal size, thanks to the bread she'd been baking. "We'll find another motivation for you."

"Unfortunately, Lucy takes her sloth seriously," Panda said, his lips thinning. "I doubt she'd be willing to work that hard."

"I really wouldn't," Lucy said hastily. "And I'm sorry, but I can't possibly help you." Not with Panda here, she couldn't.

"I see." Temple fixed her confident public smile firmly in place, a smile Lucy recognized from having employed it so frequently herself. "I suppose I'd hoped . . ." She licked her lips. "If anybody sees me . . . Finds out why I'm here. . . ." Her chin came up another inch. "Panda said you wouldn't stay."

Lucy didn't like Panda predicting her behavior.

Temple's chin came up another inch. "I really . . . shouldn't have counted on it. I . . ."

And right then it all fell apart. The Evil Queen lost her public smile. Her head dropped, her shoulders sagged, her ramrod spine lost its steel, and tears glimmered in her eyes.

Witnessing an imperious woman's pain over having her plans thwarted should have been somewhat satisfying. Instead, it was heartbreaking. Temple clearly wasn't used to falling apart, and she had no practice asking for help. Whatever had caused her to lose control of her weight in the first place was still beating her down.

Lucy didn't want to leave the island. It would mean leaving Viper behind, something she couldn't bear thinking about yet. It also meant that this time next week, she'd be wearing pumps and knocking on Fortune 500 doors, her hand outstretched. Instead she wanted to kayak whenever she felt like it, and sit down to write in the office she'd cleaned, and spread fresh honey on her bread. She wanted to carry her morning coffee down to the dock and see how Bree was faring at the farm stand. And she'd miss that little rat Toby.

Unlike Temple, Panda was more than happy with Lucy's decision. "Lucy tends to be a distraction," he said to his employer. "It'll be better this way."

Better for him.

Lucy didn't want to share her house with the Evil Queen of *Fat Island.* But more important, she didn't want to share it with the Evil Bodyguard. Still, it was a big house, and Temple looked so defeated, an emotion Lucy understood better than she wanted to. "I'll try it for a day or so," she finally said. "But I won't promise more than that."

Panda had counted on her leaving, and he wasn't pleased. "Obviously, you haven't thought this through."

"You'll stay?" Temple was transformed. Her posture straightened. Her eyes shone. "I can't thank you enough. And truly . . . Your body will thank me, too."

Lucy sincerely doubted that, but she had a more important battle to wage. Staking out her turf. "The big dormitory upstairs will be perfect for your workouts once it's cleaned up. I know you'll want Panda nearby. The second floor has four bedrooms and two big bathrooms, so there's plenty of room for both of you." Lucy wasn't giving up the downstairs bedroom, with its sliding doors that led directly outside so she could come and go without seeing either of them. If all went well, she'd only have to meet up with them in the kitchen, and she suspected Temple wouldn't be spending a lot of time there.

She ignored Panda's scowl as she offered to show Temple around. "The upstairs is bad, but nothing a couple of dump trucks and a fumigator can't take care of."

PANDA INSISTED ON ACCOMPANYING THEM, and as he spotted each change Lucy had made, his scowl grew darker. "Where's the mirror that used to hang over there?"

"Mirror?"

"And the coatrack?"

"What coatrack?" She'd tossed them both in the garage with all the other junk that had accumulated here.

When they reached the upstairs, she found an ally in Temple. "Didn't you say you've had this place for two years?" she asked as they inspected the dormitory. "Why haven't you cleaned it up?"

"I like it the way it is," he said tightly.

Temple gazed with distaste at the rows of mismatched bunk beds. Each had a bare mattress rolled up at the end. She wandered over to the longest wall, which held three large windows, all of them masked with discolored, vinyl-lined curtains. Temple pushed aside one dusty panel. "The view is incredible. You're right, Lucy. This will be a great workout room."

Lucy stated the obvious. "The caretaker passed away, so it's been a while since anyone's cleaned, but I'm sure Panda can find someone."

"I can't have anyone here," Temple said firmly. She let the curtain fall back and rubbed her dusty fingers together. "Panda and I will do it. Taking care of myself will be a new experience." And then, with a bitter edge, "I wonder if I still remember how."

The old Lucy would have volunteered to help, but Viper had no intention of being Temple Renshaw's personal assistant. She pointed out the linen closet with its piles of mismatched sheets and left them to fend for themselves.

Once she got downstairs, she put away the groceries from her backpack and told herself this just might work. As she cleaned up some dirty dishes, she heard Temple's voice coming from the hallway. "Really,

Panda, you don't have to do that." The entreaty in her voice aroused Lucy's curiosity. She peeked out.

They stood by the front door, where Panda was riffling through Temple's purse, a luxurious black satchel with heavy silver hardware. Temple fingered the neck of her tunic. "Honestly, Panda, there's no need. I'm clear about what I came here to do."

"Then you must have overlooked this." He pulled out a bar of Toblerone chocolate.

Temple tilted her head and gave him a wide smile. "Congratulations. You passed your first test. This is exactly why I'm paying you a ridiculous amount of money to work for me this summer."

He tore off the wrapper and bit a big chunk from the end. "Don't bullshit me, Temple."

Temple glued her eyes to the candy bar, her smile disappearing. Even from a distance, Lucy could feel her craving. He took another bite and slowly chewed, savoring every morsel, an act of such monumental cruelty he'd surely be damned forever. "Anything I find," he said, "you're going to watch me eat."

Temple was furious. "I don't have to put up with this!"

"Save your breath." The last of the chocolate disappeared into his mouth. He wadded up the wrapper and shoved it in his pocket. "Open your suitcases."

"There's nothing inside that shouldn't be there," she declared.

"Let's hope that's true."

It wasn't. Panda found another large chocolate bar. Even for a big man, it was a lot of chocolate, but he consumed every bite. Temple was furious. "You don't have to be such a prick."

"You didn't hire me for my warm personality. You knew this wasn't going to be a picnic."

"Fine."

She started to whip past him, but he caught her arm. "Do I need to search you, too?"

She reached into the pocket of her slacks and sneered, "Tic Tacs. They're perfectly harmless, and I've had enough of this."

"It'll only hurt for a minute."

She gave a hiss of outrage as he began running his hands down her body. "Don't you dare touch me!"

"Give it a rest." He whipped a pack of Skittles from her other pocket, then grabbed the Tic Tacs for good measure. "Compassion's for losers. Isn't that what you always say on TV?"

"I'm not paying you seventy-five thousand dollars to lecture me!"

Seventy-five *thousand* dollars? Lucy couldn't believe it. She wondered what her parents had paid, then thought of her thousand-dollar bribe and what a laugh-fest that must have given him.

"Not a lecture," he said. "An observation." Apparently his stomach had reached its limit because he shoved the Skittles in his own pocket along with the chocolate wrappers, then closed her suitcases. "I'll carry these upstairs for you."

"Don't bother!" She grabbed them away and hauled them up the stairs.

"Seen enough?" Panda said, his back still turned to the door where Lucy lurked.

"Still trying to absorb it all," she replied. "The two of you are a real riot."

He briefly inspected the spot once occupied by the baker's rack. "You can leave anytime you want. As a matter of fact, why haven't you?"

Because this was her house. "Because I'm still punishing myself for my bad judgment in people." She disappeared back into the kitchen.

It was only four o'clock, but she hadn't eaten since breakfast, so she heated up a skillet, added some oil, and tossed in one of the pork chops she'd picked up in town. It would have tasted better on the grill, but she'd thrown that rusty mess out last week.

The pork chop had just begun to sizzle nicely when Panda, still dressed in his businessman's attire, shot into the kitchen. He grabbed a towel, wrapped it around the handle of the skillet, and stalked out the back door.

"Hey!" She raced after him as he strode across the yard. "Bring back my pork chop!"

He flipped open the lid of the garbage can next to the garage, flicked his wrist, and sent her pork chop tumbling to its death. "No cooking unless it's something Temple can eat, too."

"No cooking? What do you mean, *no cooking*!"

"The smell was going through the house. She's supposedly doing a cleanse, and you're not going to torture her."

"Me! You gulped down a thousand calories in front of her!"

"Natural consequences. What you're doing is different."

She threw up her hands. "I don't believe you!"

His mouth twisted. "Maybe you'd better call Mommy and have her send in the SEALs to protect you."

Had she really kissed this man? Let him—let him—do *that?* Viper was beyond pissed, and she pointed a chipped charcoal fingernail right in his face. "You," she said, "are going to pay." And off she went.

HE WAS ALREADY PAYING. JUST being near her again was torture. He still remembered his first sight of her. The night of the rehearsal dinner. She'd been standing at Ted's side in a ladylike blue-green dress, her shiny hair many shades lighter than it was now. All he could think about was how impeccably matched the two of them were, the perfect all-American couple. It wasn't until almost two weeks later, the night at

Caddo Lake when she'd finally called her family, that he'd realized she truly wasn't going back to Ted. Stupid.

You weren't that good anyway.

What a fricking lie. He was the one who'd been inept—rushed, clumsy, out of control. Lucy had been giving and natural, with none of that phony porn star posturing women seemed to believe they needed to bring to the bedroom.

He'd counted on her taking off as soon as she saw that he'd come back, but instead of jumping on the ferry the way she should have, she'd decided to cook pork chops in his kitchen. Now he had two problem women on his hands, both of whom wanted to use his house as their hideaway. One of them was a demanding pain in the ass, but he'd handled Temple before, and he could do it again. The other was a different kind of pain in the ass, and the way he most wanted to handle her was naked.

He pushed images of a naked Lucy from his mind so he could concentrate on the job at hand. This was the last place he wanted to be, but Temple was paying him a lot of money to babysit her, and she had refused to negotiate the location. He wished he hadn't told her about the house, but he'd never imagined she'd insist on coming here, just as he never imagined her thirty pounds overweight and on the verge of ruining her career. He liked jobs that kept him on the move, jobs where there was at least the potential for a little excitement. This was a shit job, but it was also a highly lucrative one. Besides, Temple had been his first big client, and he owed her.

They'd met not long after he'd taken over the agency when her publisher had hired him for a routine security job at a Chicago bookstore where she was doing a signing. A twitchy-looking guy in the crowd had caught his attention. Panda had kept a close eye on him, and before the night was over, had stopped him from leaping over a row of chairs to carve up Temple's face. From then on, whenever Temple needed security, she insisted he provide it. Thanks to her, he'd attracted other well-heeled clients, and his business had grown to the point where he'd been able to rent the Lake Shore Drive apartment he seldom slept in, buy this house, and put his mother in the best Alzheimer's facility in Illinois.

His stomach rumbled, not from hunger but from trying to digest all that chocolate. He didn't have much of a sweet tooth. Too bad Temple hadn't been smuggling potato chips.

His thoughts drifted back to Lucy. He'd expressly told her not to change anything in the house, but she'd done what she'd wanted, and the changes unsettled him. Why had Lucy given in to Temple's request? He couldn't figure it out, but he did know that the sooner he could make her leave, the better, and the best way for him to accomplish that was to make sure she hadn't forgotten his worst qualities.

If only the prospect of reminding her didn't depress him so much.

THE EVIL QUEEN WASN'T A prima donna; Lucy would give her that. The next morning she worked side by side with Panda breaking down the bunk beds and carrying them outside. "Great cardio," she told Lucy as she hauled a set of bedrails toward the front door.

Temple had pulled her hair into a messy ponytail and traded in yesterday's black outfit for roomy navy workout pants and an oversize V-neck mesh knit top, neither of them stylish enough to have come from her own clothing line. "I'm getting the idea that you and Panda have some history," she said.

Lucy moved ahead of her to hold the front door open. "Wrong idea."

Temple wasn't fazed by Lucy's cool response. "As long as he does the job I hired him for"—she angled her cargo through the doorway—"I don't care what the two of you do the rest of the time."

Lucy wasn't used to being addressed as anyone's underling, but before she could fire back, the Evil Queen and her load of bedrails had disappeared down the front steps.

Lucy had discovered a padlock on the pantry door when she'd gone into the kitchen for breakfast, and since she hadn't been up to doing battle with Panda on an empty stomach, she'd settled for coffee. But now she was hungry. She located a carton of black cherry yogurt and a cold hot dog. Before she could finish either one, she heard a truck pulling into the drive, followed almost immediately by the sound of a door slamming upstairs, presumably Temple hiding from sight. Soon Panda and the driver were unloading what proved to be gym equipment.

Lucy had planned to bake bread for Bree and Toby, but after last night's pork chop incident, she couldn't see that happening, and she rode to the farm stand empty-handed.

Bree stood on a ladder, painting a colorful ribbon garland across the top of the farm stand's pale yellow frame, the kind of whimsical decoration that might be seen on a carousel. The colors coordinated with the old-fashioned moss-green quilt she'd tossed over the counter to showcase a row of three-bottle honey pyramids.

Toby popped out from behind the stand as Lucy got off her bike. "I saw Panda's car go by yesterday. You got a job for me?"

Toby was a complication she hadn't thought through. "Not for a while. One of my . . . girlfriends is visiting. We're going to be hanging out, so it'll be boring." The idea of the Evil Queen as a girlfriend made her shudder, but she needed to lay some groundwork in case Toby showed up unexpectedly at the house, which he would almost certainly do.

"But I can still come over and do stuff, right?"

"Toby, please stop harassing her." Bree gave Lucy a tired smile as she got down off the ladder, leaving her tray of paint pots balanced on top. Although the morning was warming up, Bree didn't have any body fat, and she wore a lightweight gray sweater over her T-shirt. Neither the tan she was acquiring nor the fresh sprinkle of freckles across her cheekbones concealed her exhaustion. "I'll do my best to keep him from bothering you."

Considering Bree's general ineffectiveness with Toby, Lucy wasn't counting on it, and she slipped an arm around his shoulder. "The thing is, Toby, my friend isn't exactly a kid person, so instead of coming over, maybe you could start showing me around the island. I know there are a lot of places I haven't seen yet."

"I guess."

Lucy took in the Carousel Honey sign and freshly painted border. "I love what you're doing. Is the sign working?"

"I've sold seven jars this morning." She scratched a bee sting on her wrist, leaving a spot of raspberry paint behind. "I'm thinking about adding more products, maybe soap or beeswax candles. Whatever I can figure out how to make."

"It's still not enough money," Toby said, with his customary belligerence. "You should leave."

Lucy quickly intervened. "The two of you have brought the farm stand back to life in just a couple of days. You should be proud of yourselves."

"It's Gram who should be proud," Toby said. "It's her honey." He stomped off toward the house. "I'm calling Big Mike!" he shouted. "He said he'd take me out on his boat."

"No!" Bree dashed to the driveway. "Toby, do not call Mike! Do you understand me? *Toby!*"

Toby had already disappeared.

With an air of weary resignation, Bree tucked away a lock of hair that had escaped her ponytail. She pulled a cigarette pack from a shelf behind the counter. "I'm no good at this."

"He's hurting," Lucy said. "That makes him a tough challenge."

"We're both hurting." She waved away the smoke, as if what hung in the air posed a bigger danger than what she was sucking into her lungs. "Sorry. Having a little pity party here." She studied Lucy more closely. "You look so familiar. I feel like I know you from somewhere, but I'm sure we've never met. When I first saw you, I thought you were a kid."

"I'm thirty-one."

Her gaze drifted to Lucy's hair, the new eyebrow ring, and the dragon tattoo on her neck.

"A case of arrested development," Lucy said by way of explanation.

"I see."

But Bree clearly didn't see, and Lucy no longer felt right about keeping her identity hidden. She decided to take a risk. "I'm . . . sort of in disguise." She hesitated. "I'm . . . Lucy Jorik."

Bree's eyes widened, her posture straightened, and she dropped her cigarette. She might be able to smoke in front of that odd girl who lived on the other side of the woods, but she couldn't do it in front of the president's daughter. "Oh . . . I . . ."

"I needed to hide out for a while," Lucy said with a shrug. "This seemed like a good place."

Bree realized she was staring. "Sorry. It's just . . . a little unexpected." She pushed at her hair again, trying to straighten it. "Why did you tell me? I'd never have guessed."

"It doesn't seem right to keep coming over here and not say anything. Hard to believe, but I have this thing about honesty."

"But . . . You barely know me. I could tell everybody."

"I'm hoping you won't." She wanted to change the subject. "That pity party you mentioned. Would you like to fill me in?"

A car slowed but didn't stop. Bree gazed after it. "It's a boring story."

"I hate to admit this, but some days hearing about other people's problems actually cheers me up."

Bree laughed, the tension broken. "I know the feeling." She wiped her hands on her shorts. "You really want to hear this?"

"Does that make me a bad person?"

"Don't say you weren't warned." She rubbed absentmindedly at a paint flake on her arm. "Last November I came home from a luncheon at our country club and found my husband packing up his car. He said he was tired of our *privileged* life, he wanted a divorce, and oh, by the way, he was going to start over with his soul mate, a nineteen-year-old office temp who was twice the woman I was."

"Ouch."

"It gets worse." The speckled sunlight coming through the trees cast her face in light and shadow, making her look both older and younger than she was. "He said he realized he owed me something for ten years of marriage, so I could have whatever was left after the debts I didn't know anything about were paid off."

"Nice guy."

"Not even when I met him. I knew that, but he was gorgeous and smart, and all my sorority sisters were crazy about him. Our families had been friends for years. He was one of GM's wonder boys before Detroit imploded." She flicked her ash into the grass. "Scott and his temp headed off to Seattle to find their bliss, and the debts ate up everything we had. I'd only finished a year of college. I had no work experience and no idea how to support myself. For a while, I lived with one of my brothers, but after a few months of barely leaving my room, my sister-in-law let me know I'd worn out my welcome."

She forgot her discomfort about smoking in front of the first daughter and reached for another cigarette. "Around the same time, Myra's lawyer contacted me and told me she'd died and left her cottage to me along with her grandson. I'd only seen Toby a few times years ago when Myra came to visit me. Yet here I am. Mistress of my domain." She looked around at the farm stand and gave a self-deprecating laugh. "Have you ever heard anything more pathetic? I was raised with all the advantages except a backbone." She pushed the cigarette back in its pack without lighting up. "I can imagine what you're thinking after everything you've accomplished in your life."

"Running away on my wedding day?"

"Especially that." She grew almost dreamy-eyed. "How did you have the guts?"

"I wouldn't exactly call it guts."

"I would." Just then a car stopped. Bree tucked the cigarette pack in her pocket. "Thanks for trusting me. I won't sell you out."

Lucy hoped she'd keep her word.

ON THE WAY HOME, LUCY realized she'd forgotten her honey, but without the prospect of warm bread to slather it on, she didn't turn around. A pile of broken-down bunk beds, old mattresses, and the ugly vinyl curtains from the dorm sat at the end of the drive, waiting to be hauled away. The delivery truck was gone, and as she entered the house she heard something heavy being dragged across the floor overhead. Too much to hope it was Panda's dead body.

She cut through the kitchen to go outside and noticed that the old refrigerator was gone. In its place stood a high-tech stainless steel side-by-side. Her unsatisfactory breakfast had left her hungry, so she opened the doors.

And discovered all her stuff was gone. Her peanut butter and jelly, her deli ham and perfectly aged Swiss cheese. No black cherry yogurt, salad dressing, or sweet pickles. None of the leftovers she'd counted on for lunch. Even Panda's marmalade had disappeared.

The freezer section was equally awful. Instead of Hot Pockets and the frozen waffles that were her weekend treat, she saw rows of pre-packaged diet meals. She pulled open the vegetable bins. Where were her carrots? Her blueberries? The fresh bunch of romaine lettuce she'd bought just yesterday? Frozen waffles were one thing, but they'd taken her lettuce?

She stormed upstairs.

Chapter Twelve

⬨

THE RUBBERY SMELL OF A gym hit her even before she paused in the doorway. The dorm had been transformed since last night. Shiny new exercise equipment sat on pristine black rubber mats, the bare floor had been swept clean, and sunlight spilled through the open windows. Panda was wrestling with one of the bent window screens, the twist of his body tugging up his T-shirt and exposing a rock-hard abdomen. What she could see of his shirt was mercifully free of smutty messages, and the fact that she found this vaguely disappointing she blamed on Viper.

Temple grunted away on an elliptical machine, sweat dripping from her temples, wet tendrils of dark hair sticking to her neck. Lucy took in the scene of workout horror. "My food seems to be missing from the refrigerator."

Temple hunched her shoulder and wiped her forehead on her sleeve. "Panda, take care of this."

"Happy to." He secured the screen and followed Lucy out of the room so quickly she knew he'd been looking for an excuse to escape. Before she could open her mouth to launch what she intended to be an un-Lucy-like tirade, he grabbed her elbow and steered her along the hall. "We have to talk downstairs. Loud voices upset Temple. Unless they're coming from her."

"I heard that," Temple shouted from inside.

"I know," Panda shouted in return.

Lucy headed for the stairs.

IT WAS PROBABLY PANDA'S IMAGINATION, but he could swear he saw dust bombs exploding from beneath the soles of Lucy's ridiculous combat boots as she stomped down the worn beige stairway carpet. A carpet he suspected she wanted him to get rid of. Which he damned well wasn't going to do.

She hit the bottom step. A purplish painted chest used to sit there, but it had gone missing, right along with the antler coatrack and that black shelving thing that was now on the porch holding some plants he hadn't bought and didn't want.

Why the hell hadn't she taken off like she was supposed to? Because she'd latched onto this place. That was the thing about people who'd been raised with money. Their sense of entitlement made them believe they could have whatever they wanted, even when it didn't belong to them. Like this house. But as much as he wanted to cast Lucy as spoiled, he knew it wasn't true. She was rock-bottom decent, even if she was screwed up right now.

As she tromped toward the kitchen, her small butt twitched in a pair of weird-looking black shorts that weren't nearly baggy enough. He wanted her in oversize clothes like those Temple was wearing. Clothes that covered up everything he didn't want to think about. Instead she wore those black shorts and an ugly gray top with these black leather ties on her shoulders.

As soon as she reached the kitchen, she whirled on him, making the ties twitch. "You had no right to get rid of my food!"

"You had no right to get rid of my furniture, and you shouldn't be eating that crap." His mood grew darker as he once again noted the clean counters, now missing, among other things, the ceramic pig dressed like a French waiter.

"Blueberries and lettuce aren't crap," she said.

"They weren't organic."

"You threw them out because they weren't organic?"

She was really pissed. Good. As long as he kept her pissed at him, she wouldn't try to suck him into one of those cozy little chats he used to pretend to hate. He splayed his hand on the counter. Her hair was so black it looked dead, the ratty purple dreadlocks were ridiculous, and her heavily mascaraed eyelashes looked like caterpillars had expired on them. A silver ring pierced one eyebrow; another pierced her nostril. He hoped like hell they were both fakes. And smearing that delicate mouth with ugly brown lipstick was a crime against humanity. But the tattoos bothered him most. That long, slender neck had no business being strangled by a fire-breathing dragon, and the thorns on her upper arm were an abomination, although a few of the blood drops had mercifully flaked off.

"Do you really want to pollute your body with pesticides and chemical fertilizers?" he said.

"Yes!" She jabbed a finger toward the pantry door. "And hand over that key."

"Not going to happen. She'd bully you into giving it to her."

"I can stand up to Temple Renshaw."

He could be a world-class prick when he wanted to, like right now, with his ceramic pig missing and those leather ties twitching on top of her bare shoulders. "You couldn't even stand up to Ted Beaudine. And he's the nicest guy in the world, right?"

She was a babe in the woods when it came to dealing with pricks. Her chin shot up, her small jaw jutted, but beneath her bluster, he saw the guilt she still couldn't shake off. "What do you mean, I couldn't stand up to him?"

This was exactly the kind of personal conversation he'd told himself he wouldn't have with her, but he didn't feel like backing off. "Your aversion to getting married didn't just hit you on your wedding day. You knew it wasn't right long before that, but you didn't have the guts to tell him."

"I didn't know it wasn't right!" she exclaimed.

"Whatever gets you up in the morning."

"Not eggs and bacon, that's for sure."

He gave her his badass sneer, but it wasn't as effective as usual because he couldn't take his eyes off those little leather ties. Just one tug . . .

"I want my food back," she said.

"It's in the trash." He pretended to inspect a broken drawer handle, then eased away from the counter. "I'll open the pantry whenever you want. Just don't eat any of your crap around Temple."

"My crap? You're the one who thinks Frosted Flakes are antioxidants!"

She had that right. He jerked his head toward the refrigerator. "Help yourself to whatever's there. We'll be getting deliveries twice a week. The fruits and vegetables are coming later today."

"I don't want her lousy organic food. I want my own."

He understood the feeling.

Overhead, the treadmill began to run. He told himself not to ask, but . . . "You don't happen to have any of your bread stashed away some-place, do you?"

"A fresh loaf of cinnamon raisin where you can't find it," she re-torted. "Eat your heart out. Oh, wait. You can't. It's not organic."

She stomped outside and slammed the door behind her.

SHE'D LIED ABOUT THE BREAD. She also hadn't slammed a door since she was fourteen. Both felt really good.

Unfortunately, she hadn't brought her yellow pad with her, and she'd promised herself she'd write for real today. She wasn't going back in through the kitchen, so she cut around behind the house and mounted the three steps that led to the deck outside her bedroom. She'd left the sliding doors open to catch the breeze. The screen caught in the track. She gave it an extra nudge and stepped inside.

Panda was already there.

"I want my bedroom back," he said as he walked out of her closet, carrying a pair of sneakers that she happened to know were a size twelve.

"I rented this house for the summer," she retorted. "That makes you the interloper, and I'm not leaving."

He crossed to the dresser. "This is my room. You can sleep upstairs."

And lose her private exit? No way. "I'm staying right here."

He tugged open the drawer that used to contain his underwear, but now held hers. He reached inside and pulled out a midnight-black thong.

"Your things are in the bottom drawer," she said quickly.

He ran his thumb over the silky crotch. As his eyes caught hers, she was hit with another of those jolts of sexual electricity that proved exactly how disconnected a woman's body could be from her brain.

"Here's the part I don't get." His big fist swallowed the thong. "Knowing the way you feel about me, why are you still here?"

"My attachment to your house overrides my complete indifference to you," she said with remarkable steadiness.

"My house, not yours," he retorted, his eyes on her right shoulder—she had no idea why. "And if you make one more change to it, you're out, regardless of what Temple says."

Letting him have the last word would have been the mature thing to do, but he was still holding her thong, and she didn't feel like being mature. "Are you offering her your *complete* line of services?"

Once again, his eyes drifted to her shoulders. "What do you think?"

She didn't know what she thought, so she shot across the room and snatched back her thong. "I think Temple's the kind of woman who's not easily conned."

"Then you have your answer."

Which told her exactly nothing.

"That's what I thought." She stuffed her thong back in the drawer, retrieved her writing supplies, and left the same way she'd come in.

My mother is a— So many things to choose from.

> *My mother is a notoriously hard worker.*

Or maybe . . .

> *My mother believes in hard work.*

Lucy clicked her pen.

> *The United States was built on hard work.*

She tried to find a more comfortable position.

And so was my mother.

Lucy crumpled the paper. Her attempts at writing were going even worse than her encounter with Panda, but this time she had an empty stomach to blame it on. She abandoned her yellow pad and rode into town, where she gorged on two chili dogs and a large order of fries at Dogs 'N' Malts, the most food she'd eaten in months, but who knew when she'd get a chance to eat again?

When she returned to the house, she found Temple in the almost empty living room watching television, a couple of DVDs of *Fat Island* on the floor by her bare feet. The brown and gold loveseat where she sat was one of the few pieces of furniture left, since Lucy had transferred the better pieces to the sunroom as replacements for what she'd thrown out.

Temple grabbed the remote and paused the television on an image of herself. "I'm just taking a fifteen-minute break." She acted as if Lucy had caught her munching a chocolate bar. "I've been working out for three hours."

The chili dogs rumbled unpleasantly in Lucy's overstuffed stomach. "You don't have to explain to me."

"I'm not explaining. I'm—" Looking exhausted, she slumped back into the loveseat. "I don't know. Maybe I am." She pointed toward the frozen image of herself on screen. "See that body," she said with such self-loathing that Lucy cringed. "I threw it away." She hit the play button and captured her sleek screen image in the middle of a furious diatribe directed at a sweet-faced, sweat-drenched, middle-aged woman who was fighting tears.

"There's the door! You want to leave? Go ahead! If you don't care, nei-

ther do I." The veins on Temple's slim neck popped, and her perfectly glossed mouth formed a snarl. *"Get on the boat and off the island. Let everybody see what a loser you are."*

The woman was openly crying now, but Temple continued to berate her. It was painful to watch. Even more painful to imagine what kind of desperation would drive someone to let herself be subjected to this kind of abuse.

The woman's tears only fueled Temple's scorn. *"Boo hoo. This is what you've done all your life. Cry about your problems instead of fixing them. Go on! Get off the island! There are thousands of people waiting to take your place."*

"No!" the woman cried. *"I can do it. I can do this."*

"Then do it!"

Temple hit the pause button as the woman began frantically pummeling a punching bag. Lucy didn't believe self-loathing was the best form of motivation, but Temple thought differently. "Irene ran her first half marathon four months after we taped that episode," she said proudly. "By the time I was done with her, she'd lost over a hundred pounds."

Lucy wondered how many of those hundred pounds Irene had been able to keep off without Temple around to scream in her face.

"God, she looked amazing." Temple turned off the television and stood, wincing slightly as she straightened. "The critics are always putting me down. They'll compare me to trainers like Jillian Michaels—say she has a heart and I don't. I have a heart. A big one. But you don't help people by coddling them, and I'll match my results against hers any day." She jerked her head toward the stairs. "I'm going to do some upper body work. From the looks of those arms, you should join me."

The face of the sobbing woman flashed through Lucy's mind. "It's not a good time for me."

Temple's lip curled. "There's never a good time for you, is there, Lucy? You can always find a reason not to take care of yourself."

"I take care of myself." Maybe it was Temple's intimidating glare, or it could have been the second chili dog, but she didn't sound convincing. "I exercise," she said in a firmer voice. "I don't love to, but I do it."

Temple crossed her arms over her chest like a prison warden. "What kind of exercise?"

"Push-ups. Some crunches. I walk a lot. Sometimes I run."

"Sometimes doesn't cut it."

"In the winter, I go to the gym." Three times a week, if she was lucky. More often twice. But hardly a week went by that she didn't get there at least once.

Temple flicked her hand toward Lucy's body as if it were spoiled meat. "Are you really satisfied with the results you're getting?"

Lucy thought about it. "I sort of am."

"You're lying to yourself."

"I don't think so. Would I like to be a little firmer? What woman wouldn't? But I keep at it. A little here, a little there. Do I obsess about it? Not really."

"Every woman in this country obsesses about her body. You can't live in our society without obsessing."

It occurred to Lucy that she was so screwed up about so many other things—what she owed her family, what she owed herself, and how she was supposed to balance the two—that she didn't have time for serious body-image issues. "I'm not into heavy workouts. I guess I have my own exercise philosophy. The 'Good Enough' approach."

Temple looked as though Lucy had cockroaches crawling over her, and even though Lucy knew it was useless to explain, she gave it a try. "I believe exercise is important, but I'm not training for a triathlon, just for general fitness. And when I make exercise drudgery, I stop altogether."

"You should force yourself."

"I'm pretty happy being weak-willed." Lucy considered suggesting that Temple might not be quite so miserable if she tried a little more of the "Good Enough" approach. The Evil Queen's weight gain couldn't be accidental, and the social worker inside Lucy wondered what had happened to make Temple lose that iron self-control.

But Temple couldn't comprehend Lucy's laid-back attitude, and Lucy took advantage of her temporary speechlessness to switch the subject. "I have a twelve-year-old friend who tends to pop up here uninvited."

Temple's eyes widened in alarm. "That can't happen."

"Without an electric fence surrounding the property, it'll be hard to keep him out. I told him I have a girlfriend visiting, so if he shows up, he won't think it's strange that you're here."

"You don't understand! No one can see me!"

"I doubt that he's part of your fan base."

"Panda!" Temple screeched. "Panda, get in here."

Panda took all kinds of time wandering in.

Temple jabbed her hand at Lucy. "I can't deal with this now. Take care of it!" She stormed out and pounded up the stairs two at a time.

Instead of addressing the subject at hand, Panda gazed around at the living room. "What happened to my furniture?"

"What furniture?"

"The furniture that used to be in here."

"Describe it."

"What do you mean, 'describe it'?"

She narrowed her eyes at him. "Describe the furniture that used to be in here."

"A couch. Some chairs. Where is it?"

"What color was the couch?"

He gritted his teeth. "It was a couch. It was couch-colored. What did you do with it?"

"If you told me what it looked like," she said with exaggerated patience, "I might remember."

"It looked like a couch!" he exclaimed.

"You don't remember," she said triumphantly. "You don't have a clue what anything in this room looked like. What anything in this house looks like. None of this means anything to you."

A muscle ticked in his jaw. "I know I had a couch and now it's gone."

"It's not gone. It's in the sunroom. Along with some chairs and a couple of other things you wouldn't recognize. You don't care about this house, and you don't deserve it."

"Tough. It's mine. And I want my pig back."

That stopped her. "Your pig?"

"The pig that was in the kitchen."

"That ugly pig with the waiter's apron and the missing ear?"

"The ear isn't missing. It's only chipped."

That stunned her. "You remember the chip in that stupid pig's ear, but you don't know what color your couch is?"

"I'm more into the ceramic arts."

"Panda!" Temple shrieked from upstairs. "Come spot me."

Viper gazed toward the stairs. "It's fascinating," she said, "how well you've adapted to being Temple Renshaw's bitch."

He stalked toward the hallway. "That pig had better be back where it was the next time I walk in the kitchen, or you'll never see your food again."

"Your pig is ugly!" she shouted after him.

"So's your mother," he shot back, which made her furious. Not really at him. More at herself. Because she almost laughed.

✎

BREE WAS CLOSING THE FARM stand for the night when the white pickup slowed, then stopped. The lettering across the door read JENSEN'S HERB FARM.

It was nearly dark, and she'd just finished packing up the last of her unsold honey in the cardboard carton she'd propped in the wheelbarrow. She'd been up since before six, trying to finish weeding Myra's overgrown garden, she'd forgotten to eat again, and she was bone-tired. Still, there were a few good things about today. She'd sold eighteen jars of honey along with some strawberries and asparagus that had survived the neglect. She also almost had a friend, not that she believed someone as famous as Lucy would ever be a real friend, but still, it was nice.

Toby had done his customary disappearing act, but as the truck door opened, he came racing down the drive. *"Big Mike!"*

She barely avoided dropping the jars as Mike Moody climbed out. After such a grueling day, this was too much. She still couldn't quite reconcile his current good looks with the fat, acne-faced teenager she remembered. If she didn't know better, she'd have pegged him as an amiable soccer dad instead of a crass, loudmouth sneak.

He grinned and waved at Toby. "Hey, kid. I brought you something."

"What?" Toby cried as Mike walked around to the back of the truck.

"What do you think?" Mike swung down the tailgate and, in a single effortless motion, pulled off a shiny silver mountain bike.

Classic Mike Moody. She knew exactly how this would play out.

Toby stared at the bike as if it would disappear the moment he looked away. She wanted to forbid him to take it, but of course she couldn't. Mike's ambush had made that impossible.

Toby's voice grew small, uncertain, unable to comprehend that something so wonderful was happening to him. "For me?"

Bree blinked her eyes against a sting of tears. He'd received a gift he hadn't needed to fight for. A gift she couldn't have given him.

As Toby reached out to touch the handlebars, Bree understood what Toby couldn't. The bike wasn't being offered out of affection but as a way for Mike to horn in where he didn't belong. He'd done the same thing when they were kids. Shown up with bags of Skittles and Lemonheads—entrance tickets to the group that wanted to exclude him.

"Brand-new," Mike said. "I saw it when I was on the mainland yesterday and thought to myself, now who could use a great bike like that? Only one name came to mind."

"Me," Toby said on a long, soft breath. His lips were parted, his eyes so focused on the bike that nothing else existed. He looked exactly as David used to look when something he regarded as amazing happened. She ached with the pain of remembrance.

Mike pulled some tools from the truck bed and they worked together—man to man—to adjust the seat height. She was so angry she felt sick. She wanted to be the one giving David's son a bicycle. She wanted to be the one who made Toby's world brighter, not this master manipulator with his overpowering cologne, designer logos, and oily charm.

Toby mounted the bike. As his spindly legs found the pedals, Mike pointed down the drive. "It's too dark to ride on the road tonight. Give it a spin in the driveway, then try it out on the path in the woods."

"Thanks, Mike. Thanks a lot!" Toby took off.

Mike still hadn't acknowledged her. Only after he'd slammed the tailgate did he look in her direction. She turned away and stacked the last of the honey into a carton.

"I brought you something, too, Bree," he said from behind her. "To help with your business."

"I don't want anything." She grabbed the wheelbarrow and began pushing it through the scrubby grass. She needed to fix the doors on the storage shed behind the farm stand so she didn't have to keep hauling everything back and forth twice a day.

"You don't know what it is."

"And I don't care." The front wheel caught in a rut, the honey jars rattled, and she barely prevented it all from overturning.

"You don't believe in second chances, do you, Bree?"

As a kid, he'd always been whiny when anyone challenged him, but now his voice had a calmness she didn't like. "What I believe is that a leopard doesn't change its spots." She struggled to get the wheel out of the rut. "I want you to stop using Toby to try to get to me."

He pushed her aside, took the handles, and steered the wheelbarrow toward the driveway. "Myra said your ex-husband left you for an eighteen-year-old."

Scott's supposed soul mate was nineteen, but correcting him wouldn't exactly help her save face. "That's what happens when you marry the wrong man," she said.

He stopped the wheelbarrow. "You don't still believe David was the right one, do you?"

He was a lot more perceptive than he used to be, and anger coursed through her. "I won't talk to you about David."

"He never would have married you. You intimidated him."

Despite Mike's surface changes, he was as clueless as ever. David, with his blazing intellect and boundless self-confidence, had never been intimidated by anyone, let alone an ordinary girl like herself.

"The WASP princess and the kid from the ghetto . . ." He slipped his thumb under the gold bracelet on his wrist. Either he'd forgotten to put on his cologne or he'd taken her criticism seriously because he smelled like peppermint gum. "David was fascinated by you, but that's all it ever was."

Her hand itched to slap him. "Stop acting like you knew him."

"Who do you think he talked to after he married Star and settled on the island?"

"You want me to believe you were David's confidant? After what you did?"

"Living in the past is never a great idea," he said, with an air of compassion she didn't believe for a moment. "It makes things harder than they need to be. I can help you."

"The only way you can do that is to leave me alone." She abandoned the wheelbarrow and strode toward the house.

"You're barely hanging on," he said, not raising his voice. "What are you going to do when the tourists leave?"

"Get off the island like everybody else."

"And go where?"

Nowhere. Her brothers loved her, but they didn't want her living with them—not by herself and definitely not with a twelve-year-old boy tagging along. She had no place to go, something Mike seemed to know.

She could hear him coming closer, his even stride so much more confident than her fast, furious steps. "You're going to need a friend here," he said as she reached the front step. "Myra's gone. David and Star are dead. And you don't seem to have a long list of pals."

Not ones she could count on. After Scott left, her friends' so-called support had been nothing more than thinly disguised attempts to learn the juicy details of her breakup. She spun around to confront him. "I hope you're enjoying your revenge. You have money and a successful business. I don't have either one. I'm sure that makes you incredibly happy."

He pulled on a solemn expression. "Would it make you happy to see somebody you once cared about in trouble?"

She thought of David and Star, how they'd hurt her, how fiercely she'd hated them, and how much she missed them. Pushing their images away, she focused on Scott and his nineteen-year-old hottie. "You bet I would."

Mike surprised her by laughing. "Whether you want to admit it or not, you need me, so you'd better start acting like a friend. I'm picking you and Toby up on Sunday for church. Nine-thirty."

"Church?"

"It's the best place for you to get reacquainted with the locals. But there are some ground rules. Don't disrespect me in public." The steadiness in his fool's eyes alarmed her. "Don't make fun of anybody in the congregation, not even if some of them start talking in tongues. And if Ned Blakely shows up with his snake and starts quoting from the Bible, you'll be polite. Church here isn't what you're used to in Bloomfield Hills, but this is Charity Island, and people worship with their whole hearts."

Tongues? *Snakes?*

Mike smiled, not one of those unpleasant smirks she remembered, but a big smile. At her expense. "I've got to get this truck back to Hank Jenkins. I'll see you on Sunday. Oh, and if you decide not to go, I'll pass the word that you want to be left completely alone."

"I do," she said fiercely.

"Are you sure about that?" He was still smiling, congenial. "Winters are long, and people here only have one another to depend on if they drive into a ditch or run out of heating oil. Or if their kid—a kid like Toby—gets sick and has to be taken off the island." He rubbed his chin. "You should be careful what you wish for, Bree."

Blackmail. She wanted to throw something as he walked away, but she'd never been a thrower or a screamer. She'd never been much of anything except a mediocre student and Scott's cheerleader.

After Mike left, she retrieved the wheelbarrow and the quilt she'd been using in her display. Only then did she see the present he'd left for her, the one he'd said would help her with her business. Not Skittles or Lemonheads. Mike Moody had stepped up to the major leagues. His current form of bribery was a new Mac notebook computer.

Chapter Thirteen

❧

Lucy wrapped a Teenage Mutant Ninja Turtle beach towel around her waist and stepped from the outdoor shower. She'd gone for a swim off the dock, but the lake water was still cold enough that she hadn't stayed in long. As she latched the warped wooden door behind her, Panda came down the steps from the screened porch. His sweat-soaked T-shirt and damp hair indicated he'd just finished one of Temple's workouts.

"I want my bedroom back," he said, taking in her wet shoulders and the too-thin top of her cheap black swimsuit.

She pulled the towel under her armpits. "You're guarding Temple. You need to be near her."

"Temple sleeps like a log, and the food's locked up." He wandered closer, moving from shade into sunlight. "There are three empty bedrooms upstairs. Choose whichever one you like. Hell, you can sleep in all of them if you want."

He had justice on his side, and she believed in fair play. But not about this. "It's my room now, and I'm not giving it up."

"Is that right?" He leaned closer, bringing with him the scent of clean sweat and male menace. "Evicting you won't bother me one bit. Remember that I'm bigger than you, I'm stronger than you, and I have no principles."

Not completely true but close enough. She didn't like the nervous flutter in her stomach, and she crossed her arms over her chest. "You could do that . . . but then you'd have to explain it to Temple."

He still looked sinister but also a bit . . . sulky? "There's a brand-new mattress on that bed."

"Now we get to the crux of the matter." The mattress was heaven. Not too soft, not too hard, and it had a cushy new feather-top, which still took second place to the room's private entrance and exit. "It seems to be the only furnishing in the house you haven't neglected."

His glare wasn't entirely convincing. "If I have to give up my bedroom, I want something in return." His eyes lingered on her exposed collarbone. "What are you offering?"

What, indeed? "Decorating advice."

"Forget it."

"Sparkly windows."

"Like I care."

She thought hard, and then . . . *Ka-ching.* "Bread."

A few seconds ticked by. He eased away, cocked his head. "I'm listening."

"If you can keep Temple down by the cove for an hour tomorrow afternoon, I'll make sure there's a loaf of fresh bread hiding behind the plants on the porch when you get back."

He considered. "She'll smell it the minute she walks in the house."

"I'll burn some candles. Bake with the windows open. Squirt a little air freshener. What do you care?"

"You think you can do it?"

"I know I can."

"Deal. Fresh bread whenever I want it, and you keep the room." He turned on his heel and headed down to the water.

Only after he'd disappeared did she begin to have second thoughts. No one knew better than she did how seriously Panda took his work. Would he really leave Temple alone on the second floor all night just for a great mattress? She couldn't imagine it.

The more she thought about it, the more she became convinced that Panda's threats had nothing to do with getting his bedroom back and everything to do with making her give up her bread. Apparently she wasn't the only one suffering from a lack of food. She stomped into the house.

He'd set her up, and she'd fallen for it.

HE SURFACED, THEN DIVED UNDER again. When was he going to apologize for what he'd said to Lucy that night? As if he didn't have enough other things haunting him, those words had turned into a verbal earworm he couldn't shake off. *You weren't that good anyway.* He needed to apologize, but he could already feel himself letting down his guard, and if he apologized, things might get cozy between them. He didn't want that. *Be the best at what you're good at.*

He began swimming back toward the dock. He was hungry, damn it, and he hated being Temple's keeper. That's why he felt like he was off his game—losing focus, the old itch to get drunk clawing away at him. Lucy's bread would set things right again. With something decent in his stomach, he'd be able to stay on top of this job that felt like it would never end. More important, he'd do a better job managing the girl with the fake dragon tattoo.

Hunger. That was his problem.

WHETHER SHE'D BEEN SET UP or not, Lucy still had baking to do. After she'd finished eating a free-range egg the next morning, along with a slice of omega-3 spelt and flax bread that tasted like beach sand, Panda let her into the pantry to fetch what she needed. "Don't think I haven't seen through your little ploy, Patrick," she said as she came out.

"As usual, I have no idea what you're talking about." He bypassed the beach sand bread for a package of tiny fat-free whole-grain tortillas, thought better of it, and set the tortillas aside for more coffee, which he carried upstairs.

While he and Temple were occupied with their morning workout in the new gym, Lucy mixed and kneaded. When the dough finally turned elastic under her hands, she set it in an oiled bowl, covered it with a clean dish towel, and hid it on the top cupboard shelf to rise.

She wanted to buy some plants in town for the porch, purchases that were too cumbersome for a backpack, so she sneaked upstairs into the bedroom Panda had chosen and swiped his keys. As she walked to his car, Temple came hurrying out. Her face was flushed from her workout, and sweat stains blotted her gray knit top. She wore no makeup, but with her almond eyes and strong bones, she didn't need much. "Would you pick up a few things for me in town?" she said. "I forgot nail clippers, and I need some polish remover. And if the new *Women's Health* is out, would you get that, too?"

"Sure."

Temple handed over the moist twenty-dollar bill she'd curled in her palm. "I assume there's some kind of bakery or coffeehouse?" Her hushed voice still managed to sound imperious.

"The Painted Frog."

"Get a chocolate muffin for me." A straightforward demand. "Or an iced brownie if they look good. Something sweet to keep me from feeling so deprived." She was obnoxiously haughty, insufferably arrogant, and so very sad. "Deprivation is the enemy of serious weight loss."

It wasn't Lucy's job to be chief of the diet police, so she tucked the bill in her pocket. She happened to agree about deprivation. Although she'd never been a slave to sweets herself, now that sugary treats were off limits, she couldn't seem to think about much else.

Panda's SUV still had a new-car smell. As she left the house, she found herself glancing at the glove box. She waved at Bree when she passed the farm stand, took another quick look at the glove box, and ordered herself not to snoop.

The Painted Frog's pastries sat in the glass display case like fanciful hats. Four varieties of muffins with puffy, sugar-crusted tops; glistening lemon bars perched on white doilies; fancifully frosted cupcakes nestled in frilly papers. She chose a dense, but not overly large, chocolate muffin for Temple, then decided on a turtle brownie topped with toasted pecans and chewy caramel for herself. She'd never been much of a doughnut eater, but she suddenly had to have a Bavarian cream. At the last minute, she added half a dozen of the Painted Frog's oversize chocolate chip cookies for Bree and Toby.

She finished the rest of her shopping, eating the brownie and doughnut between stops, then made a quick trip to Dogs 'N' Malts for fries. Who knew how long it would be before she could sneak away to eat again?

Toby was overjoyed with the cookies, and Bree was embarrassingly touched. Lucy picked up her honey and drove toward the house. But before she got there, the car, as if it had a will of its own, pulled over to the side of the road.

She stared at the glove box. What would Ted do in this situation? Her perfect ex-fiancé never did anything even remotely sneaky, so she conjured up Meg instead and flipped open the latch.

She half expected to see a loaded gun or, at the very least, a box of condoms and an abandoned red thong. Instead she found an owner's manual, a tire pressure gauge, and an Illinois vehicle registration made out to one Patrick Shade, resident of Cook County, with an address on Chicago's Lake Shore Drive.

She carried her new plants to the porch and entered her bedroom through the sliding doors, then hid the sack with the Evil Queen's muffin under her bathroom sink. Temple could figure out for herself how to get her contraband. After giving the bread a quick second knead, she shaped the loaves, set them in a pair of pans for a final rise, and tucked them back in the cupboard. Then she went down to the dock and took out the kayak. Panda wouldn't let Temple on the water by herself, and a second kayak had been delivered.

When she got back, Temple and Panda were sitting at the monstrously oversize kitchen table eating a lunch that couldn't have been all that much better than a colon cleanse. Their matching dinner plates held sparse portions from the frozen meal containers sitting on the counter. Panda pushed a morsel of dry salmon around with his fork. A lemon wedge floated in the glass of water Temple lifted to her lips. She dabbed the corner of her mouth with a cloth napkin she'd unearthed from somewhere. "I think it's important for food to look appealing," she said.

"Nothing can look appealing when you're eating it on Panda's puke-green table," Lucy retorted.

"The table stays," he said.

"Your loss." She went to her bedroom and returned with the sack of Temple's legitimate purchases. Panda snatched it away before Temple could touch it. He rooted around inside and, after satisfying himself that it held only magazines and nail clippers—none of the banned substances hidden under Lucy's sink—he handed it to his client.

The Evil Queen turned her imperious eyes on him. "Really, Panda . . . Don't you think that's a bit insulting to Lucy?"

"Could be. Don't care."

Lucy snorted.

Temple set the sack aside. "Honestly, why don't the two of you just go to bed together and get it over with?"

Panda's forkful of mushy broccoli stalled in midair. Lucy nearly choked. Panda recovered first. "You're way off base."

"Am I?" Temple propped her bent elbow on the table and tapped her chin with her fingers. "I've made a successful career out of reading people, and the chemistry between you two is hot enough to be embarrassing."

"Your imagination," Panda said. "What you're picking up is hostility. Two different people with two different outlooks. One of us is a hardheaded realist. The other isn't."

That was such crap that Lucy couldn't stand it. "We had sex, Temple. It wasn't that good."

"I knew it!" Temple chortled in triumph. "He's one of those selfish lovers, isn't it? Only out for his own pleasure."

"I am not!"

"Totally selfish," Lucy said. "Over in a flash. Once was definitely enough."

Panda's plate rattled as he dropped his fork.

Temple ignored him. "I'm surprised. He has amazing stamina during our workouts. Maybe . . ."

"That's enough." He shot up from the table. "More than enough. End of discussion."

As he stalked toward the back door, Lucy took the seat he'd vacated. "I'm not sure workout effort translates into the bedroom."

"It should," Temple said. "All that blood flow."

The door slammed behind him, and the porch floor reverberated from the blunt trauma of his footsteps. Temple's voice became an urgent whisper. "Did you get my muffin?"

"It's in a sack under the sink in my bathroom."

"What kind?"

"Chocolate."

"Perfect." She eyed Panda through the window, assessing how far he was from the house. "Was he really a bad lover?"

"I guess not." Lucy pushed his plate of barely eaten food away. "He said it was me. He said I wasn't that good."

Temple's dark brows arched. "He actually told you that?"

Lucy nodded.

"Interesting," Temple said. "Maybe you should try again?"

"Are you serious?"

Her cat's eyes grew thoughtful. "Panda is a fascinating man. I'll admit I put out a few signals when I first met him, but he ignored them. Then I met someone else . . ." Her expression clouded. "A disaster. I should have tried harder with Panda."

Lucy wondered if this "disaster" was at the root of Temple's weight gain.

Temple checked the window view one more time, then rose. "I'm going after that muffin. If he comes back inside, keep him occupied."

"How exactly am I supposed to do that?"

"Take off your clothes."

"You take off your clothes," Lucy retorted.

But nobody was taking off any clothes because Panda had reappeared. "If you're done with your girlie chat," he sneered from the doorway, "let's get back to work. Or maybe you think those pounds are going to melt away by themselves?"

"Prick." Temple cut a resentful glare toward Lucy's bedroom, then followed him down to the cove.

As Lucy waited for the bread to finish baking, she caught glimpses of Temple and Panda kayaking. Unlike Lucy, Temple deliberately steered the boat into the current. Panda paddled nearby, guarding his client against potential attack by a roving band of Great Lake pirates.

Between the doughnut and French fries, Lucy wasn't hungry, but she couldn't resist cutting the heel from one freshly baked loaf of oatmeal bread and drizzling it with some of Bree's honey. She hid both loaves on the porch behind the new plants she rearranged on the baker's rack. Panda could figure out where to store the leftovers.

She'd baked with the windows open, then camouflaged the lingering aroma by partially melting the lid of an old plastic Cool Whip container over a gas burner. When Temple came back inside, she was so frantic to get to the muffin hidden in Lucy's bathroom that she didn't notice the noxious fumes, but Panda noticed. He shot Lucy a look that clearly asked if this was the best she could do. Then his gaze settled on the ceramic pig she'd retrieved from the garage and set on top of the refrigerator. He took in the hangman's noose she'd hooked around the pig's neck, a rope-tying skill she'd picked up from Andre but intended to attribute to HGTV if he asked.

He didn't.

Temple pulled off her ball cap and stretched her arms. "I'm going upstairs to take a nap. Wake me in an hour."

"Great idea." Panda was as anxious to get to the bread as Temple was to retrieve her muffin.

Temple pretended to work out a kink in her neck. "Lucy, can I borrow that magazine you were reading? Nothing like celebrity gossip to put you to sleep."

"Sure." Lucy didn't have a gossip magazine. What she had was a hidden chocolate muffin, and she didn't feel guilty about it. One small muffin wouldn't kill Temple, and the Evil Queen needed a reward for the torture she was putting herself through.

As Temple set off for Lucy's bedroom, Panda headed for the porch.

Lucy was feeling a little sick from everything she'd eaten, and she rubbed her stomach.

"*Bastard!*" Temple screeched.

Uh-oh. The sound had come from the bedroom. Lucy stuck her head out the back door. Panda wasn't on the porch. She craned her neck toward the open deck on the other side of the screen. Sure enough, the slider door into her bedroom was open.

It was time to make herself invisible.

"*Lucy!*"

At the sound of Panda's ominous roar, she quickly reviewed her options. Escape by car or by water?

She chose escape by car, but before she could reach the front door, Panda was storming toward her through the living room with Temple at his heels. "Do you think this is a joke?" he exclaimed. "You deliberately sabotaged her. Don't you get it? This woman's career is at stake."

"It really wasn't well done of you, Lucy," the Evil Queen said haughtily. "I thought you understood how much I need a supportive environment. Obviously, I can't count on you to be there for me." Lifting her head, she bounded up the steps.

Lucy stared at her, then opened her mouth to unload, but Panda's hand shot up. "Not now. I'm way too pissed off at you." He headed for the porch.

No way was she putting up with this. She stormed after him.

He'd already found the bread.

She stomped across the porch. "If you think for one minute—"

"Damn . . ." He said the word like a prayer. "It's still warm."

She stared at him as he lifted the first loaf from behind the plants. He took in the missing heel but didn't seem upset about it . . . Or about anything, for that matter, including the smuggled muffin. "I don't suppose you have a knife," he said. "Oh, hell . . ." He ripped off a chunk and sank his teeth in. "Honest to God, Lucy . . ." He swallowed. "This is the best thing I've had to eat all week."

"Never mind about that. I'm not going to let you—"

"We need to find a better hiding place."

She splayed her hands on her hips. "Obviously not under my bathroom sink!"

"Maybe that desk in the den? Watch the door. Make sure she doesn't change her mind and come back downstairs." He took another bite. "And try not to let her get to you again."

She threw up her hands. "You two deserve each other." And then . . . "What did you do with the muffin?"

"Ate it in front of her like I told her I would. I had to stuff it in so fast I couldn't even enjoy it."

That would account for the smear of chocolate at the corner of his mouth.

"You do know this diet she's on is insane," she said.

"I'm hoping she'll figure that out, but until then I have a job to do." He tore off a second chunk. "I'll have to search you from now on."

"Search me?"

"Nothing personal."

Nothing personal, indeed!

Chapter Fourteen

❧

I DON'T SEE WHY WE HAVE to go to church," Toby said.

"Take it up with your best friend Big Mike." Bree knew she sounded petty, but she couldn't help herself. She slipped into her only remaining pair of heels, strappy bronze stilettos that would make her as tall as Mike. As a bonus, she could always use the heels to stab any serpents that might escape during the worship service.

For the past five days, she'd tried to come up with a way to get out of this, but Mike had backed her into a corner. As long as she was responsible for Toby, she couldn't afford to have Mike blackball her in the community, something he was perfectly capable of doing. He was a big man outside, but inside, he was small and petty, and he had years of practice manipulating people to do what he wanted.

"We have to go to church because of the way you act so mean to Big Mike," Toby said. "I'll bet he thinks you're going to hell."

Already there.

Just then Mike's red Cadillac pulled into the drive. She still couldn't figure out the best way to warn Toby to keep his guard up. "Mike's been nice to you," she said tentatively, "but . . . sometimes people aren't always exactly the way they seem."

He shot her a look that branded her the dumbest person on earth and dashed out the door, the tail of his plaid shirt flapping. So much for good intentions.

She'd tucked her hair into a fashionably untidy bun to accompany one of the few dresses she hadn't put up for consignment, a sleeveless caramel sheath she'd accessorized with costume hoop earrings. Her arms still felt bare without her bangles. She'd sold all her good jewelry months ago, along with her two-carat engagement ring. As for her wedding ring . . . The night Scott had left her, she'd driven to the club and thrown it in the pond by the eighteenth green.

Mike hopped out of the car to open the door for her. She handed him the computer laptop he'd given her. "Thank you," she said stiffly, "but I'm sure you can find a better use for this."

Toby clambered into the backseat. The interior smelled of good leather with only the faintest trace of Mike's cologne. She cracked open a window anyway to get some air.

Mike set the computer in the backseat without commenting. Even before they pulled out onto the highway, Toby started chattering about his bike. When he finally paused for breath, Mike said, "Why don't you ride it in the Fourth of July parade tomorrow?"

"Could I?" Toby asked Mike, not her.

"Sure." Mike glanced over at Bree. "We finished work on my float yesterday. This year's theme is 'Island in the Sun.'"

"Catchy." How she'd once loved the way this parade marked the beginning of another magical island summer.

"I always have the biggest float," he bragged. "Hey, why don't you ride on it?"

"I'll pass."

Mike shook his head and grinned, no better at picking up on social cues than he'd ever been. "Remember the year you and Star talked your way onto the Rotary float? Star fell off the back, and Nate Lorris nearly ran her over with his tractor?"

She and Star had laughed until they'd both wet their pants. "No. I don't remember."

"Sure you do. Star was always angling for a way to get the two of you on a float."

She'd always managed it, too. They'd ridden on floats for Dogs 'N' Malts, Maggie's Fudge Shop, the Knights of Columbus, and the old barbecue joint that had burned down. Once Star had even gotten them onto the Boy Scouts' float.

Toby piped up from the rear. "Gram said my mom was worthless." He delivered this statement so matter-of-factly that Bree was taken aback, but Mr. Salesman had an answer for everything.

"Your gram said that out of sadness. Your mom was restless, and sometimes she could be a little immature, but she wasn't worthless."

Toby kicked the back of the seat with no particular venom. "I hate her."

Toby's antipathy for his mother was disturbing, even though Bree felt the same. Although lately her resentment toward Star had begun to seem more like the dregs of an old head cold than a full-blown attack of the flu.

Once again, Mike stepped into the breach. "You didn't know your mother, Toby. Sure she had her faults—we all do—but there were a lot more good things about her."

"Like running out on me and Gram and my dad?"

"She had this thing called postpartum depression. Sometime women get it after they have babies. I'm sure she didn't mean to stay away for long."

Myra had never said anything to Bree about postpartum depression. She'd said Star couldn't stand being stuck with a baby and had run away so she could "cat around."

As they reached town, Bree hoped the subject of Star was closed, but bigmouthed Mike couldn't leave it alone. "Your mom and Bree were best friends. I bet Bree can tell you lots of good things about your mom."

Bree stiffened.

"I bet she can't," Toby said.

She had to say something. Anything. She forced her jaw to move. "Your mother was . . . very beautiful. We . . . all wanted to look like her."

"That's true." The glance Mike darted at her held unmistakable reproof. Mike Moody, the master of misdeeds, was judging her for not coming up with something more meaningful, but Toby didn't seem to notice.

They'd reached the church. The *Episcopal* church. The largest and most respectable congregation on Charity Island.

Bree looked at Mike. "Serpents and speaking in tongues?"

He grinned. "It could happen."

A joke at her expense. Still, some of her tension began to fade.

BREE HAD ATTENDED THE METHODIST church as a child, but organized religion with all its unanswered questions had eventually felt too burdensome, and she'd stopped not long after she got married. Mike found seats for them off to the side beneath a stained-glass window of Jesus blessing the multitudes.

As she relaxed into the rhythm of the service, her mood began to lift. For now anyway there were no beehives, no tomato plants to water or weeds to pull. No customers to entice or young boy to disappoint.

The possibility that she might not be alone on this planet, that something larger might be watching out for her, gave her a fragile comfort.

Occasionally Mike's arm, big and solid in a navy suit coat, brushed against hers. As long as she didn't look at his gold-link bracelet or big college ring, she could pretend he was someone else—one of those steadfast, dependable men with solid values and a faithful heart. He closed his eyes for the prayers, listened attentively to the sermon, and sang the first verses of every hymn without consulting the hymnal.

After the service, he worked the crowd, slapping the men on the back, flattering the women, telling one of the deacons about a house going on the market, turning church into another sales opportunity. Everybody sucked up to him, except it didn't exactly seem that way. They acted as if they genuinely liked him. The adult Mike Moody was beginning to confuse her, although he still didn't seem to have any clue about how patronizing he could be, since he called an elderly woman "young lady." On the other hand, he noticed the distress of a kid on crutches and rushed to help her before anyone else realized there was a problem. It was disconcerting.

He introduced her to everyone. A few of the parishioners remembered her family. One of the women remembered her. People were both friendly and intrusive. How was Toby doing? How long did she intend to stay on the island? Did she know the cottage's roof leaked? Marriage had made her guarded. She sidestepped their probing as best she could, a process made easier by Mike's garrulousness.

She learned he was chairman of the island's biggest charity. Both admirable and good promotion for his business, since it kept his face plastered on all the fund-raising literature. He also sponsored Little League and soccer teams in every age group, ensuring that dozens of island kids were his walking advertisements.

"How about some lunch?" he asked Toby as they climbed back into his car. "The Island Inn or Rooster's?"

"Can we go to the Dogs 'N' Malts?" Toby asked.

Mike glanced at Bree, taking her in from head to toe. "Bree's all dressed up. Let's take her someplace nice."

She didn't want to be indebted to Mike for lunch or mountain bikes or notebook computers. She didn't want to be indebted to him for anything. "Not today," she said briskly as he turned the key in the ignition. "I need to start melting beeswax for candles."

Toby predictably took issue. "That's not fair. You spoil everything."

"Now, boy, there's no need to be disrespectful," Mike replied.

"Please stop calling him boy," she said tightly.

Mike glanced over at her.

Toby kicked the back of her seat. "I'm a kid. Mike's my friend. He can call me whatever he wants."

Toby was David's son, and she wasn't backing down on this one. "No, he can't." As she looked over her shoulder at him, she saw Star's thickly lashed golden brown eyes staring back at her. "That word has a negative connotation—a bad association—in the African-American community."

Mike flinched, finally catching on, but Toby grew more belligerent. "So what? I don't live in the African-American community. I live on Charity Island."

How had she, the whitest of white women, become responsible for instilling racial pride in David Wheeler's son?

Mike, who'd started the whole thing, concentrated on pulling out of the parking lot. She plodded on. "White people used to call black men—even elderly men—'boy.' It was a way of making them feel inferior. It's very insensitive."

Toby thought about it for a moment and, no surprise, curled his lip at her. "Mike's my friend. He didn't mean to be insensitive. That's just the way he is."

Mike shook his head. "No, Bree's right. I apologize, Toby. I keep forgetting."

Forgetting to deal with his racism or forgetting Toby was half African-American?

"So what?" Toby muttered. "I'm white, too, and I don't see what's the big deal."

"The big deal," she said stubbornly, "is that your father was proud of his heritage, and I want you to feel the same way."

"If he was so proud, why did he marry my mom?"

Because Star had always wanted whatever Bree had.

"Your dad was crazy about your mom," Mike said. "And she was just as crazy about him, right up to the end. Your mom could make your dad laugh like nobody else, and he got her to read books she wouldn't have picked up otherwise. I wish you could have seen the way they looked at each other. Like nobody else existed."

He might as well have slapped her. And he wasn't done. "It took them a while to realize how much they loved each other," he said, an unfamiliar toughness clipping his words. "At first Bree was your dad's girlfriend, but let me tell you, he never looked at her the way he looked at your mother."

The real Mike Moody, with his calculated cruelty, had finally resurfaced. He kept his eyes on the road. "We'll drop Bree off at the cottage so she can get her work done, and then I'll take you to Dogs 'N' Malts. That okay with you, Bree?"

All she could manage was the barest nod.

As soon as she was inside, she sagged down on the couch and stared blindly at the Siamese cats on the mantel. She'd spent more time lately thinking about her youthful love affair than the demise of her ten-year marriage. But her affair with David had such a clear beginning and end, while the course of her marriage had been so very murky.

She slipped her heels off. The sandals she wore every day had left tan marks on her bare feet. Not that she had much of a tan. This was as dark as she got, a touch of honey and a few more freckles, which made it even more ironic that she'd been charged with raising a young black male.

Despite what she'd told Mike and Toby, she wasn't ready to tackle melting beeswax today, so after she'd changed clothes, she found paper and began sketching some ideas for handmade note cards. But her heart wasn't in it, and she couldn't come up with anything she liked. Eventually she heard Toby burst into the house and head for his room. She listened for the sound of the Cadillac pulling away from the cottage. It didn't come.

"I know you're mad at me, but what's new, right?" Mike said from the doorway.

"I don't want to talk about it." She got up from the table.

In his businessman's navy suit, he seemed bigger than ever, and despite her own height, she felt as if he were looming over her. "What I told Toby about David and Star was true."

She began gathering up her drawing materials. "Only to you."

He tugged absentmindedly on his necktie. "You want to believe you and David were Romeo and Juliet, but the truth is, you were a rich white girl from Grosse Pointe, and he was a black kid from Gary." He shifted his car keys from one hand to the other. "David was fascinated by you, but he never loved you."

She stuffed the notepad in the junk drawer. "Are you done?"

"It was different with Star." Mike filled the room, sucking up her air. "Neither of them had money. They were both ambitious, charismatic, maybe a little ruthless. They understood each other in ways you and David couldn't."

"Then why did she leave?" The junk drawer banged as she shoved it in. "If they were such passionate lovers, why did Star run off?"

"He took a job in Wisconsin after she'd begged him not to. She always hated it when he was gone, and she wanted to punish him. I doubt she planned on being gone for long. She sure didn't count on sliding off the road and going through the ice in that drainage canal."

Bree wasn't buying it. "They found a man in the car with her."

"A drifter. She was always picking people up. My guess is he was hitchhiking."

She didn't want to believe his story. She wanted to believe what Myra had told her, that Star had gotten bored with David and left him for good. Shame curled in the pit of her stomach. "I don't know why you keep bringing all this up. It happened years ago. It means nothing to me."

He knew that wasn't true, but he didn't argue. "I'm a religious man," he said matter-of-factly. "I believe in sin, and I believe in repentance. I've made amends as best as I know how, but it hasn't changed anything."

"And it won't."

His gold bracelet caught a stray sunbeam, and he nodded, not so much at her, more to himself, as if he'd made a decision. "I'm going to leave you alone from now on."

"Right." She didn't believe it. Mike never left anyone alone.

In the old days, he'd avoided meeting anyone's eyes. Not now. And something in his steady gaze threw her off balance. "I'd appreciate it if you'd let me stay in touch with Toby," he said with an unsettling dignity. "I should have checked with you before I told him he could ride his bike in the parade. I have a bad habit of charging ahead without thinking things through." A matter-of-fact statement, neither hiding his flaws nor beating himself up for them. "The parade steps off at ten. He needs to be in the school parking lot by nine. I'd come get him, but I'm head of the committee, and I have to be there early."

She studied a worn spot on her sandal. "I can handle it."

"All right."

That was it. No salesman's pitch to win her over. No bribes of Lemonheads, Skittles, or Eskimo pies. He called out a brief good-bye to Toby and then he was gone, leaving her with the uneasy feeling that she was now truly on her own.

Ridiculous. He'd be back. Mike Moody always came back, whether you wanted him to or not.

Chapter Fifteen

I 'M NOT GOING!" TEMPLE DECLARED from the gym floor where she was doing a mind-boggling set of one-handed push-ups at Lucy's feet while hip-hop played in the background. Even Panda agreed that opera didn't make the best workout music.

"You need to get out." Lucy dangled the short brown wig she'd swiped from the Evil Queen's closet in front of the owner's nose. "Shutting yourself up like this isn't healthy. Witness your hissy fit yesterday just because I brought a couple of sprigs of honeysuckle into the house."

"They smelled like Jolly Ranchers."

"Save your breath." Panda returned the monstrous weights he'd been lifting to the rack. "She prides herself on being insane."

Temple rose, switching from push-ups to jump squats. Strands of wet dark hair stuck to the back of her neck and her face glistened. "If you understood what I'm going through, you wouldn't suggest this. You have no idea, Lucy, what it's like to be so famous."

Lucy rolled her eyes just like Toby.

Temple got the point and gave a dismissive wave. "You have second-hand fame. It's different for me."

Panda snorted. His sweat-soaked T-shirt clung to his chest, and the hair on his legs lay damp against his skin. It had been only a week, but Lucy could swear his already buff body was starting to show those creepy overdeveloped muscles. When Lucy had inquired why he was torturing himself so much, he'd asked her what the hell else he was supposed to do with his time? The enforced isolation was wearing on him nearly as much as Temple, and as each day passed, both of their moods had grown darker.

"I've been on the island for a month," Lucy said patiently, "and I haven't had a problem."

"It's how you look. People are afraid of you."

Lucy loved the idea and paused a moment to admire the new thorn and blood-drop tattoo she'd applied yesterday to replace the one that had started to flake. In another couple of days, she'd have to fix her dragon. And maybe add a tattoo sleeve on her other arm . . . "Nobody expects to see either Lucy Jorik or Temple Renshaw at a Charity Island Fourth of July parade," she said, "and if nobody expects to see you, they don't see you."

When she'd stopped at the farm stand yesterday, Toby had been decorating his bike while Bree examined a bedraggled bee costume that Toby's grandmother used to wear in parades. "The question is . . . ," Bree had said to Lucy as she straightened an antenna, "how desperate am I to attract new customers?"

Until last night, Lucy had intended to go to the parade alone, but after Temple had thrown the Scrabble board across the sunroom and Panda had threatened to dump Lucy in the lake if she didn't stop making nooses for his French waiter pig, she'd modified her plan. "The brutal fact is, you've only been here a week, and you've both turned into bad-tempered, snarly bitches. Not that either of you had that far to go."

Panda's towel snapped as he threw it across the gym. "I'm the easiest guy in the world to get along with. But Lucy's right, Temple. If you don't take a break soon, somebody is going to die. And it won't be me." He grabbed a water bottle and chugged.

"Do you really expect me to stake my future on the dubious protection of a wig? I'm not doing it." Her jump squats gave way to side planks.

Lucy sighed. The Evil Queen was demanding, temperamental, and difficult, and Lucy should hate her guts, but the social worker inside her couldn't. Beneath all that bluster was a lost soul trying to cope with a life that had gone out of control, a lost soul who understood exactly how crazy she was but couldn't figure out what to do about it.

Lucy and the Evil Queen had a lot in common, although the Evil Queen knew what she wanted to do with her life, and all Lucy knew was what she didn't want to do—knock on more doors begging for more money and more legislation that would help children. Which made her the lowest of the low.

Panda set the bottle aside and gazed at Lucy. "What if her disguise was more than a wig?"

"What do you mean?"

"I mean . . ." Panda turned to Temple. "Your pal, the president's daughter, has had lots of experience hiding her identity, and I don't mean just her current stomach-churning disguise." He took in Lucy's now-neon-pink dreads. "If you persuade her, I'm sure she'll share her secrets."

An hour later, the three of them were on their way into town. Temple slouched in the backseat, her long hair concealed under the short brown wig, her face shielded by sunglasses and an unremarkable straw sunhat. Lucy wore her black tank, the one embellished with a skull and roses; a pair of denim Daisy Dukes she'd frayed and spiced up with safety pins; her nose ring and *two* eyebrow rings. Panda wore his black Nike ball cap, his hair curling slightly from beneath the bottom edge. Lucy had asked him to ditch his aviators because they made him look too much like Secret Service.

Temple's gray yoga pants fit a bit more loosely than when she'd arrived, but not her purple knit top, which stretched tightly across her middle, thanks to the small pregnancy pillow Lucy had secured beneath it.

Beachcomber Boulevard was closed to traffic for the parade, and Panda looked for a parking place on a side street. "Remember what I said, Temple. You don't leave my sight, not even for a second. Lucy, you're Temple's cover, so you stick with her. Don't talk to anybody, but if something happens, Temple's your pregnant friend from back east."

"My story is better," Lucy said. "She's one more woman you knocked up and plan to abandon first chance you get."

Panda ignored that. "Don't even think about trying to give me the slip, Temple. If you have to use the Porta Potti, we all go."

Temple pushed down her sunglasses and gazed at the back of his neck over the top rim. "I would die before I used a Porta Potti."

"I'm with you on that one," Lucy said.

Temple glanced nervously out the car windows at the people passing on the sidewalk, some of them carrying lawn chairs, others pushing strollers. "You're too paranoid, Panda. I haven't worked this hard to blow it on street food."

"Reassuring, but that doesn't change the rules."

Lucy tugged on the waistband of her shorts. Despite living in a house with nothing but diet food, she'd managed to regain the weight she'd lost before her wedding. She turned to inspect Temple's disguise again and saw her compressed lips. "Will you knock it off?"

Temple frowned. "What are you talking about?"

"The exercise you're doing right now. Squeezing your thighs or contracting your stomach or something like that."

"I'm doing my Kegels." Temple gave a condescending smirk. "And if you cared about your pelvic floor, you'd be doing them, too."

"I swear to God," Panda declared, "if my next job involves a woman—even a female gerbil—I'm not taking it!"

Lucy smiled and propped her elbow on the seat back. "Here's the good news, Temple. When Panda is around, no one looks at anybody else."

"Exactly why Lucy and I need to go off by ourselves," Temple declared.

"Oh, yeah, that'll work," Panda said dryly. "The second you two are out of my sight, you'd both be mainlining funnel cakes."

So true. Which explained Lucy's weight gain. Being surrounded with nothing but diet food left her so unsatisfied that she gorged herself when she came to town. So far she'd avoided Panda's threatened body searches by turning out her pockets and patting herself down in front of him. To her relief, he hadn't pushed her.

"Your paranoia is a sickness," the Evil Queen declared as Panda eased into a tight parking space. "You should get therapy."

Lucy eyed Temple. "No offense, but you might want to go along with him."

Panda smiled, his first of the morning, then cut the ignition and returned to his lecture. "We watch the parade, take a walk around the harbor, get back in the car, and go home better people."

Now Lucy was the one who snorted.

"It could happen," he said with a lack of conviction.

They found a viewing spot near the end of Beachcomber Boulevard away from the smell of fried food and the worst of the tourist crowd. As Lucy had predicted, the people nearby were more interested in Panda than either of the women, although Lucy attracted more notice than Temple, something that irritated the Evil Queen. "I know it's illogical," she whispered, "but I'm used to being the center of attention."

Lucy laughed and whispered back, "Now's as good a time as any to consider adding a mental health component to your workout."

"If I were sane," Temple said on a sigh, "I wouldn't know who I was."

And that was the thing about Temple Renshaw. Exactly when you wanted to write her off as an obnoxious diva, she'd say something that twisted your heart. The fact that she was both brutally insightful and totally clueless kept her from being insufferable.

The day was windy for a parade. The pennants hanging from the lampposts snapped in the breeze, and the canopies over the food tents billowed like overstuffed stomachs. A local politician led off the parade as grand marshal, followed by a marching band and a group on horseback. The first of the floats came into sight, a Native American scene sponsored by Jerry's Trading Post. The next float featured a forest of crepe paper palm trees listing wildly in the wind and a grass hut bearing the sign BIG MIKE'S ISLAND BROKERAGE: HOUSES AND BOATS. Big Mike Moody stood at the front having the time of his life waving to the crowd and throwing out candy bars.

A dancing hot dog from Dogs 'N' Malts strutted next to a pirate promoting Jake's Dive Shop and a giant walleye representing the Island Inn. Lucy had forgotten about Bree until she saw a honeybee following the Girl Scouts. Antennae topped with bouncy black balls rose from her tight-fitting black hood. The wind tried to carry away her sign advertising Carousel Honey, but she hung on. She looked only a little embarrassed as Lucy waved at her.

The bicycle brigade was up next, and Toby was so excited to see Lucy he nearly lost his balance. He'd been to the house twice since Temple had arrived, but both times Lucy had set off with him on her bike before he spotted Temple. Lucy blew him a couple of kisses for fun, and he grinned good-naturedly.

Six elderly members of the American Legion passed. Seeing them, and being around so many American flags, made Lucy miss her mother. She cheered loudly.

Panda leaned down and whispered, "Way to keep a low profile."

But she'd stopped worrying about being recognized, and even Temple no longer seemed so anxious. "There are some seriously over-weight people here," she said. "It's like *Fat Island* brought to life."

"Close your eyes and do your Kegels," Lucy advised before Temple decided to stage an intervention.

When the parade ended, none of them was ready to go home, but the idea of mixing with the crowd made Temple nervous. Lucy suggested a trip to the lighthouse instead. Since Panda was even less anxious to get back to Goose Cove than Lucy, he readily agreed.

The wind blew stronger at the lighthouse point than along the parade route, and ropes chimed against the flagpole. Although the building was open to visitors in honor of the holiday, most of the tourists were still in town, and the parking lot held only a few cars. The three of them climbed the winding metal staircase inside the tower to an open, fenced galley just beneath the black dome and giant lens. They'd left their hats in the car to keep them from blowing off, and Temple reached up to anchor her wig. "What a beautiful view."

Behind the flying clouds, the sky shone a brilliant blue. The metal railing was warm from the early afternoon sun, but the wind whipped angry waves across the jetty, and only the larger pleasure boats dotted the choppy water. Temple left them to circle the galley.

"Makes you feel sorry for people who never get to see the Great Lakes," Panda said as he slipped his aviators back on.

Lucy felt exactly the same way, but she didn't want to talk to him, so she merely nodded.

A pair of terns beat their wings over the water, searching for a meal, while a gull circled stubbornly above them, ready to steal their catch. Panda propped his forearms on the rail. "I owe you an apology."

"So many to choose from."

He stared straight ahead, his eyes shadowed behind the dark lenses. "What I said to you three weeks ago . . . That night . . . I was pissed because you'd locked the door. I was pissed about a lot of things, none of them your problem."

She'd suspected his ugly words had more to do with him than her, but they'd still hurt. "Sorry. Don't remember."

"That night at the motel . . . You were great that night. I was the one who—"

"Really," she said icily. "I don't want to hear it."

"I'm sorry. Again, I'm sorry."

"Not necessary." She refused to soften her expression even though she was glad he'd offered an apology.

Temple passed behind them, her third trip around the galley. "I'm going down. If that's all right with you, Warden."

Panda peered over the railing. "I don't see a ready food supply, so go ahead."

Temple disappeared. Lucy wasn't ready to leave, but she didn't want to talk to him either, so she moved a few yards away. He refused to take the hint. "Lucy, I know—"

"Temple needs to figure out how to police herself," she said before he could go on. "Sooner or later, you have to ease up on the reins."

"I know. Maybe next week."

A gust of wind blew a crumpled newspaper across the parking lot, and her resolve not to engage in a conversation with him wavered. "You like her, don't you?"

He straightened, resting only the heels of his hands on the rail. "More like I owe her. She's sent a lot of business my way."

"You like her, too."

"I guess. She's crazy, but she's gutsy, too. Sort of like you, although in your defense, your crazy is a little less in-your-face than hers."

"You being a model of sanity."

He leaned out, watching Temple as she emerged from the light-house. "At least I know what I want out of life, which is more than you seem to."

She abandoned her attempt to keep the conversation impersonal. "What is that? What do you want?"

"To do my job well, pay my bills on time, and keep the bad guys from hurting the good guys."

"You were doing all that on the police force, so why give it up?"

He hesitated a moment too long. "Lousy pay."

"I don't believe you. Fighting the bad guys had to have been more interesting than guarding Temple from fat grams. What's the real reason?"

"I got burned out." He pointed to the water's edge. "Riprap. That's what they call the rocks they use to hold back erosion."

In other words, he wanted her to stop asking questions. Which was fine. She'd had enough sharing for one day. "I'm going down."

He followed her to the bottom. As they stepped out into the sun-light, she saw Temple doing some deep walking lunges into the wind. Another set of visitors had arrived. A mother stood near the jetty argu-ing with her son while his younger sister chased a seagull.

Lucy heard the frazzled young woman say to the boy, "I don't have any more juice boxes, Cabot. You finished the last one in the car."

"Sophie finished it." The kid stamped his foot. "And you gave her the grape! Grape's my favorite!"

As the boy demanded her attention, the little girl ran into the wind, arms outflung, curly hair skinned away from her face. She was around five, more interested in the joy of the day, the violent crash of waves over rock, than her brother's tantrum.

"That's enough, Cabot," the mother snapped. "You have to wait."

His sister threw up her arms, racing closer to the rocky shoreline as the wind plastered her pink T-shirt to her small chest.

"But I'm thirsty," the boy whined.

An unexpectedly fierce gust made Lucy take a step backward. Out of the corner of her eye, she watched the little girl stagger, lose her balance, and with nothing more than the softest cry, stumble onto one of the treacherous boulders lining the edge of the water. Lucy gasped as her small arms flailed. The child clawed to find a hold, but the rocks were too slippery, and within seconds, she'd tumbled into the rough water.

Even before her head vanished under the churn, Panda had begun to run. Lucy raced after him. The mother finally saw what was happening and screamed. She started to run but was farther away.

Panda scrambled onto the slippery boulders, trying to locate the child as he moved. A wave crashed around his legs. He must have seen something because he kicked against the jagged rocks and launched himself into the water in a powerful dive.

Lucy clambered onto the wet rocks, barely keeping herself from falling in, too.

Panda surfaced. He was alone.

Lucy was dimly aware of the mother's cries behind her. Panda went under again. Lucy scanned the water for a glimpse of pink, saw nothing. Panda came back up, grabbed some air, and dove.

And then Lucy saw something. Maybe just a reflection, but she prayed it was more. "There!" she screamed when he resurfaced.

Panda heard her, twisted in the direction she was pointing, and went under again.

He stayed there forever. She tried to spot him, but he'd gone deep.

The waves crashed over the rocks, but their roar couldn't block the mother's heartbreaking cries. Seconds ticked by, each one an hour long, and then he came up, the child anchored against him.

The little girl's head hung listlessly against his white T-shirt. Lucy felt time stop. And then the child began to choke.

Panda kept her head well above the churning surface while she coughed and gagged. She started to flail. He put his mouth to her ear, talking to her. He was slowing everything down, giving her time to get her breath back, to understand that she was safe before he tried to pull her through the rough surf back to the jetty.

She clutched him around the neck, burying her face against him. He kept talking. She seemed to be breathing easier now. Lucy couldn't imagine what he was saying. She spun toward the mother, who'd scrambled to Lucy's side. "Wave to her," Lucy said. "Let her see everything's okay."

The mother managed to muster an unsteady croak. "It's all right, Sophie!" she yelled into the wind. "Everything's all right." Behind her, the boy watched in wide-eyed shock.

Lucy doubted Sophie could hear her mother above the crashing waves, but the child wasn't fighting Panda's grip on her. He had to be tiring, but he kept talking to her as he began struggling toward the shore against the tumbling surf.

The mother tried to crawl past Lucy to the jetty's edge, but her thin sandals didn't have the grip of Lucy's boots, and she kept slipping. "Get back," Lucy ordered. "I'll get her."

Panda drew close. He caught Lucy's eye. A wave hit her in the knees as she crouched down. She braced herself, reached out. He lifted the child and with almost superhuman strength, managed to press her into Lucy's arms. Sophie blindly fought this new stranger's grip, but Lucy held tight until Panda pulled himself up. The mother was scrambling toward them, but Sophie threw herself at Panda. He gathered her up and carried her off the rocks onto the path, his strong, tanned arms incongruous against the little pink T-shirt.

Even then, she clung to him. He dropped to a crouch and cradled her. "You're safe, champ. It's over. Did you leave any water in that lake, or did you swallow it all? I'll bet you swallowed it. I'll bet there's no lake left . . ."

He went on like that. Nonsense. Insisting she'd drunk the lake dry until she finally turned to look, saw it wasn't true, and began to argue with him.

Her mother took longer to recover. She alternated between hugging her child as if she'd never let her go again and repeatedly thanking Panda through her tears. In the distance, Temple had given up her walking lunges in favor of jogging and was heading back toward them, oblivious to what she'd missed.

Panda listened patiently to the mother's frantic chatter about where they were from and why her husband wasn't with them. He talked to Sophie again and her brother. When he was eventually satisfied that the mother was capable of driving, he helped her load the kids in the car. The mother grabbed him in an awkward hug. "God sent you to us today. You were His angel."

"Yes, ma'am," he replied, all stern-faced cop.

The woman finally pulled out of the parking lot. Beads of water still clung to Panda's beard stubble, but the ends of his hair had already started to curl. "Just so you know . . . ," Lucy said, "I'm not mad at you anymore."

He gave her a tired smile. "Give me a couple of hours, and I can fix that."

Tight little buds of warmth began unfurling inside her.

Temple appeared, red-faced and out of breath. "Why are you wet?"

"Long story," he said.

As they drove home, Lucy thought about his patience with the hysterical mother. But most of all, she thought about his gentleness with Sophie. The way he related to kids didn't fit what she thought she knew about him. Even Sophie's bratty little brother . . . When the boy had lost patience with not being the center of attention, Lucy had wanted to throttle him, but Panda had engaged him in a discussion of the lifesaving techniques every "man" should know.

Panda was a chameleon. One minute, a surly, barely articulate biker; the next, a no-nonsense bodyguard to the world's most demanding client; and today, a combination superhero and child psychologist.

He unsettled her. Disarmed her. Confused her. She knew people couldn't be pigeonholed, but she'd never known anyone who resisted a label more than he did.

LUCY FROWNED AT THE MICROWAVE-SHRIVELED green bean draping the clump of chicken on her plate that night. Temple gazed longingly toward the refrigerator, as if she hoped a stream of hot fudge would magically pour out of the water dispenser.

Panda had been quiet all through dinner, but now he pushed his plate away. "I have a surprise for the two of you."

"Tell me it involves pastry," Lucy said. "Or letting me cook real food." Salad was the only contribution she was permitted to make to a meal—all vegetables, no cheese, no olives, no croutons or creamy salad dressing.

"Nope." He kicked back in his chair. "We're going out on the water to watch the fireworks."

"I'll pass," Temple said. "Two kayaks for three people isn't my idea of fun."

"No kayaks." He got up from the table. "I'll meet you both down at the dock. No excuses."

While Temple finished her dinner Lucy grabbed a sweatshirt and went outside to see what Panda was up to. A black-hulled cabin cruiser, maybe twenty-five feet long, was moored at the dock, a boat that hadn't been there last time she'd looked down here. "Where did this come from?" she asked.

Panda tossed a pair of life preservers in a locker on the deck. "I talked to Big Mike a couple of days ago. His guys delivered it while we were at the parade and hid it in the boathouse. I leased it for the rest of the summer."

"What's this?" Temple said, coming down the steps.

After he'd explained, Temple began calculating how many calories waterskiing burned.

Lucy couldn't stand it. "I'll make a deal with you, Temple. If you promise not to use the word *calorie* for the rest of the night, I'll work out with you tomorrow. For a little while," she quickly added.

"Deal," Temple said. "Really, Lucy, you won't believe what a difference rigorous exercise makes in—"

"You also can't talk about exercise, fat grams, cellulite, or any of the rest of that crap," Lucy said. "Basically, you can only talk about sloth."

"I'm all over that." Panda started the engine.

He handled the boat as easily as he handled everything except human relationships. The wind had calmed, the sky had cleared, and the stars were just beginning to come out. He goosed the throttle when they hit open water and headed toward the point that divided them from the town harbor. As they rounded it, they were met with a flotilla of pleasure boats waiting for the show to start, their lights bobbing like fireflies above the water. Some of the boats flew yacht club burgees; others displayed patriotic pennants.

When they were just inside the harbor—close enough to see the show but away from the other boats—Panda turned the bow into the current, set the anchor, and cut the engine. In the sudden silence, laughter and music drifted across the water.

Temple grabbed a cushion and crawled to the bow, leaving them alone.

Chapter Sixteen

THE FIRST OF THE FIREWORKS exploded above them, an umbrella of red and violet. Lucy rested her head against the back of the bench seat that ran across the stern of the boat. Panda did the same, and they watched in surprisingly comfortable silence. "What you did today with little Sophie was pretty great," Lucy eventually said as a shell of stars withered above them.

She felt him shrug. "You're a good swimmer. If I hadn't been there, you'd have gone in."

She liked how certain he sounded. She glanced over at him and watched a trio of silver comets shimmer in his eyes. "The surf was rough. I don't think I could have pulled her out."

"You'd have done what you had to," he said curtly, and then, "People need to watch their kids better."

The sharp edge to his voice seemed unwarranted. "Children move fast," she said. "Hard for any parent to watch them every second." Sailboat spars jingled in the silence between booms, and water slapped the boat's hull. "You understand kids. I guess that surprised me."

He crossed his ankles. Purple palms dropped a trail of stars, and orange peonies unfolded. "You can't be a cop and not deal with kids."

"A lot of gang stuff?"

"Gangs. Neglect. Abuse. You name it."

She'd seen a lot of troubled kids through her work, although she suspected not as many as he had. It was odd. She was so accustomed to regarding Panda as an alien being that she'd never thought about what they might have in common. "Sophie didn't want to let you go."

A silver weeping willow glittered against the dark night. "Cute kid."

Blame it on the night, the fireworks, the emotional aftermath from what could have been a terrible tragedy, because her next words came out unplanned. "You'll make a great dad someday."

A short harsh laugh. "Never going to happen."

"You'll change your mind when you find the right woman." She was sounding too sentimental, and Viper came to her rescue. "You'll know her when you see her. Opposable thumbs. Not too choosy."

"Nope." He smiled. "One of many good things about modern science."

"What do you mean?"

"Vasectomy. The medical profession's gift to guys like me."

A fusillade of explosions split the air. This was so wrong. She'd seen him today with the kids, witnessed what a natural he was. He should never have done something so permanent. "Don't you think you're too young to make that kind of decision?"

"When it comes to kids, I'm a hundred years old."

She'd been involved with child advocacy too long not to know what cops faced, and in the dim light she thought he looked haunted. "I saw too many dead bodies," he said. "Not just teens but infants—five-year-old kids who hadn't lost their baby teeth. Kids blown up, missing limbs." She cocked her head. "I saw parents on the worst day of their lives," he went on, "and I've promised myself I'll never have to go through that. Best decision I ever made. It's hard to do your job when you wake up every night in a cold sweat."

"You saw worst-case scenarios. What about the millions of kids who grow up just fine?"

"What about the ones who don't?"

"Nothing in life comes with a guarantee."

"Wrong. A snip here, a snip there. It's a damn good guarantee."

The sky lit up with the grand finale, the bangs, crackles, and whistles ending their conversation. She respected people who understood themselves well enough to know they wouldn't make good parents, but instinct told her that wasn't the case with Panda.

Her Lucy-ness was getting in her way again. This had nothing to do with her, other than serving as an omen, a harsh reminder that a lot of men felt the way Panda did about fatherhood, and despite what she'd done to Ted, she still wanted to get married and have children. What if she fell in love with a man like Panda who didn't want to be a father? One of so many variables she wouldn't be facing if she hadn't bolted from that Texas church.

Temple scrambled back from the bow to join them, and they headed home. Panda stayed behind on the boat, so Lucy and Temple walked up to the house together. "There's something about fireworks," Temple said as they reached the top of the stairs. "They make me sad. That's weird, right?"

"Everybody's different." Lucy didn't feel all that cheery herself, but the fireworks weren't to blame.

"Fireworks make most people happy, but there's something depressing about watching all that color and beauty die out so fast. Like if we're not careful, that's what will happen to us. One minute you're blazing hot—on top of your game. The next minute you're gone, and nobody remembers your name. Sometimes you have to think, what's the point?"

The porch screen door dragged as Lucy opened it. Light from the fake Tiffany lamp hanging in the kitchen spilled out through the windows. "You're depressed because you're starving. And by the way . . . I think you look terrific."

"We both know that's not true." Temple threw herself down on one of the chaises Lucy had covered with a crimson beach towel. "I'm a pig."

"Stop talking about yourself that way."

"I call it like I see it."

The wind had overturned one of the herb pots, and Lucy went to the baker's rack to right it. The scents of rosemary and lavender always reminded her of the White House East Garden, but tonight she had something else on her mind. "Being vulnerable isn't a sin. You told me you'd met someone, and it didn't work out. That puts a lot of woman in a tailspin."

"You think I found solace for my broken heart at the bottom of a Häagen-Dazs carton?"

"It's been known to happen."

"Except I'm the one who broke it off," she said bitterly.

Lucy picked up the watering can. "That doesn't necessarily make it any less painful. I speak from experience."

Temple was too wrapped up in her own tribulations to acknowledge Lucy's troubles. "Max called me gutless. Can you believe that? Me? Gutless? Max was all—" She made quick air quotes. "'Now, Temple, we can work this out.'" Her hands dropped. "Wrong."

"Are you sure?"

"More than sure. Some problems can't ever be worked out. But Max . . ." She hesitated. "Max is one of those people who not only see the glass as half full, but half full of a mocha caramel Frappuccino. That kind of rosy outlook isn't realistic."

Lucy wondered if it was geography that stood in their way—Max on the East Coast, Temple on the west. Or maybe Max was married. Lucy wouldn't ask. Although she was dying to know.

But the old Lucy's tactfulness only extended so far. She set aside the watering can and crossed to the chaise. "I haven't watched much of *Fat Island* . . ." She'd hardly watched any of it. "But I seem to remember that psychological counseling is a component of the program." She remembered, all right. The show had a female psychologist who wore a red bikini and counseled the contestants from a tiki hut—all caught on camera, of course.

"Dr. Kristi. She's a fruitcake. Major esophageal damage from too many years of sticking her finger down her throat. All shrinks are nuts."

"Life experience is sometimes what makes them good at their job."

"I don't need a shrink, Lucy. Although I do appreciate the way you keep pointing out how nuts I am. What I need is willpower and discipline."

Lucy wasn't playing the good girl on this one. "You also need counseling. Panda can't stand over you forever. If you don't figure out—"

"If I don't figure out what's eating me—blah, blah, blah. God, you sound just like Dr. Kristi."

"Is she still sticking her finger down her throat?"

"No."

"Then maybe you should listen to her."

"Fine." Temple crossed her arms over her chest so aggressively it was a wonder her ribs didn't crack. "You think I need counseling? You're some kind of social worker, aren't you?"

"Not for years. I work as a lobbyist now."

Temple waved away the distinction. "Go ahead and counsel me. Let's hear it. Tell me how I can stop wanting to shove every piece of high-fat, high-sugar, carb-loaded crap down my throat."

"I'm afraid you'll have to figure that out for yourself."

Temple leaped off the chaise and stormed into the house, banging the door behind her like an angry teenager. Lucy sighed. She didn't need this tonight.

A few moments later, Panda came up the steps from the dock. She'd had enough conversation, and she slipped inside.

SHE WAS ASLEEP WHEN HER cell rang. She fumbled for the bedside light, then reached for her phone.

"Hey, Luce. I hope I didn't wake you up." Meg's cheery chirp didn't quite ring true. "So how's it going?"

Lucy shoved the hair out of her eyes and peered at the bedside clock. "It's one in the morning. How do you think it's going?"

"Really? It's only midnight here, but since I have *no idea* where you are, it's a little tough to allow for time differences."

Lucy caught the barb, but Meg didn't have room to criticize. It was true that Lucy hadn't told her best friend where she was—hadn't told her much at all—but Meg was being just as evasive. Still, Lucy knew Meg was worried about her. "It won't be much longer. I'll tell you as soon as I can. Right now everything's a little . . . too confusing to talk about." She rolled to her side. "Is something wrong? You sound worried."

"Something's wrong, all right." Another long pause. "What would you think about—" Meg's pitch rose half an octave as she rushed through her words. "What would you think about me hooking up with Ted?"

Lucy shot up in bed, wide awake now, but not certain she'd heard right. "Hooking up? As in——?"

"Yes."

"With Ted?"

"Your former fiancé."

"I know who he is." Lucy shoved back the sheet and dropped her legs over the side of the bed. "You and Ted are a . . . couple?"

"No! No, not a couple. Never. This is just about sex." Meg was talking too fast. "And forget it. I'm not exactly thinking clearly right now. I should never have called. God, what was I thinking? This is a total betrayal of our friendship. I shouldn't have——"

"No! No, I'm glad you called!" Lucy jumped up from the bed. Her heart was racing, her spirits soaring. "Oh, Meg, this is perfect. Every woman should have Ted Beaudine make love to her."

"I don't know about that, but—— Really? You wouldn't mind?"

"Are you kidding?" Lucy was dizzy, light-headed, giddy at this astonishing gift from the gods. "Do you know how guilty I still feel? If he sleeps with you . . . You're my best friend. He'd be sleeping with my best friend! It'll be like getting absolution from the pope!"

"You don't have to sound so broken up about it," Meg said dryly.

Lucy did a little hop skip over the shorts she'd abandoned on the floor.

And then in the background, she heard it. Ted's voice, deep and steady. "Tell Lucy hello from me."

"I'm not your messenger boy," Meg snapped back.

Lucy swallowed hard. "Is he there right now?"

"That would be a yes," Meg replied.

The old guilt washed over her. "Tell him hello from me then." She sank back on the edge of the bed. "And that I'm sorry."

Meg stopped talking directly into the phone, but Lucy had no trouble hearing her. "She said she's having the time of her life, screwing every man she meets, and dumping you was the best move she ever made."

Lucy jumped up. "I heard that. And he'll know you're lying. He knows things like that."

Ted's response to Meg's fabrication was as clear as a bell. "Liar."

"Go away," Meg snarled at him. "You are totally creeping me out."

Lucy clutched the phone. "Did you just tell Ted Beaudine that he was creeping you out?"

"I might have," Meg said.

Ohmygod! Ohmygod! Ohmygod! Lucy tried to pull herself together. "Wow . . . I sure didn't see this coming."

"See what coming?" Meg sounded annoyed. "What are you talking about?"

"Nothing." Lucy gulped. "Love you. And enjoy!" She hung up, jumped up, pressed the phone to her chest. And danced around the room.

Meg and Ted. Meg and Ted. Meg and Ted.

Of course.

Of course, of course, of course! Ted wasn't a player. He didn't sleep with women he wasn't seriously attracted to. And he was attracted to Meg, Lucy's screwball, screw-up best friend, who wandered the world without a plan and cared nothing about earning anyone's good opinion.

Meg Koranda and Mr. Perfect. Her rough edges and his smooth surfaces. Her impulsiveness and his forethought. Both of them blessed with brains, loyalty, and gigantic hearts. It was a crazy, unpredictable match made in heaven, although from the sound of their conversation, neither of them seemed to realize it. Or at least Meg didn't. With Ted, it was hard to tell.

Lucy had no trouble imagining the battles they were having. Meg blunt-spoken and confrontational; Ted laid-back on the surface, steely underneath. And as she thought about them, the missing pieces of her own relationship with Ted finally fell into place. The only rough edge between them had been Lucy's inability to relax with him, her feeling that she had to be on her best behavior to justify being Ted's partner. Meg wouldn't give a damn about anything like that.

They just might be perfect for each other. If they didn't screw things up. Which, since Meg was involved, seemed highly probable. But whether they worked out or not, one thing was certain. If Meg and Ted were in bed together, Lucy was finally off the hook.

AFTER THAT, SHE WAS TOO worked up to get back to sleep. The house's spotty air-conditioning had left her bedroom uncomfortably warm. She opened the sliders, fetched her flip-flops to protect her bare feet from the splintery deck, and stepped outside.

Threatening clouds tumbled in the sky. She pulled her damp cami away from her breasts. With the wind, the distant flash of lightning, and the dark mystery of the lake for company, she finally felt liberated from her guilt.

A movement caught her eye, a figure—broad of shoulder, narrow of hip, with a distinct long-legged stride—coming around the side of the house. As he passed the picnic table, he paused to look back, but she was standing too deeply in the shadows for him to see her. He crossed the yard, moving more quickly. When he reached the top of the stairs, he paused, looked back again, then headed down to the water.

Maybe he had insomnia, too, but why was he being so furtive? She decided to find out. She stepped off the deck. On her way across the yard, she tripped over the horseshoe stake. It hurt like crazy, but no way was Viper letting a little thing like a stubbed toe hold her back.

Limping slightly, she made it to the steps. She didn't see him below, only the single post light glowing at the end of the dock. It reminded her of *The Great Gatsby* and the fascination English teachers had with that book instead of something most teenagers might actually want to read.

As she descended to the dock, she was careful not to let the slap of her flip-flops betray her, although that seemed unlikely with so much wind. When she reached the bottom, she carefully made her way across the creaky boards toward the dim glow of mustard light oozing from the open end of the weathered boathouse.

The fishy smell of storm-whipped waters joined the odors of old rope, mildew, and gasoline that had seeped into the wood. An opera she didn't recognize was playing softly. As she slipped inside the boathouse, she saw Panda sitting on the bench seat in the stern of the powerboat, his back to her, his bare feet propped on a cooler. He wore a T-shirt and shorts, and his hand was buried inside a giant bag of potato chips. "I'll only share," he said without turning, "if you promise not to talk."

"Like my only pleasure in life is talking to you," she retorted. And then, because she liked the idea of being rude, "Frankly, Panda, you're not intelligent enough to be all that interesting."

He recrossed his ankles on the cooler. "Tell it to my Ph.D. adviser."

"You don't have a Ph.D. adviser," she said as she climbed into the boat.

"That's true. Getting my master's was all my brain could handle."

"Your *master's?* You are so lying." She plopped onto the cushion next to him.

He smiled.

She stared at him. Long and hard. "Tell me you don't really have a master's degree."

His smile turned into fake apology. "Only from Wayne State, not an Ivy." He snapped a potato chip between his teeth, then bent down to flick off the music. "It's one of those night and weekend degrees favored by us working slobs, so it doesn't count in your world."

That *bastard*. She glared at him. "Damn it, Panda. I liked you so much better when you were stupid."

"Look on the bright side," he said as he held out the chip bag. "I'm still no Ted Beaudine."

"None of us are." She reached inside and grabbed a handful. "He and my best friend are hooking up."

"Meg?"

"How do you know M——?" She moaned as the salt from the chip hit her tongue. "Oh my god, these taste so good."

"Meg and I had an entertaining chat at your farce of a rehearsal dinner."

"I'm not surprised. You're totally her type." She stuffed more chips in her mouth.

"Meg's my type, too," he said as a clap of thunder shook the boathouse. "Can't see her with Ted, though."

But Lucy could, and right now that was all that counted. Rain began pummeling the roof. She grabbed more chips and curled her toes around the edge of the cooler next to his feet. "Do you have any other goodies stashed away down here?"

"I might." His eyes were on her bare legs, and he didn't seem all that happy with what he saw. They were tanner than usual, but there was nothing wrong with them, other than a bruise on her shin starting to turn yellow. She also had a small chip in the blue polish on her big toe from tripping over the horseshoe stake. She hadn't worn blue polish since she was a teen. She remembered painting Tracy's baby toes that same color when it was just the two of them.

His gaze moved up her legs to her striped sleep boxers. His frown reminded her of the bra and panties she wasn't wearing underneath. "What are you offering?" he said, his eyes lingering on her thighs with that same expression of displeasure.

"Offering?" She tugged on the boxer's soft cotton leg openings, unwisely as it turned out, because pulling them down showcased a fair amount of stomach. Or maybe she'd done it on purpose to retaliate for his attitude. She no longer knew what she was thinking when it came to Patrick Shade. She dropped her feet to the deck. "How many loaves of bread have I baked for you?"

"The bread covers your rent, not my junk food."

"Says you."

"I guess I could share." His gaze was on the move again, skimming her body until he reached her collarbone, dropping back to her breasts, where the thin fabric barely hid anything. He no longer seemed quite so critical, and as another clap of thunder shook the boathouse, she felt something shift inside her, a treacherous vibration, a risky thrum that had nothing to do with the stormy weather.

His eyes met hers. He nudged off the cooler lid with his bare foot, a gesture that shouldn't have been nearly so enticing. She broke his gaze and looked inside, but instead of seeing an icy nest filled with beer and soda, she saw a treasure chest of chips, pretzels, Doritos, licorice whips, malted milk balls, cheese curls, and a jar of peanut butter. "El Dorado," she whispered.

"Forbidden fruit," he replied, but when she looked up, he was staring at her, not at his stash.

The rickety old boathouse became a secret cave—dimly lit and seductive. A trickle of rain coming through the leaky roof splashed her shoulder. He reached out, dabbed a drop with the tip of his finger, and dragged the moisture into the hollow of her collarbone. Her skin pebbled. "Stop it," she said without any conviction.

He didn't pretend not to know what she was talking about. A raindrop hit her thigh. He saw it but looked away and reached into the cooler. "You're probably not interested in this." He pulled out the peanut butter.

"So wrong." Even she wasn't sure whether she was talking about the peanut butter or something more dangerous.

The boat swayed at its mooring, and a shift in the wind sent a wet blast through the open end of the boathouse. Drips from the leaky roof had begun hitting the deck and, more damaging, the food stash. "Come on." Panda picked up the cooler and carried it to the boat's cabin, ducking as he entered.

Their relationship had changed today, and following him was fraught with peril. She liked thinking of him as the bad guy, but today had altered that. On the other hand, his vasectomy, not to mention that incredible body, made him irresistible.

Viper followed him.

The cabin was small, with only a tiny galley and a V-shaped berth in the bow. Panda set down the cooler and sank into the navy-blue vinyl cushions. He gave her a lazy smile, then opened the peanut butter jar, scooped up a glob with a pretzel rod, and held it out to her.

Two consenting adults . . . One vasectomy . . . An ex-fiancé who, on this very night, was making love to her best friend . . . The stars were in perfect alignment.

Lucy accepted the pretzel and sat on the cushion across from Panda. "I don't even like peanut butter very much."

"It's the deprivation," he said. "It makes you want what's forbidden all that much more." The way he gazed at her across the narrow space—straight into her eyes—made his meaning clear.

She had the perfect smutty prop in her hand, a pretzel stick with a dollop of peanut butter clinging to the tip. Another woman might have made the most of it, but Viper didn't feel like it. She snapped off the end between her teeth. "I'm the only one eating."

"I got a head start." He opened a bag of licorice whips but didn't take any out. He simply gazed at her. Not at her legs or her breasts. Just at her, which felt even more intimate. His voice came to her in a husky vapor. "This isn't a good idea."

"I know."

"I keep trying not to think about how much I want you."

Her skin prickled. "How's that going?"

"Not well."

The cabin was too warm, too close, but she wasn't leaving. Darts of heat zipped through her. She wanted this man with his tarnished eyes, inky hair, and powerful body. But she wouldn't make the first move.

That wasn't a problem for him. Ducking his head, he closed the short distance between them, took what was left of the pretzel from her hand, and put it aside. "You make me crazy," he said.

"Glad to hear it," she replied, "but I really don't want to talk now."

He smiled his outlaw's smile, settled into the cushions, and pulled her up with him into the point of the bow. Only the faintest light penetrated their cave, enough for her to see the brief flash of his teeth before he turned her beneath him and lowered his head to kiss her.

She hadn't wanted his kiss in that ratty Memphis hotel room, and his guilt-filled kiss at the airport had brought only confusion, but this was perfect.

Her lips parted. Their tongues met in a dirty dance of thrust and parry—a delicious overture to sin. His hands were under her cami, hers under his T-shirt. She felt muscle and tendon, bone and sinew. He abandoned her mouth and used his teeth to torture her nipple through the thin cotton. He wedged his bare thigh between hers. She rubbed against it, locked her arms around him.

A crack of lightning hit too close, bringing with it a brief return to sanity. She moved her lips against his shoulder. "We can't do this without a condom."

His breath fell warm across her nipple. "I thought you didn't want to talk."

"Vasectomy or not, you need—"

"All taken care of," he said in a husky rasp.

Did he carry them with him? The implication temporarily distracted her, but then he was kissing her again, and the question slipped away.

The thunder rumbled overhead. The boat rocked at its mooring. They pulled at their clothes, and when they were naked, explored. That night in Memphis had been as much about cutting her ties with Ted as it had been about sex, but this was different. Not an anonymous coupling with a virtual stranger. She knew her lover now, and tonight was inevitable.

Her breasts nested in his hands . . . His hips gripped under her palms . . . Their kiss deepened. He nudged her thighs open, and she didn't consider resisting.

He parted her with his fingers. Unfolded. Searched. Invaded textures moist and soft.

She moaned. Let him play. And when she could stand it no longer, she became the aggressor, rolling to her side, using cheek, hands, and lips to savor the feel and strength of him.

When he could tolerate no more, he twisted her beneath him again. Fumbled with something. Mounted. He hooked his hands behind her knees, separating them, raising them. His body pressed to hers. The hard core of him, full and thick.

Smutty little words hoarsely uttered.

Soft, rough commands.

And he was inside her.

Outside, the storm howled. Inside, it raged just as fiercely. Finally it erupted.

HER SWEETNESS WAS TOO MUCH for him. As she dozed in the dim light, he studied the fall of her dark lashes on her pale skin, made even paler by that black hair. He traced the curve of her cheek with his knuckle. Beneath all that tough talk, she was confused and vulnerable.

A warning siren fired in his brain. An explosion. The grit of sand, taste of whiskey, bite of memory. He shoved the darkness away.

She opened her eyes and gazed into his. "That was nice."

Too sweet. Too good.

"Nice?" He dropped his arm over the side of the cushions and touched the bag of candy. One of the licorice sticks had fallen out. He picked it up and nudged her ear with his lips. "Get ready to retract that."

"Why?"

He dangled the licorice in front of her. "You keep forgetting that I have a mean streak."

She stirred beneath him, those green-flecked eyes alive with interest. "I guess I'm in trouble now."

"Big-time."

He nipped her bottom lip with his own, and then he whipped her with the licorice stick. Flicks at her nipples. The soft skin of her stomach. Her open thighs. Between.

"Evil," she moaned when he stopped. "Do it some more."

And so he did until she snatched the licorice away and returned the pleasure. Except he'd unleashed her secret dominatrix, and she wasn't nearly as careful as he'd been. When he told her he'd had enough, she told him to beg, and what could he do after that but punish her?

He bent her over the cushions, gave her rear a soft smack, and exacted retribution. Or tried to. Because the whole episode was getting foggy in terms of who was doing the punishing and who was being punished.

Outside the boathouse, the storm began to calm, but inside, it had just begun.

Chapter Seventeen

LUCY SNIFFED LIKE A DISAPPROVING aunt. "That was way too perverted for me."

"I could tell." Panda tried to remember the last time he'd lost himself like this with a woman. They were wedged in the stuffy berth, their bodies pressed together, their skin sticking to the vinyl cushions, and even though he could feel her, it wasn't enough. He extracted his arm, rolled to his elbow, and flipped on one of the small, battery-powered lights mounted in the bow.

She lay on her side, the naked line of her shoulder, waist, and hip forming a golden curve, her dragon tattoo alien on the smooth column of her neck. Her small nose, mercifully free of its nostril ring, wrinkled in disdain. "Don't ever do that again."

He touched her bottom lip, swollen from his kisses. "Midnight tomorrow?"

"If I don't have anything better to do."

"I hate it when a woman plays hard to get."

She traced a vein that ran down his arm. "Really I just want your food stash. If I have to put out to get to your Cheetos, so what?"

"A pragmatist."

"Stop using big words. It depresses me." She bent her arm beneath her head, revealing the rosy side of her breast where his beard had abraded her skin. He wouldn't hurt her for anything, but his dark side felt a primitive satisfaction in seeing the mark he'd left on her.

Her question shocked him out of his lethargy. "Where did the condoms come from?"

He should have known she'd latch onto that. "My pocket. You want some more chips?"

"You carry condoms around?"

"Not always. Sometimes. Who needs an STD, right?"

She pulled on one of her ratty pink dreadlocks. "So, you carry them in case you and Temple decide to add a little variety to your workouts?"

He hit her full force with his badass sneer, hoping to shut her up. "That's right."

"Bull. The two of you would eat nails before you'd screw each other."

"Nice talk."

She pinned him with those shrewd eyes. "You didn't know I was coming down here tonight, yet you were ready for action. That leads me to believe that you actually do carry those things around."

"That's what I said, isn't it?"

"Yes, but you didn't say why."

Shit. He gave up. "Because you drive me out of my mind, that's why. I never know what the hell you're going to do next. Or what I'm going to do. Now shut up about it."

She smiled, lifted her arm, and tugged on a couple of his pain-in-the-ass curls, her expression tender enough to bring him back to cold reality. He was an ex-cop. She was the president's daughter. He was scrap metal. She was pure gold. Beyond all that, he had a dead zone a mile wide inside him, while she bubbled with life. "Lucy . . ."

"Oh lord . . ." She rolled her eyes and flopped to her back. "Here we go. The speech." She deepened her voice in exaggerated imitation of him. "Before this goes any further, Lucy, I need to make sure you don't get the wrong idea. I'm a cowboy, wild and free. No little filly can ever tame a man like me." She sneered. "As if I'd want to."

"That's not what I was going to say." It was exactly what he'd intended to say—not so sarcastically, but she had the general idea.

"Let's get this straight, Patrick." The tip of her finger poked his bicep. "I may be screwed up about my future right now, but I know it includes kids. That rules you out, so all the complications your paranoia is conjuring up are a waste of your limited brain power. You're for entertainment, Mr. Shade. The missing ingredient in my lost summer. And here's what you need to understand." She flicked his chest. "When you cease to pleasure me, I'll find somebody who can. Clear?"

"Pleasure you?"

"I like the sound of it." Her eyes grew serious. "This is about sex. Nothing else. You'd better be clear about that, or this stops right now."

"Me?!" It was exactly what he wanted to hear—what he needed her to know—but he didn't like her attitude. What had happened to the well-bred runaway bride he'd picked up? "When it comes to you, nothing can just be about sex," he said.

"That's what you think. I want sex. The dirtier, the better." Her eyes landed on his crotch. "Got any more licorice?"

He should have flipped her to her back right then and given it to her, but her flippancy irritated him. "I'm tired," he heard himself say, barely believing those words had come out of his mouth.

"Figures," she retorted. "You're a lot older than me."

"Not a lot." He sounded like a petulant asshole, but before he could decide what he wanted to do about that, she was sliding out of the berth, her bare skin squeaking against the vinyl.

"Thirty-six and going downhill," she chirped. "That's okay. I've changed my mind."

He didn't want her to change her mind, but she was already humming a happy little tune and pulling on what passed for her clothes. First, she tugged that skimpy white top over her head. The hem caught on one rosy nipple, hung there for a moment, then sprang free. Next, she took way too much time wiggling into the bottoms. When she reached the door of the cabin, she turned back to him.

"Get some rest, lover boy. I have big plans for you. Let's see if you're man enough to keep up."

He smiled as she disappeared—happy, if only for the moment.

LUCY SKIPPED UP THE STEPS, so full of herself she could hardly stand it. The rain had cleared, and a sliver of moonlight tried to cut through the clouds. She'd never talked to a man like she'd talked to Panda. She'd laid out her terms, said exactly what she wanted to, and hadn't cared a bit how he felt about it.

She dashed across the lawn, this time giving the horseshoe stake a wide berth. She couldn't imagine Ted ever doing to her what Panda had done. Although she could imagine him doing it to Meg. Not that she wanted to. She grimaced and shook off the image.

She and Panda . . . Two mismatched people . . . One vasectomy . . . This was exactly what she wanted from her lost summer. A chance to be really bad.

As she stepped up on the deck, she thought about how people made bucket lists—everything they wanted to accomplish before they died. It occurred to her that she was working her way through a kind of reverse bucket list, doing things she would already have gotten out of her system if she'd been part of another family. Crazy hair, unsuitable clothes, tattoos. She'd dumped the perfect boyfriend, dropped out, and now she'd taken an unacceptable lover. She'd thought she didn't believe in meaningless hookups, but had she only convinced herself of that because meaningless hookups were unrealistic for the president's daughter? No wild monkey sex for Lucy Jorik.

Until now.

Could this be the key? What if doing all the things she'd missed was precisely what she needed before she could move on with the next part of her life?

She locked the sliding doors behind her, changed into dry clothes, and climbed into bed, but she was too worked up to sleep. A reverse bucket list . . .

She got out of bed and grabbed her yellow pad. This time she had no trouble finding the right words, and before she was done, she had a perfect list. This was exactly what she needed.

She flipped off the light and smiled to herself. Then she thought of the licorice whip and shivered. She turned into the pillow, got out of bed again, and unlocked the sliders.

No doubt about it. She'd gone bad. And it felt so good.

"READING TIME," BREE SAID, OPENING the door to the cottage's small front porch just as she'd been doing for the past two weeks, ever since she'd made up her mind about this.

"It's summer," Toby protested. "I'm not supposed to read books in the summer." But even as he complained, he got off the living room carpet and followed her outside.

The porch was only big enough for a pair of ancient brown wicker chairs and a small wooden table. She'd set up a lamp from her bedroom so she could read after Toby went to bed, but she was so tired by the end of the day that she generally dozed off first. She had better luck keeping up with her new adult reading list between breaks from molding candles, painting note cards, or experimenting with a new beeswax furniture polish.

As she opened the book they'd been reading, she asked herself once again why she was putting herself through all this. It wasn't as if she didn't have enough to worry about. It was mid-July. She wouldn't be able to begin harvesting this year's honey until early August, if she was lucky, and as always, she was frantic about money. She'd been trying to create new products, but that took a financial investment for materials, and how many of her products would actually sell? At least she'd begun to see tiny cracks in Toby's dislike of her, the same cracks that had formed in her own resentment toward him.

The wicker armchair creaked as he pulled his grubby bare feet up on the edge of the cushion. "I can read good. You don't have to read to me like I'm a kid."

"I like reading aloud," she said. "That way, I can learn at the same time as you."

"I already know all this stuff."

That was total crap. He knew even less than she did, although she was learning more every day.

With the help of the island librarian, she'd located a few books on transracial child rearing only to discover they focused primarily on whether or not it was right for white families to adopt black children. Hardly helpful. Most of the rest of what she'd been able to discover didn't go much further than an explanation of hair care, something Toby was handling just fine for himself. Not one of them answered her most fundamental question—how was a pale white woman like herself supposed to instill a sense of racial pride and identity in this golden-brown child?

She was working on instinct.

He slung one leg over the chair arm, waiting for her to begin. So far, he'd finished short, kid-friendly biographies of Frederick Douglass, Booker T. Washington, and Martin Luther King, along with the story of the Negro Baseball League. He'd rebelled when she'd found a book about the abolitionist Sojourner Truth, so she'd begun reading it aloud to herself. Within a few pages, he'd forgotten his prejudice against "books about girls," and when she'd reached the end of the first chapter, he'd pestered her to keep going.

Even though she was tired from a day that had begun too early, she read for nearly an hour. When she finally closed the book, Toby started picking at his big toe. "Did you get another movie for us to watch this weekend?"

"*When We Were Kings*." She made a face. "It's about boxing, a famous match between Muhammad Ali and George Foreman."

He forgot about his toe as his face lit up. "Really?"

"I know. Disgusting. Let's watch *The Princess Diaries* instead."

"No way!"

He grinned at her—a real grin—and one more loop in the snarl of negative feelings that resided inside her loosened its grip. Sometimes—not often, but sometimes—he smiled at her the same way he did at Lucy.

"Don't take any crap from him," Lucy had advised. "At the same time, look for chances to touch him. He'll pull away. Do it, anyway."

Bree had tried resting her hand on his shoulder when he was sitting at the kitchen table, but it felt forced, and as Lucy had predicted, he wiggled away, so she'd stopped. She wasn't giving up the rest, however. An uncharacteristic stubbornness had taken hold of her. He was going to learn about the heritage he'd received from his father whether he wanted to or not.

He dropped his feet to the floor and scratched his ankle with his toe. "You don't have to watch the movie with me. You can go work on your painting or something."

Right now, that "something" included waiting for a dozen nonreturnable glass bumblebee Christmas ornaments to arrive. Every time she thought about the Internet order she'd placed over the library computer she felt sick. She was getting more customers every day, but who knew if any of them would want to buy Christmas ornaments in the summer?

"We always watch movies together," she said.

"Yeah, I guess you should probably watch. Being white and everything, you've got a lot to learn."

She did her best to imitate Lucy's sarcastic looks. "Like you know so much, Mr. Brown Man."

He liked being called a man, and he grinned. She smiled back at him, and he kept smiling until he realized what he was doing and exchanged the smile for a scowl. "Me and Big Mike are going horseback riding tomorrow."

She still couldn't believe Mike had befriended Toby out of the goodness of his heart. On the other hand, he'd kept his word, and the only times he'd spoken to her since they'd all gone to church two weeks earlier had been during a few brief telephone exchanges when he'd made arrangements to pick Toby up.

Toby scowled at her. "If you weren't so mean to him, he'd let you go with us."

"I can't get away from the farm stand."

"You could get away if you wanted to. Lucy would watch it for you."

Toby had been calling Lucy by her real name ever since he'd overheard Bree call her that, but since daughters of past presidents weren't on his twelve-year-old radar screen, he'd only commented that he'd known all along Viper couldn't be her real name.

Bree's growing friendship with Lucy meant even more to her than the help Lucy offered. She watched the farm stand so Bree could have a break. Together, they'd figured out how to reattach the big wooden doors on the storage shed that jutted off the back of the farm stand. Now she could lock up at night instead of having to haul her goods back and forth from the house. Bree also appreciated Lucy's lack of judgment as she watched Bree try to deal with Toby.

Toby slouched farther into the wicker chair. "Mike told me to see if it was okay for him to take me to church again this week, but I don't want to go. Church is boring."

Bree had loved the service at the Episcopal church and yearned to go back, but she didn't want to run into Mike. She toyed with the cover of the Sojourner Truth book. "Maybe we need to find a church that's not boring."

"All church is boring."

"You don't know that for sure. I've been thinking we should try a new church."

"I don't want to try a new church. I'll go to the old one with Big Mike."

"Not this week." Bree had been dubious when Lucy introduced the idea, but now she made up her mind. "On Sunday, we're going to Heart of Charity."

His eyes widened in outrage. "We can't do that. That's the black people's church!"

So much for all the books they'd been reading. And, really, what was the point? If claiming his father's heritage wasn't important to Toby, why should it matter to her?

Because it did.

❧

Lucy smelled of the almond oil she'd used to help Bree make hand cream. It masked the scent of the fresh loaf of bread in the sack dangling from her handlebars. She visited the cottage daily to spell Bree at the farm stand and take another stab at perfecting honey-based caramels. Once she was satisfied with the results, she'd try dipping them in chocolate and topping them with sea salt. So far, her efforts weren't going well, but she had hopes. She also baked bread in Bree's kitchen, using the excuse that the stove at the house wouldn't keep true temperature. She was willing to trust Bree with her own secrets, but Temple's weren't hers to share.

What she hadn't been doing was writing. She couldn't seem to figure out where to start. Nealy was one of the most fascinating women in the world, but Lucy ended up throwing out whatever she wrote about her after a few sentences. Her father wanted a personal account, not a Wikipedia entry. Something was very wrong, but she had no idea what.

When she wasn't trying to write or helping out at the farm stand, she was thinking about her reverse bucket list. Just that morning she'd slept late, and before she lost her nerve, she'd prank-called two people. *"This is a recording. I'm confirming your order for one hundred pounds of fresh manure. If you want it dumped anyplace except your driveway, call us back immediately. Our number is—"* And she'd hung up.

Totally juvenile. Moderately satisfying. Especially since she'd used Panda's phone to make the calls in case they got traced.

As she pulled up to the house, she saw Temple pass by the upstairs windows. Last week Toby had appeared unannounced and seen Temple running up and down the steps to the dock carrying ten-pound weights. Temple was predictably upset—first because she'd been spotted and second because Toby had no idea who she was.

"He's twelve," Lucy had told her.

"That's the way it starts out. First a kid doesn't know your name. The next thing you know, it's a forty-year-old soccer mom, and your career is over."

"You're a lunatic," Viper told her. "A fruitcake for the ages." And then, more kindly, "You've already lost at least fifteen pounds, and—"

"Barely fourteen."

"—and despite what you want to believe, you look fantastic." She ignored Temple's derisive snort. "You're doing what you came here to do, and you should be on top of the world. Instead, you're meaner than ever. How do you expect to handle real food once you don't have Panda policing you?"

"Things'll be different. I'll handle it." She'd stormed off.

Lucy knew a lot of women ate their way through breakups, and although Temple hardly ever mentioned Max, their split had to be at the root of her troubles.

Panda's car was just turning into the drive. He'd begun leaving Temple alone for short periods of time, generally going for a run or taking the kayak out. More recently, he'd made two brief trips into town. She climbed off her bike and watched him step from the car.

The muscles underneath his tight-fitting gray T-shirt were out of control, and although his abs were temporarily covered up, she happened to know they were extraordinary. She, on the other hand, had gained back another five pounds. After a lifetime of never thinking about her weight, she'd been brought low by living in a house full of diet food. Once she was around the real stuff, such as her failed honey caramels, she lost control.

Her weight gain, however, hadn't affected her current choice of outfit, a trashy blue and black tie-dyed bra top that showed more boob-age than a bathing suit and shorts that didn't even start until the top of her hip bones. She might as well show them off while they were still visible.

As Panda sauntered toward her, he took in her outfit, from trashy top to platform flip-flops. He cocked his head toward the garage. "Let's go."

"Go?" She casually unclipped her nose ring and slipped it in her pocket.

"You know the routine."

"That doesn't mean I have to go along with it."

"I have a job to do."

She tilted her head and tugged on one of her dreads. "Screw your job."

"Big mistake." He caught her arm and forcibly steered her through the shadows at the side of the house toward the garage. When they reached the warped side door, he kicked it open. "Inside."

"I don't want to go inside. I want—"

"I don't care what you want." He slammed the door behind them.

Murky rays of afternoon light struggled to ooze through a cobweb-draped window. The cluttered garage held old furniture, boxes, broken beach chairs, and a leaky canoe. The air smelled of dust and motor oil, while Panda smelled of blueberries and heat. He turned her and, settling his hand between her shoulders, pressed her to the wall. "Spread those legs."

"You're scaring me."

"Good."

"I have no contraband on me. I swear."

He gave her his nastiest, most intimidating snarl. "Then you don't have anything to worry about."

"I— I guess not." She set her palms against the rough boards but kept her legs together.

He kicked them apart. "Don't play ignorant. You know the drill." His breath ruffled the hair brushing her ears, and his voice was a soft rasp. "I don't like it any better than you."

Not much, you don't.

Her eyes drifted shut as he slid his hands along her sides, from her armpits to her thighs. "I told you," she said. "I'm clean."

"Why don't I believe you?" He reached around her, his hands stopping just under her collarbone. And then he lowered his palms and cupped her breasts.

She looked at him over her shoulder. "Don't say what you said last time."

"What was that?" He nuzzled her ear.

"You said, 'There's nothing here.'"

He smiled, slipped his thumbs inside her bra cups, and found her nipples. "I was so wrong."

By the time he stopped tormenting her breasts and moved to new territory, her knees were weak and her skin hot. He made a play of running his hands over her hips and thighs before he found his prime target. "I think I feel something."

He wasn't the only one. "This is illegal," she said, wiggling her hips.

"Resisting arrest." His hands tugged at the zipper on her shorts. "Now I'll have to do a body cavity search."

"Oh, no. Not that." She couldn't have sounded less convincing.

"You brought it on yourself." He kneed her legs together and tugged off her tight shorts along with her panties.

"I try to be a good person, but it's hard."

"You have no idea." He pressed against her to make his point.

It was amazing how many places he found to explore. Enough for her to offer a weak protest. "A candy bar would never fit *there*."

"Always a first time," he said hoarsely, his breath coming as fast as her own.

"Police brutality," she managed as he fumbled with the front of his shorts.

"This will only hurt for a minute."

It wouldn't hurt at all. As for the "minute . . ." Not likely. Panda had enormous staying power.

"Brace yourself." He tilted her hips.

"Wait . . ."

"Too late." He took her from behind.

His groan drowned out her gasp. He pressed his lips to the nape of her neck. She pushed against him as he braced her body in his big hands. Surrounded by the dust and debris of other people's lives, they played their game, their bodies locked as they used each other, gave, used again. It was primitive sex. Raw and raunchy. Bad-girl sex. Exactly the way she wanted it.

"DON'T LOOK AT MY STOMACH," she said as she pulled her panties back on.

He brushed her cheek with his finger. "Because?"

"It's round."

"Ah."

"You don't have to say it like that." She shoved her legs in her shorts, sucked in her stomach, and zipped them. She'd started the whole strip-search thing when she'd dragged him into the garage after he'd made a quick trip into town. She'd told him she'd gotten a tip that he was trying to smuggle Slim Jims. He said there was nothing slim about his Jim. She'd backed him against the wall and said that was for her to decide. Eventually she had to concede he was right.

"It's your fault I'm gaining weight," she said. "Having nothing but diet fucking food in the house makes me crazy."

His eyebrow gave a gratifying lift, but he didn't comment on her obscenity. "What about all that crap I feed you every night in the boat?"

"Exactly," she said. "If I had decent food, I wouldn't be gorging myself on your junk food stash."

"You're right. It is my fault. I promise. No more chips. No more licorice whips. I'm cleaning up my act."

"Don't you dare."

He laughed and pulled her into his arms, as if he wanted to kiss her. But they only kissed when they were in bed—deep tongue kisses that mimicked what was happening with their bodies. Sex with Panda was like being in a porno movie but without a third party involved. He let her go and wandered over to inspect a pile of junk. His restlessness had returned. Unlike herself, the island's enforced confinement was chafing at him. He wanted action.

She slipped back into her platform flip-flops as he studied a mirror framed in broken seashells and asked, "Didn't this used to be in the downstairs bathroom?"

"No." She loved lying. It was a whole new experience.

"Bull. This was there yesterday."

"Really, Panda, you have lousy powers of observation for a cop."

"Hell I do. Stop rearranging my house. And stop messing with my pig."

"You didn't like the eye patch? I think it's—" She broke off as she saw Panda pick up a folded piece of yellow notepad paper from the grubby garage floor. She hurried toward him, hand extended. "Must have fallen out of my pocket when you ripped my shorts off."

"I didn't rip— What the hell is this?" Like the suspicious person he was, he'd unfolded the paper and started to read.

"Give that to me!" She tried to grab it from him, but he held it out of reach and read over her head.

" 'Reverse bucket list'?"

"That's private."

"I won't tell a soul." He scanned the page and grinned. "Frankly, I'd be embarrassed to."

When he finally lowered the paper it was too late. He'd read everything.

> *REVERSE BUCKET LIST*
> *Run away from home**
> *Dress like a skank**
> *Sleep around*
> *Use f-word whenever possible**
> *Get drunk in public*
> *Make out in public*
> *Smoke a joint*
> *Pick a fight**
> *Prank call**
> *Go to bed without taking off makeup**
> *Swim naked*
> *Sleep late**
> *Scratch, burp, etc.**

"Go to bed without taking your makeup off." He blew a long whistle. "That's living in the danger zone."

"Do you have any idea what kind of damage that does to your skin?"

"Any time now, I'm sure you'll work up the nerve." He jabbed the paper with his finger. "What do all these asterisks mean?"

Good Lucy would have tried to change the subject, but Viper didn't give a damn what he thought. "The asterisks mark things I'd done by the time I was fourteen but sadly abandoned. I intend to rectify that, and if you think it's stupid, that's your problem."

The corners of his mouth twitched. "Stupid? Make prank calls? Now why would I think prank-calling is stupid?"

"I probably won't do that one," she said innocently.

He took in her tie-dyed bra top. "You've got 'dress like a skank' under control. Not complaining, mind you."

"Thanks. I had to order a few things off the Internet, but it's working out for me."

"Definitely." He snapped his fingers at the paper. "Smoking pot is illegal."

"I appreciate your concern, Officer, but I'm sure that didn't stop you from doing it."

He scanned further down. "You never swam naked?"

"Sue me."

"You'll let me know, won't you, when you're ready to try?"

"If I fucking remember."

"If you're going to use the word, at least use it at the right time. You sound ridiculous." He frowned. "'Make out in public'? Not with me you won't."

"S'okay. I'll find somebody else."

"Like fucking hell," he growled. "And you can mark off 'sleep around,' since you're doing that with me."

"No way. 'Around' implies more than one partner."

"Already forget about Ted?"

"Doesn't count. He proposed."

Panda looked like he had something to say about that, but didn't. Instead he pointed to a doodle she'd made in the margin. "What's that?"

Damn. She slapped on her new sneer. "Hello Kitty."

He grinned. "Badass."

THE BASIL PLANT ON THE baker's rack was getting a little droopy. She hopped up from the chaise to water it, pulled some dead leaves off the geranium, and then resettled. She wiggled her pen between her fingers and started to write.

> *My mother's dedication to children's causes had its roots in her teenage years when she visited sick children in hospitals and refugee camps . . .*

Something Lucy's grandfather was writing about in detail and wouldn't appreciate Lucy duplicating.

She tore up the page, pulled her reverse bucket list from her pocket, and jotted down a new item.

> *Blow off homework.*

Then she added an asterisk.

BREE HAD NEVER FELT MORE out of place. It was fine for African-Americans to attend white churches—it gave white congregations a pleasant feeling of inclusiveness—but being the only white person in the island's sole black church made her uncomfortable. She'd never enjoyed standing out. She liked to blend. But as the usher led them down the center aisle of the Heart of Charity Missionary Church, she didn't see another face as pale as her own.

The usher handed them bulletins and gestured toward a pew in the second row. So much for her plans to sit in the back.

After they were seated, her discomfort grew. Was this how it felt to be a black person going solo into the white world? Or maybe her own insecurity was at play, and all her reading had made her more racially conscious than she needed to be.

Heart of Charity Missionary was the second oldest church on the island, a squat, red brick building that would never win points for style, although the airy sanctuary looked as though it had been recently remodeled. The walls were ivory, the high ceiling paneled in blond wood. A purple cloth covered the altar, and three silver crosses hung on the front wall. The congregation was small, and the air smelled of perfume, aftershave, and stargazer lilies.

The people sitting nearby smiled in welcome. The men wore suits, the older women hats, and the younger women bright summer dresses. After the opening hymn, a woman she assumed was the minister, but who turned out to be a deacon, greeted the congregation and announced upcoming events. Bree felt herself flush as the woman looked at her. "We have some visitors today. Would you introduce yourselves?"

Bree hadn't been prepared for this, and before she found her voice, she heard Toby speak up. "I'm Toby Wheeler," he said. "And this is Bree."

"Welcome, Toby and Bree," the woman said. "God has blessed us bringing you to join us today."

"Whatever," Toby muttered under his breath as the congregation delivered a chorus of "amens." But unlike her cynical ward, Bree felt herself begin to relax.

The service began in earnest. She was used to cool, cerebral religion, but this was hot religion, loud in supplication and praise. Afterward, she lost count of the number of people who came up to greet her, and not one of them asked what a paleface like herself was doing in their church. A woman talked to Toby about their Sunday school program, and the minister, a man Bree recognized from the gift shop in town, said he hoped they'd come back.

"What do you think?" she asked Toby as they headed back to her used Chevy Cobalt.

"It was okay." He pulled his shirttail out of his pants. "But my friends are at Big Mike's church."

The only friends he talked about were a set of twins who weren't on the island now. Myra hadn't done him a service by keeping him so isolated. "Maybe you could make some new friends here," she said.

"I don't want to." He jerked open the car door. "I'm calling Big Mike and telling him I'm going to church with him next week."

She waited for the familiar weight of defeat to claim her. But it didn't happen. Instead she grabbed the car door before he could slam it shut and leaned down. "I'm the boss, I like this church, and we're coming back next week."

"That's not fair!"

He tried to wrestle the door away from her, but she held on, and in the same tone she'd heard Lucy use, she staked her ground. "Neither is life. Get used to it."

"ALL SHE CAN THINK ABOUT is black, black, black," Toby complained to Lucy, those thickly lashed golden eyes flashing in outrage. "Like that's all I am. This black kid. Not even me. She's prejudiced. She's a ray-shist."

"Racist," Bree called out from behind the counter where she was nailing a new set of shelves in place after moving her precious bumblebee Christmas ornaments to safety. They'd been such a success that she'd placed a second order.

"A racist," he repeated. "Just like Ames in *Roots*."

"The sadistic overseer." Bree popped up long enough to explain.

"Right." Lucy smiled. Bree had been watching the old miniseries with Toby this week, and it was hard to say which of them was more caught up in it. "Kids need to know about their heritage," Lucy said.

"Being African American is part of your heritage just like it is my brother Andre's."

"But what about the white part?" Toby countered. "What about that?"

Bree's head reappeared. "I told you. Your grandmother's people were Vermont farmers."

"Then why don't we study Vermont farmers?" he retorted. "Why is one part of me more important than the other?"

Bree held her ground. "Not more important. But significant." She ducked behind the counter again.

Despite their squabbling, Lucy detected a change in their relationship. They looked each other in the eye and talked more frequently, even though their conversation was often adversarial. She'd also noticed changes in Bree. She stood straighter, smoked less, and spoke with more confidence. It was as if the therapeutic powers of her honey were giving her strength.

So far that day, Lucy had tried to convince Temple to stop exercising five hours a day and consider Lucy's "Good Enough" approach, but not surprisingly, Temple wasn't buying it. Lucy had more success with the bread she'd baked in Bree's kitchen. Now she was helping Bree finish painting four old Adirondack chairs in Easter egg colors of periwinkle, light blue, peach, and nursery yellow. They would offer a comfortable place to relax in the shade of the old oak that sheltered the farm stand. Bree also hoped their cheerful colors would attract the attention of drivers passing by.

Maybe the chairs were working because she heard a car stop behind her. She turned and saw a dark gray SUV with Illinois plates. Her heart gave a little leap. As far as she knew, this was the first time Panda had stopped here on any of the sorties he'd made into town since he'd loosened the reins on Temple. Now he got out and ambled toward her.

"So this is where you've been spending your time." He nodded at Toby. "Hey, Toby. Lucy make any more bread today?"

Toby had begun to feel at ease with Panda. Last week they'd even gone out on the kayaks together. "Whole wheat. But it's still good."

"I know. I like the heels."

"Me, too."

"Done." With one final slam of the hammer, Bree rose from behind the counter. "Oh, sorry," she said as she spotted Panda. "I was making so much noise I didn't hear a car. Can I help you?"

Lucy stepped forward. "Bree, this is Patrick Shade, aka Panda. Panda, Bree West."

"West?" The smile on Panda's face faded. He grew unnaturally still. He gave a brusque nod and, without another word, got in his car and drove off.

Chapter Eighteen

✦

THE SUV DISAPPEARED FROM SIGHT. Bree quickly turned back to the shelves that lined the farm stand and began rehanging the bumblebee Christmas ornaments on the tree branch display she'd erected above her pots of lip balm, beeswax candles, and flower-shaped soaps. She hung them crookedly, not trying to balance the arrangement.

As Toby went off to get a drink, Lucy tried to figure out what had just happened. "Do you and Panda know each other?"

The branch display began to tilt precariously. Bree grabbed two of the ornaments and moved them. "I've never met him."

"But you know him?"

Bree shifted another ornament. "No."

Lucy didn't believe her. "You'd think by now you could trust me a little."

Bree moved the soap basket a few inches to the left. Her shoulders lifted as she took a deep breath. "I used to live in his house."

Lucy was stunned. "The Remington place?"

Bree fumbled in her pocket for her cigarettes. "Sabrina Remington West. My full name."

"Why didn't you ever mention this?"

Bree gazed toward the trees in the general direction of her old house. She was quiet for so long that Lucy didn't think she was going to answer. Finally she said, "I don't like talking about it or even thinking about it, which is crazy, because I think about it all the time."

"Why's that?"

Bree shoved her hands deeper into the pockets. "I have a lot of memories attached to the house. Complicated ones."

Lucy understood complicated memories.

"I spent every summer there when I was growing up," Bree said. "I stopped coming when I was around eighteen, but the rest of my family used it for years until my father died and Mother went into a nursing home. Finally it got too expensive to maintain, so my brothers put it on the market."

"And Panda bought it."

She nodded. "I knew about him, but we'd never met. It was a shock finally seeing him." She examined her broken fingernails. "It's hard to think of someone else living there." She regarded Lucy apologetically. "I should have told you, but I'm not used to confiding in people."

"You didn't really owe me an explanation."

"Not true. Your friendship has meant more to me than you can ever imagine." Once again, she started patting her pockets. "Damn it, where are my cigarettes?"

"You left them at the cottage, remember? You're trying to stop."

"Shit." She sagged into the pale yellow Adirondack chair and said, almost defiantly, "I knew Scott was having affairs."

It took Lucy a moment to adjust to the change of subject. "Your husband?"

"In name only." Her mouth twisted bitterly. "I was flattered when he fell in love with me, but we'd been married for barely two years before he started screwing around. I found out right away."

"That must have hurt."

"It hurt all right, but I made excuses for him. He had an advanced degree. I'd left college after my freshman year to marry him, so I decided I wasn't smart enough to hold his interest. But it kept happening and, believe me, all of those other women weren't smart."

"What did he say when you confronted him?"

She set an elbow on the chair and curled her hand tightly around the end of the arm. "I didn't. I pretended not to know." Her voice was full of pain. "Can you imagine? How gutless is that?"

"You must have had a reason."

"Sure. I didn't want to give up my life." She stared blindly toward the road. "I'm one of those women the feminist movement passed by. I had no career ambitions. I wanted what the women I saw around me had while I was growing up. A husband, children—good luck with that. Scott refused to even talk about kids." She rose from the chair. "I wanted a beautiful house. Never having to worry about money. Knowing exactly where I fit. I wanted that security so much I was willing to sell my self-respect to get it. Even at the end . . . A year ago . . ." She stopped, hugged herself, her expression bleak. "I wasn't the one who walked out. He walked out on me. I was still hanging on, the faithful doormat wife."

Lucy's heart filled with pity. "Bree . . ."

Bree refused to look at her. "What kind of woman lets herself get treated that way? Where was my pride? My backbone?"

"Maybe you're finding it now."

But Bree was too caught up in self-loathing to accept comfort. "When I look in the mirror, all I feel is disgust."

"Clean off your mirror and take another look. I see an amazing woman who's building a good business and also taking responsibility for a kid who's not exactly easy."

"Some business. A broken-down farm stand in the middle of nowhere."

"It's not broken-down. Look around. This is the Taj Mahal of farm stands. The honey is the best I've ever tasted, new customers are stopping all the time, you keep adding more products, and you're making a profit."

"Which I'm plowing right back into new jars and Christmas ornaments, not to mention soap molds and a few gallons of cocoa butter for the lotions. What happens when Labor Day comes and the tourists leave? What happens when winter's here and Toby stages a full-out teenage rebellion?"

Lucy had no easy answer for that. "You've figured everything else out. I'm betting you'll figure that out, too."

Lucy could see that Bree wasn't buying it, and her own need to make other people feel better asserted itself. "What if Scott showed up today and said he'd made a mistake? What if he said he wanted you back, and he'd never screw around on you again? What would you do?"

Bree thought it over. "If Scott showed up?" she said slowly.

"Just supposing."

"If Scott showed up . . ." Her jaw set. "I'd tell him to go screw himself."

Lucy grinned. "Exactly what I thought."

LUCY WAITED UNTIL PANDA FINISHED his afternoon workout before she went upstairs to find him. Bree's story explained her reaction to meeting him, but not his to seeing her. He stood in the middle of the small, overcrowded bedroom he'd taken for himself. As he pulled his damp

T-shirt over his head, the sight of that sweaty, too-ripped chest distracted her. But only momentarily. "Why were you so rude to Bree?"

He sat on the side of the bed to take off his sneakers. "I don't know what you're talking about."

"Sure you do." One of his sneakers hit the floor. "When I introduced Bree, you threw yourself in your car and raced off like a teenager trying to beat curfew. You didn't even say hello."

"I've got no manners." His second sneaker landed with a thud.

"You have perfectly good manners when it suits you."

He balled up his socks. "I have to take a shower."

"It can wait."

But apparently not, because he walked right past her and across the hallway to the bathroom. The lock clicked behind him.

He kept away from her for the rest of the afternoon. She repaired her black fingernail polish, dyed her bangs magenta, and reapplied her dragon tattoo. Then she went upstairs to bother Temple, which turned out to be a big mistake. A brutal workout and a stinging lecture on the stupidity of Lucy's "Good Enough" exercise philosophy left her drenched in sweat and pissed off.

Temple refused all of Lucy's offers to make anything but a plain green salad, and that night they ate more frozen dinners of dry turkey, mushy brown rice, and mashed parsnips. Lucy fell back on her favorite expression from when she was fourteen. "This blows."

"So does being fat," Temple replied self-righteously.

"You blow, too," Lucy grumbled.

Panda lifted an eyebrow. Temple reached across the table to pat Lucy's hand. "Somebody's got PMS."

Panda slammed his elbow on the table. "I swear to God, if I hear any more about PMS, cramps, or even female acne, I'm going to blow something up."

Temple waved a breezy hand toward the door. Panda glowered.

Lucy hadn't been able to get him alone yet, and she didn't want to talk about what had happened at the farm stand in front of Temple, so she picked another target for her bad mood. "I hate this table."

"Tough," Panda said.

Temple snorted. "He likes being surrounded by squalor. It reminds him of his hideous childhood."

"How hideous?" Lucy said. "He never tells me anything."

"My father was a drug dealer shot by a dissatisfied customer when I was two," he said matter-of-factly. "My mother was an addict. We had rats in our apartment. That's the part Temple likes best."

"*And* he stole food so they could eat," Temple said gleefully. "Isn't that sad?"

Lucy pushed her plate away. It didn't seem right for Temple to know more about him than she did. "What else did you learn?"

"He graduated from college with honors," Temple said.

Panda frowned, clearly displeased by any information that didn't portray him as a menace to society. "How do you know that?"

"Google." She sniffed. "You don't think I'd have kept hiring you if I hadn't investigated you?"

"By Googling me? You're a crackerjack detective, all right."

"He was also in the army," Temple went on. "Boring. Unfortunately, I couldn't find anything about his romantic history. I think we can safely assume a trail of broken hearts has been left behind."

"Or unmarked female graves," Lucy said, which only made him smile.

How could Temple work out with him every day and not want to rip his clothes off? Instead, whenever she took a break, she tended to stare out the window. Lucy studied the long tendon that ran down the side of his neck. The one she liked to bite. He caught her at it and gave her a look that said he knew exactly what she was thinking.

❧

PANDA DIDN'T COME THROUGH HER sliding door that night, and the boat-house remained dark. It was the first time they hadn't been together since their affair had begun, which led her to wonder . . . If his connection with Bree only involved real estate, why was he being so secretive?

Rain peppered the windows the next morning, matching her mood. What was it that he didn't want her to know? She needed their affair to be completely straightforward—no murky corners or dark mysteries she might find herself pondering when they weren't together. She pulled on an old yellow slicker that one of the Remingtons, maybe Bree herself, had left behind in an upstairs closet, and she set off across the wet grass. But instead of heading for the woods, she turned toward the three acres of land on the north side of the house, a rockier area she hadn't origi-nally realized was part of his property. By the time she reached the top of the steep slope, she was out of breath.

Panda stood at the edge of the bluff in what she'd come to think of as his brooding place. He wore a high-end dark gray rain jacket and jeans. His head was bare, hair wet and wind tousled. She took in his swarthy, rain-slicked face. He didn't look happy to see her.

"I missed my sex last night," she said. "I'm thinking about firing you."

PANDA HAD FIGURED SHE'D FORCE a confrontation, but he'd hoped to buy a little time before it happened. He should have known better. Shit. If he didn't get away from this place soon—away from her—he was going to lose it. He'd tried to talk Temple into letting him out of his contract, but she'd refused. When this was over, he was getting back to doing what he did best, protecting clients from real danger.

The wind flipped up the collar of his jacket. "I wouldn't advise firing me," he told her. "I've got a sex tape."

She didn't smile. In a yellow slicker, with a black-lined hood pulled over her ridiculous hair and three inches of black cuffs turned up, she looked like a wet bumblebee. "You're lying," she said. "Tell me why you had your little freak-out when you saw Bree."

"Would I lie about something as serious as a sex tape?"

"In a heartbeat. I know Bree's family owned the house. She told me all about it."

He should have made the connection between the woman named Bree that Lucy visited at the cottage and Sabrina Remington West, but this asinine assignment had dulled his thinking. "Video cameras are small," he said. "I'm exceptionally good at hiding them."

Again, no smile. She meant business, and he didn't like that. "Bree told me she'd never met you," she said. "So why did you run off like that?"

He came up with the most plausible explanation. "She reminded me of an old girlfriend."

"What old girlfriend?"

He ignored the slick of raindrops on her cheek to work on his sneer. "I don't ask about your lurid past. Leave mine alone."

"You don't ask about my lurid past because you know you'd fall asleep if I told you about it." She paused. "Something I intend to fix."

He frowned. "You told that woman who you are. Do you really think she's going to keep it to herself?"

"She has for a month. And other than Temple's dubious companionship, Bree is the only friend I have on the island.

What did that make him? "Who needs friends here?" he said. "We'll all be leaving in a couple of weeks." He ramped up his argument. "You're getting way too cozy with people. You ride into town whenever you like, talk to whoever you want. It's not smart."

"I like talking, and this conversation isn't about me. It's about you, and if you don't tell me the truth, I'll start digging around. Believe me, my resources are a lot more powerful than Google."

He wished she hadn't moved so close to the edge of the bluff, but if he told her to step back, she'd bite his head off. He yearned for the quieter, more compliant woman he'd first met. "Why do you even care?" he said.

"I don't like mysteries."

"Leave it alone, Lucy."

Her hood blew back. "Here's what I think. I think you have some kind of connection to the Remington family. That's why you bought this house, and that's why you don't want anything changed."

"The house has roots, and I don't. It's what I like about it and why I'm not getting rid of the table you're so obsessed with."

Fortunately she moved a few steps away from the edge. "Could be true," she said. "Now tell me the rest."

Like hell he was telling her the rest. As he watched the wind slap that yellow slicker against her small body, he couldn't imagine spilling his guts about any of it. Curtis, the army, how it felt to be a cop walking into some rat-hole apartment to tell a mother her kid was dead. How it felt not being able to trust yourself. He'd rather tell her how beautiful she was. Even her messy hair and fake tattoos couldn't destroy the sweet feistiness of that face or the allure of those green-flecked eyes.

He reminded himself that all this sweetness, that spirit, was destined for somebody else. Someone who hadn't spent so many years mucking around in the shadows. Someone who could never hurt her.

"There's no rest to tell." He reached out and pulled her hood up, sending rainwater down the back of her neck. "You laid out the terms for this affair. Don't tell me you've gone soft and fallen for me."

He watched her closely—not sure what he wanted to see—both relieved and disappointed that her expression remained unchanged. "I've fallen for your body," she said, "even if you are starting to look like a warning poster for illegal steroids. The body is definitely spectacular—all but the part between your ears."

She was so full of life, so smart, so screwed up. For years, she'd been pushing herself into a mold that didn't quite fit, trying so hard to be the perfect daughter, and now she was floundering. As for the two of them . . . For all her big talk about her asinine reverse bucket list, she wasn't cut out for a dead-end affair. She needed real intimacy, something he couldn't give her, and damn it, if she wouldn't look out for herself, he'd do it for her.

He turned his smile into the facsimile of a leer. "You're a hot number, babe. Hell on wheels when you're naked, but a pain in the ass once you've got your clothes on. If you want real communication, pull down your pants."

She blinked at his crudeness. His stomach twisted, but he was doing what he needed to. Still, he had to will himself not to take her into his arms and kiss the raindrops from her cheeks.

"Interesting." She pushed her hood back and lifted her chin. "Keep your secrets, Panda. I really don't care all that much."

She disappeared, sending him into the foulest of moods.

THE SKIES CLEARED, AND LUCY let Toby talk her into going out with him on Big Mike Moody's boat. The idea of spending the afternoon in the funk of his salesman's cologne didn't appeal to her, but it was better than stomping around the house.

Did Panda really believe she wouldn't see through his crap—that calculated insult and ridiculous sneer? It was his way of reminding her to keep her distance, as if she needed a reminder. This affair was supposed to be another check mark on her reverse bucket list, but by holding on to his secrets, he'd made her do exactly what she didn't want—think too much about him.

She forced a smile as she and Toby approached the roomy blue and white powerboat docked in the municipal harbor. Toby's eyes shone with anticipation. "Permission to come aboard."

"Permission granted." Mike's grin showcased his straight, gleaming teeth. He wore khaki shorts, a white Polo with a green logo, and boat shoes. Expensive Revo sunglasses hung by a strap around his tanned neck.

She'd traded her skank clothes for her black bathing suit and a white terry cover-up, but she'd kept her nose ring. He took the tote that held her sunblock, a towel, her ball cap, and some cookies she'd bought at the Painted Frog. Unfortunately, he also held out his hand to help her aboard, but the cologne pollution she remembered was noticeably absent, along with his gold bracelet and college ring.

"Glad you could come with us today, Miss Jorik."

She was disappointed. "Bree told you who I was."

"No. Remember how I said I never forget a face? It finally came to me a couple of weeks ago." He gestured toward her dragon tattoo. "You've got a real good disguise going for you."

Toby dashed to the stern to check out the fishing gear. She pulled her ball cap from her tote. "Nobody in town's recognized me, so the news doesn't seem to have spread."

"I figured if you wanted people to know who you were," he said earnestly, "you would have told them."

His openness was refreshing, and she found herself warming to him.

Once the boat was out of the harbor, he let Toby take the wheel. Eventually they passed around the south end of the island. When they were closer to shore, Toby got his rod and began to cast, with Mike giving him pointers. Lucy went over the other side to swim and to not think about Panda.

The next few hours passed pleasantly, but the fish weren't biting, and eventually Toby gave up and went in to swim himself. As Lucy lounged on the deck, she realized her initial impression of Mike had been wrong. He wasn't a phony at all. Instead, this good-looking, gregarious salesman was one of those people who genuinely looked for the best in everyone, even the sixteen-year-old who'd rear-ended his Cadillac the previous week while texting his girlfriend. "All teenagers do stupid things," he said as they bobbed at anchor while Toby snorkeled. "I sure did my share."

She smiled. "You're too good to be true."

"Afraid not. Just ask Bree."

She couldn't come up with a polite way of saying that Bree never mentioned him, but Big Mike wasn't quite as clueless as he seemed. "She hasn't told you about me, has she?"

"Not really."

He unzipped a soft-sided cooler he'd brought with him. "I grew up on this island. Except for college, I've lived here all my life." They bounced on the wake of a passing speedboat. "My parents were drunks—couldn't help themselves—and I was a big, clumsy island oaf with no idea how to make friends." He took out a bag of sandwiches from the island deli and set it on a table built into the deck. "Bree was one of the summer kids. Every year I'd count the days until she and her brothers arrived. They were great guys, exactly the kind of kid I wanted to be. Always knew exactly what to say, always fit in. But mainly it was Bree I waited for."

He pulled a bottle of sauvignon blanc from the cooler and picked up a corkscrew. "You should have seen her then, so full of life, always laughing, not tense and sad like she is now. Instead of walking from one place to another, she danced." He pulled the cork. "Star, Toby's mother, was supposed to be the most beautiful girl on the island, but when Bree was around, I couldn't look at anybody else, even though I knew she was way too good for me."

"She is not." They hadn't seen Toby climbing up the swim ladder that hung over the stern, the snorkel mask on top of his head.

"She's had a hard time, Toby," Mike said as he filled a plastic cup with wine and handed it to Lucy. "You need to look at things from her viewpoint."

Toby jumped onto the deck, water dripping from his skinny frame. "She never stands up for you. I don't know why you're always sticking up for her."

Because that's the kind of man he was, Lucy thought. He forgave the kid who rear-ended him, pardoned his alcoholic parents, and now was defending Bree for not returning the feelings he seemed to still hold for her.

Mike ripped open a bag of potato chips. "You'd better grab your sandwich before I eat it."

Toby and Mike traded jokes as they devoured the chips and sandwiches, along with the cookies Lucy had brought. Toby was a different kid around Mike—funny and communicative, with no traces of his customary sullenness. When they were done, Toby hunkered down on the rear bench and, as the sun began to set, dozed off.

Mike took the wheel, and they headed back. Lucy sat next to him, sipping her third glass of wine and enjoying the shimmer of the fading sun on the water. Out of nowhere, he said, "I did a crummy thing to Bree when I was seventeen." He spoke just loudly enough so that Lucy could hear him over the noise of the engine but Toby couldn't. "She was in love with David, Toby's father, and I was so jealous I started hating them both." He backed off on the throttle. "One night I spied on them, then spilled the beans to her mother about what they were doing, or at least what I knew they'd be doing if I'd stuck around to watch. The next day, Bree was gone. She never came back, not until a little over two months ago. So it isn't hard to see why she can't stand the sight of me."

Lucy curled her fingers around the plastic cup. "Are you still in love with her?"

He considered the question. "I think real love has to work two ways, and that's sure not how it is with her. But I don't like seeing her struggle." He gave Lucy an apologetic smile. "All I've done is go on about myself. Usually, I'm not like this, but you're easy to talk to."

"I don't mind." In one afternoon, Mike had told her more about himself than Panda had ever revealed.

As they approached the harbor, Mike gave a sigh of satisfaction. "I've traveled lots of places, but I never get tired of that view. I can't imagine living anywhere else."

"You've got to have second thoughts about that in the winter."

"I spend a couple of weeks in Miami every year, but I'm always anxious to get back. Cross-country skiing, ice fishing, snowmobiles. In other parts of the country, people hibernate in the winter. Up here in Michigan, that's when we come out to play."

She laughed. "You could sell sand in the middle of the desert."

"People know they can trust me." He glanced over at her, and unlike Panda's, his eyes stayed above her neck. "I'm the richest man on the island," he said matter-of-factly. "I don't take that for granted. Anybody who lives here knows if they've got trouble, I'll do my best to help them out."

"Don't people take advantage of that?"

"Every once in a while somebody takes me for a sucker, but I'll tell you what . . . I'd rather have that happen than not be there for a person who really needs help."

Which said everything about Mike Moody. What she'd initially regarded as braggadocio was a true generosity of spirit. Unlike Patrick Shade, Big Mike wasn't afraid to let people see who he was, warts and all.

❧

PANDA HEARD HER FOOTSTEPS ON the deck. As usual, she was entering the house through her bedroom doors instead of coming in the front like a normal person. His relief at knowing she was safe barely overshadowed his resentment. Worrying about what she was up to had ruined his afternoon.

He fixed his attention on the paperback thriller he'd propped on his chest and pretended to read. He didn't look up as the sliders opened, but he could see all he needed to out of the corner of his eyes.

She looked windblown and happy. The white terry cover-up she wore over her swimsuit had a food stain on the front. She'd tied it crookedly at the waist so that it gaped open over one breast. The way it nestled in her swimsuit top was as erotic as anything the skin magazines could conjure up.

She took him in as he lay on her bed but didn't say anything. He crossed his ankles and tilted his head toward the chest of drawers. "I brought my pig along to spruce up the room."

"I don't want your pig."

"You can't mean that. It's a great pig."

"Each to his own." She tugged at the leg of her suit. She smelled of sunblock and lake.

He set aside his book and dropped his legs over the side of the bed, casual as all hell. "You were gone a long time."

"I told Temple where I was going." She yawned and tossed her tote in the corner. "I need a shower."

He followed her into the bathroom, propped his shoulder against the doorjamb. "She said you were going fishing with Mike Moody. He's an ass."

That pissed her off way too much. "No, he's not. He only seems that way because he comes on so strong. He's a great guy."

Exactly what he didn't want to hear. "Yeah, just ask him."

She jerked at the tie on her cover-up. "You don't know anything. Mike is a good man with a huge heart. And unlike you, he's not afraid to have a real conversation."

He snorted. Men didn't have real conversations with women unless they wanted to get in their pants.

Lucy puckered her lips, all prim and proper. "Please leave so I can take a shower."

They took showers together. She knew that. But he damned well wasn't going to argue with her about it. "You got it."

He shut the door behind him, grabbed the book he had no intention of reading, and left the room.

He worked at his computer until one in the morning, catching up on paperwork, but he still had trouble falling asleep. Every time he closed his eyes, he saw that damned list of hers plastered against the back of his lids with the words "Sleep around" pulsing away.

Chapter Nineteen

◆

THE KITCHEN TABLE MOCKED HER as it squatted in its customary spot on the cracked vinyl floor. It looked like a fat green warthog with a broken leg. Lucy slapped at the counter with a dishrag. "Just once, do you think you could make coffee without getting the grounds everywhere?"

Panda turned from the kitchen window where he'd been scanning the backyard for armed robbers, escaped murderers, or even a rabid skunk, anything that would satisfy his craving for action. "Just once, do you think you could make the coffee instead of me?" he retorted.

"I'm trying to eat," Temple said from the table. "Would you both shut up?"

Lucy turned on her. "And you . . . Would it kill you to have a box of Cheerios around, or is that too much temptation for Her Majesty?"

Temple licked her yogurt spoon. "Panda, get rid of her."

"My pleasure."

"Don't bother. I'm leaving." Lucy flounced across the kitchen. "I'm going someplace where I'm *appreciated*." She tried to produce a decent burp but failed.

"I hear there's a new kindergarten in town," Panda called after her.

"You should know." Lucy slammed the back door on them both and headed for the cottage. The only bright spot in that encounter was how good it felt to act infantile.

Something had shifted between them, and not just because Panda hadn't been waiting for her in bed last night when she'd come out of the shower. She'd started feeling a resentment toward him that had no place in a summer fling. Temple knew more about him than she did, and Lucy didn't like that. She wanted his confidences. His trust. Maybe it should be enough to know he'd take a bullet for her, but not when she knew he'd do the same for Temple, or anyone else he felt responsible for.

Bree was opening up the farm stand when Lucy got there a few minutes later. As Bree set out the Carousel Honey sign, Lucy inspected the new note cards. They showed an old-fashioned straw skep, the forerunner of the modern hive, sitting under a blossoming cherry tree abuzz with fanciful bees. "These are great, Bree. Your best yet."

"Do you think so?" Bree repositioned a small metal table under the shady oak. She painted there between customers.

"Definitely. They're going to sell like crazy."

"I hope so. Labor Day's only a month away, and then . . ." She made a vague, helpless gesture.

Lucy wished Bree would let her cover the initial printing costs of mass-producing some of the note cards. But even though Lucy had presented it as a business proposal, Bree was too proud to accept. On the positive side, Bree had found a new sales outlet through Pastor Sanders, the minister at Heart of Charity Missionary Church and owner of the local gift shop. He'd just started carrying some of her products.

"How did your nautical excursion with Mike go yesterday?" Bree said, too casually.

"Great. I had fun."

"Then Mike must have fallen overboard."

Lucy pretended not to notice the edge in Bree's comments. "Nope."

"Too bad." Bree snatched up a bag of tiny sampling spoons and poured them into a basket she set next to a dish of the individually wrapped chocolate-dipped honey caramels Lucy had finally perfected.

Lucy spoke carefully. "I like him."

"That's because you haven't been around him long." She wrenched the lid off a fresh container of comb honey she set out for customers to sample. "I've known him since he was younger than Toby."

"Yes, he said he wasn't exactly Mr. Popular."

"You have no idea."

"I sort of do. He told me what he did to you."

She went still. "He told you?"

Lucy nodded. "He's an interesting person. Unusual. As open about his mistakes as he is about his accomplishments."

"Yes, I'm sure he loved telling you how important he is."

"Not really."

Bree finished arranging the honeycomb and spoons, along with some stick pretzels for dipping into a cocoa-flavored honey she'd started putting out as an experiment. "I don't like Toby spending so much time with him."

"Mike cares about Toby."

"Yes, they have a real love fest going on," she said bitterly.

Lucy cocked her head. "Are you jealous?"

"Of course I'm jealous." She swatted a fly swooping too close to the honeycomb. "Mike doesn't have to nag him into taking a shower or going to bed at a reasonable time. Mike only does the fun stuff, and I'm the wicked witch." She stopped, her expression troubled. "I know I'm right about Mike. People don't change that much. But . . ." Another of those helpless gestures. "I don't know . . . Things are getting confusing. I'm not even sure why."

Lucy had a few ideas about that, but she kept them to herself.

BREE LOCKED UP THE FARM stand for the night. The frames in the hives were heavy with honey. Earlier today, she'd cleaned Myra's old hand-cranked extruder, and at dawn tomorrow, she'd start this year's harvest. The work would be backbreaking, but that didn't bother her as much as the implications of harvesting honey for next summer. She'd accepted the fact that she had to stay on the island, but she was far from sure she had enough money saved to survive the winter until she could sell this new crop.

She gazed around at what she'd created—her little fairy castle farm stand with its carousel ribbon trim and Easter egg Adirondack chairs. It shocked her how happy this world she'd created made her. She liked watching her customers settle into the painted chairs and enjoy samples of her honey. She enjoyed seeing them testing her lotions, sniffing her soaps, and pondering her candles. If only she could live in a perpetual summer, with no threat of winter, no obsessing over money, no worries about Toby. She sighed, gazed at what she could see of the sunset through the trees, and headed for the house.

The first thing she noticed as she stepped inside was that the kitchen smelled delicious, like real food. "Toby?"

He wore his favorite jeans and T-shirt along with a baseball cap and a pair of red oven mitts with the batting coming out of one thumb. He took a casserole dish from the oven and set it on the stove next to a pair of wrinkled baked potatoes. "I made dinner," he said.

"By yourself? I didn't know you could cook."

"Gram taught me some stuff." Steam rose from the casserole as he pulled off the aluminum foil. "I wanted Mike to come eat with us, but he had business."

"He has a lot to do," she managed, without sarcasm. "What did you fix?"

"Cowboy casserole, noodles, and baked potatoes. Plus we have the bread Lucy made today."

Not exactly carb light, but she wasn't going to criticize. She washed her hands, avoiding the pan of cold, soggy noodles in the sink, then took two plates from the cupboard. She pushed aside a copy of *Black Soldiers in the Civil War* to set them on the table. "It smells delicious."

The cowboy casserole turned out to be a concoction of ground beef, onion, pinto beans, and, judging from the empty can on the counter, tomato soup. Six months ago, she'd never have eaten anything like this, but despite some undercooked onions and overbrowned ground beef, she had seconds. "A great meal, Chef," she said when she finally put down her fork. "I didn't realize how hungry I was. Anytime you feel like cooking, you go right ahead."

Toby liked having his work appreciated. "Maybe. How come you don't cook?"

Exactly when was she supposed to add that to her schedule? But the truth was, she'd never liked to cook. "I'm not much of a food person."

"That's why you're so skinny."

She gazed around at the kitchen with its dated pickled oak cabinets and yellowing vinyl floor. How odd to feel more comfortable in this shabby cottage than she'd ever felt in the luxurious house her cheating husband had bought. As for the money she'd once spent so freely . . . Not a penny of it was as precious as what she was earning for herself with her own hard work and imagination.

"Your mother liked to cook, too," she said.

"Really?" Toby stopped eating, fork poised in midair. His eagerness made her feel petty for not talking to him about Star. Just as Mike had asked her to.

"Gram never told me that," he said.

"Sure. She was always trying out new recipes—not just cookies and brownies, but things like soups and sauces. Sometimes she'd try to get me to help, but mainly I just ate what she made."

He cocked his head, thinking that over. "Like you're eating what I made."

"Exactly." She searched her mind. "She wasn't crazy about bees either, but she loved cats and dogs."

"That's like me, too. What else about her?"

She stole the man I loved. Or was that merely what Bree wanted to believe because it was easier to think bad of Star than to admit that David had never really loved her?

She made a play out of pleating her napkin. "She liked to play cards. Gin rummy." Star cheated, but Toby had heard enough negatives about his mother. "She loved Janet Jackson and Nirvana. All we did one summer was dance to 'Smells Like Teen Spirit.' She stunk at softball—none of us wanted her on our team, but we always let her because she made us laugh. She liked to climb, and when we were younger, she'd hide from me in that big old tree in the front yard."

"My tree," he said with so much wonder that her heart ached.

She told him what she should have understood from the beginning. "Your mom wasn't perfect. Sometimes she didn't take life as seriously as she should, but I can tell you this. She never intended to leave you. She always meant to come back."

Toby dipped his head so she wouldn't see his eyes filling with tears. She reached out to touch him, then thought better of it. "Let's go to Dogs 'N' Malts for dessert."

His head came up. "Could we?"

"Why not?" She was so stuffed she could barely move, but just once, she wanted to be the fun person in Toby's life.

They climbed into her car, and she drove to town. Toby ordered a super-size concoction of ice cream, M&M's, sprinkles, peanuts, and chocolate sauce. She ordered their smallest vanilla cone. As luck would have it, Mike showed up not long after they'd sat at one of the picnic tables. "Hey, Toby. Sabrina."

Sabrina?

Toby jumped up from the bench. "Sit with us, Mike!"

Mike glanced toward Bree. She wasn't going to be the bad guy, and she nodded. "Sure. Come and join us."

A few minutes later Mike returned with a small chocolate sundae and settled next to Toby, which put him directly across from her. Her heart twisted as Toby shot her a pleading look, imploring her not to ruin this. Mike avoided looking at her altogether.

Her cone was beginning to drip, but she couldn't take another lick. She didn't like feeling as if there was something wrong with her because she refused to join the Mike Moody fan club. Even Lucy liked him. But how could Bree forget the past? Except wasn't that beginning to happen? Each day it grew more difficult to reconcile the adult Mike Moody with the boy she remembered.

A young couple—the husband carrying a baby in a Snugli—stopped to talk to him, followed by an older man hauling an oxygen tank. Everybody was glad to see Mike. Everybody wanted to say hello. Toby waited patiently, as if he'd been through this before. Finally they were alone. "Toby, this sundae is so good I think I'll have another." Mike dug in his pocket and handed over a five-dollar bill. "Mind getting one for me?"

As Toby went off, Bree noticed that Mike had barely touched his first sundae. He finally looked at her. "I was coming out to see you tomorrow."

"I thought you were done with me." She managed not to sound too petulant.

"This is about Toby." He pushed aside his ice cream. "The Bayner boys aren't coming back to live on the island."

It took her a moment to place the name. "The twins who are Toby's best friends?"

"His only real friends. Their parents are splitting up, and his mother is staying in Ohio with them. Toby doesn't know about it yet, and this is going to hit him hard."

"Great. One more problem I have no idea how to solve," she said.

He wiped his mouth with his napkin. "I might be able to help out."

Of course he could. Mike could fix everything, something she should have thought harder about before she'd dismissed him.

He balled the napkin. "I never liked how Myra kept him so isolated, but she was odd that way, and she refused to talk about it. Toby's with other kids at school, but she wouldn't let him invite them to the cottage or go to their houses. The only reason the twins were friends was because they lived close enough to walk. She overprotected him."

"What am I supposed to do about it?" It was odd asking Mike for advice, but he didn't seem to find it strange.

"I coach a soccer team," he said. "It'll be a good place for him to start making new friends. Let Toby join."

She'd already become a beekeeper. Why not add soccer mom to her résumé? "All right."

He seemed surprised that she'd agreed so quickly. "I'm sure you have some questions. I'm not the only coach. There's another—"

"It's fine. I trust you."

"You do?"

She pretended to examine a ragged fingernail. "You've been a good friend to Toby."

"Here you are." Toby popped up at Mike's side with the sundae. Mike surreptitiously moved the first one under his napkin and took up the plastic spoon to start on the second. Toby asked him about fishing rods, and they were soon immersed in conversation.

Long after she should have been asleep that night, Bree was still sitting on the back step, staring out into the darkness, thinking about Mike and the upcoming winter. Her honey was selling better than she could have hoped, and the bee Christmas ornaments were a surprise hit. Pastor Sanders was displaying her products in his gift shop without charging her a percentage. He said he'd take his commission in honey and give it away to any of his parishioners who needed their spirits lifted.

She was saving every penny she could, but she was spending it, too. And not just for more jars. After days of agonizing, she'd placed a big order for some very expensive hand-blown glass globe ornaments that she intended to paint with island scenes and—cross her fingers—sell for three times what she paid for them. But with only a month left before Labor Day, when her customers would disappear, the purchase was a huge risk.

She still had a dribble of cash coming in from the consignment shop at home where she'd left most of her clothes. With luck, that money, combined with steady sales at the farm stand for the rest of the month and a big profit from the hand-painted ornaments she'd just received, might carry her through the winter. If Toby didn't keep growing out of his clothes, and the old furnace kept running, and the leaky roof didn't get worse, and her car didn't need brakes, and . . .

Winters are long, and people here only have one another to depend on.

It had been easier dismissing Mike's words in June than it was now, with fall creeping closer each day. If the worst happened, she had nowhere to turn. She needed Mike.

The more she thought about it, the more she realized that ignoring him was a luxury she could no longer afford. She had to change direction. She had to convince him that she no longer hated his guts. Even if it killed her.

Toby's sleepy voice drifted through the screen door. "What're you doing out here?"

"I—couldn't sleep."

"Did you have a bad dream?"

"No. What about you? Why are you up?"

"I don't know. Just woke up." He yawned and came out to sit next to her. His shoulder brushed her arm. The sleepy, sweaty boy smell of him reminded her of summer nights with her brothers when they'd sneak into one another's rooms and tell ghost stories.

He spoke through another yawn. "Thanks for the ice cream tonight."

She cleared the lump in her throat. "You're welcome."

"A lot of kids are scared of the dark, but not me," he announced.

She wasn't either. She had too many real things to be afraid of.

He leaned over to examine a scab on his ankle. "Could we maybe invite Mike over for dinner soon?"

She began to bristle, then realized he'd handed her the perfect method to begin mending her relationship with Mike. One way or the other, she had to make him believe she'd put the past behind her.

"Sure we can." She briefly wondered when she'd become so coldblooded, but standing on principle now seemed to be a luxury only the wealthy could afford. "I think it's time we both got some sleep." She rose from the step.

"I guess." He got up. "Do you think he'd like cowboy casserole?"

"Definitely."

They went inside, and as Toby headed for his bedroom, she called out to him the same way she did every night, "Good night, Toby."

This time he answered her back. "G'night, Bree."

❧

AUGUST SETTLED IN FOR GOOD, bringing more sunny, humid days along with the occasional fierce thunderstorm. Most nights, Lucy and Panda met on the boat or in her room, but an unsettling intensity had replaced their playful kinkiness. There were no more strip searches, no more licorice whips. And during the day they bickered.

"Did you use yesterday's grounds to make this coffee?" Panda said as he splashed the contents of his newly poured cup down the sink.

"You bitch if I make the coffee. You bitch if I don't," Lucy retorted.

"Because you refuse to follow directions."

Temple gave a long-suffering sigh from her perch on top of the kitchen step stool where she was eating half a thinly sliced apple. She'd slicked her hair into its customary long ponytail, a style that put her almond-shaped eyes and increasingly sharp cheekbones on full display. She'd been on the island a little over six weeks. The fleshy cushion beneath her chin had disappeared, and her long, toned legs testified to her hard work. But instead of being happy, she'd grown tenser, more short-tempered, sadder.

"*Your* directions," Lucy said to him.

"Which work a hell of a lot better than whatever it is you're doing," he retorted.

"In your opinion."

"Children!" Temple exclaimed. "Do not make me spank."

"Let me," Panda drawled.

Lucy curled her lip at him and left the kitchen to take the kayak out. She resented the tension between them. She wanted the fun back. Without fun, what was the point of this affair?

She was glad when the water got so choppy she had to focus all her attention on paddling.

TEMPLE APPEARED FOR DINNER THAT night in a clean version of the workout clothes she wore all day. Her body was muscular perfection. Her black racer-back top exposed arms with every tendon defined, and her matching Spandex shorts rode low enough to showcase a hollowed-out, muscle-rippled abdomen. She and Panda together were a matched set—both of them overexercised, restless, and surly.

Lucy muttered something about two nutcases on human growth hormones. Temple glanced at Lucy's waist and made a reference to an aimless loser with middle-aged spread. Panda growled at them both to shut up so he could eat tonight's crap in peace.

Unlike Panda, Lucy had no complaints about the underseasoned frozen beef stew—thanks to the sweet potato fries and giant sugar cookie she'd downed in town. Temple began a halfhearted lecture about the link between childhood illnesses and adult immunity, and when she asked Panda if he'd ever had chicken pox. Lucy couldn't resist butting in. "Privacy intrusion. Panda doesn't talk about his past."

"And that galls you," Panda retorted. "You won't be satisfied until you know everybody's business."

But he wasn't everybody. He was her lover.

"He's right, Lucy," Temple said. "You do like to poke around in other people's heads."

Panda flipped sides by pointing a fork at his employer. "Somebody needs to poke around in yours. The longer you're here, the bitchier you get."

"That's a lie," Temple retorted. "I've always been bitchy."

"Not this bitchy," Lucy said. "You've lost twenty pounds, and—"

"Twenty-four," Temple said defiantly. "No thanks to either of you. Do you have any idea how depressing it is listening to you snarl at each other?"

"Our snarling doesn't have anything to do with your problem," Lucy said. "You have a textbook case of body dysmorphia."

"Ewww . . . ," Temple scoffed. "Big words."

Lucy shoved away her plate. "You look fantastic everywhere except inside your head."

"In your opinion." Temple made a dismissive gesture toward her own body. "You can spin it any way you want, but I'm still fat!"

"When will you not be fat?" Lucy cried. "What ridiculous number has to flash on the scale you carry around in your head to finally make you feel okay?"

Temple licked her fingers. "I can't believe Miss Porky is lecturing me about weight."

Panda didn't like that. "She's not porky."

Lucy ignored him. "Your body is beautiful, Temple. There's not an inch of you that jiggles."

"Unlike your hips," Temple shot back, but without any real sting.

Lucy gazed at her untouched plate with disgust. "My hips will be just fine as soon as I can eat like a normal person again."

Temple turned to Panda. "She's some kind of alien. How can she gain twenty pounds and not have it make her crazy?"

"I haven't gained twenty pounds," Lucy retorted. "Ten max." But sweet potato fries and sugar cookies weren't her real enemy. Her enemy was the guilt she felt over the pages she hadn't written, the family she was virtually ignoring, and the panic she experienced whenever she thought about leaving Charity Island.

Panda pushed back from the table. "If you'll both excuse me, I'm going outside to shoot myself."

"Do it near the water," Lucy said, "so we don't have to clean up after you."

She and Temple finished their sad excuse for dinner in glum silence. Temple stared out the window, and Lucy picked at the kitchen table's vomitous green paint.

The Great Escape

❧

LATE THE NEXT AFTERNOON, AS Lucy pulled some weeds by the porch and contemplated a trip to a bar in town so she could work on her reverse bucket list, she heard a car pull into the driveway. It didn't sound like one of their regular delivery vans. She set aside her trowel and went around the house to investigate.

A woman with short, bright red hair and a stocky figure stepped out of a silver Subaru. She wore a loose-fitting white top, serviceable tan capris that would have looked better on someone with longer legs, and athletic sandals. A chunk of turquoise hung from a leather cord around her neck, and silver rings flashed on her fingers. Lucy nodded in greeting and waited for the woman to identify herself. Before that could happen, the front door opened and Mr. Bodyguard stepped out.

The woman turned away from Lucy to face him. "Patrick Shade?"

He stopped at the top of the steps. "Can I help you?" he said, without answering her question.

She came around to the front of her car. "I'm looking for a friend."

He nodded toward Lucy. "Unless you're looking for one of us, you have the wrong house."

"She's here. I know she is."

Their visitor's stocky build reminded Lucy that Temple had enemies. What if this woman were a disgruntled former client? Or a *Fat Island* television viewer turned stalker?

Panda kept himself firmly planted between the visitor and the door.

"It took me weeks to find her," the woman said stubbornly. "I'm not going away."

He moved slowly down the steps. "This is private property."

He hadn't raised his voice, but that didn't make him any less intimidating. She backed against the car, more desperate than threatening. "I have to see her."

"You need to go now."

"Just tell her I'm here. Please. Tell her Max is here."

Max? Lucy stared. *This* was Max?

But Panda didn't seem surprised by the woman's revelation. Was he wearing his professional poker face or had he known all along that the person Temple pined for was a woman?

Of course he'd known. Someone as thorough as Panda wouldn't let a detail like that escape him.

The woman turned toward the house and shouted, "Temple! Temple, it's Max! Don't do this. Come out and talk to me!"

Her pain was so visceral Lucy felt it in her own heart. Surely Temple would hear her and come out. But no sound came from the house, no movement. The door stayed shut. Lucy couldn't stand it. She cut around the side and entered through the back.

She found Temple upstairs in her bedroom standing off to the side of the front window where she could watch the driveway without being spotted. "Why did she have to come here?" She sounded both fierce and broken. "I hate her."

Everything Lucy hadn't understood was now clear. "No, you don't. You love her."

A lock of Temple's hair came out of her clip as she spun around, every muscle of her overexercised body taut. "What do you know about anything?"

"I know this has been tearing you apart all summer."

"It'll get better. It's simply a matter of time."

"Why did you break up?"

Temple's nostrils flared. "Don't be naïve. Do you think I want the world to know that I—I fell in love with another woman?"

"You'll hardly be the first celebrity trainer to come out of the closet. I doubt it'll ruin your career."

"It'll ruin *me*."

"How? I don't understand."

"This is *not* what I want to be."

"A lesbian?"

Temple flinched.

Lucy threw up her hands. "Jeez, Temple, welcome to the twenty-first century. People fall in love."

"Easy for you to say. You fell in love with a man."

For a moment Lucy actually thought she was talking about Panda, but then she realized Temple must mean Ted. "We don't always choose whom we fall in love with. Lots of women are lesbians."

Her lip curled, even as her eyes were shiny with unshed tears. "I'm not lots of women. I'm Temple Renshaw."

"And that puts you a cut above ordinary humans?"

"I don't settle for second best. It's not how I'm made."

"Do you really think Max is second best?"

"Max is wonderful," she said fiercely. "The best person I've ever known."

"Then what?"

Temple remained stubbornly silent, but Lucy wouldn't let her get away with that. "Go ahead and say it."

"I don't have to. Political correctness doesn't change the reality. Homosexuality is a defect. A flaw."

"Got it. You're too perfect to be gay."

"I'm not talking to you about this any longer."

Lucy was filled with pity. The standards Temple had set for herself were impossible for anyone to meet. No wonder she was miserable.

Tires crunched in the gravel. Temple closed her eyes and leaned back against the curtain. Lucy looked out the window. "Congratulations. The best person you've ever known just drove away."

PANDA WAS SAWING AT A dead tree and spoiling for a fight when Lucy came out to talk to him. "I suppose you think I should have told you about Max, too?" he said.

"Yes, but I also understand client confidentiality. I know—"

A loud crash came from the house. He threw down the saw and raced inside. Lucy ran after him. As she reached the front hallway, she heard thuds coming from overhead, then something slamming against the floor. She followed him up the steps.

Temple stood in the middle of the gym, eyes wild, hair undone, the destruction of her prison-kingdom all around her. An overturned weight bench, scattered floor-mats, a hole in the wall. Temple snatched up a ten-pound weight and was about to hurl it through the window when Panda grabbed her.

It was a battle of the gods. Hercules versus Xena Warrior Princess. But as strong as she was, he was far stronger, and it didn't take long for him to pinion her against his chest.

All the fight went out of her. When he finally released her, she collapsed at his feet. He shot Lucy a silent appeal for help, and she did the only thing she could think of.

Her bread was hidden in the den where Panda could get to it. She'd baked it just that afternoon at the cottage. She carried it to the kitchen where she unwrapped it, cut off the chewy heel, and drizzled it with honey from the jar she'd hidden in the cupboard.

Temple was slumped against the wall, her head resting against the arms she'd folded over her bent knees. Lucy knelt next to her and offered it. "Eat this."

Temple's teary red eyes reflected only betrayal. "Why are you sabotaging me?" she said hoarsely.

"This isn't sabotage." Lucy struggled to find the words. "It's—it's life."

Temple ate it. Not gulping it down but savoring each small bite. While Panda leaned against the doorjamb and watched, Lucy sat cross-legged at Temple's side and tried to think what to say. In the end, she said nothing.

"That was good," Temple said in a small voice. "Can I have another?"

Lucy thought for a moment. "No, but I'm making dinner tonight."

Temple's shoulders slumped in defeat. "I can't do this any longer."

"I know."

Temple buried her face in her hands. "It's all going to come crashing down. Everything I've worked for."

"Not unless you want it to," Lucy said. "You've fixed your body. All you need to do now is fix your head." She rose and faced Panda. "I'll be back in an hour. Unlock the pantry."

Chapter Twenty

❦

THE HOUSE WAS QUIET WHEN Lucy returned from town. She unpacked the groceries and a small charcoal grill from Panda's trunk. While the coals heated, she tossed a worn cloth over the picnic table, set it with a hodgepodge of dishes, and shucked four ears of corn.

When she was back in the kitchen, she poured herself a generous glass of wine and unwrapped some freshly caught, but mercifully cleaned and de-headed, trout she'd bought at the marina. She stuffed the trout with spinach leaves, some wild chives she'd found growing in the back, and a few lemon slices. After brushing the fish lightly with olive oil, she set the pieces on a platter waiting for the grill. She wasn't sure she was doing the right thing, but she did know Temple couldn't keep on like this any longer—obsessed, tormented, and destined to regain all the weight she'd lost as soon as she left this *Fat Island* she'd created.

Panda appeared while she was making a quick salad, this one supplemented with pine nuts, slivers of ripe pear, and a creamy crumble of forbidden feta. "Do you really think this is a good idea?" he asked.

"Got a better one?"

He watched glumly as she mixed up a light dressing from a splash of olive oil and a fruity balsamic. "Why did I ever take this job?"

"Because you owed her." She handed him the platter of stuffed trout. "The grill's outside. Don't overcook it."

He gazed at the trout, his expression vaguely dumbfounded. "Do I look like a guy who knows how to grill?"

"Just don't poke at the pieces until they're ready to flip. You'll figure it out. It's in your male genes."

He stalked outside, muttering under his breath. She checked the water she'd set to boil the corn. Instead of sabotaging Temple's diet, she wanted to awaken her senses to something other than deprivation.

Temple wandered into the kitchen, her hair scraggly and eyes red, looking more like the scullery maid than the Evil Queen. Lucy poured her half a glass of wine from the bottle of sauvignon blanc she'd just bought and handed it over without speaking. Temple brought it to her nose, inhaled, then took a small sip. She closed her eyes and savored.

"We're eating outside tonight, and I want flowers on the table." Lucy gave her a lumpy blue pottery vase that looked like a grade-school art project. "Scrounge around and find something."

Temple was too drained to protest.

Her effort consisted of hosta leaves, Queen Anne's lace, and a few black-eyed Susans. Predictably, the end result didn't fit her definition of perfection, so she hated it, but Lucy couldn't imagine an arrangement more suited to the faded red-rooster tablecloth and unmatched dishes.

The picnic table, turned for a lake view, sat under the oak. Panda took the bench across from Lucy and Temple. Lucy set an ear of corn on

Temple's plate and her own, but gave him two. "I forgot to buy butter," she lied. "Try that instead." She pointed to the lime wedges lying on a child's plastic Sesame Street plate.

As she'd hoped, the explosive sweetness of the corn combined with the tang of fresh lime juice and a sprinkle of sea salt made up for the lack of butter. She wanted to feed Temple's soul but not sabotage her body. Despite a few charred places, Panda had done a good job grilling the fish, and the interior was moist and flavorful.

"God, this is so good." Temple uttered the words like a prayer.

"Amen." Panda moved on to his second ear of corn, eating far more tidily than either Temple or Lucy.

Temple examined her cob for a kernel she might have missed. "How did you learn to cook like this?"

Lucy didn't feel like bringing up the subject of White House chefs. "Trial and error."

After Temple had chased the last remaining pine nut around her empty plate with a moistened fingertip, she studied Lucy with genuine curiosity. "What's in this for you? We all know I'm crazy. Why do you care what happens to me?"

"Because I've grown weirdly fond of you." Besides, trying to fix other people was a great distraction from trying to fix herself. With her deadline less than a month away, she hadn't written even a page of the material her father wanted, she wouldn't let herself think about going back to work, and she barely talked to her family. All she'd accomplished was to bake a lot of bread, perfect her honey caramels, and have a dead-end affair with a man she was using as a sexual convenience.

"Lucy's been taking care of people all her life," Panda said. "It's in her DNA." He studied her in a way that made her uncomfortable. "She saved her kid sister. She got her parents together. Hell, if it hadn't been for Lucy, it's doubtful her mother would have become president." He brushed a fly away. "You could say that by the time Lucy was fifteen, she'd changed the course of American history."

His vision of her made her uncomfortable, and she got up from the table. "How about dessert?"

"There's dessert?" Temple sounded as if she'd just heard that the Easter Bunny was real.

"Life is meant to be lived."

Lucy returned from the kitchen with a square of dark chocolate that she broke into three small pieces. "You gave him more," Temple grumbled. And then, "Forget I said that."

But as Lucy and Temple nibbled at their own chocolate, Panda's square remained untouched. He crushed his napkin and dropped it on his plate. "I'm handing in my resignation."

The chocolate stuck in Lucy's throat. Temple's breakdown . . . The meal Lucy had just fixed . . . He'd found the excuse he'd been looking for to leave the island and, in the process, get away from her.

"Like hell you will." Temple sucked a chocolate smear from her finger.

"You hired me to stop exactly this sort of thing," he said calmly. "Cheese, chocolate, corn on the cob . . . I didn't do my job."

"Your job's changed."

His calmness evaporated. "Exactly how has it changed?"

She made a vague gesture. "I'll figure that out."

"Forget it!" He pushed himself up from the table and stormed across the yard toward his brooding place.

As he disappeared up the rocky slope, Temple looked at Lucy. "If you want to land this guy, you'll have to work faster. Your time's running out."

"Land him? I don't want to land him."

"Now who's hiding from the truth?" She reached for the chocolate he'd left, thought better of it, and tossed it over the bluff. "Patrick Shade adores you, despite his grumbling. He's one of the sexiest men on the planet. He's also ethical, caring, and just screwed up enough to be interesting. You're in love with the guy."

"I am not!"

"Now who needs a shrink?"

Lucy tossed her legs over the picnic bench and grabbed her plate. "This is the thanks I get for feeding you real food."

"Unless you want to lose the best man you'll ever meet, you'd better pick up your game."

"I don't have a game. And Ted Beaudine was the best man I ever met."

"Are you sure about that?"

Lucy stormed toward the house. "You clean up. I'm going into town. And no more exercise the rest of the night!"

THE COMPASS SAT A BLOCK off Beachcomber Boulevard, a weather-beaten one-story building with fishing nets draped across the front and pitted brass ships' lanterns mounted on either side of the door. A sign advertised LIVE MUSIC AND HAPPY HOUR ALL DAY.

In love with Panda? Total rubbish. She knew the difference between real love and an affair.

The interior smelled of beer and buffalo wings. More fishing nets hung on the walls, along with plastic floats, fake compasses, reproduction ship's wheels, and a collection of bras. The wooden tables were pressed close together with an open space at the rear for the band. The bar, which had a reputation as a hangout for the younger vacation crowd, was just beginning to come alive.

Lucy watched the band tune up while she sipped a watermelon margarita. Why would Temple even think such a thing? Just because Panda was hot? So were a lot of men, maybe not to the same degree—definitely not to the same degree—but love was more than sex. Love implied common interests, an ease being with each other, a shared sense of values. Okay, so she and Panda did have some of that—a lot of that—but . . .

She was relieved when a beefy jock type sidled up to her. "What's your name, foxy lady?"

"I go by Viper."

"Like windshield viper?" He was already visibly drunk, and he blew a series of hee-haws through his nose.

"No," she replied. "Like, if-you-piss-me-off, I'll-kick-your-ass Viper." She blew her own silent hee-haw.

Only as the kid backed away did it occur to her that, between her dreads, tattoos, and tough talk, she might be too scary for the average male, which kind of defeated her purpose in coming here. But as she watched jock boy retreat, she had to admit she loved the idea that goody-goody Lucy Jorik could frighten anybody away.

She'd dressed in full-out goth-skank mode: a little black skirt that barely covered her butt, a one-shoulder black halter top with a grommet border, and her only pair of heels—studded black platform mules. With her tats on full display, nose and eyebrow rings in place, heavy dark eyeliner, she definitely stood out from all the college girls in their cute little shorts and flip-flops.

She drifted toward a kennel of males: a golden retriever, a greyhound, a pit bull, and a couple of mongrels. All of them were watching her. She almost asked permission to join them before she remembered who she was. "I'm Viper." She set her beer on the table and took the only empty chair. "If you hear any stories about me, they're probably true."

❧

WHERE THE HELL WAS SHE? By midnight, Panda had checked every bar in town before he remembered The Compass. Lucy had taken his car, so he'd had to come into town by boat, leaving Temple alone. For all he knew, Temple had downed the rest of the chocolate Lucy had bought. He no longer cared.

He surveyed the crowd and spotted her right away. She was dancing in front of the band with a skinny, long-haired kid who looked like a young Eddie Van Halen. If you could call that pelvic grind she was doing "dancing." Both the lead guitarist and bass player were singing right to her, a cover of Bon Jovi's "Runaway." She looked tough, dangerous, and barely legal in her trashy top and trashier shoes. Her skirt wasn't much more than a handkerchief and showed way too much leg, along with a new tat of a snake coiling up one calf, its fanged head pointed toward Nirvana. Hard to remember that two and a half months ago this tough-as-nails man-eater had been wearing pearls and preparing to settle into domestic bliss with the most respectable guy in Texas.

He was attracting his own kind of attention, but he'd long ago lost his taste for coeds. The song came to an end. She hooked her arms around the young stud's neck, leaned into him, and kissed the son of a bitch. Long and hard.

Panda plowed through the crowd and gave the punk a nudge on the shoulder. "Get lost."

She turned her head just far enough to lift her phony-pierced eyebrow at him, then tightened her hold on the kid's neck and stuck her lips near his earlobe. "Ignore him. He's not as tough as he looks."

Panda didn't have to stare at the kid more than a few seconds before the kid figured out that wasn't true. The boy broke Lucy's hold. "Later, okay?"

Lucy watched the kid hurry off, then glared at Panda. "Go away," she shouted over the music. "I'm drunk, and I was just getting ready to make out with him."

He gritted his teeth. "Congratulations. At this rate, you'll be done with your list in no time."

She stomped her metal-studded shoe. "Damn it, he's leaving, and I was going to sleep with him. Now it'll have to be the greyhound."

Like hell. He didn't know who the greyhound was, only that this she-devil wasn't sleeping with anybody but him tonight. "Here's the thing, babe . . . I don't share my woman."

She looked way too outraged. "I'm not your woman. And I'm not your *babe*!"

He kissed her before she could say any more. She tasted like booze and cinnamon lipstick. But she didn't throw herself into the kiss the way he wanted. Instead she nipped his bottom lip with her teeth and backed off. "Nice try, Patrick, but no dice. I'm partying with new friends, and you aren't invited."

"Hold on. You told me you wanted to make out in public."

"And you said you wouldn't."

"Changed my mind." He was a shitty dancer, but he figured what she'd been doing wasn't exactly dancing, so he pulled her against him.

She refused to cooperate. "Buy me a drink first."

"You've had enough."

She glued her feet to the ground. "No drink, no dance. Get me a kamikaze."

He gritted his teeth and stalked over to the bar. "Make me something that tastes like a kamikaze," he told a female bartender who looked like a prison guard. "But without the booze."

"What are you?" she growled. "Some kind of religious nut?"

"Just make the damned drink."

The final concoction tasted more like an orange Popsicle than a real kamikaze, but maybe Lucy wouldn't notice. He spotted her perched on some guy's lap. The kid was tall and almost comically skinny, with a long nose and longer neck. The greyhound.

He bought himself a beer and sauntered over to the table. The greyhound saw him coming and got up so fast he nearly dumped her. Panda nodded at him and handed Lucy her drink. "I see you're up to your old tricks, *babe*."

She gave him the stink eye.

"A word of advice, boys . . ." He sipped his beer. "Check your wallets before you let her get away. She can't help herself."

As they reached for their pockets, he set down his beer and pulled her back to the dance floor, where the band had launched into an off-key ballad. She smirked at him. "No need to make out with me. Like I told you, I've already done that. With *two* of them."

"I'm impressed." He cupped his hands around her butt and moved his mouth closer to her ear. "How about getting felt up in public? Is that on your list, too?"

"No, but . . ."

He squeezed. "You should put it there."

He was hoping for a little embarrassment on her part, but he didn't see it. He backed her to the wall next to a wooden whale and kissed the hell out of her. This time he got a reaction. She wrapped her arms around his neck, right where they belonged. She seemed a little dazed, or maybe that was him. He tugged at her earlobe with his lips. "Let's get out of here."

She acted as though he'd dumped a bucket of ice water over her head. "No way, dude. I'm staying."

"Think again, *dude*," he retorted. "You're going with me."

"And how exactly are you going to pull that off?"

She had a point. As much as he might want to, he couldn't exactly throw her over his shoulder and drag her out without attracting the attention of at least a few good Samaritans, right along with the prison guard behind the bar, who probably had a handgun tucked away somewhere.

Lucy sauntered off, ass wiggling. She found another table, this one holding an older and tougher crowd. His temper surged. She was a big girl, and if this was the way she wanted it, to hell with her.

He began to elbow his way toward the door, then paused. Some of the women were watching her a little too closely, probably because they didn't like the male attention she was attracting. But maybe they were trying to place her face, and if that happened . . . He imagined cell phones pulled out, cameras clicking away, people pressing in on her . . .

He ordered a club soda, leaned against the bar, and watched her until the men at the table got uneasy and stopped talking to her. She tried another table, but he had his glare on good and strong, and they didn't roll out the welcome mat either. Instead of calling it a night, she came toward him, the ass-wiggling a thing of the past. Her footsteps were firm, her eyes steady, and beneath all that makeup, she looked like a woman who knew her way around the world's power centers.

"Thanks to whatever it was you ordered for me, I'm sober," she said with deadly seriousness. "I know exactly what I'm doing, and I don't need your protection." She lifted her chin. "I've spent a decade under guard. That's more than enough. As of right now, we've broken up. I want you to leave."

A blinding fury claimed him, the kind of fury he'd thought was behind him. He slammed his drink down on the bar. "You've got it, sister."

LUCY HAD GOTTEN RID OF Panda, but she'd also lost her party spirit. Why did he have to show up and spoil everything? Still, she shouldn't have flown off the handle like that. It was Temple's fault. Her smug certainty that Lucy had fallen in love with him had made Lucy panicky.

She shouldn't be. Temple was wrong. Lucy wasn't the kind of woman to fall in love with one man two and a half months after she'd been in love with another. And she especially wasn't the kind of women to fall in love with someone who was so guarded that he refused to reveal anything about himself. Still, some part of her wished she hadn't announced they were breaking up quite yet, even though summer was nearly over and he'd be leaving soon.

She waited long enough to be sure she wouldn't run into him outside before she left the bar. The parking lot was full. Since she'd taken his car, she half expected to see that he'd driven off in it and left her stranded, but he hadn't. He was still taking care of her. Her eyes prickled even though she knew it was better to get their breakup over with now.

She didn't want to go home, didn't want to talk to anybody. She glanced toward the car but couldn't make herself get in. If she'd had sneakers with her, she could have gone for a walk to clear her head, but her heels weren't designed for a nighttime hike. Still, the air was warm, the moon full. She picked her way through the cars and around to the side of the bar, harshly lit with a single flood.

The building perched above an inlet. If she owned the place, she'd have put an open patio back here. Instead, she saw a pair of Dumpsters, an equipment shed, and a broken-down picnic table. Judging by the crushed cigarette packs and litter of butts on the ground, this was where the employees took their smoke breaks.

She made her way carefully over the uneven ground to the picnic bench and sat. The damp wood was cool against her bare thighs, and the air smelled of lake and cooking oil. She heard the roar of motorcycles, and for a moment, she wanted to believe one of them belonged to Panda, her own Sir Galahad rushing to rescue her from the dismal swamp of her own thoughts.

She gazed at the lights from the homes across the water. After his blowup with Temple, she wouldn't be surprised if Panda was gone by this time tomorrow. But what about Lucy herself? How long was she going to stay? She envisioned herself standing on the bluff behind the house, autumn leaves falling around her, then snowflakes. She saw spring arriving; another summer. Years passing. Her hair turning gray, face wrinkling, the strange old lady who'd arrived one summer and never left. Eventually they'd find her mummified body buried under a mountain of petrified homemade bread.

She shivered. A loud voice intruded. "Hold on. I gotta take a piss."

"You always gotta take a piss."

"Fuck you."

Footsteps crunched in the gravel. A man with an unkempt beard and a bandanna wrapped around his head appeared behind the building. As his companion stopped by the Dumpster, the bearded one spotted her. "Hey."

They both wore boots, scruffy jeans, and scruffier hair. These guys weren't the lawyers and high school guidance counselors who turned biker on weekends. They were the real thing, and from their unsteady walks, they were both drunk.

Lucy Jorik would have been frightened, but Viper knew how to handle situations like this. "Hey, yourself."

"You care if I take a piss?" the bearded biker said in a voice louder than necessary. "You can watch if you want."

The man by the Dumpster snickered. "Trust you, man, to find a chick back here."

Viper wasn't easily cowed, but she wasn't stupid either. The bar was too noisy for anyone to hear her, and she was keeping this conversation short. "I've got better things to do." She rose from the bench.

Dumpster man swaggered toward her. "He'll let you hold it for him."

As she smelled the liquor on them, her uneasiness grew, but Viper didn't believe in showing fear. "I couldn't find anything that little."

They hooted with laughter. Even though her knees had started to shake, she loved how tough she was. This summer hadn't been a waste after all.

Except her wisecrack had opened the door to a camaraderie she didn't want, and they were both closing in on her. "I like you," the bearded one said.

Dumpster man had a narrow, sloping forehead and a uni-brow. "Come on inside and have a drink with us."

She swallowed. "Sure. Let's go."

But they didn't move, and the smell of liquor and body odor was making her queasy.

"You got an old man?" The one with the beard scratched his stomach like Panda used to, except this was the real thing.

"An old lady," she retorted. "I don't go for guys."

She thought she was being smart, but the look they exchanged wasn't encouraging, and Beard Man's eyes were creeping all over her. "You just haven't found the right one. Isn't that right, Wade?"

"Yeah, like I haven't heard that before." She managed a sneer.

A fence blocked the far side of the bar, so she'd have to slip past both of them before she could get to the parking lot. She'd always felt safe on the island, but she didn't feel safe now, and her Viper face was slipping. "Let's get that drink."

"No hurry." Wade, the Dumpster man, rubbed his crotch. "Scottie, go pee."

"Can't. I got a boner."

Their stench made her want to retch. Her heart had started to race. "I need a drink," she said quickly. "You can come with me or stay out here."

But as she tried to slip past them, the one named Wade grabbed her arm. "I like it out here." He squeezed until it hurt. "You really a dyke?"

"Leave me alone." Her voice was suddenly high-pitched, all the toughness gone.

A man interrupted. A knight in shining armor calling out from the corner of the building. "Everything okay back here?"

"No!" she exclaimed.

"Girlfriend's drunk," Wade shouted back. "Don't pay her no attention." He palmed the back of her head and smashed her face into the reek of his T-shirt so she couldn't cry out.

Her knight in shining armor turned out not to be a knight at all, but one more person who didn't want to get involved. "Okay, then." She heard his steps fade away.

She had no Panda to protect her, no Secret Service. *Be careful what you wish for.* The pressure on the back of her head against his chest didn't ease. She couldn't scream. Could barely breathe. She was on her own.

She started to struggle. Pushed hard against him, twisted, got nowhere. She tried to gasp for air but came up short. The more she struggled, the tighter he held her. She fought harder. Lashed out with her shoe. The hard toe connected.

"Bitch! Grab her legs."

Her head was suddenly free, but as she started to scream, a hand clamped over her mouth from behind, wrenching her neck. One of them caught her legs. Her shoes dropped off as her feet left the ground. She was screaming in her head, a silent scream that did her no good at all.

"Where do you want to take her?"

"Behind those trees."

"I go first."

"Bullshit. I saw her first."

They were going to rape her. They dragged her, one of them holding her legs, the other seizing her by the neck, cutting off her air. She clawed at his arm, digging in her fingernails, but the bruising pressure on her windpipe didn't ease. They pulled her deeper into the cover of the trees. The hold on her ankle loosened. Her foot scraped the ground, and something sharp cut her heel. She felt a hand on her thigh. Heard grunts and curses. She summoned a thread of air, enough for a mewing cry. Kicked out.

"Fuck! Hold her."

"Bitch."

"Keep her quiet."

"Shut up, bitch."

Hands pressing, fingers clawing, and her consciousness beginning to slip away . . .

The world exploded. "Let her go!"

The bikers dropped her to the ground and spun to confront this new threat.

Barely conscious, she sucked in air and pain. Through her mental fog she saw Panda. He hurled one of them into the dirt. The other charged him. Panda threw a punch that made him stagger, but the guy was a goon, and he came right back. Panda landed a vicious jab to his middle that knocked him into a tree.

This was no gentlemen's fight. Panda was an assassin, and he knew exactly what he was doing. The man on the ground tried to get up. Panda slammed a foot down on his elbow joint. The biker howled in agony.

The other one was still on his feet, and Panda had his back turned. She tried to get up, call out to warn him, but Panda was already spinning, his leg shooting out like a piston, catching the biker in the groin, crumpling him. Panda leaned down, caught him by the neck, and banged his head against the tree.

The one with the broken elbow came up on his knees. Panda grasped him by his bad arm, dragged him to the long slope that led down to the water, and rolled him over. She heard a distant splash.

Panda's breath was coming harder now. He went back for the other one and started hauling him toward the water. She finally found her voice, a scratchy thready affair. "They'll drown."

"Their problem." He hoisted the second one over the edge. Another heavy splash.

He came toward her, his chest heaving, trickling blood from the corner of his mouth. He knelt beside her, and the hands that had been so brutal moved gently along her body from her neck to her limbs to the gouge on her heel. "You're going to hurt," he said softly, "but I don't think anything is broken. I'm carrying you to the car."

"I can walk." She hated how weak she sounded.

He didn't argue. He simply picked her up and cradled her against his chest. The images wouldn't fit together—the lover she knew and the brutally efficient assassin who'd crushed two men.

He must have had a spare car key because he didn't ask for the one she'd tucked in her pocket. A couple came out of the bar and stared at them. He opened the passenger door and carefully lowered her into the seat. He took his time fastening her seat belt, still protecting her.

He asked no questions as they drove home, didn't tell her what an idiot she was to come here alone or reproach her for being so rotten to him. She didn't know why he'd returned to the bar, couldn't think about what would have happened if he hadn't. She huddled against the door, nauseated, shaken, still terrified.

"I had a half brother," he said into the quiet gloom. "His name was Curtis."

Startled, she turned her head to look at him.

"He was seven years younger than me." His hands shifted on the wheel. "A dreamy, gentle kid with a big imagination." He spoke softly as they sped along the dark road. "Our mother was either drugged out or on the prowl, so I ended up taking care of him."

This was her story, except it was coming from him. She rested the back of her head against the door and listened, her heart rate beginning to slow.

"Eventually we ended up in foster homes. I did everything I could to keep us together, but things happened, and as I got older, I started getting into trouble. Picking fights, shoplifting. When I was seventeen, I was caught trying to sell half a gram of marijuana. It was like I wanted to get thrown into jail."

She understood and said softly, "A good way to escape the responsibility."

He glanced over at her. "You had the same kind of responsibility."

"A pair of guardian angels showed up in my life. You didn't have that, did you?"

"No. No guardian angels." They passed Dogs 'N' Malts, closed up for the night. She was no longer shaking quite so badly, and she unclasped her hands. He flipped on his high beams. "Curtis was murdered while I was in juvie," he said.

She'd suspected this was coming, but it didn't make it easier to hear.

Panda went on. "It was a drive-by shooting. Without me around to protect him, he started ignoring curfews. They let me out to go to his funeral. He was ten years old."

If it hadn't been for Nealy and Mat, this might have been her story and Tracy's story. She licked her dry lips. "And you're still trying to live with what happened. Even though you were only a kid at the time, you still blame yourself. I understand that."

"I figured you would." They were alone on the dark road.

"I'm glad you told me," she said.

"You haven't heard all of it."

For months she'd tried to get him to spill his secrets, but she was no longer sure she wanted to hear them.

He slowed for the road's sharpest curve. "When Curtis's sperm donor found out my mother was pregnant, he gave her five hundred dollars and split. She loved the jerk and wouldn't go to a lawyer. Curtis was nearly two before she realized her big love wasn't coming back. That was when she started using."

Lucy did the math. Panda had been nine when he'd become his brother's caretaker. A protector, even then.

"When I got older," he said, "I found out who the bastard was and tried to call him a couple of times, tell him how bad things were for his kid. He acted like he didn't know who I was talking about. Told me he'd have me locked up if I kept harassing him. Eventually I found out where he lived and went to see him." He shook his head. "It's not easy for a city kid to get to Grosse Pointe on public transportation."

Grosse Pointe? Lucy sat up straighter, an odd feeling coming over her.

"It was a big house, looked like a mansion to me. Gray stone with four chimneys, a swimming pool, and these kids chasing each other around the front yard with water guns. Three boys in their teens. A girl. Even in shorts and T-shirts they all looked rich."

The pieces fell into place.

"The Remingtons," he said. "The perfect American family."

The car's headlights cut through the night.

"I'd walked the last couple of miles from the bus stop," he said, "and I hid across the street. They all had that lean, WASPy look. Curtis and I were both dark like our mother." The shuttered farm stand whipped by on their left. "While I watched, a landscape crew pulled up at the house and wheeled a mower off the back of the truck. Four kids in the family, and they hired somebody to cut their grass."

He turned into the drive. The house loomed, not even a light over the front door to welcome them. "I found another hiding place where I could watch them in their backyard. I stayed until it got dark." He killed the engine but made no move to get out of the car. "I felt like I was watching a TV show. It was his wife's birthday. There were balloons and presents, this big glass-top table set with flowers and candles. Steaks on the grill. I was so damned hungry, and none of them looked like they had a care in the world. He had his arm around his wife most of the evening. He gave her some kind of necklace as a present. I couldn't see what it looked like, but from the way she acted, I figured it cost a lot more than five hundred dollars."

Her heart welled with pity for him. And something more. Something she wouldn't consider.

"The sickest part is that I kept going back. Maybe a dozen times over the years. It was easier after I got a car. Sometimes I'd see them, sometimes not." He curled his fingers over the top of the steering wheel. "One Sunday I followed them to church and sat in the back where I could watch them."

"You hated them, and you wanted to be part of them," she said. "That's why you bought this house."

His hand came off the steering wheel, and his mouth twisted. "A stupid decision. It was a bad time for me. I shouldn't have done it."

Now she understood why he refused to change anything in the house. Consciously or unconsciously, he wanted to live inside the museum of their lives.

He got out of the car and came around to help her. Even though she was feeling steadier, she was grateful for his hand as he led her through the front door and into the bedroom.

He understood without her telling him how much she needed to wash away the men's filth. He helped her undress. Turned on the water.

When she was in the shower, he pulled off his clothes and got in with her. But there was nothing sexual in the tender way he washed her, dried her, tended to the cuts on her feet. Not once did he remind her of what she'd said to him at the bar or criticize her for wandering off the way she had.

After he'd helped her into bed, he touched her cheek. "I need to talk to the police. The house is locked, and Temple's upstairs. Your cell is by your bed. I won't be gone long."

She wanted to tell him she could take care of herself, but that was so blatantly untrue that she said nothing. Viper, despite all her tough girl posturing, had proved to be completely helpless.

Later she awoke to the sound of his footsteps on the stairs. She looked at the clock. It was four-thirty. He'd been gone almost two hours. She flinched as she tried to find a more comfortable position, but her ribs were tender, her neck stiff, her back sore. None of that hurt as much as thinking about what Panda had endured as a child.

She eventually gave up trying to fall back to sleep and got out of bed. He'd done a good job bandaging her foot, and putting her weight on it barely hurt. She made her way to the sunroom, where she curled up on the couch.

As the light leaked over the horizon, she turned her thoughts from Panda to her own foolishness —the last thing she wanted to examine. But last night's ugly experience had ripped away the veil of her self-deception and shown her the absurdity of the false identity she'd created for herself. What a joke—that hard-boiled swagger and pugnacious attitude. She'd never felt more like a fool—the biggest phony on the island. When it had come to protecting herself, she'd failed abysmally. Instead she'd been a helpless, frantic mess who had to be rescued by a man. The truth tasted bitter in her mouth.

She found her yellow pad. After a few false starts, she wrote a brief note. She owed him that—and so much more. She tossed a few things into her backpack and, as the sun came up, made her way through the woods.

Her sneakers were soaked with dew by the time she reached the cottage just as Bree was emerging from the honey house. Bree's hair was uncombed, her clothes rumpled, her sticky hands held far away from her body. But her gasp of alarm indicated that Lucy looked a lot worse.

Lucy slipped her backpack off her shoulder. "Could I stay here for a while?"

"Of course you can." She paused. "Come inside. I'll make coffee."

LATER THAT MORNING, WHILE BREE was at the farm stand, Lucy went into the bathroom and cut the dreads from her hair. Standing naked on the white tile floor, she worked at her tattoos with a combination of rubbing alcohol and baby oil. Finally the last remnants were gone.

Chapter Twenty-one

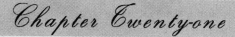

P ANDA CRUMPLED THE NOTE SHE'D written and tossed it in the trash, but throwing the damned thing away didn't erase it from his mind.

> *Thank you for everything you did for me last night. I'll never forget it. I've gone to the cottage to stay with Bree for a while and try to get a fresh perspective. I'm glad you told me about your brother.*
>
> L.

What the hell? Not even a *Dear Panda* or a *Yours sincerely?* The message it delivered was loud and clear. She wanted him to leave her alone. Which he was more than happy to do.

He slammed the cupboard door, trying not to think about what would have happened if he hadn't gone back to the bar last night. By the time he'd reached his boat at the marina, his temper had cooled just enough that he'd started to worry about her again. He'd made up his mind to get her out of that bar, no matter what she said.

He splashed coffee into his mug, decent coffee because he'd made it. He had work to do, and he forced himself into the den, where he booted up his computer. After he'd left her last night, he'd gone with the local cops to locate the two scumbags who'd attacked her. He'd known the water wasn't deep enough to drown them when he'd tossed them in, and sure enough, it hadn't taken long to find them staggering back to the bar to get their bikes. No surprise either, there were warrants out on both of them, which made it easier to convince the police chief to keep Lucy's name out of it.

He couldn't concentrate on work, and he pushed himself back from the desk—old man Templeton's desk, although he'd stopped thinking so much about that. He decided to go up to the gym and take out his frustration on Temple. If she hadn't talked him into coming here, none of this would have happened.

But he set off for the lake instead. *Be the best at what you're good at and stay away from what you're not.* Right now, caring too much about the daughter of the president of the United States topped the list of everything he wasn't good at.

THE ORGANIST WAS PLAYING A familiar hymn, although Bree couldn't recall its name. She smiled at a woman she'd spoken with during last week's coffee hour. Bree was growing to love Heart of Charity Missionary. Although she still sometimes felt like an outsider, the emotion-filled service gave her comfort. She wished Lucy had come along this morning, but after Lucy had shed her tattoos, Bree had cut her hair, trying to camouflage the areas where she'd chopped off her dreads, and now Lucy was too recognizable.

When Bree had stepped out of the honey house and seen Lucy standing there so pale and bruised, she'd thought Panda had beaten her. Lucy had quickly disabused her of that notion with a brief, disturbing account of what had happened at The Compass, but she hadn't said much more, and Bree wasn't pressing her.

Toby turned around in the pew, and she saw why he hadn't given her his normal flack about going to church. "You came!" he said in a loud whisper as Mike settled next to him.

"Sure I did." Even though temperatures were already in the low eighties, he wore a light tan sports coat, pale blue dress shirt, and a blue-and-brown-striped necktie. She wasn't exactly sure when he'd discarded his big college ring and ostentatious gold bracelet. She'd never mentioned either one, no matter how much she'd wanted to, but they were gone. He also smelled great. Like good shaving cream.

He nodded politely at Bree, whatever amorous feelings he'd once harbored for her clearly gone. She studied him as he looked away, something she'd been doing a lot of over the past two weeks. She couldn't feel good about the way she was using him. By acting friendly and pretending she'd forgotten about the past just so he'd be there for her if she needed him, she was the worst kind of hypocrite.

Since the night he'd appeared at Dogs 'N' Malts, he'd become a regular visitor to the cottage. Sharing a few meals with him hadn't been as difficult as she'd thought. He spent most of the time talking to Toby. He treated her politely, but that was all. No more apologies, no more references to the past. He was a man who'd said his piece and didn't repeat himself. She'd even gone out on the boat with him and Toby after Lucy had insisted on watching the farm stand.

To her surprise, it had been the best day of her summer. The three of them had dived into the lake together. Mike was an excellent swimmer, and Toby loved horsing around with him. She'd watched the flex of Mike's shoulders as he'd tossed Toby in the water and felt the most peculiar stirring, like an embryonic chick who'd grown just big enough to make the first small crack in its shell. Later that day, while the boat bobbed at anchor and they munched on junk food, she'd had to fight back tears just because Toby had reminded her to put on more sunscreen.

Deacon Miller rose to welcome the congregation. She and Toby no longer warranted a special introduction, but Mike was a newcomer. "We are so blessed to have you with us today, Mike," Deacon Miller said. "We all remember how you helped us buy our new organ."

The congregation broke out in a lusty chorus of amens.

"It was the least I could do after all those potlucks," Mike said, displaying none of the discomfort she'd felt during her first visit. "Best church food on the island."

Agreeing nods all around. Wasn't there anybody who didn't like him?

Pastor Sanders rose for the opening prayer. Her products had only been in his gift shop for two weeks, but her lotions and honey were selling well enough that he'd asked for more—only a small order because Labor Day was near, but an order nonetheless.

As bad luck would have it, his sermon that morning centered on forgiveness, a subject that reminded her of Mike.

"I'm a religious man," he'd said. *"I believe in sin, and I believe in repentance. I've made amends as best as I know how, but it hasn't changed anything."*

"And it won't," she'd told him.

Sitting here in this sacred place, she no longer felt so righteous.

When the service was over, Toby attached himself to Mike, and Mike worked the crowd, just as he'd done at the Episcopal church. He knew everyone, and everyone knew him. He introduced her to members she'd yet to meet, including one of the real estate agents who worked for him and several former clients.

It was finally time to leave, and they stepped out into the blazing late morning sun. "Is it okay if I take Toby to see my new dog?" Mike said, once again forgetting to ask her these kinds of things when Toby wasn't listening.

Toby's eyes immediately lit up. The abandoned puppy had been a frequent topic of conversation between them. Toby had tried to dissuade Mike from turning it over to a rescue group on the mainland. In the end, Toby had won. "You've got to come, too, Bree," he declared before she said he could go. "Can she, Mike?"

She tugged on one of her hoop earrings, not looking at Mike. "I should . . . get back and relieve Lucy."

Toby grew mulish. "Lucy already told you she'd stay all morning."

Once again, she'd set herself up as the bad guy. She was sick of it. "You're right. I'd love to see the dog."

Toby grinned and raced down the sidewalk. "I'm riding with Mike."

Mike gazed at her. He'd slipped on his sunglasses, so she couldn't see his eyes. "You don't have to go with us."

"I know that." She couldn't bring herself to say that she almost wanted to go. "But Toby wants me to, so I will."

Mike gave a brusque nod and went off to join Toby, leaving her to trail after them in her own car.

Mike's luxurious log home sat far above the lake on the island's less populated west side. Each level held a porch or balcony built of varnished logs. Mike led them around to the back, where a long wooden table big enough to hold a dozen people sat in the shade of the covered patio. As Bree took in the lake view, Mike went inside and, a few moments later, reappeared with the puppy, an adorable short-haired mutt sporting alarmingly oversize paws.

She couldn't hold back a smile as she watched Toby and the dog get reacquainted. "I wonder how Dr. King would feel about having a dog named after him?" she said.

Mike pretended to take her comment seriously. Or at least she thought he was pretending. "Martin's an exceptional dog. I think Dr. King would be okay with it."

"You're keeping the dog because of Toby, aren't you?"

Mike merely shrugged.

She needed Mike a lot more than he needed her, and she pressed on. "He was upset about his friends not coming back. Thank you for volunteering to break the news. Martin has really helped cheer him up."

He tossed his sports coat over the nearest chair. His tan dress shirt was virtually unwrinkled, with none of the sweat rings under his arms the day's heat should have produced. "I might as well tell you that I put my foot in it again," he said, not quite looking at her as he loosened his tie. "I wanted to give him something to look forward to, so . . ." His faintly guilty expression wasn't encouraging. "I asked him if he'd take care of Martin whenever I leave the island."

"What's wrong with that?"

He pulled off the tie. "The logistics."

She got it. Mike lived too far away for Toby to bike to his house, especially in the winter, and it would be impractical for Bree to drive him back and forth several times a day. "So the dog will have to stay with us at the cottage," she concluded.

"Sorry," he said. "I should have asked you first."

She made herself nod even as she eyed Martin's enormous paws with a sense of foreboding. "It's okay," she said.

Toby wrestled the puppy for a stick. He was outgrowing his only pair of decent pants, and it wouldn't be long before he needed shoes. She pushed the thought away. "Tell me about your house."

"It's one of the most expensive on the island, one of the biggest—" He stopped, his customary enthusiasm deserting him. "Sorry. I didn't mean to brag. When you sell real estate, you get used to lining up your talking points."

She was surprised that he'd recognized how he was coming off, but he seemed more tired than embarrassed. She didn't know what to make of that, so she asked to see the inside of the house.

Mike tossed Toby a dog leash. "How about taking Martin for a walk while I show Bree around?"

As Toby clipped the leash to the pup's collar, Bree followed Mike through the glass doors. They stepped into an enormous great room with log walls, a high-beamed ceiling, and a massive stone fireplace. The magazine-worthy decor was both masculine and comfortable, with a color scheme of chocolate, cinnamon, and bittersweet. Old-fashioned snowshoes, topographic maps, and forged iron wall sconces hung on one wall; a big picture window with a view of the lake occupied another. A round coffee table rested in front of a deep leather couch draped with a black-and-gold-checked Pendleton blanket. The hearth held a twig firewood basket and a roughly carved wooden statue of a black bear.

"It's beautiful," she said.

"I always wanted a North Woods house. Cool and dark in the summer. Warm and comfortable in the winter."

"Pure Michigan." She smiled. "I'd say you accomplished your goal."

"I hired a decorator. A great guy. He and his partner visit once a year and throw out the kind of stuff I tend to pick up on my own. I still can't figure out what's wrong with a couple of U2 posters and a stuffed carp." His eyes were laughing at her, but as she smiled back, he looked away. "The truth is, I don't have what you call first-class taste, as I'm sure you've noticed."

True. Mike only had first-class kindness. "It's a big house for a bachelor," she said.

"I had a family in mind when I built it. I was engaged at the time."

That surprised her, although it shouldn't have. A man as attractive and successful as Mike wouldn't have trouble finding women—at least women who hadn't known him when he was younger. "Anyone I know?" she asked.

"No." He nudged an ottoman out of the way so she wouldn't have to step around it. "Her family summers in Petoskey. Breaking that engagement was the hardest thing I ever did."

"*You* broke the engagement?"

"You figure I was the one who got dumped, right?"

"No. Not at all." That's exactly what she'd thought. "I just didn't know you'd ever been engaged."

"We had different values. She didn't like island life or most of my local friends. But she had good qualities, too."

"Just not enough for you to marry her."

He refused to put down his former fiancée. "She took it hard. I still feel bad about it."

And he would. The adult Mike Moody didn't like hurting people. Maybe he never had.

He reached up to open his collar button, a simple gesture, but so completely masculine that she felt a little queasy. The sensation threw her off so much that she asked a question she'd never otherwise have posed. "Have there been a lot of women?"

"A lot? No. As much as I enjoy sex, I never slept with a woman I didn't care about. If that makes me an oddball, I can live with it."

It didn't make him an oddball; it made him a decent guy. But she still wished he hadn't brought up sex. All right, so she was the one who'd brought it up, but he didn't have to give her any details. She wanted to believe he . . .

She didn't know what she wanted to believe, and she was glad when his cell rang.

"A client," he said, glancing at the display. "I have to take this."

He retreated to the next room. She studied the untidy pile of books on the table. John Steinbeck, Kurt Vonnegut, a couple of motivational books, the Bible. There were some newsmagazines, *Sports Illustrated, GQ.* Everything looked as though it had been read, and she seemed to remember Mike trapping David into more than one conversation about books.

Through the glass doors, she could see him in the next room talking on the phone. He was the only consistent male role model in Toby's life, the closest thing Toby had to a big brother. Or a father. She could no longer doubt Mike's affection for Toby, but would it last? How would Toby react if Mike disengaged himself?

Each day it became more difficult to get her bearings. She could no longer tell what was self-serving about Mike and what was genuine. But she did know what was self-serving about herself . . . She felt a flush of shame.

He finished his phone conversation and rejoined her, but it quickly became evident that he was more interested in getting back to Toby and the dog than he was in talking to her.

Lucy sat on an old beach towel she'd spread under a cherry tree in the neighboring orchards just out of sight of the cottage. For three days, she'd been checking the local news, but she'd seen nothing about bodies washing ashore, so she assumed the thugs who'd attacked her had survived. Too bad. Today she'd cranked the extractor, bottled honey, and cooked, but before she started tonight's dinner, she'd slipped away to spend a little time here, lying on her back and looking at the clouds through the branches.

One of Bree's bees landed in a spot of clover not far from her arm and dipped its proboscis into the heart of a flower. As bruises from her attack had begun to fade, everything that had been so murky was becoming clear. For years she'd lived in a skin that didn't fit her, but the skin she'd adopted this summer had proved to be just as wrong. Had she really thought that slapping on a few tattoos and playing at being fearless would somehow transform her into the free spirit she wanted to be? This summer had been nothing more than a fantasy. Panda was nothing more than a fantasy.

She rolled to her side. Her arm looked different without its rose and thorn ink, like it belonged to someone else. She picked up the pristine pad of yellow paper that lay next to her. This time she didn't feel like running off to bake bread or take the kayak out. Instead she sat up, balanced the pad on one knee, clicked her ballpoint pen, and finally began to write in earnest.

> *A lot of what happened that summer, you already know. The way Nealy, Mat, Tracy, and I met has been widely documented by journalists, scholars, biographers, a few novelists, and an awful television movie. But it's always Nealy and Mat's story, with me in a supporting role. Since this is my father's book about Nealy, you might expect more of the same, but I can't write about my mother without writing about myself . . .*

PANDA STEPPED UP HIS WORKOUTS to mark off the hours until he could finally leave the island. When he wasn't lifting weights or out for a run, he worked around the house. He repaired the broken screen on the back porch, fixed a couple of rotted windowsills, and talked to half a dozen potential clients on the phone. It was Wednesday. Lucy had only been gone since Friday, but it felt like weeks. He'd driven by the farm stand a couple of times, but he'd seen only Toby or Sabrina West, never Lucy. Every part of him yearned to stalk over to the cottage and drag her back here where she belonged.

He glanced out the window. Temple was down on the dock again. It had been so long since she'd made a snarky remark that he was starting to worry about her. She wasn't working out as much these days, and she barely spoke. He needed Lucy here to talk to her. To talk to him. For all Lucy's complaining that he never told her anything, she could read his mind better than anyone.

What if she wasn't taking care of that cut on her heel? And for all he knew, she might have a concussion. A dozen things could be happening to her over there, none of them good. Bree knew who Lucy was, and he suspected Mike Moody did, too. All either of them had to do was make one phone call and the press would be swarming. He wanted Lucy where he could watch her, damn it. And take her to bed.

He'd always been a serial monogamist. He was used to going long periods without a woman, and sooner or later he'd get used to this. But he didn't want to. He wanted to feel her moving under him, over him, hear the catch of her breath, the soft moans, the entreaties. He wanted to hold her. Taste her. Make her laugh. He wanted to talk to her, really talk.

That brought him up short. She was too damned softhearted. If he really talked to her, she might start thinking about his well-being instead of her own. He couldn't allow that to happen.

BREE HEADED BACK TO THE cottage from the farm stand. Lucy had disappeared, and Toby was on duty. He complained bitterly about being overworked, but Bree had turned mean lately, and she'd told him she liked making kids suffer.

"Make sure you don't get shortchanged," she'd reminded him.

He'd given her one of his looks, since they both knew he was quicker with numbers, and she was far more likely to have that happen to her.

She'd been halfway down the drive when something had made her stop and call back to him. "Hey, punk!"

"What do you want now?"

"Your mom was really good at math, too," she'd said.

He'd stood completely still before he turned away. "Whatever."

Despite his phony nonchalance, Bree knew he loved hearing about his parents, and she'd been dredging up every story she could remember.

She couldn't recall exactly when she'd stopped wanting to reach for her cigarettes whenever she thought about David. The pain and that aching sense of regret had faded so gradually she'd barely noticed.

Just before she reached the honey house, she heard a rustle. Branches moved in one of the clump maples that bordered the woods. There was no breeze this afternoon, so it could have been a squirrel, but——

The branches swayed again, and she caught a glimpse of a woman—a tourist who'd lost her way? She went to investigate.

A particularly foul stream of curses assailed her ears as she pushed through the weeds. She came upon a dark-haired woman trying to disentangle her purple yoga pants from the blackberry brambles. As soon as the woman looked up, Bree experienced a jolt of recognition. First Lucy Jorik had popped up and now Temple Renshaw? What was going on? She hurried over to help.

The woman tugged at the knit fabric of her pants. "Why would you keep something this vicious around?"

Bree descended to teen-speak. "Uh, like for the blackberries?"

Renshaw snorted, then cursed again and sucked a scratch on the back of her hand.

Bree knew her from *Fat Island,* a show she hated but that Scott had loved. He'd taken pleasure in the way Temple tormented the contestants, boasted about his own fitness, and drooled over the vapid, bikini-clad psychiatrist who supposedly counseled them. *"That is one hot shrink,"* he'd said more than once. *"If you had tits like hers, I'd be a happy man."*

Instead of telling him that if he had a shred of decency, she'd be a happy woman, she'd nursed her hurt in silence.

Finally free of the brambles, Temple gazed past Bree toward the cottage. "I'm looking for a friend."

Bree was immediately on guard. "Friend?"

"Black hair. Tattoos. Chubby thighs."

Temple could only be talking about Lucy—although Lucy had great legs—but Bree wasn't giving out any information. "Chubby thighs?"

Temple climbed through the weeds toward the cottage, not waiting for an invitation. "A lot of women carry weight there. It's so unnecessary."

Bree followed her, both put off by her high-handed manner and curious. As Temple reached the yard, she took in the hives and the ripening tomatoes in the garden. She wore no makeup to hide the hollows under her eyes, and her hair, long and lustrous on-screen, was pulled into a haphazard ponytail. The muscles and tendons in her upper torso were too gristly for Bree's taste, and her tight-fitting workout clothes clung to an unnaturally rippled abdomen. She looked better on television.

Temple examined the scratch on her hand. "She left a note at the house saying she was coming here. I have to talk to her."

Lucy had mentioned a friend who was staying at the house, but she hadn't offered any details, and Bree had forgotten about it. She'd certainly never imagined Lucy's friend was Temple Renshaw.

Temple looked her square in the eye. "Is she around?"

Bree wasn't good at standing up to assertive people, but she didn't know whether Lucy wanted to see this woman or not. "There's nobody here now but me."

Temple shoved back a lock of dark hair that had escaped her ponytail. "Fine. I'll wait."

"I'd rather you didn't."

Temple ignored her. She crossed the yard and dropped down on the back step—the same place where Bree used to spend so much time.

Bree couldn't throw her off the property physically, so she shrugged and echoed Toby. "Whatever."

TOBY WAS WORRIED. THE GLASS ornaments Bree had hand-painted with scenes from the island and sold for thirty-five dollars each were all gone, but instead of saving the money, she'd bought more to paint. It was stupid. Labor Day was three weeks away, and the tourists would be gone after that. She didn't have time to sell more, and then what were they going to do for money? This had been the worst summer of his life. He was never going to see Eli and Ethan again. Even Mike hadn't been around much lately. He was too busy with clients.

A gray SUV stopped. As the door opened, he saw the driver was Panda. Now that he'd gotten to know him better, Toby wasn't so scared of him. Panda let Toby take a kayak out, and the two of them had paddled around the cove and even into the lake. Panda also let Toby help chop down a dead tree. Toby hoped he'd be as cool as Panda when he grew up. He liked the way Panda walked, like he was real tough and never had to worry about anything. He liked his shades. Nobody would ever mess with a guy liked Panda.

"How you doing, pal?" Panda said as he approached. "Made any money?"

"Sixty-eight dollars this afternoon."

"That's good." He looked around. "I thought Lucy might be working here today."

Toby shrugged. "I don't know where she is."

Panda nodded like he was thinking that over, although Toby couldn't really see what there was to think about. "How is she?" he asked.

"Okay, I guess." The scab on Toby's knee was itching. He scratched around it.

"Is she walking okay?"

"What do you mean?"

"I mean, is she limping or anything like that?"

"I don't know. I guess not."

Panda shoved his hand through his hair, like he might be getting a little upset. He was acting weird. "But she's talking to you?"

"Sure."

"So . . . Did she say anything to you about . . . anything?"

"Lots of stuff."

"Like what?"

Toby thought about it. "She said she didn't think anybody should go around saying the *n*-word, not even if they're black like me. Her brother, Andre, is black. Did you know that?"

"I did."

"She doesn't think a lot of hip-hop artists are good role models for kids, but I think they are. They make a lot of money and everything." Panda kept looking at him, like he expected Toby to say more, but Toby didn't know what else he was supposed to say. "She put a mashed-up sweet potato in some bread she made, but it still tasted good."

Panda kept staring at him. Toby was starting to wish he'd go away. "She told Bree that she likes to ride horses."

Panda wandered over to the honey and stared at it, like he was really interested in honey. "Did she say anything about me?"

His scab was itching again. "I don't know. I guess not."

Panda nodded, stared at the honey some more, then grabbed a bottle. Only after he was back in his car did Toby see that he'd paid for it with a twenty-dollar bill. "Hey!"

But Panda was pulling away.

LUCY HEARD THEIR VOICES BEFORE she reached the cottage. She'd hoped to write another few pages this afternoon, but an overpowering urge to eat something sweet had driven her back to the house. She was finding it more difficult to adjust to her former healthy eating habits than she'd ever imagined possible. In the old days, she seldom ate when she wasn't hungry, but two months of "dieting" had made her obsess about food. Now, when she was uncomfortable, tired, or unhappy, all she wanted to do was stuff her mouth. No wonder most people gained their weight back after they dieted.

As the voices grew louder, she readjusted the beach towel she'd bunched under her arm and stopped to listen.

"You should leave now," she heard Bree say.

"Not until I see Lucy," Temple retorted.

"She's gone."

"I don't believe you. Her things are still in her bedroom at the house."

Bree hesitated. "Only because she doesn't want them anymore."

"Tell me another one. Where is she?"

"I'm not her keeper. How am I supposed to know?"

Lucy listened in bemusement as the timid field mouse stood up to the Evil Queen. What had happened to the insecure woman Lucy had first met? Lucy reluctantly stepped out of the trees. Temple slammed her hands on her hips. "There you are! I'm furious with you."

"Leave her alone," the field mouse said.

Temple stalked toward Lucy. "It was bad enough for you to walk out on Panda, but I didn't do anything, and you had no right to walk out on me. Did you stop for one second to think how I'd feel when I heard you'd run away without a word? I'm so furious with you that I don't care if I ever speak to you again."

"Then why are you here?" Bree's jaw set in a newly stubborn line.

Temple spun on her. "Stay out of this. It has nothing to do with you."

"This is my house, and Lucy's my guest. That makes it my business."

Lucy forced herself to step in. "Have the two of you been properly introduced? Bree West, this is Temple Renshaw. Temple, Bree."

"I know who she is," Bree said tightly.

Lucy regarded her ruefully. "Believe it or not, Temple really isn't quite as rude as she seems."

"Don't you dare apologize for me," Temple retorted, taking in Lucy's chin-length and much neater hairdo—compliments of Bree and her scissors. "I'm still infuriated with you."

"I understand," Lucy conceded. "And you're right. I'm sorry. I should at least have left you a note."

Temple sniffed. "You deserve to be sorry. When are you coming home?"

"She's not," Bree said firmly. "She's staying here."

"That's what you think."

Listening to the two of them argue over her made Lucy feel better than she had in days. Temple turned her back to Bree. Some of her aggression faded, and her brow knit with concern. "What did he do to you? He told me what happened at that dive you went to, but I know he didn't tell me everything." And then, to Bree, with forced politeness, "Would you mind going away so Lucy and I can talk?"

Lucy reluctantly put a halt to their tiff. "Stop glowering at her, Temple. She has every right to be here. I was planning to talk to you. I just didn't want to go back to the house to do it."

Wrong thing to say. Temple's brow shot up in righteous anger. "Then obviously our friendship isn't important to you."

"That's not true." Lucy dropped her beach towel in a patch of shade and sat on it. As the spicy scent of basil drifted toward her, she filled Temple in on more of the details of what had happened at The Compass. When she was done, she hugged her knees to her chest. "I thought I was so tough."

"You're not seriously blaming yourself for not being able to fight off those gangsters," Temple said.

"Other women do it."

"In the movies."

Her indignation was comforting, but Lucy couldn't give herself a free pass.

In a single graceful movement, Temple dropped beside her on the beach towel. "I don't understand why Panda was so stingy with the details."

"Client privilege, I'm sure." Lucy swallowed her bitterness. "Basically, that's how he still sees me. As his responsibility."

"He protected you," Temple said adamantly. "So why are you so pissed with him?"

"I'm not," she said. "I'm pissed with myself."

"Sure. Blame the victim," Bree interjected.

"It's not that," Lucy said. "All summer I pretended I was so tough. Joke's on me, right?"

Temple brushed that away. "What about Panda? Why did you walk out on him?"

"Because our relationship was as phony as my tattoos."

"It didn't seem phony to me." Temple looked over at Bree. "Anybody who sees them together can tell how hot they are for each other."

Lucy didn't like that. "I dumped my fiancé at the altar, and two weeks later, I jumped in bed with another man. Nice, right?"

"Normally, no," Temple said. "But when the man is Panda . . ."

Lucy wasn't letting anybody make excuses for her. "It's time for me to deal with what's real in my life and what isn't. Panda's not."

"He seems real to me. And you're in love with him."

"Stop saying that!" she cried. "Believe me, love isn't what I feel for Panda." That word belonged to Ted. She'd worshipped him, and she definitely didn't worship Panda. How could you worship someone when all you wanted to do was rip his clothes off? Or laugh with him, or snarl at him, or exchange those looks of perfect understanding? With Panda, she felt like bad Lucy, good Lucy, and Viper all rolled into one. Who needed that kind of confusion?

Bree loomed over the beach towel, rescuing her from further explanation. "Lucy is staying here," she told Temple.

"No, she's not." Temple jumped to her feet. "I want her back."

"Too bad. I need her."

"You think I don't?"

"Tough. You can visit her here whenever you like."

Lucy's eyes stung. "As much as I love watching the two of you fight over me, you really shouldn't."

Bree moved toward the side of the house. "I have to check on Toby. There's iced tea in the refrigerator." She spun back to Lucy. "You stay here. Don't let her bully you."

A smile tugged at the corners of Temple's mouth as Bree disappeared. "I like her." Her smile quickly faded. "What do you hope to accomplish by running away? You keep telling me I need to face my problems, but what do you do when things get tough? Big talker runs away."

"Be nice."

"Fine," Temple said in a huff. "If that's your attitude, I won't tell you about the phone call I made."

"Tell me," Lucy said, because she knew Temple wanted her to ask.

"You don't deserve to know."

"Tell me anyway."

She did, and Lucy sprang up off the towel. "Are you sure about this?"

Temple glowered. "I thought you'd be happy. Isn't this what you wanted?"

Not exactly. But Lucy kept that thought to herself.

PANDA SLAPPED DOWN THE SCREWDRIVER as the doorbell rang. The only person he wanted to see right now was Lucy, and she wouldn't be ringing the doorbell. He'd just finished wrestling with the kitchen table, and removing the bulky legs wasn't going well.

On his way to the front door, he frowned at a cheap seascape hanging on the wall. He'd grown used to paintings disappearing and furniture mysteriously transporting itself from one room to another. Why hadn't Lucy gotten rid of this? Worst of all was his pig. It still wore the same clown nose she'd stuck on it last week.

He reached the door and glanced through the sidelight. A bombshell blonde stood on the other side.

There was something familiar about her, although he knew they'd never met. Maybe it was her figure. Hard to forget a body like this. Big breasts, tiny waist, narrow hips. And spectacular legs, what he could see of them.

He tried to place her as he opened the door, but something about her appearance was throwing him off. Her long blond hair shouldn't be pinned up so neatly, and she wore too many clothes.

Then he recognized her. His stomach sank.

She held out her hand. "You must be Mr. Shade. I'm Kristina Chapman." She cocked her head to the side and smiled, as though they were sharing a private joke. "Dr. Kristi."

Chapter Twenty-two

WOMEN EVERYWHERE, AND EACH ONE of them was a nightmare. Temple, with her dark moods; Dr. Kristi, who'd probably earned her counseling license over the Internet, although she insisted she was legit; Lucy, the biggest pain of all, living on the other side of the woods with Sabrina Remington, the daughter of the man he hated.

Nine days and not a word from her. Telling himself it had to end anyway didn't help.

Temple came downstairs. She was red-eyed and passed him in the hallway without speaking. He didn't like seeing her like this. "Let's go for a run," he said brusquely.

"Later." She sagged into the living room chair and reached for the television remote.

Not long after, while he contemplated where he was going to find a table to fill the newly empty spot in the kitchen, he saw Dr. Kristi in the backyard with a book. She'd been swimming earlier, but instead of wearing her infamous red bikini, which would have provided him with at least some small compensation for putting up with her intrusion, she was wearing an unimpressive green-and-white one-piece.

Temple appeared in the kitchen on her way outside. He jerked his head toward the backyard. "You could have told me you were inviting her here. To *my* house."

"I knew you wouldn't mind." Before he could disabuse her of that notion, she swept past him. "I'm going to the cottage."

"Make yourself useful this time."

"Bring her back yourself," she retorted, just before she slammed the door.

He'd like nothing better than to do that, but then what? Lucy needed a happily-ever-after, something he wasn't capable of delivering. Still, he had to see her before he left the island, although he had no idea what he'd say.

Through the window, he saw Temple approach Dr. Kristi, who closed her book and rose. He couldn't hear what Temple said to her. He didn't really care. He didn't care about much these days.

LUCY WAS BRINGING A COUPLE of glasses of iced tea out to the farm stand when Temple appeared, followed by a tall, busty blonde who could only be Dr. Kristi. The psychologist wore a sleeveless green cover-up over a matching bathing suit. Her blond hair was slicked back from her face, setting off perfect cheekbones and plump, pouty lips.

Lucy had been expecting something like this for the past four days, ever since Temple had told her that she'd asked Dr. Kristi for help. Lucy had urged her to call someone reputable instead of the *Fat Island* shrink, advice Temple had obviously ignored.

Bree sat at the worktable she'd set up in the shade where she was furiously hand-painting the island lighthouse on one of her precious glass ornaments. She had less than two weeks to sell them. She straightened when she saw who'd arrived.

Temple was dressed in her customary yoga pants and tank. She plunged into introductions. "Kristi, this is my friend Lucy. And that's Bree."

Kristi nodded at Bree. "You're the beekeeper. It's a pleasure." And then, to Lucy, "I've looked forward to meeting you, Ms. Jorik. Temple's told me a lot about you."

"None of it good." Temple sprawled into the nursery-yellow Adirondack chair.

"Liar," Lucy retorted, placing the iced tea glasses on Bree's table.

"You're right," Temple muttered. "It's sad to admit I've made an overweight runaway my role model."

"She's not overweight." Bree tore her eyes away from Kristi's porn star lips.

Overweight or not, Lucy couldn't imagine being anybody's role model, although she'd certainly learned some important life lessons this summer.

Temple assured her that Dr. Kristi wouldn't blow her cover. After that, a silence fell over the group. Kristi examined Bree's products. She seemed comfortable with the silence, but none of the rest of them were. Temple stared at her feet, Bree fiddled with her paintbrush, and Lucy tried to think of something to say before she remembered she didn't have to be cruise director for this motley crew.

Temple hopped up from the chair and gazed at Bree, her expression belligerent. "I'm gay."

Bree blinked.

Temple sat back down and stared at her feet again.

Lucy sucked in her breath. She understood what Bree couldn't. This was Temple's coming-out.

Another silence fell over the group. Temple lifted her head but didn't meet any of their eyes. "I'm in love with a woman."

"Uhm . . . Congratulations?" Bree turned the word into a question, then slanted an inquiring look at Kristi. "To both of you?"

It took Temple a moment to follow Bree's train of thought, and then she shuddered. "For god's sake, it's not Kristi."

"That was rather hostile," Kristi said firmly.

"What do you care?" Temple retorted. "You're straight."

Kristi took a seat in the peach-colored chair. "Which doesn't mean I enjoy being dismissed like that."

Bree glanced at Lucy, clearly questioning what kind of loonies she associated with.

"Sorry," Temple said.

Dr. Kristi gave a gracious nod. "Apology accepted."

Lucy leaned toward Temple. "Have you talked to Max?"

Temple waved a dismissive hand, as if Lucy's question were too stupid to waste time answering. Kristi cleared her throat. Temple glanced toward her, then mumbled, "Max hung up on me. She wants revenge."

Lucy thought about it. "I guess that's understandable. What are you going to do now?"

Temple fidgeted in the chair, and when she finally replied, she sounded as if she'd swallowed a bug. "I'm going to beg."

Bree nearly tipped over her painting table as she came out of her chair. "Never beg! Never! It'll rot your soul."

Dr. Kristi regarded Bree with a seriousness very much at odds with her pornographic lips. "You sound as though you're speaking from experience."

Bree's jaw set in its newly stubborn manner. "Ex-husband."

"Do you want to tell us about it?" Kristi asked.

"Hey!" Temple said. "You're my shrink."

Kristi waved off her protest. "I work best in groups."

And that's what she did. For the next hour, Lucy found herself in the middle of a group therapy session that Dr. Kristi led with surprising skill. They touched on the lessons Bree had learned from her humiliating relationship with Scott as well as Temple's need for perfection. Lucy restricted sharing the guilt she felt for hating her lobbying work so much. Dr. Kristi offered the comforting observation that more people should take a break from their ordinary lives to assess their future path. Gradually Lucy realized that Dr. Kristi was very good at what she did, one more shock in a summer filled with them.

Eventually the psychologist declared their time was up, as if this had been a regular appointment. Lucy tried to be tactful. "We don't see this side of you on television."

One of Kristi's pale, beautifully shaped eyebrows arched. "Yes, the tiki hut and red bikini do tend to call my professionalism into question."

"Why do you do it?" Bree asked.

"I suffered from bulimia when I was a teenager," Kristi said matter-of-factly. "That's how I ended up specializing in eating disorders. I took the job on *Fat Island* so I could pay off my student loans, planning to quit after the first season. But I fell in love with the money." She crossed a long, slender leg. "I try to justify staying even though I know the producers care a lot more about giving my body camera time than showing much of the actual counseling component of the show. But our contestants have serious emotional issues, and I know if I leave, the producers won't bother examining the credentials of the person they choose to replace me. As long as she's blond and looks great in a bikini, they'll hire her. So I stay."

"Kristi thinks none of our long-term success stories would have happened without her," Temple said tartly.

Kristi leveled her with a look. "The *few* long-term successes we've had . . . When *Fat Island* became so popular, I used the power I'd built to insist the show pay for real behavioral counseling. The contestants are a wreck after Temple's done with them—destined for long-term failure, which I think she's beginning to understand. Realistically, people with jobs and family can't keep up with a two- or three-hour workout every day. And most of them can't make a long-term commitment to healthy eating without ongoing support."

The Evil Queen toppled. "I'm rethinking my approach, okay?"

"It's about time." Dr. Kristi turned to Bree. "Does knowing Temple is gay affect your opinion of *Fat Island*?"

"She's too polite to tell you the truth," Temple said.

"That's what you think." Bree's red hair caught the sunlight as her chin came up. "I hated the show before, and I still hate it."

Kristi nodded. "You see, Temple. The world won't stop spinning because you've finally found the courage to live genuinely."

"Blah, blah, blah," Temple said, but her heart wasn't in it.

Eventually the conversation shifted to less explosive topics, and while Dr. Kristi asked to sample Bree's new flavored honeys, Temple dragged Lucy aside. "Kristi's attracted to Panda," she hissed when they were out of earshot. "She's got her eyes all over him."

Lucy bit the inside of her lip. "Is Panda attracted to Kristi?"

"Have you looked at her? What man wouldn't be attracted? Last night she wore her hair down, and she never does that if she's not on camera. You need to come home right now and protect your turf."

Lucy gazed at a completely ordinary swallowtail butterfly as if she'd never seen such a creature. "I don't have a turf."

"You're an idiot," Temple jeered.

But Lucy saw the concern in her eyes, not that she was stupid enough to mention it. "And here I thought you were turning into a kinder, gentler person."

"Later."

Lucy barely managed a smile.

BREE SPENT THE LATE AFTERNOON extruding more honey from the heavy frames, and she didn't have a chance to clean up before dinner. Lucy insisted on doing the dishes afterward, and Bree put up only a cursory protest. She was heading for the shower when she overheard Mike and Toby talking on the front porch. She stopped to listen.

"I think you should ask Bree out on a date," she heard Toby say. "I know she didn't like you at first, but she's changed her mind. Did you see her at dinner? She laughed at all your jokes."

Bree moved nearer the front curtain where she could better hear Mike's response.

"I wouldn't make too much of it," he said. "Lucy laughed, too."

"But Bree laughed more," Toby observed. "And she's always looking at you. You should ask her to go out to dinner or something. Not to Dogs 'N' Malts, but like to the Island Inn or someplace nice."

"I can't do that, Toby," Mike replied with an uncharacteristic stubbornness.

"Why not?"

"Because I can't." A dish clattered in the kitchen. Mike's chair creaked. "Bree's worried about what will happen this winter. She wants to make sure she can count on me if she needs help. I'd do exactly the same thing if I were in her shoes."

And Bree thought she was being so clever . . . She should have realized no one built a business as successful as Mike's without having some insight into people's motivations.

Toby wouldn't give up. "I still don't see why you can't take her out to dinner."

"Because she'd have to say yes, even if she didn't want to."

"She'd want to," Toby insisted. "I know she would."

"Toby, this might be hard to understand. . . ." His voice was patient, the way it always was when he explained anything to Toby. "I'm not interested in Bree that way."

He wasn't?

She heard a chair scrape followed by the solid tread of his steps across the porch. "Martin!" Mike shouted. "Come back here! Toby, go rescue him before he gets to the highway."

She'd never quite believed Mike's recent display of indifference. She'd counted on his steadfastness, consoled herself that—even though Scott had long ago lost interest in her—Mike would yearn for her forever. What a fool.

She pressed her hand hard against her chest. She couldn't bear another rejection, not from Mike of all people. Her heart thudded against her palm. She came out from behind the curtains, pushed open the screen door, and stepped onto the porch.

Toby was at the far end of the drive with the dog. Mike stood on the top step, a lock of light brown hair drifting across his forehead. Even in worn jeans and a white T-shirt advertising JAKE'S DIVE SHOP, he was an arresting figure, tall and imposing, his strong profile illuminated by the porch light.

The hinges squeaked. She walked toward him. Across the porch . . . To the step . . . "Come with me," she whispered over the crazy thudding of her heart.

He opened his mouth. Started to refuse?

"No," she said. "No words." She caught his arm, drew him away from the house, out of sight of the boy and the dog, into the trees. She was fueled by panic, by exhaustion, by the fear that everything she'd built would slip from her grasp.

Her height had made her accustomed to meeting people eye to eye, but she stopped in a small depression that made her look up at him. Even in the dim moonlight that filtered through the leaves, she could see the resistance in his eyes.

"Bree . . ."

She slid her arms around his neck, pulled his head down, and silenced him with her mouth.

This, her kiss said, *is to remind you of what you've always wanted and never had.*

But as his lips covered her own, she was reminded instead of what she'd never had. Fidelity. Honor. Kindness. And something far less noble. An exhilarating, sensual pleasure free of the shame she'd experienced during her marriage.

Hot blood rushed through her veins, and all her senses caught fire. His kiss was the kiss of a man who loved to give pleasure. A kiss as unselfish as it was erotic.

He was hard, and she relished his arousal, relished knowing the hands splayed over her hips didn't carry the memory of countless other women's bodies. His mouth moved to one cheek then the other, kissing the afternoon's honey from her skin. He reclaimed her lips, and she pressed herself against him.

He pulled back without warning. Only a few inches, but enough.

"Bree, you don't have to do this." He unwrapped her arms from around his neck. "I'll watch out for you and for Toby. I don't need to be bribed this way."

She was humiliated, furious that he would think such a thing of her, even though he had every reason to. The only argument she could muster in her defense was the truth. "It wasn't a bribe."

"Bree, don't do this to yourself." He sounded tired, a little impatient. "It's not necessary."

She'd started this, which made it unconscionable to take her pain out on him, but the words spilled from her in a dark torrent. "You listen to me, Mike Moody. I spent years begging for a man's love, and I'll never *ever* do that again. Do you understand?"

"*Mike!*" Toby shouted from the house. "Mike, where are you?"

Mike stared at her, his eyes suddenly old and tired. Then he walked away. "I'm here," he said as he stepped out of the trees.

"What are you doing over there?" Toby asked.

Mike's shoes crunched in the gravel on the driveway. "Nothing important."

Bree rested her cheek against the rough bark of the tree, shut her eyes, and willed herself not to cry.

AT DR. KRISTI'S INSISTENCE, TEMPLE restricted her workouts to ninety minutes a day. This left her with free time she'd otherwise have spent brooding over Max's continued refusal to talk to her, so for the past few days, she and Dr. Kristi had started hanging out at the farm stand for an hour or so each afternoon. When Lucy finished her writing for the day, she joined them.

While Bree hand-painted a beach scene on one of her Christmas globes, the rest of them sprawled in her Easter egg chairs and combined group therapy with girl talk. They comforted Temple over Max's rejection and told Lucy she should give up her lobbying work. They didn't understand the obligation she felt to help children who hadn't been as lucky as she'd been. Bree never mentioned Mike, although she talked freely about her marriage.

"It feels good to have girlfriends," she said one afternoon. "I didn't have any when I was married. I knew all they wanted was for me to explain why I kept turning a blind eye to Scott's cheating."

"Bastard could never pull that shit on you now," Temple said, crossing an ankle over her knee.

"No." Bree looked suddenly sad, then seemed to shake herself out of it as she gazed at Kristi. "I haven't had much business this afternoon. Are you sure you wouldn't consider—"

"No!" Kristi declared.

Temple and Lucy exchanged looks, entertained by Bree's attempts to convince Dr. Kristi to wear her red bikini as a way to draw in more business.

"You wear it," Kristi said hotly. "See how you like it."

"If I looked like you, I would." Bree got back at Kristi by putting her on the confessional chopping block. "I don't understand how you of all people can ever feel inadequate about men. You could have any one of them you want."

Lucy immediately thought of Panda.

Kristi shoved her sunglasses on top of her head. Even her ears were perfectly shaped. "That's what you think. The kind of men I'm attracted to aren't attracted to me."

"Corpses?" Lucy said, taking the empty periwinkle chair.

Temple laughed, but Kristi pursed her pouty lips like the prim nerd she was inside that knockout body. "Go ahead and mock. I like men with brains. Thoughtful men who read real books and have interests beyond playing beer pong. But guys like that won't come near me. Instead, I get all the players—actors, athletes, zillionaire fifty-year-olds looking for a trophy wife."

Lucy rubbed an ink stain on her thumb, then decided to hell with it. "What about Panda?"

"A fascinating exception," Dr. Kristi said. "He looks like he should be the leader of the beer pong gang, but it doesn't take long to realize how intelligent he is. Last night we spent an hour talking about Puccini. He has an incredible grasp of politics and economics. And a social conscience. Did you know he still works with street gangs? Too bad he's completely unavailable emotionally."

"Because he's in love with Lucy," Temple said pointedly.

"Right," Lucy drawled. "That's why he keeps coming over here to see me." Even though she knew it was better for him to stay away, it rankled that he hadn't even made an attempt to contact her.

"Temple hadn't told me about your relationship when I made a play for him," Kristi said earnestly. "I don't believe in poaching."

"If you really want a man," Bree said, "you should do what Lucy did. You should disguise yourself. Make yourself ugly so regular guys aren't afraid to approach you."

Lucy pointed out the obvious. "Making Kristi ugly would take a Hollywood special-effects team."

A silver Subaru sped by. Temple gasped and shot out of her chair.

"What's wrong?" Kristi said.

Temple's hand flew to her throat. "That was Max!"

"Are you sure?" Bree asked.

But Temple was already running toward the house.

The three of them gazed at one another. Finally Lucy said exactly what they were all thinking. "I'd give anything to see what happens next."

"You and me both," Bree said. But just then a van filled with women and kids stopped. With a glance of regret toward the woods, Bree went to help them.

Which left Lucy.

"Stay right where you are," Dr. Kristi said. "This is a private affair between Temple and Max."

"I know," Lucy replied. "But—" She jumped up from the chair and made a dash for the path.

"Don't let them see you!" Kristi called out as Lucy disappeared.

Lucy knew this was crazy. She didn't want to go near the house. But she also needed to believe in happy endings, and if there was going to be one, she wanted to see it firsthand.

She turned onto a narrow track that led toward the garage. She moved carefully, dodging a stack of rotting firewood, a grown woman who'd lost her mind. She peeked around the corner of the garage just as Max emerged from her car. Her short red hair was as rumpled as her olive cargo shorts and ill-fitting tan blouse. Temple shot out of the woods and then froze, every insecurity that lurked behind her Evil Queen's bluster written on her face. "Max . . ." The word sounded like a prayer. "Max, I love you."

Max stayed where she was, her unyielding expression testifying she was just as strong-minded as her lover. "Enough to stop hiding? Or are all those messages you've been leaving for me crap?"

"Not crap. I do love you."

"Enough to go out in public with me?"

Temple nodded.

"Enough to get married?" Max said stubbornly. "And throw a big party? And invite everybody we know?"

Lucy saw Temple's throat work as she swallowed. "That much," she whispered.

But Max wasn't done with her. She made a brusque gesture toward her stocky figure. "I'm not making myself over for you. What you see is what you get, chub and all."

"I love what I see. I love you."

Max twisted one of the silver rings on her fingers. "This could destroy your career."

"I don't care."

"You do care," Max said, but she softened as she saw the tears glistening in Temple's eyes.

"Not as much as I care about you," Temple replied.

Max finally melted, and they were in each other's arms.

Watching two women exchange such a passionate kiss was a little icky but also completely satisfying. Lucy backed away to give them privacy.

Chapter Twenty-three

WITH THE EXCEPTION OF A man walking with a dog, Lucy had the beach to herself. Smaller and less accessible than the south beach, this spot on the west side of the island was mainly used by the locals, but even though it was Saturday, a thickly overcast sky had kept all but a few away. She'd settled in a sheltered spot at the base of a sand dune, her chin resting on her bent knees. Max had arrived two days earlier, and she and Temple had left yesterday afternoon. This morning, Kristi had taken off. Lucy was going to miss them. Maybe that accounted for her melancholy mood. She was making steady progress with her writing, so she had no reason to feel depressed about her work. By mid-September, she should finally be able to leave the island.

She sensed someone approaching. Her heart skipped a beat as she saw Panda walking toward her. Toby must have told him where she was.

Even though the sun had buried itself beneath the clouds, he wore dark glasses. He was clean-shaven, but his hair had grown wilder in the eleven days since she'd last seen him. It seemed like months. The knowledge she worked so hard to suppress struggled toward the surface. She shoved it back into the darkest recesses inside her where it could do no harm. While her own heart raced, he ambled toward her as casually as a tourist out for an evening stroll.

If he was mad at her for running out on him, it didn't show. He nodded and took in her shorter hair, no longer quite as dark but still not back to her natural light brown color. She wasn't wearing makeup, her fingernails were a wreck, and she hadn't shaved her legs in a couple of days, but she didn't let herself tuck them under her hips.

They gazed at each other, maybe only a few seconds, but longer than she could bear. She pretended to examine a trio of ladybugs crawling along a piece of driftwood. "Come to say good-bye?"

He stuffed a hand in the pocket of his shorts. "I'm leaving in the morning." He gazed out at the water, as if he couldn't stand looking at her longer than he needed to. "I'm starting a new job in a week."

"Great."

Another uncomfortable silence fell between them. At the water's edge, the beach-walker tossed a stick into the lake, and his dog went after it. Whether she wanted to or not, there were things she needed to say before he left. "I hope you understand why I had to move out."

He sat in the sand next to her and pulled a knee up, leaving a wide space between them. "Temple explained it to me. She said it was because I was an asshole."

"Not true. If it hadn't been for you that night—" She dug her toes into the sand. "I don't like to think about it."

He picked up a beach stone and rolled it in his palm. The dune grasses bent toward him as if they wanted to stroke his hair. She looked away. "Thanks for what you did."

"I don't need any more thanks," he said gruffly.

She rubbed her arm, her skin gritty beneath her fingers. "I'm glad you told me about your brother."

"I wanted to take your mind off what happened, that's all."

She pushed her feet deeper into the sand. "I think you should tell Bree about Curtis before you leave."

He dropped the beach stone. "That her old man had no conscience? Not going to happen."

"She's a big girl. She knows he screwed around on her mother, and she needs to know about this. Let her decide whether or not to tell her brothers."

The stubborn set of his jaw told her she was wasting her breath. She poked at a zebra mussel shell, feeling as undesirable as this invasive Great Lakes intruder. "With everything that happened, I never asked why you came back to the bar."

"To get my car. I was pissed with you."

"I made such a fool of myself that night. All summer, really, with my badass act."

"It wasn't an act. You are a badass."

"Not true, but thanks." She sifted some sand through her fingers. "One good thing came out of the experience. I learned that trying to slide into another skin wouldn't fix me."

"Who says you need fixing?" He displayed a comforting degree of indignation. "You're fine just the way you are."

She bit the inside of her lip. "Thanks."

Another long silence fell, an awful, unbreachable chasm that spoke volumes about the distance that had grown between them. "How's your writing going?" he asked.

"Pretty well."

"That's good."

More silence, and then he rose. "I need to finish packing. I came here to tell you that you're free to stay at the house when I leave."

That was the only reason? Her chest aching, she looked up and saw her reflection in his dark glasses. "I'm fine at Bree's," she said stiffly.

"You care about the place more than I do. If you change your mind, here's a key."

She didn't reach for it—couldn't make herself—so he dropped it in her lap. It landed on the hem of her shorts, the yellow happy-face key fob staring up at her.

He reached for his sunglasses, as if he were going to take them off, but changed his mind. "Lucy, I— " The stubbornness she knew so well thinned his lips. He rested a hand on his hip and dipped his head. The words that emerged were as rough as if he'd rubbed them with sandpaper. "Stay safe, okay?"

That was all. He didn't look at her again. Didn't say more. Simply walked away.

Her fingers curled into fists. She squeezed her eyes shut, too angry to cry. She wanted to throw herself at his back and wrestle him to the ground. Slap and kick. The callous, unfeeling bastard. After everything that had happened, after everything they'd said and done, this was his exit line.

She finally managed to make her way back to the parking lot. She biked to the house, peddling as furiously as Miss Gulch on her way to collect Toto. No wonder he'd never come to the cottage to check up on her. Out of sight, out of mind. That was Patrick Shade's way.

Bree was at the farm stand. She took one look at Lucy's face and set aside her paintbrush. "What happened?"

It was over. Finished. Accept it. "Life," Lucy retorted. "It sucks."

"Tell me about it."

Lucy resisted the urge to hurl her bike across the driveway. "I need to get out. Let's have dinner at the Island Inn. Just the two of us. My treat."

Bree looked around at the farm stand. "I don't know . . . It's Saturday night. There's a fish fry on the south beach, so there'll be a lot of traffic . . ."

"We won't be gone long. Toby can handle things for a couple of hours. You know how much he loves being a big shot."

"True." She cocked her head. "All right. Let's do it."

Lucy stomped around the small bedroom where she'd been staying. Eventually she forced herself to open the matchbox closet and study the clothes Temple had brought over. But she couldn't go back to her Viper outfits, and she didn't have much else with her. Even if the closet had held her old Washington wardrobe, the tailored suits and pearls wouldn't have felt any more right than Viper's green tutu and combat boots.

She ended up in jeans with a breezy linen blouse she borrowed from Bree. As they left, Bree stopped her car at the end of the drive to throw last-minute instructions out the driver's window. "We won't be gone long. Remember to ask people to be careful with the ornaments."

"You already told me that."

"Watch the change box."

"You told me *that* about a thousand times."

"Sorry, I . . ."

"Go," Lucy ordered, gesturing toward the highway.

With one last worried glance, Bree reluctantly stepped on the gas.

Lucy hadn't come into town since she'd cut her dreads from her hair and scrubbed off her tattoos, and Bree automatically took the chair that looked out into the dining room so Lucy could face the wall. But it had been almost three months since her wedding, the story had died down, and Lucy couldn't bring herself to care whether or not anyone recognized her.

They ordered grilled portabellas and a barley salad sweetened with peaches. Lucy gulped down her first glass of wine and started on her second. The food was well prepared, but she had no appetite, and neither, it seemed, did Bree. By the time they drove back to the cottage, they'd given up the effort to make conversation.

The farm stand came into sight. At first they didn't notice anything was wrong. Only as they came closer did they see the destruction.

Toby stood in a sea of broken honey bottles—far more bottles than had been out on display. He turned in a jerky, aimless circle, the honey-splattered quilt Bree tossed over the counter hanging from one hand, his game player in the other. He froze as he saw the car.

Bree jumped out, the motor still running, a scream ripping from her throat. *"What happened?"*

Toby dropped the quilt into the mess. The Adirondack chairs lay on their sides near the splintered remains of the Carousel Honey sign. The door of the storage shed that jutted off the back gaped open, its shelves emptied of several hundred bottles of next year's crop Bree had stashed there to give her more working room in the honey house. Toby was streaked from head to toe with honey and dirt. A trickle of blood ran down his hand from broken glass. "I only left for a minute," he sobbed. "I didn't mean—"

"You *left?*" She charged forward, her shoes crunching in the glass.

"Only for a minute. I-I had to get my N-Nintendo. Nobody was stopping!"

Bree saw what he was holding, and her hands fisted at her sides. "You left to get a *video game?*"

"I didn't know— I didn't mean— It was only for a *minute!*" he cried.

"Liar!" Her eyes blazed. "All this didn't happen in a minute. Go! Get out of here!"

Toby fled toward the cottage.

Lucy had already turned off the engine and jumped out of the car herself. The wooden shelves hung askew, and broken honey bottles were everywhere, even out on the highway. Shattered lotion jars spattered the drive; the luxurious creams and scented potions smearing the gravel. The cash box was gone, but that wasn't as devastating as the loss of hundreds of bottles of next year's crop. The glass from the bottles mingled with the silver shards of Bree's precious, fragile Christmas ornaments.

Bree knelt, her skirt trailing in the muck, and cradled what was left of a delicate globe. "It's over. It's all over."

If Lucy hadn't insisted they go out this evening, none of this would have happened. She couldn't think of anything comforting to say. "Why don't you go inside? I'll deal with the worst of this."

But Bree wouldn't leave. She stayed crouched over the debris of goo, glass, and ruined dreams.

With guilt hanging over her head like a shroud, Lucy fetched a pair of rakes and a shovel. "We'll figure out something tomorrow," she said.

"There's nothing to figure out," Bree whispered. "I'm done."

LUCY MADE BREE CALL THE POLICE. While Bree told them what had happened in a flat, listless voice, Lucy began scraping the worst of the glass back from the highway. Bree finished answering their questions and hung up. "They're coming out tomorrow to talk to Toby." Her expression hardened. "I can't believe he let this happen. It's unforgivable."

It was too early to plead Toby's case, and Lucy didn't try. "It's my fault," she said. "I'm the one who insisted we go out." Bree brushed away her apology with a shaky hand.

They worked in the ghostly illumination of a pair of floodlights mounted on the front of the farm stand. Cars slowed as they passed, but no one stopped. Bree dragged away her splintered sign. They righted the chairs, tossed the damaged candles and ruined note cards into trash bags. As night settled in, they began attacking the broken glass with rakes, but the ocean of ruined honey made the glass stick to the tines, and a little after midnight Lucy pulled the rake from Bree's hands. "That's enough for now. I'll bring a hose out in the morning and spray everything down."

Bree was too demoralized to argue.

They walked back to the house in silence. They had honey everywhere—on their skin, on their clothes, in their hair. Clumps of dirt and grass stuck to their arms and legs, along with slivers of glass and other muck. As Lucy peeled off her sandals, she saw a square of pale blue cardboard stuck to the heel.

I'm a one-of-a-kind Christmas ornament.
Please be careful when you pick me up.

They took turns sticking their feet under the outside faucet. Bree leaned down to rinse off her hands and forearms, then glared toward the back window. "I can't talk to him right now."

Lucy understood. "I'll check to make sure he's okay."

"How could he have been so irresponsible?"

Because he was twelve, Lucy thought. And because Lucy should never have encouraged Bree to leave him alone with so many rowdies on the island for the weekend.

Even though she'd rinsed off, Lucy's feet still stuck to the vinyl floor as she crossed the kitchen. She turned down the hall. Toby's door was open. He usually kept it closed so Bree wouldn't nag him about the mess. With a sense of foreboding, Lucy looked inside.

The room smelled of strawberry bubble gum and boy-funk. The last few days' clothes lay in a heap on the rug, along with a discarded bath towel. The bed was unmade as usual. And empty.

She searched the house. He was gone. She shoved her sticky feet into her sneakers, located a flashlight, and went back outside to find Bree staring into space, smoking a cigarette.

All she does is sit on the back step and smoke. That's what Toby had told her, but Lucy hadn't seen Bree do either in weeks. "He's not in the house."

Bree's head shot up. "What do you mean? Where is he?"

"I don't know."

Bree came off the step. "I'm going to kill him! Doesn't he know he's only making things worse?"

"He's probably not thinking too clearly."

Bree ground out her cigarette. "Because of me. Because of what I said to him." She turned toward the woods just as Lucy had done on the day they'd met. "Toby!" she shouted. "Come back here right now! I mean it!"

Not exactly the way to lure a frightened kid home. On the other hand, Bree sounded like a million other angry mothers.

Not surprisingly, Toby didn't appear. Finally Bree grabbed a flashlight of her own, and they separated to search the perimeter of the yard, the root cellar, and the woods around the house. They went into the neighboring orchard and shone the flashlight down the ravine. "I'm calling Mike," Bree declared. "Toby's over there now. He has to be."

But he wasn't.

"Mike hasn't seen him," Bree said when their brief call was over. "He's going out to look. What am I going to tell him? That I screamed at Toby and told him to go?"

"You're only human."

"Maybe he's at your house. Check over there while I wait for Mike. Please."

Lucy couldn't bear the idea of seeing Panda again, and if anything other than Toby's safety had been involved, she would have refused, but she couldn't refuse this. She followed the path she'd traveled so many times in the daylight, but at night the woods were no longer as friendly. "Toby!" she called into the silence. "Toby, it's Lucy. Bree isn't mad anymore." Not true, but good enough. "I want to talk to you."

The only response came from the rustle of night creatures and the hoot of an owl.

She emerged from the woods. It was one in the morning, and the sky had cleared. With no light pollution, the stars shone brightly overhead. Until she'd come to the island, she'd forgotten what a real star-spangled sky looked like.

The house was dark, and she prayed it would stay that way. As she moved deeper into the yard, she shined her flashlight around. Her hands were still tacky even though she'd washed them, and her clothes stuck to her skin. She even had honey in her eyebrows.

A shadow moved on the porch. A shadow too large to belong to Toby. Her heart sank. She couldn't go through this again. Except she had no choice. She stiffened her spine and directed the beam toward the screen. "Toby's disappeared," she said brusquely. "Have you seen him?"

The shadow stood. "No. How long has he been gone?"

"Since around nine." She briefly explained what had happened, glad she couldn't see him clearly.

"Let me get my shoes on." A few moments later, he emerged with a flashlight of his own. Its beam swept over her. "You're a mess."

"Really? I wasn't aware."

He ignored her sarcasm. "The front door's locked. I don't think he could have gotten in the house."

"He has a talent for breaking and entering. Check while I look in the garage." No way was she going in the house with him. She made her way to the garage, but as she stepped inside, she was flooded with memories of the afternoon they'd made such kinky love here. She couldn't imagine ever being so uninhibited again.

She searched the interior of the garage, then went outside to check the area around the woodpile. The longer Toby went missing, the more anxious she became. In so many ways, Toby was her doppelgänger. She knew what it was like to be a kid who felt alone in the world, and she knew how dangerous that kind of desperation could be.

Panda emerged from the house. "It's clear inside."

"Maybe the boathouse."

But that, too, proved fruitless. They split up to circle the yard and the woods nearby. Lucy had tucked her cell in her pocket, and she called Bree, but the agitation in her friend's voice told her nothing had changed.

"What if he went to the beach?" Bree said. "Anything could have happened. The thugs who vandalized the farm stand— Maybe he ran into them. I called the police back, but they won't do anything till morning. Why did he have to make things worse? That's all he's done, right from the beginning, is make things worse."

Panda came up behind Lucy. "Ask her if his bike is still there."

Lucy did.

"Hold on," Bree said. "Mike's beeping in. I'll call you right back."

Lucy's phone rang again within minutes. "Toby's bike is gone. Mike's out on the highway, but so far he hasn't seen anything."

Lucy relayed the information.

Panda took the phone from her, every inch the cop. "Bree, it's Patrick Shade. Can I have Mike's cell number?"

Lucy looked frantically around for something to write with, but

Panda didn't seem to need pen or paper. "Got it. Is there any particular place Toby tends to go when he's upset?"

He listened and nodded. "Okay. What was he wearing?" He listened again. "Go to his room and look around. See if he took anything with him. A backpack? Clothes? Anything at all. Call me back when you're done."

"He's going to be fine," Lucy said to herself as he disconnected. "I know he's fine."

Panda was already talking to Mike. "Toby has his bike. Where are you now? All right . . . Check the south beach, and then stop here and we'll work out what to do next."

Lucy tried to imagine where she'd have gone if she were Toby. Even though he'd grown up on the island, she couldn't imagine him huddling in the woods all night. He'd look for someplace where he'd be alone but where he'd also feel safe.

She remembered the rocky bluff Panda had made his brooding place. It was more open than the woods, and the rocks offered some shelter. While Panda headed toward the highway, she climbed the slope.

The air was still at the top, and she could hear the lap of waves below. She swept the beam over the rocks, praying for a glimpse of him. Nothing.

In a few hours, it would be dawn. Increasingly worried, she returned to the house. Panda was coming down the drive with Toby's bike. She ran toward him. "Did you find him?"

"Only the bike. It was hidden in the trees about thirty yards up the road."

She thought of the bikers, along with the other lowlifes who came to the island to get drunk and make trouble. "What if he left it there and hitched a ride?"

"I don't think so. I found some footprints. It's too dark to follow them, but my guess is that he was coming here."

"We've looked everywhere."

He gazed toward the woods. "Maybe he waited until after we'd searched before he settled in."

Safe. Sheltered.

She and Panda moved together.

Chapter Twenty-four

LUCY FOLLOWED HIM DOWN THE steps to the dock and into the boathouse. The creaks of the boat at its mooring had been the sound track of their lovemaking, but unlike her, Panda didn't seem to be plagued by painful memories. He directed his flashlight toward the cabin door. She was almost certain she'd latched it after she'd searched here earlier, but now it was slightly ajar. He eased it open and shone his flashlight inside. She peered around him.

Toby lay curled in the front berth, the one in the bow, sound asleep.

Her relief left her momentarily light-headed. Panda passed her cell phone back. She retreated to the stern and called Bree. "We found him in the boathouse," she said breathlessly. "He's asleep."

"Asleep?" Bree sounded more furious than relieved. "Don't let him get away! I'm coming."

Lucy didn't like what she was hearing, but Bree hung up before Lucy could advise her to calm down first.

Panda emerged with a very groggy, very dirty Toby. The boy's clothes were filthy. Dried blood crusted his arm and smeared his cheek. His legs were covered with honey-saturated grime, and patches of hair were glued to his head. "I didn't hurt anything on the boat," he muttered, looking frightened.

"I know you didn't," Panda said gently.

Toby tripped on the steps up to the house and would have fallen if Panda hadn't steadied him. Just as they reached the top, Mike came running around the side of the house. When Toby saw him, he began to stumble toward him.

"Toby!" Mike exclaimed. "What were you thinking? You should never have——"

Their reunion was interrupted by a banshee's scream as Bree shot out of the woods. *"Toby!"*

Mike froze. Toby instinctively stepped backward, away from all of them, only to butt up against the picnic table.

She looked like a wild woman, clothes caked with grime, red hair flying. "How could you do something so awful?" she screeched as she dashed toward him across the yard. "Don't you dare do anything like this again!" Before any of them could stop her, she grabbed him by the arms and started to shake him. "Do you have any idea what could have happened to you? Any idea at all?" Her fingers dug into his flesh; his head jerked.

All of them lunged for her, but before they could touch her, she wrenched Toby tight against her. "Anything could have happened to you. Anything!" She started to cry. "You scared me so bad. You shouldn't have left. I know I yelled at you. I was out of control. I'm sorry. But you shouldn't have run away."

She pushed him back a few inches, cradled his cheeks in her hand, and turned his face up, her voice choked with emotion. "Promise me you won't ever run away from me again. If we have a problem, we'll talk about it, okay? Promise me."

Toby stared at her mutely, his eyes huge.

She rubbed her thumbs across his grimy cheekbones. "Do you hear me?"

"I promise." A big tear spilled over his bottom lid. "But we lost everything," he whispered. "Because of me."

"We didn't lose you, and that's what's most important." She pressed her lips to his forehead. "We'll figure something out about the rest."

All the fight left him. He wilted against her. His arms snaked around her waist. She hugged him tightly and buried her lips in the top of his head. He'd finally found safe harbor, and his small body began to shake as he tried to hold back his sobs. Bree crooned something only he could hear.

Mike stood apart from the rest of them, an outsider once again. Toby hadn't looked at him once since Bree had arrived.

"Let's go home," Lucy heard Bree whisper to Toby. "I'll make us some pancakes. We'll sleep late tomorrow. How about that?"

His words came out on a hiccup. "Your pancakes aren't too good."

"I know."

"I don't care," he said. "They're good enough for me."

She kissed the top of his head. Their arms around each other, they walked toward the woods. Just before they stepped into the trees, Bree stopped. She looked back at Mike. Lucy saw her begin to lift her hand only to let it fall back to her side. Another long moment passed, and then she and Toby disappeared.

Mike stayed where he was, alone in the pool of dim yellow light. Lucy had never seen anyone look so devastated. "I wanted to adopt him," he finally said in a disconcertingly quiet voice. "I was going to talk to her about it tomorrow." He gazed toward the trees. "She could have sold the cottage and made a fresh start somewhere else. I thought she'd like that."

Lucy understood. After what they'd just witnessed, Mike knew that Bree loved Toby every bit as much as he did and that she'd never let him go.

Lucy heard herself say, in a voice very much like Dr. Kristi's, "Making her happy is important to you, isn't it?"

He nodded. "Always has been. From the moment I set eyes on her. She only remembers what a clueless idiot I was. She's forgotten about the times the other kids weren't around when she'd draw for me or we'd talk about music. Goofy stuff."

"She cares for you," Lucy said. "I know she does."

"Pretense. She puts up a good front because she needs me."

"I don't think that's true. She's changed as much as you have."

He wasn't buying it. "It's late. I'd better get home." He dug into his pocket for his car keys.

This was wrong. Lucy knew it. But as he turned to leave, she couldn't think of anything to say that would make it right.

Panda had been quiet during their exchange, but now his voice cut through the hushed night. "I could be wrong, Moody, but it looks to me like your days of being a clueless idiot aren't over."

She turned to stare at him. She was supposed to be the perceptive one, not Panda.

Maybe because the words had come from another man, Mike stopped. He looked back at Panda, who shrugged. Mike glanced toward the path. And then he began to move.

BREE HAD JUST REACHED THE back steps when she heard a loud rustling in the woods. Toby leaned against her side, warm and solid. Beloved. She turned and saw Mike come out into the yard. Her chest constricted.

He stopped at the edge of the trees and stood there. If he was waiting for her to run into his arms, he'd be waiting a long time. She cradled Toby tightly against her body and gazed at Mike. "I've lost just about everything," she said quietly. "You can believe I'm using you for a meal ticket. Or you can believe the truth. What's it going to be?"

Toby went unnaturally still, as if he'd quit breathing.

Mike's hands slipped into his pockets, his salesman's confidence deserting him. "I know what I want to believe."

"Make up your mind," she said. "You're either part of this family or you're not."

Still he didn't move. Instead of looking at her, he looked at Toby. Then he began walking slowly. But he didn't make it all the way to the back steps. Instead he stopped halfway. "Toby, I love Bree." His throat worked as he swallowed. "I'd like your permission to marry her."

Bree gasped. "Hold it! I'm—I'm glad you love me, but it's way too soon—"

"Really?" Toby exclaimed. "*Really?* I say yes!"

She couldn't believe the leap of faith Mike was making, the courage he displayed in offering his heart to someone he had no right to trust. But it was three o'clock in the morning, and they were exhausted. It was too early to talk about the future. She needed to set him straight. Except in order to do that, she first had to stop smiling, and she couldn't seem to manage that.

As Mike gazed into her eyes, she pressed her cheek against the top of Toby's soft head. "I love you, too. With all my heart. But for now, I'm only interested in pancakes."

Mike cleared his throat, which didn't stop the swell of emotion in his voice. "How about I make them? I'm really good at it."

She looked down at Toby. Toby looked up at her. "I say yes," he whispered.

She had Toby in her arms, but her eyes found Mike's. "I guess I'll have to say yes, too, then."

His blazing smile cut through all the darkness left inside her. She held out her hand. He took it. And the three of them went inside.

LUCY COULDN'T GO BACK TO the cottage tonight. Whatever was transpiring there needed to unfold without an outsider looking on. She straightened her shoulders. "I'm going to bunk down in the boat for what's left of the night."

Panda stood by the picnic table, one foot on the bench. "You can stay in the house."

"The boat'll be fine." But before she went anywhere, she had to clean up. Not just from the dirt and honey but from the tiny slivers of glass cutting her. Even though the outside shower only had cold water and she had nothing to change into, she didn't want to go in the house. She'd wrap up in one of the beach towels and change at the cottage in the morning.

She walked past him toward the shower, hating this stilted awkwardness, hating him for causing it, hating herself for being so hurt by it. "The shower's not working," he said from behind her. "The pipe broke last week. Use your old bathroom. I never got around to moving back downstairs."

That seemed strange, since she'd been out of the house for almost two weeks, but she wasn't asking questions, wasn't saying more to him than she needed to. As much as she dreaded going in the house, she couldn't sleep while she was such a mess, and without a word, she made her way inside.

The kitchen door gave its familiar creak, and the old house embraced her, still smelling faintly of damp, coffee, and the ancient gas stove. He flipped on the overhead light. She'd vowed not to look at him, but she couldn't help herself. His eyes were red-rimmed and his beard stubble villainous. But it was what she didn't see behind him that surprised her. "What happened to your table?"

He acted as if he needed to search his memory. "Uh . . . Yeah . . . Woodpile."

"You got rid of your precious table?"

His jaw tightened, and he sounded unnecessarily defensive. "I kept getting splinters from it."

He'd thrown her off balance, and she was even more disconcerted when she noticed something else was missing. "What about your pig?"

"Pig?" He'd acted as though he'd never heard the word.

"Fat little guy," she snapped. "Speaks French."

He shrugged. "I got rid of some stuff."

"Your pig?"

"What do you care? You hated that pig."

"I know," she sneered. "But hating it gave my life focus, and now that's gone."

Instead of delivering a counterpunch, he smiled and took her in. "God, you're a mess."

His tenderness made her heart constrict, and she threw up her defenses. "Save it for somebody who cares." She stalked toward the hall.

He moved behind her. "I want you to know . . . I . . . care about you. It's going to be hard not seeing you. Talking to you."

His gruff, begrudging admission was salt in her open wounds, and she whirled around. "Fucking me?"

"Don't say that."

She curled her lip at his indignation. "What? Didn't I use the word right?"

"Look, I know I pissed you off at the beach, but . . . What was I supposed to say? If I were a different person . . ."

"Stop right there." She thrust up her chin. "I already dumped you. This isn't necessary."

"You were in a vulnerable place this summer, and I took advantage of that."

"Is that what you think?" She wouldn't let him shatter her pride, and she charged toward him. "Believe me, Patrick, my eyes were wide open through our tawdry little affair."

But he wouldn't let it go. "I'm a Detroit roughneck, Lucy. You're American royalty. I've been through too much. I'm not good for you."

"Got it," she sneered. "You were put through hell as a kid, hell as a cop, so you're taking a pass on life's messy stuff."

"That's not true."

"It's true, all right." She needed to shut up, but she hurt too much to stop. "Life is too hard for you, isn't it, Panda? So you live it at a coward's distance."

"It's more than that, damn it!" He clenched his teeth, ground out the words. "I'm not exactly . . . emotionally stable."

"Tell me about it!"

He'd had enough of her, and he headed for the stairs. She should have let him go, but she was drained, furious, and out of control. "Run away!" she called after him, too out of control to see the irony in accusing him of what she'd done herself. "Run away! You're a champ at that."

"Damn it, Lucy . . ." He spun around, his eyes dark with a misery that should have stirred her pity but merely fired her anger because all that pain spelled the death of something that should have pulsed with life.

"I wish I'd never met you!" she shouted.

His shoulders dropped. He braced one hand on the banister, then let his arm fall. "Don't wish that. Meeting you was . . . There are things that happened."

"What things? Either spill your precious secrets or go to hell!"

"I've already been there." His fingers were white where they gripped the banister. "Afghanistan . . . Iraq . . . Two wars. Double the fun."

"You told me you served in Germany."

He came down off the bottom step, walked around her, moving just to move, ending up in the living room. "That was easier than telling the truth. Nobody wants to hear about the heat and sand. Mortar attacks, rocket grenades, IEDs exploding without any warning tearing off legs, arms, leaving holes where a heart should be. I have images seared on my brain that'll never go away." He shuddered. "Mutilated bodies. Dead kids. Always dead kids . . ." His words trailed off.

She curled her fingernails into her palms. She should have guessed.

He stopped by the living room fireplace. "When I got out, I joined the police force, thinking nothing could be as bad as what I'd already seen. But there was more blood, dozens of Curtises—all dead before their time. The migraines got worse, the nightmares. I stopped sleeping, started drinking too much, got into fights, hurt people, hurt myself. One night I was so drunk I begged a guy to blow my head off."

The pieces fell into place, and she leaned against the door molding. "Post-traumatic stress disorder."

"A textbook case."

This was what he'd been hiding—the fate of so many who'd come back from those wars. She struggled for some kind of detachment. "Did you see a therapist?"

"Sure. Ask me how much it helped."

She had to seal off her own feelings. If she didn't, she'd fall apart. "Maybe you need to try someone else," she said.

He uttered a bitter laugh. "Find me a therapist who's seen what I've seen—done what I've done—and I'm there."

"Therapists deal with issues they've never experienced all the time."

"Yeah, well, that doesn't quite work with guys like me."

She'd read about the difficulties of treating veterans with PTSD. They'd been trained to be guarded, and even the ones who knew they needed help were reluctant to open up, especially to a civilian. Their warrior mentality made treatment problematic.

"One guy I served with . . . He's spilling his guts, right? Next thing he knows, the shrink's turning green and excuses himself to throw up." He headed toward the window. "The doctor I saw was different. She was a specialist in PTSD, and she'd heard so many stories that she'd learned to detach. She detached so much that it felt like she wasn't even there." Some of the anger seemed to leave him. "Pills and platitudes aren't enough to fix that kind of crazy."

She started to tell him it was all in the past, but that was obviously untrue, and he had more to say.

"Look at this house. I bought it during one of the manic times. My adult revenge for Curtis. Some revenge, right? Remington had been dead for years. Who the hell knows what I was thinking?"

She knew. All those trips to Grosse Pointe to spy on the family he hated . . . and the family he so much wanted to be part of.

He gazed out the window at nothing. "This guy I know . . . His wife touched him in the middle of the night, and he woke up with his hands around her throat. And a woman I served with . . . She grabbed her baby from day care, convinced the kid was in some kind of mortal danger, and took him on a five-hundred-mile road trip without telling anybody, including her husband. Nearly ended up in jail for kidnapping. Another guy . . . He and his girlfriend were having an argument. Nothing important. But out of nowhere, he slammed her into the wall. Broke her collarbone. Do you want that to happen to you?" Bitter lines bracketed his mouth. "Luckily, time took care of the worst of it for me. I'm okay now. And that's the way it has to stay. Now do you understand?"

She locked her knees, braced herself. "Exactly what am I supposed to understand?"

He finally looked at her, his expression stony. "Why I can't give you any more than I already have. Why I can't give you a future."

How did he know that was what she wanted when even she didn't?

"You look at me with those eyes I could swim in," he said, "and you ask for everything. But I'm never letting myself go back to that dark place." He moved away from the window, a few steps closer to her. "I'm not capable of big emotions. I can't be. Now do you understand?"

She said nothing. Waited.

His chest heaved. "I don't love you, Lucy. Do you hear me? I *don't* love you."

She wanted to smash her hands over her ears, clutch her stomach, crash into the walls. She hated his brutal honesty, but she couldn't punish him for it, not in light of what he'd just told her. She pulled on a reservoir of strength she hadn't known she possessed "Get real, Panda. I walked out on Ted Beaudine. Do you really think I'm going to lose sleep over you and our hot little summer fling?"

He didn't flinch. Didn't say anything. Just looked at her, those mineral blue eyes cloaked in darkness.

She couldn't bear another second of this. She turned away, not letting herself move too quickly. Into the hallway . . . Out the front door . . . She walked blindly into the night, the awful knowledge she'd tried so hard to suppress oozing to the surface.

She'd let herself fall in love with him. Against all reason, all common sense, she'd fallen deeply in love with this emotionally stunted man who couldn't love her back.

She ended up in the boat, not curled asleep in the bow where Toby had hidden himself, but sitting up, wide awake—the whole furious, sticky, heartbroken mess of her.

Chapter Twenty-five

~

H IS CAR WAS GONE THE next morning, along with him. Lucy stumbled into the house, threw her clothes into the washer, and took a shower, but she had a splitting headache and she didn't feel any better when she came out.

All she could find to wear was her black bathing suit and one of his T-shirts. She wandered through the empty house barefoot. He'd taken most of his clothes, his work folders, and the commuter coffee mug he carried around in the morning. So many emotions overwhelmed her, each one more painful than the last—her pity for what he'd been through; her anger at the universe, at herself, for falling in love with such a damaged man. And her anger at Panda.

Despite his words, he'd misled her. With every tender touch, every shared glance and intimate smile, she'd felt him telling her he loved her. Lots of men had been through traumatic experiences, but that didn't mean they ran away.

Her anger made her feel better, and she nursed it. She couldn't afford to pity him or herself. Far better to turn that pity into antagonism. *Run, you coward. I don't need you.*

She decided to move back into his house that same day.

Despite her misery, she couldn't forget her promise to help Bree clean up from last night's vandalism, but before she could get to the cottage, Mike called and told her that he and Toby were handling the mess—no girls allowed. She didn't protest.

She waited until afternoon to get her things from the cottage. She discovered a dreamy-eyed Bree sitting at the kitchen table with a notepad, an equally infatuated Mike at her side. The faint beard-burn on Bree's neck and Mike's tender, proprietary manner didn't leave much doubt about what the two of them had been up to last night while Toby slept.

"You can't leave," Bree said when Lucy revealed her intention. "I'm working on a plan to save my business, and I'm going to need you more than ever."

Mike tapped a legal pad covered with notes in Bree's precise handwriting. "We don't want you in that big house by yourself," he said. "We'll worry about you."

But the two of them could barely take their eyes off each other long enough to talk to her, and Toby was no better. "Mike and Bree are getting married!" he announced when he came into the kitchen.

Bree smiled. "Settle down, Toby. Nobody's getting married to anybody yet."

The looks Mike and Toby exchanged suggested they had other ideas about that.

Lucy wouldn't spoil their happiness with her own misery. She promised to come over the next afternoon and waved good-bye.

She continued to nourish her anger, but after a few days of furious, solitary walks and lengthy bike rides that still didn't wear her out enough to sleep, she knew she had to do something else. Finally she opened the laptop Panda had left behind and got back to work. At first she couldn't concentrate, but gradually she found the distraction she needed.

Maybe it was the pain from her breakup with Panda, but she found herself thinking more and more about the earlier pain she'd endured from spending the first fourteen years of her life with a biological mother who was a professional party girl.

"Lucy, I'm going out tonight. The door's locked."

"I'm scared. Stay here."

"Don't be a baby. You're a big girl now."

But she hadn't been a big girl—she'd been eight—and over the next few years, she'd become the only responsible person in their dismal household.

"Lucy, damn it! Where's that money I hid in the back of my drawer?"

"I used it to pay the damn rent! Do you want us to get kicked out again?"

She'd always believed her sense of responsibility had begun after Sandy had died, when she'd had to take care of Tracy on her own, but now she understood it had begun long before that.

She wrote until her muscles cramped, but she couldn't write forever, and as soon as she stopped, heartache overwhelmed her. That was when she tightened her cloak of anger. With it firmly in place, she could keep breathing.

PANDA HAD BEEN LOOKING FORWARD to his new job managing security for a big-budget action film shooting in Chicago, but two days after he started, he got the flu. Instead of staying in bed where he belonged, he worked through the fever and chills only to end up with pneumonia. He worked through that, too, because going to bed with nothing to think about except Lucy Jorik wasn't an option.

Be the best at what you're good at . . . A great motto right up to the day he'd met her.

"You're an ass," Temple told him during one of her too-frequent phone calls. "You had a chance at happiness, and you ran from it. Now you're trying to self-destruct."

"Just because you think you've gotten your life together doesn't mean everybody wants to," he retorted, glad she couldn't see how gaunt he looked, how tense he was.

He had more job offers than he could handle, so he hired two former cops to work for him. He sent one on an assignment in Dallas, the other to babysit a teen actor in L.A.

Temple called again. He dug into his pocket for a tissue to blow his nose and jumped in before she could harangue him about Lucy. "How's filming the new season going?"

"Other than having the producers constantly screaming at Kristi and me," she said, "it's going great."

"The two of you put them over a barrel. You're lucky they didn't have time to replace you or you'd both be looking for new jobs."

"They'd have been sorry," Temple retorted. "Audiences were getting bored with the old show, and they're going to love this new approach. It's got heart. Kristi still has to wear her red bikini, but she has a lot more screen time, and she's using it brilliantly." He heard her crunch into something. An apple? A piece of celery? The cookie she allowed herself each day? "I've made the workouts so much more fun," she said. "And I actually cried today! Real tears. That's going to be ratings gold."

"I have a lump in my throat just thinking about it." His drawl turned into a cough he quickly muffled.

"No, really," she said. "This contestant—her name's Abby—she was abused horribly as a child. It just . . . got to me. They all have stories. I don't know why I didn't take the time to listen more closely before."

He knew why. Paying attention to other people's fears and insecurities might have forced her to examine her own, and she hadn't been ready to do that.

She went on, mouth full. "Usually after a couple of weeks filming, I'm hoarse from screaming at people, but listen to me."

"I'm doing my best not to." He took a slug of water to suppress another coughing fit.

"I thought Lucy was crazy when she talked about her 'Good Enough' approach to exercise, but she hit on something. I'm working on a long-term exercise program that's more realistic. And . . . Get this . . . We have a great hidden-camera segment where we teach the audience how to read food labels by staging these phony fights in supermarket aisles."

"That'll get you an Emmy for sure."

"Your bitterness isn't attractive, Panda. Mock as much as you want, but we're finally going to be able to help people long term." And then, because she still wanted him to think she was as tough as ever, "Call Max back. She's left three voice mails, and you haven't returned any of them."

"Because I don't want to talk to her, either," he grumbled.

"I phoned Lucy yesterday. She's still at the house."

Another call buzzed in, which gave him an excuse to hang up on her. Unfortunately, this call came from Kristi. "No time to talk," he said.

She ignored him. "Temple was amazing in our interview. Completely raw and open."

It took him a moment to figure out she was talking about the lengthy counseling session she and Temple had just finished filming. The producers planned to use it to kick off the new season, knowing Temple's lesbian revelation would kick up a storm of extra publicity.

"We bring Max on toward the end," Kristi said, "and watching the two of them together is enough to soften the hardest hearts. Audiences are going to love this new side of her. And I got to wear a dress."

"A tight one, I'll bet."

"You can't have everything."

"I only want one thing," he growled. "I want you and your she-devil friend to leave me the hell alone."

A brief, censorious pause. "You could live a more authentic life, Panda, if you'd do what I've advised and stopped transferring your anger to other people."

"I'm hanging up now so I can find a window high enough to jump out of."

But as much as he complained about them, some days it felt as if their intruding phone calls were all that kept him anchored. These women cared about him. And they were his only fragile link to Lucy.

FALL CAME EARLY TO CHARITY Island. The tourists disappeared, the air grew crisp, and the maples began to display their first blush of crimson. The writing that had once been such a struggle for Lucy turned out to be her salvation, and she was finally able to send off her completed manuscript to her father.

She spent the next few days biking around the island and walking the empty beaches. She wasn't sure exactly when it had happened, but through her pain and her anger, she'd somehow figured out how she intended to shape her future.

No more of the lobbying she detested. She was going to listen to her heart and once again work one-on-one with kids. But that couldn't be all. Her conscience dictated that she keep using her secondhand fame to advocate on a larger scale. This time she intended to do that through something that truly fulfilled her—through her writing.

When her brutally honest newspaperman father read the manuscript and called her, he confirmed what she already knew. *"Luce, you're a real writer."*

She was going to write her own book, not about herself or her family, but about real kids in peril. It wouldn't be some dry, academic tome, but a page-turner full of personal stories from kids, from counselors, all with the goal of shining a brighter spotlight on the welfare of the most vulnerable. Her name on the spine would guarantee plenty of publicity. That meant thousands of people—maybe hundreds of thousands—who knew nothing about disadvantaged kids would gain real insight into the issues they faced.

But having a clearer direction didn't bring her the peace she craved. How could she have let herself fall in love with him? A bitter knot burned so fiercely in the center of her chest that she sometimes felt as though she'd burst into flames.

With the manuscript mailed off and October fast approaching, she called her mother's press secretary, who hooked her up with a reporter from the *Washington Post*. On the next-to-last day of September, Lucy sat in the sunroom, her phone pressed to her ear, and gave the interview she'd been avoiding.

> *It was humiliating . . . I panicked . . . Ted is one of the finest men I've ever met. . . . . . . spent the last few months working on my father's book and trying to get my bearings back . . . going to be writing my own book . . . advocate for kids who have no voice . . .*

She didn't mention Panda.

After the interview, she called Ted and had the conversation she couldn't have had with him before. Then she began to pack.

Bree had been to her old vacation house several times since Lucy had moved back in, and she came over the day after the interview to help her close up. In only a few months, she, Toby, and Mike had become woven into the fabric of Lucy's life, and she knew she'd miss them. But as close as she felt to Bree, Lucy couldn't talk to her about Panda, couldn't talk to anybody, not even Meg.

Bree perched on the counter, watching Lucy clean out the big stainless steel refrigerator. "It's funny," she said. "I thought coming inside this house would destroy me, but all it does is make me nostalgic. My mother fixed so many bad dinners in this kitchen, and Dad's grilling didn't help. He burned everything."

Bree's father had done a lot worse than burn hamburgers, but that wasn't Lucy's story to tell. She held up a barely used jar of mustard. "Want this?"

Bree nodded, and Lucy set the mustard in a cardboard box, along with the other leftover groceries she was sending to the cottage.

Bree pushed the sleeves up on the heavy sweater she was wearing against the early fall chill. "I feel like a woman of leisure not having to spend all day at the farm stand."

"Some leisure. You've been working like crazy." Bree had lost a third of next year's honey to the vandals, a group of punks who'd been caught as they drove onto the ferry. But thanks to the summer's dry weather and warm days, she'd still managed to harvest more than a thousand pounds.

"I'll love Pastor Sanders forever," she said.

The Heart of Charity minister had arranged a meeting for Bree with a wholesaler on the mainland who supplied a chain of Midwest gift shops. The woman had loved Bree's samples: the flavored honeys, lotions, candles, and note cards, the beeswax furniture polish, and the one hand-painted Christmas ornament that had survived the vandals.

"The new carousel labels sealed the deal," Bree said. "She loves them. Said they give all the products a whimsical elegance. But I still didn't expect such a big order."

"She has good taste."

"I don't know what I'd have done if she hadn't ordered. Well, I do know, but I'm glad I didn't have to." She nodded again as Lucy held up an unopened bag of carrots. "I can't abide the idea of being financially dependent on Mike. Been there, done that, not doing it again."

"Poor Mike. All he wants is to take care of you, and all you want is to take care of yourself. You're going to have to marry him soon."

"I know. But the thing about Mike Moody . . ." A dreamy smile came over her. "He's steadfast. That man is not going anywhere."

Lucy swallowed her pain. "Other than in and out of your bedroom window every night."

Bree actually blushed. "I told you about that in confidence."

"The same way you told me what a lusty lover he is. Something I could have gone to my grave not knowing."

Bree paid no attention to Lucy's objections. "I really believed Scott when he said I was the one with the problem, but now all I feel is pity for his poor little nineteen-year-old." The dreamy smile was back. "Who would have thought a straitlaced, religious guy like Mike could be so—"

"Lusty," Lucy said, cutting her off.

Bree's face clouded. "If Toby catches us . . ."

"Which he's bound to do sooner or later." Lucy added a block of Parmesan cheese and—resisting the urge to shatter it against the wall—an unopened jar of Panda's orange marmalade.

"Mike's getting more nervous about sneaking around. He actually threatened to withdraw his, uhm, services . . . until I agree to set a date. Blackmail. Can you imagine?"

Lucy closed the refrigerator door. "What's holding you back, Bree? Really?"

"I'm just so happy." She swung her legs, thought it over. "I know I have to get over my aversion to marriage, and I will. Just not yet." She slid off the counter. "You'll come back to the island to see us, won't you?"

Lucy never wanted to come back to the island again. "Sure," she said. "Now let's get this stuff over to the cottage. And no long-drawn-out good-byes, okay?"

"Absolutely not."

But they both knew it wouldn't be that easy to hold back tears. And it wasn't.

EVENTUALLY PANDA STOPPED COUGHING AND his energy began to return, but he felt as if he had a limb missing. His reflexes were no longer sharp—not bad enough for anyone else to notice, but he knew. At the shooting range, his aim wasn't as true, and if he went for a run, he lost his rhythm for no reason. He knocked over his coffee mug, dropped his car keys.

He read Lucy's interview with the *Washington Post*. No mention of him, and why should there be? But he didn't like the way her face was all over the news again.

He noticed a couple threads of gray in his hair. As if that weren't depressing enough, his job wasn't going well. The actress who played the secondary lead in the film had started hitting on him and wasn't taking no for an answer. She was out-of-this-world beautiful, with a body that almost rivaled Dr. Kristi's, and tumbling in bed with a new female would be the best way to wipe out memories of the last one, but he couldn't even think about it. He told her he was in love with someone else.

That night he got drunk for the first time in years. He awoke in a panic. Despite all his care, the ghosts he'd been able to keep at bay for so long were coming back. He called the only person he could think of who might be able to help.

"Kristi, it's me . . ."

LUCY FOUND AN APARTMENT AND a job in Boston while Nealy's press secretary dodged an avalanche of calls from the media. *Ms. Jorik is beginning a new job soon and too busy for additional interviews.* Lucy intended to stay too busy until her first book tour.

On her last night at home in Virginia, she sat with her parents on the patio of the estate where she'd grown up. Nealy wore one of Lucy's old college sweatshirts to keep warm but still managed to look patrician as she sipped from a mug of hot tea, her normally neat honey-brown hair rumpled from the early October breeze.

Her mother's fair complexion and *Mayflower* lineage provided a marked contrast to her father's darker good looks and steel-town toughness. Mat put a log on the fire in the new fire pit. "We took advantage of you," he said bluntly.

Nealy cuddled her warm tea mug. "It happened so gradually, and you were always so cheerful about stepping in, that we were oblivious. Reading what you wrote . . . It was clearheaded and heart-wrenching."

"I'm glad you're going to keep writing," her father said. "You know I'll help however I can."

"Thanks," Lucy replied. "I'm going to take you up on that."

Out of nowhere, her mother hit Lucy with one of the roundhouse punches that were her political specialty. "Are you ready to tell us about him?"

Lucy tightened her grip on her wineglass. "Who?"

Nealy didn't hesitate. "The man who's taken the sparkle out of your eyes."

"It's . . . not that bad," she lied.

Mat's voice dropped to an ominous rumble. "I'll tell you one thing . . . If I ever see the son of a bitch, I'm going to kick his ass."

Nealy lifted an eyebrow at him. "One more reminder of how grateful we all are as a country that I was elected president instead of you."

PANDA WALKED AROUND THE BLOCK twice before he worked up the nerve to go inside the three-story brown brick building. Pilsen had once been home to Chicago's Polish immigrants but now served as the heartbeat of the city's Mexican community. The narrow hallway was covered in bright graffiti, or maybe they were murals—hard to tell in a neighborhood where bold public art figured so prominently.

He found the door at the end of the hallway. A hand-lettered sign read:

I'M ARMED AND PISSED OFF
WALK IN ANYWAY

Where the hell had Kristi sent him? He pushed open the door and stepped into a room decorated in early Salvation Army with a cracked leather couch, a couple of unmatched easy chairs, a blond wood coffee table, and a chain-saw-carved eagle sitting beneath a poster that read:

U.S. MARINES
Helping bad guys die since 1775

The man who emerged from an adjoining room was about Panda's age, rumpled and beginning to bald, with a big nose and Fu Manchu mustache. "Shade?"

Panda nodded.

"I'm Jerry Evers." He moved forward, arm extended, his gait slightly uneven. Panda's gaze inadvertently strayed to his leg. Evers shook his head, then tugged up the leg of his baggy jeans to reveal a prosthesis. "Sangin. I was with the Three-Five."

Panda already knew Evers had been in Afghanistan, and he nodded. The Marines in the Fifth Regiment had been hit hard in Sangin.

Evers waved the file he was holding in the general direction of an upholstered chair and laughed. "You were in Kandahar *and* Fallujah? How'd you get to be such a lucky son of a bitch?"

Panda pointed out the obvious. "Others had it worse."

Evers snorted and slumped down on the couch. "Fuck that. We're here to talk about you."

Panda felt himself being to relax . . .

By the first of November, Lucy had settled into life in Boston and the apartment she'd sublet in Jamaica Plain. When she wasn't writing, she was at work, and even though she was tired all the time, she'd never been more grateful for her new job and busy schedule.

"What do you care?" The seventeen-year-old sitting on the couch across from her sneered. "You don't know nothin' 'bout me."

The spicy scent of tacos wafted into the counseling room from the kitchen where, each day, the Roxbury drop-in center served dinner to fifty or so homeless teens. They also offered showers, a small laundry area, a weekly medical clinic, and six counselors who helped the runaways, couch hoppers, and street kids as young as fourteen find shelter, get to school, work on their GEDs, secure Social Security cards, and look for jobs. Some of their clients had substance abuse problems. Others, like this girl with the beautiful cheekbones and tragic eyes, had fled terrible physical abuse. The counselors at the drop-in center dealt with mental health issues, medical issues, pregnancy, prostitution, and everything in between.

"And whose problem is it that I don't know anything about you?" Lucy said.

"Nobody's problem." Shauna sank deeper into the couch, her expression sullen. Through the window in the door, Lucy could see some of the kids pulling down the Halloween decorations: flying bats, black cardboard witches, and skeletons with red glitter eye sockets.

Shauna took in Lucy's short black leather skirt, hot pink tights, and funky boots. "I want my old social worker back. She was a lot nicer than you."

Lucy smiled. "That's because she didn't adore you like I do."

"Now you're just being sarcastic."

"Nope." Lucy gently laid her hand on the teenager's arm and spoke softly, meaning every word. "You are one of the universe's great creations, Shauna. Brave as a lion, cunning as a fox. You're smart and you're a survivor. What's not to love?"

Shauna whipped her arm away and eyed her warily. "You're crazy, lady."

"I know. The point is, you're a real champion. We all think so. And whenever you want to get serious about keeping a job, I know you'll figure out how to do it. Now go away."

That outraged her. "What do you mean, go away? You're supposed to be helping me get my job back."

"How am I supposed to do that?"

"By telling me what to do."

"I have no idea."

"What do you mean, you don't have no idea? I'm turning you in to the director. She'll fire your ass. You don't know nothin'."

"Well, since I've been here less than a month, that might be true. How can I do better?"

"Tell me the things I have to do to keep a job. Like showing up on time every day and not disrespecting the boss . . ." For the next few minutes, Shauna lectured Lucy, repeating the advice she'd received from other counselors.

When she finally wound down, Lucy nodded in admiration. "Wow. You should be the counselor instead of me. You're good at it."

Her hostility vanished. "You really think so?"

"Definitely. Once you get your GED, I think you could excel at a lot of jobs."

By the time Shauna left, Lucy been able to solve at least one of the teen's problems. It was such a small thing, but it posed a monumental barrier to a homeless kid. Shauna didn't own an alarm clock.

Lucy gazed around at the empty counseling room with its worn, comfortable couch, cozy armchair, and graffiti-inspired mural. This was the work she was meant to do.

She left the center later than usual that night for her apartment. As she headed for her car, she popped open her umbrella against the chilly evening drizzle and thought about the writing she still needed to do before she could collapse into bed that evening. No more haunting the halls of Congress; no more banging on corporate doors to see big shots who wanted to meet her only so they could brag that they knew President Jorik's daughter. Turning a book into her public platform was far more satisfying.

She sidestepped a puddle. A floodlight illuminated her car, one of only two vehicles still left in the parking lot. She'd nearly finished her book proposal, and half a dozen publishing houses had already asked to see it. Considering how many writers struggled to get published, maybe she should feel guilty about that, but she didn't. The publishers knew that her name on the spine of a book would guarantee big press and big sales.

She'd decided to tell the personal stories of homeless teens through their eyes—why they'd fled their families, how they lived, their hopes and dreams. Not only disadvantaged kids like Shauna, but the less publicized suburban teens living a nomad's existence in affluent communities.

As long as she focused only on her work, she was energized, but the moment she let her guard down, her anger returned. She refused to let it go. When she was bone tired, when her stomach refused to accept the food it needed, when tears sprang to her eyes for no reason . . . Anger was what got her through.

She'd nearly reached her car when she heard the sound of someone running. She spun around.

The kid came out of nowhere. Wiry, hollow eyed, in dirty, torn jeans and a rain-soaked dark hoodie. He grabbed her purse and shoved her to the ground.

Her umbrella flew, pain shot through her body, and all the fury she'd been holding inside her found a target. She screamed something unintelligible, pushed herself off the wet asphalt, and chased after him.

He hit the sidewalk, passed under a streetlight, and glanced back at her. He hadn't expected her to give chase, and he ran faster.

"Drop it!" she shouted in a rush of adrenaline-fed rage.

But he kept running, and so did she.

He was small and fast. She didn't care. She was juiced on vengeance. She raced down the sidewalk, her boots slapping the pavement.

He swerved into the alley between the drop-in center and an office building. She went right after him.

A wooden fence and a Dumpster blocked the exit, but she didn't retreat, didn't think about what she'd do if he had a gun. *"Give that back!"*

With an audible grunt, he pulled himself on top of a Dumpster. Her purse snagged on a sharp corner. He dropped it and threw himself over the fence.

She was so rage-crazed that she tried to climb the Dumpster after him. Her boots slipped on the wet metal, and she scraped her leg.

Sanity slowly returned. She gulped in air, her fury finally spent.

Stupid. Stupid. Stupid.

She retrieved her purse and limped back toward the sidewalk. Her leather skirt had offered some protection when she fell, but she'd torn her hot pink tights, scraped her leg, skinned both knees and hands. Still, despite the ringing in her ears, nothing seemed to be broken.

She reached the sidewalk. *Stupid.* If Panda had seen her run into that alley, he'd have gone ballistic. But if Panda had been nearby, the kid wouldn't have gotten close to her.

Because Panda protected people.

An awful dizziness swept through her.

Panda protected people.

She barely made it to the curb before she collapsed, her boots sinking into the rushing gutter, her stomach heaving, the words he'd spoken coming back to her.

" . . . out of nowhere, he slammed her into the wall. Broke her collarbone. Do you want that to happen to you?"

She cradled her forehead into her hands.

"I don't love you, Lucy . . . I don't love you."

A lie. It wasn't that he didn't love her. It was that he loved her too much.

With a clap of thunder, the sky opened. Drenching rain pounded her shoulders through her trench coat, stung her scalp like sharp pebbles. The soldier who tried to strangle his wife . . . The man who'd beaten up his girlfriend . . . Panda saw himself as a potential danger to her just like them, another enemy she needed to be protected from. And he intended to do exactly that.

Her teeth began to chatter. She considered the possibility that she was making this up, but her heart knew the truth. If it hadn't been for the steadfast anger she'd so carefully nurtured, she would have seen through him earlier.

A white van slowed and stopped. She looked up as the driver's window came down and a middle-aged man with a grizzle of gray hair stuck his head out. "You okay, lady?"

"I'm . . . fine." She struggled to her feet. The van moved on.

A flash of lightning split the night, and with it, she saw the anguish in Panda's eyes, heard the phony belligerence in his voice. Panda didn't trust himself not to hurt her.

She turned her face into the grimy, rain-soaked sky. He would lay down his life to protect her even from himself. How could she fight an iron will like that? She could see only one way. With an iron will of her own.

And a plan . . .

Chapter Twenty-six

❧

WHEN THE FILM SHOOT ENDED, Panda went back to the island, as if that would bring him closer to her. The house sat wet and lonely in the gloomy November afternoon. Leaves plugged the gutters, spiderwebs decked the windows, and tree branches littered the ground from a recent storm. He turned on the furnace and walked through the quiet rooms, his shoulders hunched, his hands in his pockets.

He hadn't gotten around to finding another caretaker, and the furniture held a light coat of dust, but Lucy's touch was everywhere: in the bowl of beach rocks on the sunroom coffee table, the comfortably rearranged furniture, the clutter-free shelves and tables. The house no longer felt as though it were waiting for the Remingtons to come back, but it didn't feel like his either. It was hers. It had been since she'd first stepped inside.

The rain stopped. He pulled an old extension ladder from the garage and cleaned out the gutters, barely avoiding falling off when he slipped on a rung. He threw one of Temple's disgusting frozen dinners in the microwave, popped a can of Coke, and tortured himself by going to bed in Lucy's old bedroom, the one that used to be his. The next day he ate a cold breakfast, drank two mugs of coffee, and set off through the woods.

The cottage had a fresh coat of white paint and a new roof. He knocked on the back door, but Bree didn't answer. Through the window, he saw a pot of flowers on the kitchen table and some school papers, so she and Toby were still living here. Since he didn't have anything else to do, he sat on the front porch and waited for her to come back.

An hour later, her old Cobalt came into sight. He rose from the damp wicker chair and wandered to the steps. She stopped her car and got out. She didn't seem upset to see him, merely puzzled.

She looked different from the person he remembered—rested, almost serene, no longer quite so thin. She wore jeans and an oatmeal-colored fleece jacket with her hair pulled up in one of those casual buns. She walked toward him with a new confidence.

He dug his hands into his pockets. "The cottage looks good."

"We're getting it ready to rent out next summer."

"What about your bees?" Lucy would care about that.

"I made an arrangement with the family that owns the orchard next to the cottage to move the hives there."

He nodded. She waited. He shifted his weight to the other foot. "How's Toby?"

"The happiest kid on the island. He's at school now."

He tried to think of what to say next and ended up asking the question he'd never intended to utter. "Have you talked to Lucy?"

She was just like Temple. She nodded but didn't offer any information.

He pulled his hands from his pockets and came down off the steps. "I need to talk to you about something."

Just then, Mike's Cadillac drove in. Mike jumped out, arm extended, looking as if seeing Panda again was the highlight of his day. "Hey, stranger! Great to have you back."

His hair was shorter, no longer so carefully styled, and except for a watch, he'd given up his jewelry. He looked easy, happy, a guy without any demons. Panda stifled his resentment. It wasn't Moody's fault that he'd managed to do what Panda couldn't.

Mike slipped an arm around Bree. "Did she tell you we finally set a date? New Year's Eve. Toughest sale I ever made."

Bree arched an eyebrow at him. "Toby made the sale."

Mike grinned. "Chip off the old block."

Bree laughed and kissed the corner of his mouth.

"Congratulations to both of you," Panda said.

The day was warming up, and Mike suggested they sit on the porch. Panda took the chair he'd just abandoned, and Bree claimed the matching one while Mike perched on the railing. He talked about how well Bree was doing with her business, then offered up a list of Toby's recent accomplishments. "He and his teacher are working together on a black history unit."

"Toby knows more than she does," Bree said proudly. "But you came here to talk to me about something?"

Having Mike around complicated an already difficult task. "It's okay. I can come back later."

Bree frowned. "Is it about Lucy?"

Everything was about Lucy. "No," he said. "It's a private matter."

"I'll leave," Mike said genially. "I have some errands to run anyway."

"Don't go." She gazed at him. "Despite appearances, Mike is the most discreet person on the island. And I'll end up telling him whatever you tell me anyway."

Panda hesitated. "Are you sure? This . . . has to do with your family. Your father."

She looked wary. "Tell me."

And so he did. He sat there in the creaky wicker chair, leaning toward her, his forearms braced on his knees, and told her about her father's relationship with his mother, then about Curtis.

When he was done, Bree had tears in her eyes. "I'm so sorry."

Panda shrugged.

Mike came to stand beside her. Bree searched her pockets for a tissue. "After my father died, Mother made sure we all knew what a rotten husband he'd been, so it's not exactly a surprise. But none of us imagined he had another child." She blew her nose.

Mike curled his hand over the back of her chair and gave Panda a steady gaze, his easygoing demeanor vanishing as he assessed whether this information posed any harm to the woman he loved. "Why did you buy the house?"

Panda liked him for wanting to protect her, so he told them the truth. "Some kind of twisted revenge. I hated your father, Bree. I told myself I hated your whole family, but that was jealousy." Panda shifted in the chair and then he shocked himself. "I wasn't thinking too clearly when I bought the house. After I got out of the military, I had problems with post-traumatic stress."

He said it as if he were confessing a tendency toward head colds.

Their expressions were a mixture of concern and sympathy, but they didn't run screaming from the porch or dash around looking for a weapon to protect themselves. He had Jerry Evers to thank for this. Kristi had found the right guy for him to talk to, a no-bullshit shrink who'd seen combat himself and understood exactly how terrified Panda was that the demons he'd fought would reemerge and make him hurt other people.

Bree was more interested in Panda's revelation about Curtis. "Do you have any pictures of him?"

He hadn't thought of that, but he liked that she'd asked. He reached for his wallet. "I'll send you some when I get back to Chicago. This is the only one I have on me."

He took out Curtis's final school photo. It was tattered, a little faded, the word PROOF still faintly visible across his T-shirt. Curtis was smiling, his adult teeth a tad too big for his mouth. Bree took it from him and studied it carefully. "He . . . looks like my brother Doug." Her eyes filled with tears again. "My brothers need to know about Curtis. And they need to know about you, too. When you're ready, I want you to meet them."

Something else unexpected. "I'd like that," he heard himself say.

As she held out the photo to return it, her thumb moved gently across the image.

"Keep it," he said. And somehow that felt exactly right, too.

HE WAS OUT ON A run late the next morning when his cell rang. He never used to bring a phone along, but now that he had people working for him, he had to stay in touch, and he didn't like it. His business might be thriving, but he still preferred working alone.

He glanced at the display. An East Coast area code. He didn't recognize the number, but he knew that area code. He immediately slowed and answered. "Patrick Shade."

The voice he'd been yearning to hear came buzzing through, very clear, very loud, and very angry. "I'm *pregnant*, you son of a bitch."

And then the connection went dead.

He staggered to the side of the road, dropped the phone, snatched it up, and hit redial. His hands were shaking so badly, it took two tries.

"What do you *want*?" she screeched.

Oh, God. He had to be the grown-up. He opened his mouth to say—who the hell knew what?—but she was still yelling, and he never got a chance.

"I'm too furious to talk to you right now! You and your *vasectomy*." She spit out the word.

"Where are you?"

"What do you care?" she retorted. "I'm done with you, remember?" She hung up on him again.

Jesus . . . Lucy pregnant. With his baby. He felt as if he'd been plunged into a pool of warm, rippling water.

When he tried to call back, he got her voice mail. He already knew where she'd moved, and not much later, he was at the ferry dock. Six hours after that, he was in Boston.

It was evening and already dark when he pulled his rental car up to the apartment where she was supposed to be staying. There was no answer when he hit the buzzer in the lobby.

He tried a few other buttons and eventually hit gold, an old guy with nothing better to do than spy on his neighbors. "She left this morning with a suitcase. You know who she is, right? President Jorik's daughter? Real nice to everybody."

He called her again from the sidewalk, and this time she picked up. He didn't give her a chance to speak. "I'm in Boston," he said. "The security in your building is shit."

"So are you."

"Where have you gone?"

"I ran home to Mommy and Daddy. Where do you think I went? And I am so not ready to talk to you."

"Tough." This time he hung up on her.

PHYSICAL COURAGE CAME EASILY TO him, but this was something else entirely. He'd known he had to clear the air with Bree before he could take the next step toward getting Lucy back, but he'd planned to give himself another week to talk to Jerry Evers and make sure Jerry was as convinced as Panda that the darkness wasn't coming back. Then he'd intended to write up a script and memorize it so he didn't screw up again. Now here he was, on a late flight to Washington, completely unprepared and with his entire future at stake.

He arrived at Dulles long after dark. Even though he was too juiced to sleep, he couldn't show up at the Jorik home in his current condition, so he checked into a hotel and lay awake for what was left of the night. When dawn arrived, he showered and shaved. With nothing more than a cup of coffee in his stomach, he set out for Middleburg, a wealthy community in the heart of Virginia's hunt country.

As he drove along winding roads, past wineries and prosperous horse farms, he grew increasingly miserable. What if it was too late? What if she'd come to her senses and realized she could do so much better than him? By the time he reached the Jorik estate, he was sweating.

The house was invisible from the road. Only the tall iron fence and elaborate electronic gates announced that he'd reached his destination. He parked in front of them and took in the video surveillance cameras. As he reached for his cell he knew one thing for certain. If he buckled now, it was all over. No matter what he had to do, he couldn't let her see what a wreck he was.

She picked up on the fifth ring. "It's six-thirty in the morning," she croaked. "I'm still in bed."

"No problem."

"I said I wasn't ready to talk to you."

"Now that is a problem. You have one minute to get these gates open before I ram them."

"Send me a postcard from Gitmo!"

Another hang-up.

Fortunately, he didn't have to follow through on his threat because, thirty seconds later, the gates swung open. After a brief conversation with a Secret Service agent, he drove along the curving lane that cut through the heavily wooded property to the house, a large brick Georgian. He parked in front and got out. The chilly air carried the smell of fall leaves, and the clear morning sky promised sunshine, which he tried to convince himself was a good omen. Not an easy task when he felt sick to his stomach.

The front door opened, and there she was. His stomach jumped to his throat. Everything that had been murky to him was now crystal clear, but obviously not to her . . . Instead of inviting him in, she came outside, a black windbreaker tossed on over bright red pajamas printed with green bullfrogs.

The last people he wanted to face right now were her parents, so having this showdown outside was an unexpected gift. She'd shoved her bare feet into a pair of sneakers, and her hair was a beautiful, shiny light-brown rumpus. She wore no makeup, and a sleep-crease marked her cheek. She looked pretty, ordinary. Extraordinary.

She stopped between a pair of pillars at the top of three wide steps. He walked toward her along the brick sidewalk. "Who died?" she said, taking in his suit.

She had to know he wouldn't show up at the home of the president of the United States in jeans and a T-shirt. "No time to change."

She came down off the steps and into the crimson and yellow leaves scattered along the walk. Despite her small features and the frog pajamas, she didn't look anything like a teenager. She was a fully grown woman—alluring, complicated, and angry, all of which scared the hell out of him.

She jutted her jaw at him as belligerently as a prizefighter. "There's a big difference between *having* a vasectomy and *planning* to have a vasectomy."

"What do you mean? I never said I'd already had one."

She blew that off. "I'm not arguing with you about it." She tromped onto the damp, leaf-covered grass, moving in the direction of a tree that looked like it could have sheltered Thomas Jefferson while he proofread the Declaration of Independence. "The fact is," she said, "somewhere along the line one of your little buggers hit a home run, and now you're going to be a father. What do you think about that?"

"I-I haven't had time to think."

"Well, I have, and I'll tell you what's not going to happen. I'm not pretending I went to a sperm bank, and I'm not getting rid of this baby."

He was horrified. "You sure as hell aren't."

She went on, still highly pissed. "So what are you going to do about it? Crack up again?"

The way she belittled his past mental problems, as if they weren't all that important, made him love her even more, if such a thing were possible.

"Well?" She tapped her foot in the wet grass, just as if she were his third-grade teacher. "What do you have to say for yourself?"

He swallowed. "Good job?"

He expected her to take a swing at him for that. Instead, she pursed her lips. "My parents are *not* going to be happy."

Surely an understatement. He spoke carefully, fully aware that he was treading on dangerous territory. "What do you want me to do about this?"

She went supersonic. "That's it! I'm done with you!"

She stomped back toward the house, and since he couldn't manhandle a pregnant woman like he'd manhandle an unpregnant one, he cut around her. "I love you."

The brat stopped in her tracks and sneered at him. "You *care* about me. Big difference."

"That, too. But most of all, I love you." His throat grew tight. "I've loved you from the moment I found you in that Texas alley."

Those green-flecked eyes flew wide open. "That's a lie."

"It isn't. I'm not saying I knew I loved you, but I felt something important right from the beginning." He wanted to touch her—God, did he ever want to touch her—but he was afraid that would only make things worse. "Every moment we've been together, I fought to do the right thing. I can't tell you how tired I am of that. And I think you love me, too. Am I wrong?"

This was the question that haunted him. What if he was wrong? What if she'd meant it when she'd said he'd only been a fling? His instincts told him otherwise, but he was all too aware of the power of self-delusion. He braced himself.

"So what?" Lucy had elevated sneering to an art form. "I thought I loved Ted Beaudine, and look how that turned out."

He got so light-headed he could barely respond. "Yeah, but he was way too good for you. I'm not."

"Okay, that's true."

He wanted to pick her up, dump her in his car, and drive off, but he doubted either she or her mother's Secret Service detail would go for that. He dragged in some air and made himself say what he needed to. "Kristi found a counselor for me who's a veteran. He's seen combat. We hit it off right away. I won't say everything's perfect, but I will say he's convinced me I'm saner than I thought."

"He's *wrong*," Madam Sensitive declared. Still, he thought he detected a softening in those big brown eyes, although that might be wishful thinking.

"Tell me how you want to handle this mess," he said, stopping just short of pleading. "You know I'll marry you if that's what you want. I'll do anything for you. Just tell me what you want."

Any tenderness he'd imagined vanished, replaced by an icy hauteur. "You're hopeless." She stomped through the leaves and up the steps toward the front door. She didn't slam it in his face, so he deduced he was supposed to follow her inside for more ass kicking.

The imposing entrance hall held a sweeping staircase, impressive oil paintings, and antique furniture that shouted old money, but the abandoned backpacks, bike helmets, and single multicolored kneesock tossed in the corner spoke of younger occupants. She flung her windbreaker on a chair that looked like a loaner from the Smithsonian and turned to face him again. "What if I'm lying?"

He'd stopped trying to wipe the leaves from his shoes on the Oriental carpet that stretched across the doorway. "Lying?"

"What if I'm not pregnant," she said, "and I'm making this whole thing up. What if I finally saw through that charade you built to protect me—as if I weren't perfectly capable of protecting myself—and what if I really do love you and this is the only way I could think of to get you back? What would you do then?"

He forgot about his wet shoes. "Are you lying?"

"Answer my question."

He wanted to strangle her. "If you're lying, I'm going to be more pissed than you can imagine because, despite everything I've said, I want a baby with you. Tell me the truth right now!"

Her eyes seemed to melt. "Really? You really do want a baby?"

Now he was the belligerent one. "Don't screw with me about this, Lucy. It's too important."

She turned away. *"Mom! Dad!"*

"We're in here." A male voice boomed from the back of the house.

He was seriously going to kill her, but first he had to follow her through the grand house into a roomy, sun-splashed kitchen that smelled of coffee and something baking. The squared-off bay window held a trestle table that looked out over the autumn garden. President Jorik sat at one end, the *Wall Street Journal* open in front of her, another paper folded at her side. She wore a white robe and gray slippers. Even without makeup, she was a beautiful woman, in addition to being an imposing one. Her husband sat across from her in jeans and a Saturday-morning sweatshirt. Although her hair was combed, his wasn't, and he hadn't yet shaved. Panda hoped like hell they were both on their second cup of coffee, or this was going to go even worse than he expected.

"Mom, Dad, you remember Patrick Shade." Lucy said his name as if it were spoiled meat. "My guard dog."

He couldn't afford to be awestruck by either of them, and he nodded.

President Jorik pushed aside her *Wall Street Journal*. Mat Jorik closed the cover of his iPad and pulled off his reading glasses. Panda wondered if they knew about the baby . . . or if there even was a baby. Leave it to Lucy to toss him into the lions' den without a clue. At least he'd been spared the presence of her sisters and brother. It was Saturday, so they must be sleeping in. He wished her parents had stayed in bed, too. "Ma'am," he said. "Mr. Jorik."

Lucy wanted her pound of flesh. She flopped into an empty chair next to her father, leaving Panda standing in front of them like a peasant brought before royalty. She glared at her mother. "You will never guess what he just said. He said he'd marry me if that's what *I* want."

President Jorik actually rolled her eyes. Her husband shook his head. "Even stupider than I figured."

"He's not stupid." Lucy propped her feet on the wooden trestle under the table. "He's . . . Okay, he's sort of stupid, but so am I. And he has a big heart."

Panda had heard enough. He gave Lucy what he hoped was his most menacing glare, then turned to her parents. "I'd like permission to marry your daughter."

Lucy narrowed her eyes at him. "You're way ahead of yourself. First you have to tell them all the reasons you're unworthy."

Up until now, he hadn't understood much of what she was doing, but he did understand this. She wanted him to rip off the Band-Aid fast.

"Would you like some coffee, Patrick?" President Jorik gestured toward the pot on the counter.

"No, ma'am." She'd been his commander in chief, and he realized he was automatically standing at attention. The position felt good, and he stayed that way, feet together, chest out, eyes forward. "I grew up rough in Detroit, ma'am. My father dealt drugs, and my mother was an addict who supported her habit any way she could. I did some drugs myself. I have a juvenile record, spent time in foster homes, and I lost my brother to gang violence when he was way too young. I barely made it through high school, then went into the military. I served in Iraq and Afghanistan before I joined the Detroit police." He was going to get it all out if it killed him. "I have a college degree from Wayne State, and—"

"College *degrees* . . ." Lucy interrupted. "He has his master's. That used to bother me, but I've decided to overlook it."

She was deliberately making him sweat bullets, but he was perversely glad she was forcing him to lay it all out. He switched to parade rest, hands clasped behind his back, his eyes just over their heads. "As I said, Wayne State. The only time I've been near an Ivy was working security for a Hollywood actress at the Harvard-Yale football game."

"He's got good table manners," Lucy said. "And, let's face it, he's hot."

"I can see that," her mother agreed in a shockingly suggestive voice, which made him wonder exactly how different she and Lucy really were.

He plowed on. "There was a time when I stayed drunk for too long and got into too many fights because of it." He clenched his hands behind his back. "But the main thing you need to know about me . . ." He made himself look at them. "I had problems with PTSD." He swallowed. "It seems to be behind me, but I'm not taking any chances, and I'm in counseling again. For a long time, I was afraid to care too much about anybody for fear I'd hurt them, but I don't feel like that anymore. I do cuss, though, and I have a temper."

President Jorik glanced at her husband. "No wonder she fell in love with him. He's just like you."

"Worse," Lucy said.

Her father kicked back in his chair. "I'll take your word for it."

Panda wasn't letting any of these Joriks sidetrack him. He unclasped his hands. "With my past, I'm sure I'm not what you have in mind for your daughter."

"Mr. Shade, none of your past is news to Mat or myself," the president said. "You don't really think we would have hired you to guard Lucy if we hadn't had you thoroughly investigated."

That shouldn't have taken him aback, but it did.

"You're a decorated soldier," she said. "You served your country bravely, and your record with the Detroit Police Department is exemplary."

"*But,*" Lucy said, "he can be a real idiot."

"So can you," her father pointed out.

Panda let his arms fall to his sides. "I also love your daughter very much. As you can see. Because if I didn't, I sure as hell—pardon me, ma'am—wouldn't be going through all this. Now, with all due respect, I need to talk to Lucy privately."

Ms. Maybe-I'm-Pregnant-Maybe-I'm-Not suddenly turned wary. "Muffins first. You love muffins."

"Lucy. Now." He jerked his head toward the doorway.

She hadn't finished punishing him, and she took forever getting out of her chair, looking exactly like a sulky teenager, which seemed to amuse her parents. "She used to be such a sweet girl," her mother said to her father.

"Your influence," he said right back to the former president.

If it hadn't been for the baby issue, he wouldn't have begrudged any of them their fun.

Her father wasn't done. "Maybe you two would like to settle this in Mabel?" He made it both a question and a mandate.

The president smiled at her husband.

Panda had no idea what was happening, but Lucy seemed to understand. "I guess." She displayed zero enthusiasm as she sauntered toward the back door.

He strode past her in what he hoped was an assertive manner, held the door open, then followed her across a stone terrace and into a backyard with well-defined gardens and mature shade trees. Lucy's sneakers swished in the fallen leaves as she followed a brick path around what he guessed was an herb garden toward a large garage. As they got closer, she cut behind it onto a dirt path that led to an ancient yellow Winnebago. He finally remembered. This was Mabel, the motor home Lucy and Mat Jorik had traveled in all those years ago when they'd picked up Nealy Case at a Pennsylvania truck stop.

The door creaked on its rusty hinges as Lucy opened it. He stepped inside the drab, musty interior. There was a tiny kitchen; a saggy, built-in couch with faded plaid upholstery; and a door at the back that must lead to a bedroom. The small banquette table held a baseball cap, a notebook, a bottle of green nail polish, and an empty Coke can. Her siblings must use this place as a hangout.

If he asked Lucy why her mother had suggested they come here,

Lucy would give him one of those looks that said he was a moron, so he didn't ask. "This thing run?"

"Not anymore." She plunked down on the sofa, picked up a paperback copy of *Lord of the Flies,* and began to read.

He tugged on his shirt collar. The place might be sentimental to the Joriks, but it was claustrophobic to him. *Are you really pregnant? Do you really love me? What the hell did I say that was so wrong anyway?* All questions he wanted to ask, but couldn't yet.

He opened his collar button. His head nearly touched the ceiling, and the walls were closing in on him. He wedged himself sideways onto the banquette bench across from her. Even from here, he could smell the fabric softener from her red pajamas, a scent that shouldn't have been erotic but was. "I told Bree about her father," he said.

She didn't look up from the book. "I know. She called me."

He stretched his cramped legs across the motor home. She turned a page. His nerves had stretched to the breaking point. "Now that you've had your fun, are you ready to talk seriously?"

"Not really."

If anybody else had given him such a hard time, he'd have either walked away or punched them, but he'd hurt Lucy badly, and she deserved whatever blood she could draw. She'd drawn a lot.

He made himself accept the fact that there was no baby. She'd lied. As painful as that knowledge was, he had to accept it. He couldn't even let himself be angry, because her lie had accomplished what he hadn't yet worked up the courage to do. Bring them together.

With a sense of resignation, he gave her the ammunition she needed to attack. "You won't like this, but at the time, I really did think I was doing the right thing by breaking it off with you."

She slammed the book shut, her icy reserve shattered. "I'm sure you did. No need to ask Lucy what she thought about the situation. No need to give her a vote or a voice. Go ahead and make all the decisions for the little woman yourself."

"I didn't exactly see it like that at the time, but I get your point."

"Is that how this partnership is going to work? *If* there's a partnership. You making the decisions for both of us?"

"No. And there's definitely going to be a partnership." He suddenly felt steadier than he could ever remember. If he needed proof of his new stability, all he had to do was remember the exhilaration he'd felt when Lucy had called to tell him she was pregnant. He'd experienced no fear, no doubts at all. Knowing she'd lied was a blow, but he'd fix that the first chance he got by making her well and truly pregnant.

"You took away my power, Panda. Instead of laying out all the pros and cons and asking for my opinion, you cut me out of the discussion. You treated me like a child."

Even in pajamas with every button fastened, she didn't look anything like a child, but he couldn't start thinking about what was under that red flannel or he'd lose his focus. "I've learned a lot since then."

"Is that so?" Real tears glistened in her eyes. "Then why didn't you come to see me? Why did I have to be the one to call you?"

He wanted to take her in his arms and never let her go, but he couldn't do that yet. Maybe never if he didn't get this right.

He squeezed off the bench and crouched in front of her. "I was working up my nerve to see you. I told you the biggest lie of my life when I said I didn't love you, but I was scared to death I'd hurt you. Things have changed since then. I've stopped being afraid of loving you. Now go ahead and yell at me."

She sniffed at the offense. "I never yell."

He was too smart to point out the fallacy of that statement. "I'm glad, because you're not going to like this next part." He tried and failed to find a more comfortable position. "Leaving you was hell, but as it turned out, it was the best thing I could have done for myself—for both of us—because I finally had something at stake that was bigger than worrying about all my symptoms coming back." A branch tapped the roof of the motor home. "I figured out that, at some level, I believed I deserved to suffer. I lived, and a lot of my buddies didn't. Once I understood that, other things became clear, and for the first time, I started to believe in possibilities instead of inevitability."

He could see the last of her defenses beginning to melt, but she still had some struggle left. "I would never have put you through what you've put me through."

She was kind of doing that now, but since she'd only begun torturing him yesterday and he'd been putting her through hell for months, he couldn't complain. "I know, sweetheart." He took her cold hands. "You can't imagine how miserable I've been without you."

That made her happier. "You have?"

He rubbed his thumbs into her palms. "I need you, Lucy. I love you, and I need you."

She thought that over. "You do know, don't you, that you're on your knees."

He smiled. "Yes, I do know that. And while I'm down here . . ." His smile faded as his collar started choking him again. "Luce, please marry me. I promise to love you and cherish you and respect you. I'll laugh with you and make love with you and honor you with every breath I take. I know we'll argue, but in the end it won't matter because I'd give up my life for you." Now he was sweating bullets. "Damn, I've never done this before . . ."

She cocked her head. "What about protecting me? That's what you do best, so why aren't you promising that, too?"

He couldn't take it anymore, and he yanked off his necktie. "About that . . ." He loosened another collar button. "I . . . can't figure out exactly how to say this."

She waited, giving him time, her eyes so tender that the words came out more easily than he expected. "You're my safe harbor. You don't need protecting half as much as I do, so how about you take over that job for a while?"

She stroked his hair, her fingers like feathers, her eyes giving him the world. "I'll do my best."

"What about the rest?" he said, his voice unsteady as his life hung in the balance. "Are you tough enough to marry me?"

She brushed her fingertips along his cheek. "Tougher than you can imagine."

His relief was so intense he felt dizzy, but he gradually steadied as she murmured her own love back to him. Then she got up from the couch, crossed to the door, and clicked the lock. As she turned back to face him, her fingers began opening the buttons on her pajamas.

He rose to his feet. A moment later his suit coat hit the floor.

Her pajama top fell open as she came toward him. She looped her arms around his neck, kissed him, the sweetest kiss of his life, full of passion and promise and the love he'd been looking for since he was born. But when their lips finally parted, she looked troubled again. "There's more."

"I sure as hell hope so," he murmured, caressing the small of her back, just under her pajama top.

"No, not that." She rested her hands on his shirtfront. "Once I stopped being furious with you long enough to realize that you really did love me, I had to figure out a way to get your attention."

He understood. "It's all right, sweetheart. I know you're not pregnant."

But that didn't seem to satisfy her. "I came up with a plan. Temple and Max agreed to help me kidnap you, and—"

"*Kidnap* me?"

She looked suddenly smug. "We could have done it, too."

When hell froze over. "If you say so."

"The point is"—she tugged on one of his shirt buttons—"about me being pregnant . . ."

"I intend to take care of that real soon, but please don't lie to me again."

She opened one of his buttons and then another. "The thing is . . . I really wasn't feeling well, so I started counting, and then I went to the doctor, and then . . ."

He stared at her.

Her mouth dissolved in a soft smile. She lifted her arms and cradled his face in her hands. "It's true."

Epilogue

L UCY RESTED HER HEAD AGAINST Ted Beaudine's broad shoulder and
gave a contented sigh. "Who'd have imagined after all we went
through that we'd end up together like this?"

"Life works in mysterious ways," he said.

It was late May, the three-year anniversary of their almost wedding, although that wasn't why they'd all gathered at the lake house,
which gleamed with a fresh coat of bright white paint and sparkling
navy shutters. Instead they were celebrating Memorial Day weekend
and the beginning of another summer.

Toby and two of his teenage friends dashed after Frisbees, with
Martin loping at their heels. One of Bree's nephews chatted awkwardly
with Lucy's youngest sister, while Tracy and Andre looked on in amusement. Lucy gazed at Ted's clean-shaven jawline. "No offense, but I'm so
glad I'm not married to you."

"None taken," he replied cheerfully.

In the distance, she could hear the faint sound of hammering. In another month, the roomy log buildings would be finished and ready for their first set of campers. "Frankly, I don't know how Meg does it," she said. "Living with your perfection has to be tough on someone like her."

Ted nodded somberly. "It's a burden, that's for sure."

She smiled and gazed across the yard toward the new barbecue pit, where her parents were chatting with a slightly awestruck Temple and Max. "Being married to Panda is a lot easier," Lucy said.

"I'll have to take your word for it," Ted replied. "He kind of scares me."

"He does no such thing, but I'm sure he'd take that as a compliment."

Ted squeezed her shoulder. "It's good we weren't this comfortable with each other when we were engaged, or that wedding might really have happened."

They both shuddered.

Meg and Panda came toward them. Who could have imagined that her surly bodyguard would have turned into such an exemplary husband?

Because Meg had been a terrible influence on Ted, he planted a kiss on top of Lucy's head just to see if he could make trouble. That backfired, however, because Lucy liked to cause trouble, too. "Your husband is hitting on me," she called out to her best friend. "By the way, how does it feel to be his second choice?"

Meg offered up her smart-aleck smirk. "I could totally have had Panda if you hadn't pulled your disappearing act. He was definitely coming on to me the night of your so-called rehearsal dinner."

"Well . . . You did look hot that night," Lucy agreed while Panda and Ted swapped glances that declared them both the most fortunate and the most put-upon of spouses.

"It's weird," Meg said. "We should so be married to each other's husbands."

This time all four of them shuddered.

"I'll tell you what's weird." Bree came up next to them, Mike at her side, a sleeping baby tucked in the Snugli he wore as proudly as an athletic jersey. "The four of you. I've never seen such strange relationships. Mike, aren't they all a little weird."

"Now, Bree . . . Some people might say that about us."

"You're too good to be true." Bree gave him a private smile that locked out the rest of the world.

Toby peeled away from his friends. "He's not that good. He got into my M&M's stash last night."

Mike grinned, grabbed Toby around the neck, and gave his head a gentle knuckle rub without disturbing Toby's baby brother. "You need to find a better hiding place, son."

In the past three years, Toby had shot up ten inches, and girls had started calling the house, which drove Bree crazy. But Toby had his head screwed on remarkably straight for a fifteen-year-old, and Lucy wasn't worried.

Between babies and blossoming careers, they'd experienced so many wonderful changes in their lives. But there had been difficult times, too. Lucy still grieved the loss of her grandfather Litchfield, and Bree had miscarried early in her first pregnancy. Fortunately, the joyous birth of Jonathan David Moody a little over a year later had eased the pain.

One of the changes that had most shocked everyone except Lucy had been Panda's decision to hire more employees so he could go back to school for a counseling degree. He now took only the security jobs that kept him near home and devoted the rest of his time to the more important work of helping other wounded warriors get their lives back, something he discovered he had a talent for.

Lucy found that motherhood meshed well with her growing writing career. She was a natural storyteller with an inherent ability to make the lives of the kids she helped come alive. She'd just started her third book, this one focusing on the eighteen- and nineteen-year-olds who'd aged out of foster care and had no place to go. She'd also become the go-to authority on at-risk children, which made her a popular guest on television news and talk shows. At the same time, she continued to work one-on-one as a volunteer at a Chicago drop-in center so she didn't lose touch with the work she loved the most.

Other than their family, the biggest project she and Panda had undertaken was the island summer camp they'd nearly finished building on the land where Panda had once had his brooding place. The camp would allow siblings who'd been separated in foster care to spend a few precious weeks together every summer. It would also serve as a retreat for troubled veterans and their families as they struggled to find a new normal in their lives. Panda and Lucy understood exactly how many difficulties they'd face dealing with so many kids and adults in crisis, but they'd hired some extraordinary people to help out, and neither of them was afraid of a challenge.

The camp was being funded by the Litchfield-Jorik foundation, whose assets had grown substantially after Lucy turned over a large portion of the money she'd inherited from her grandfather. "There goes our yacht," Panda had said when the paperwork was finished.

But between his business and Lucy's writing career, they were financially comfortable, and neither of them had any interest in a more luxurious lifestyle. Nor did their imp of a daughter, who was perfectly happy clomping around in whatever pair of shoes her parents had left out.

Panda's bodyguard instincts kicked in seconds before Lucy's maternal ears perked up. "I'll get him," he said.

Lucy nodded and headed instead for their two-year-old daughter, who was gleefully attempting to snatch a bedraggled stuffed dinosaur from a loudly protesting miniature replica of Ted Beaudine. Panda reached the screen porch where his son had been napping. The baby quieted as Panda put him to his shoulder, and the old house that had once felt so unwelcome seemed to embrace them both. He gazed out at his yard, where the people who meant everything to him had gathered.

Lucy had managed to distract their daughter, a pint-size lion tamer with Panda's dark curls and her mother's adventurous spirit. The afternoon ferry chugged toward the harbor. A pair of gulls swooped over the water in search of a meal. Lucy lifted her head and looked toward the porch. As their gazes met, her mouth curled in a soft smile of contentment that made his heart swell.

Be the best at what you're good at.

Who could have known he'd be so good at this?

Author's Note

You readers are a pushy lot! After I wrote *Fancy Pants* and *Lady Be Good*, you demanded to see more of the delectable Ted Beaudine, and after I wrote *First Lady*, you demanded to see more of Lucy Jorik. It seemed so logical to hook them up in *Call Me Irresistible* . . . Oh, well . . . We know how that worked out. I hope you're as happy as I am that Lucy finally got her own book.

In a career that's been as blessedly long as mine, so many people have cheered me on and held me up—family; friends; my longtime editor, the wise and wonderful Carrie Feron; the incomparable teams at HarperCollins, William Morrow, and Avon Books who are incredibly generous with me. An overdue thank-you to my ever-patient copy editor, Shelly Perron. Anything that slips past her is, unfortunately, my fault. The same goes for my incredibly able assistant, the remarkable Sharon Mitchell.

What could I have done without my writing buddies: Lindsay

Author's Note

Longford, Robyn Carr, Jennifer Greene, Kristin Hannah, Jayne Ann Krentz, Cathie Linz, Suzette Vandeweile, Julie Wachowski, and Margaret Watson? I've been very fortunate to have Steve Axelrod and Lori Antonson as my agents for lo these many years. I'm grateful to my publishers all over the world who have treated my books so well. A special thank-you to Nicola Bartels, Inge Kunzelmann, and the phenomenal team at Blanvalet Verlag in Munich. *Alles Liebe!*

Additional thanks to all those who helped me with *The Great Escape*. Nicki Anderson, your life-affirming work as a trainer couldn't be more different from that of a certain character in this book. My sister, Lydia Kihm, is an inspiration as she shares her passion for the work of Teens Alone, a superb Minnesota-based organization that does so much to help at-risk kids. Thank you, Lieutenant Colonel Victor Markell, United States Army, for helping me out. And John Roscich, I continue to be grateful for your willingness to guide my characters through their various legal troubles.

To my readers . . . I love the many ways the Internet lets me connect with all of you around the world. If you haven't yet found me on Facebook or Twitter, please say hello. If you'd like to keep abreast of my public appearances and future books, please sign up for my newsletter at www.susanelizabethphillips.com.

Happy reading,
Susan Elizabeth Phillips